Moon Rise

Lycanthropic
Book 4

Steve Morris

This novel is a work of fiction and any resemblance to actual persons living or dead, places, names or events is purely coincidental.

Published by Landmark Media, a division of Landmark Internet Ltd.

stevemorrisbooks.com

ISBN-10: 1687105456
ISBN-13: 978-1687105455

The Lycanthropic Series

Acknowledgements

Huge thanks are due to Margarita Morris, James Pailly and Josie Morris for their valuable comments and help in proof-reading this book.

Chapter One

Beneath London, waning moon

Leanna Lloyd awoke with a jump, startled from sleep by a slithering mass that covered her face, chest and arms. Fast and furry, it dragged itself across her skin in the pitch blackness, making her heart rate spike higher in wordless terror. She gasped and almost swallowed a long, twitching tail, making her gag. Hundreds of tiny feet pattered over her naked body. Sharp teeth grazed her skin. Opening her eyes wide, she glimpsed a dozen beady eyes, glinting back at her in the darkness.

She shrieked and leapt to her feet, brushing the rats away from her, dragging them from her hair, which they clung to relentlessly, and kicking her legs violently to shake them off. They fell away in a black furry horde, scurrying away down the low tunnel, scampering through the shallow water, leaping over each other in their rush to escape.

She stood breathless, her heart galloping in her tight

chest, fighting the urge to scream. Slowly, she brought her body back under control, remaining calm even as another wave of rats surged through the sewer, rushing over her bare feet like flooding water.

On the opposite side of the curved tunnel, Mr Canning sat lazily, his knees pulled up so that she couldn't glimpse his nakedness. He was chewing on a rat, teasing slivers of flesh from its fat little body, dripping blood from his mouth, studying her insolently. 'They're really quite tasty, my dear, once you get used to them. Rather like chicken, perhaps, although richer in flavour, more piquant.' He scooped up a running rat, bit off its head and offered it to her. 'Go on, try one. I think you'll be pleasantly surprised.'

She stepped away from him with distaste and drew her arms around herself protectively, trying to cover her nudity. Neither she nor he wore a single item of clothing. 'Have you been sitting there all this time, looking at me?' She could hardly keep the disgust from her voice.

He ignored her question and began to devour the second rat, pulling at its coarse fur with his teeth, spitting out bones, tearing off its tail with his dirty fingers.

She and Canning had dived into the sewer system just as the first of the nuclear warheads had exploded over London the previous evening. They had entered the sewers together in wolf form, escaping from the devastation with seconds to spare. Now they were trapped beneath ground. The moon had set, and they had returned to human form.

What had she done to deserve such a grotesque companion? She gazed in revulsion at Canning's gross body. He was not a young man, and not even good for his age. His distended belly spilled over his hairy crotch, and his skin was wrinkled and age-mottled. His grey, dishevelled hair was plastered across his high forehead, revealing the black eye patch that he wore at all times, even when in wolf form.

He continued to stare back at her as he chewed at his

meal, letting small bones slither down his bearded chin and over his chest. When he had finally finished he tossed the remains of the second rat aside and rinsed his fingers in the filthy water that ran down the drain in the middle of the tunnel. 'It hardly seems worth keeping up appearances now, does it?' he asked.

She could feel his eyes crawling over her body. It felt just like the rats scurrying over her skin. She needed to find some clothes from somewhere. But where? She glanced up at the metal ladder that led back up to street level. It was the way they had descended into the sewer, but they could not go back that way. When the warheads had exploded, the blast had surely shaken every last building to its foundations. The city that had stood for centuries above their heads must now be reduced to rubble and ghosts. She couldn't begin to imagine the extent of the destruction.

Canning guessed her thoughts. 'We must go on, my dear. Ever onwards, never back.'

Leanna looked up and down the dark tunnel. She had lost all sense of direction since going underground. 'Do you know the way?'

'I know many ways, said Canning slyly. 'Where would you like to go?'

'We must find the quickest route out of London.'

He gestured in the direction that the rats had gone. 'Our furry friends appear to be leaving the city too. I suggest we follow them. After you, my dear.'

'No. You go first.'

'Why? Don't you trust me?' asked Canning, his eyes glinting mischievously.

'Of course not!'

If she had learned one lesson this last night, it was to trust no one. The list of those who had betrayed her was long, and growing ever longer. There was James Beaumont, the boy werewolf who had turned against his own kind to save the lives of human children. James' friends, Melanie and Ben, who had fought alongside him, and thwarted her attempt at vengeance. Doctor Helen Eastgate, who had burned Leanna's face with acid. Vixen, leader of the Wolf Sisters, who had turned Warg Daddy's head and led him astray. Not forgetting Warg Daddy himself, the greatest traitor of all. But he was dead now, and one day soon the others would be too.

She hoped she would not have to add Mr Canning to her list of traitors.

Canning laughed scornfully. 'So you do not trust me, even though I saved your life just a few short hours ago. You do not show much gratitude, my dear. But what makes you think that I trust you?'

'You have no choice,' she sneered.

'Do I not?' He pondered his own question for a moment. 'You may be right there. We have no choice but to trust each other now, else how shall we be able to sleep at night? Our journey out of London will not be quick or easy. We must reconcile our differences and work together, if we are to make it out alive.'

She considered his words. The idea of spending days trapped in this dismal sewer with only him and the rats for company was repellent. Yet how else was she to escape the city? He was right in one regard – she needed him to guide her out of London. 'You know your way around these sewers?' she asked.

'Very well.'

'And you are confident they will lead us to safety?'

'I cannot guarantee it. But they are our only hope.'

A sudden noise made them both prick up their ears. A far-off splashing sound, echoing in the tunnel.

'Is that more rats?' she asked.

'Ssh!' He held up his hand for silence.

Leanna bristled. He had no right to give her commands. She would have to educate him on that matter very soon. But she did as he said, falling silent, listening closely as the sounds grew louder.

A light flickered some way off down the passageway. Two lights. The splashing sound steadily resolved itself into two pairs of feet, sloshing along the sewer. Soon, two figures came into view.

The beams from their lights fell on Leanna and Canning, picking out their pale forms. The newcomers stopped in their tracks.

'Oh, thank God,' came a woman's voice, echoing off the hard brick surfaces of the tunnel. 'There's someone else alive down here.' She started toward them again, her feet moving faster than before. 'Helloo! Are you all right, there? Do you need help?'

The splashing noises came to an abrupt halt again.

A man spoke this time. 'Look at them, Sandy. They aren't wearing any clothes. How can they survive in this cold with no clothes on?'

'I don't know, Stu. Let's go and help the poor things.'

Leanna waited until the flashlight beams came right up to them. They shone in her eyes briefly, then dropped away.

'Don't shine your light on them like that, Stu. Show the poor things some respect.' The woman, Sandy, came right up to Leanna. 'You poor, wretched thing. You don't even have any shoes. You must be frozen. Let me give you some of my spare clothes. Is there anything else you need? Food? Water? Are you hungry?'

Leanna spoke coldly in reply. 'I do not need your food and I do not need your pity.'

The woman pulled away in surprise before recovering her poise. 'It's okay. I understand. You've had a terrible shock. We all have. But we're here for you now. We can help you and your friend. We can all help each other. Isn't that right?'

'No,' said Leanna. 'We do not need your help. We need only your clothes, your possessions, and the flesh off your bones.'

'Wh … what?'

The man, Stu, was speaking again. 'Get away from her, Sandy. Keep your distance. The girl's some kind of psycho.'

Leanna shot out a hand and grabbed the woman's wrist before she could draw away. She gave a squeal of pain as Leanna tightened her grip.

'I am no psycho,' hissed Leanna. 'I am a queen. Queen of the werewolves. My plans have suffered a setback, but now my star is rising once again. You will help me by giving me everything you own. And then I shall take your body for my feast.'

Chapter Two

Gatwick Airport, West Sussex, waning moon

When Police Constable Liz Bailey arrived at Gatwick Airport, once the UK's second busiest airport, and now officially redesignated as the southern evacuation camp, dawn was already breaking, and the low sunlight stabbed painfully at her eyes. She pulled her dark glasses on to shield the early rays of the day.

They had driven through the night to get here after leaving the smoking remains of London behind. Her father, Kevin, who had been a long-distance truck driver, had taken the wheel of the police patrol car, and Liz was grateful to him for that. Transforming into a vampire last night beneath the cold light of the full moon had left her completely drained.

It wasn't just tiredness that threatened to overwhelm her. She had battled against a pack of werewolves to save her family, yet even her most valiant efforts had failed to protect her police partner, Dean, from being killed in the melee. His loss had been too sudden and too recent for her to begin to process, and she had pushed all thoughts of him from her mind during the journey, seeking solace in silence.

None of her fellow passengers had said much since witnessing the nuclear explosions that had engulfed their homes, turning London into a heap of rubble and ash. What use were words amid such unfathomable destruction?

Mihai, the ten-year-old Romanian boy who Liz had adopted, had slept for much of the journey. He stirred from sleep now, and offered her a tentative grin, his dark nut-brown eyes peeping brightly at her from beneath his unruly head of chestnut hair. She returned his smile gratefully, relieved that he was safe, and thankful that he seemed at last to have accepted her vampiric nature. It probably helped that she had saved him from being eaten by werewolves last night.

Also in the car were Samantha, Dean's heavily pregnant widow, and her two-year-old daughter, Lily. While Lily had slept soundly, curled up with her head in her mother's lap, Samantha had spent the night awake, staring dully at nothing, no doubt trying somehow to make sense of her husband's sudden and violent death. Liz could barely imagine how she must feel.

She herself felt guilt every time she caught Samantha's gaze. She had made a promise to Dean to keep Samantha and Lily safe. She had fulfilled that promise, and yet she had been unable to keep Dean himself from harm. He had died a horrible death, the victim of a werewolf attack.

Kevin brought the car to a halt, joining a line of cars waiting at the airport entrance. Soldiers wearing maroon berets manned a checkpoint at the gate, slowly processing the queuing vehicles before allowing them through and into the safety of the emergency camp beyond. The procedure was slow and Kevin shut off his engine while they waited.

Directly in front of the police car, the armoured hulk of the Foxhound, the military vehicle that had escorted them out of London, had also come to a halt. The door of the armoured car opened and out stepped Corporal Llewelyn Jones, or "Clue-Ellin", as he had told Liz to call him. Llewelyn and his men had fought bravely in the battle last night, and Liz knew that without the soldiers' help, none of them would have made it out alive.

Liz got out of the police car and waited for him to join her. The morning sun fell against her face, and even at this time of year, barely out of winter, the weak rays felt strong enough to burn her skin. She put her back to the sun and turned to face Llewelyn.

Corporal Jones sauntered over to her unhurriedly. Built like one of the mountains from his Welsh homeland, he seemed unruffled by the night's trials. Apart from a scratch on his face, he looked none the worse from battling werewolves and escaping from a ruined city. 'All in a day's work,' he had told her before leaving London. His boyish grin and light, sandy-coloured hair were reassuringly the same as ever.

'Hey, Liz, how you doing?' he greeted her in his deep melodic voice.

'Not so bad. Yourself?'

'You know. SHTF.'

'What?'

'Shit hit the fan,' he explained. 'But somehow we made it out of there.'

'Not all of us,' said Liz, unable to stop thinking of Dean.

Llewelyn acknowledged her loss with a nod. 'I'm sorry about your colleague. Half of my boys were killed too,' he said sadly.

Liz nodded. Of the eight Welsh Guards who had fought in the battle against the wolf pack, four were dead, and one was injured with a gunshot wound. 'How is Griffiths?' she enquired.

'He lost some blood, but we patched him up as best we could. Hopefully he'll get some proper medical attention once we're inside the camp.'

Behind them, the Land Rover driven by Jones' second-in-command, Lance Corporal Hughes, pulled up. With him sat Vijay Singh, the Sikh boy that Liz had got to know from the local school, and his friend Drake Cooper. Vijay's sister, Aasha, was also in the Land Rover, with the rest of the Singh family travelling in the Foxhound.

Liz waited anxiously to see if the lance corporal, also known as the Dogman, would come to join them, but mercifully he and his dog, Rock, stayed inside the vehicle. The pair of them had taken a strong dislike to her. She would be glad never to see that dog again. Any dog, for that matter.

'So, Liz,' said Jones, 'I think it's about time you told me what exactly the hell happened last night.'

She knew what he was talking about, and it was time for her to come clean with him. 'I'll tell you,' she said, 'but you might laugh when you hear what I have to say.'

'Laugh?' He shook his head solemnly. 'I saw you turn into some kind of mad killing machine. No chance I'm going to be laughing about it.'

She nodded. Llewelyn had been standing right next to her when she'd transformed under the light of the moon. God knows what he'd thought. Some of his men had tried to shoot her dead on the spot, and she'd only just managed to escape from them. She was still covered in blood from the werewolves she had killed with her bare hands and teeth.

She took a deep breath and began to talk. 'So, a few months back, I was part of the police team investigating the Ripper murders in London. You remember them?'

The wave of serial killings known as the Ripper murders had been one of the first warning signs of the impending werewolf threat. Liz wondered now whether the police might have been able to nip the werewolf outbreak in the bud if they'd somehow been more effective at that critical phase. Perhaps if she herself had taken reports about Mr Canning, the killer headmaster of the local school, more seriously then the outcome might have been different. But she had done her best at the time. She could hardly blame herself.

'Of course,' said Jones, nodding. 'It was all over the news.'

'Dean and I almost caught one of the killers red-handed one night. He was literally in the middle of devouring his victim when we found him.' She remembered how the man had squatted over his victim's body like a ghoul, sipping blood straight out of his heart. 'We chased him across Clapham Common but he managed to escape by jumping over a ten-foot wall. I grabbed hold of him briefly but he scratched me on the arm.'

Jones listened, attentive.

'So afterwards I started to have headaches, aches and pains, a fever. I thought I'd caught the flu. Eventually I collapsed and spent several days unconscious, being looked after by my father. Except I wasn't simply unconscious. According to Kevin, I stopped breathing at one point. He couldn't find a pulse. I literally died.' She paused, not able to look at him.

'You died?' prompted Llewelyn.

'That's what Kevin says. But you know, my father's not the world's greatest nurse.' She laughed nervously, but Jones didn't join her. 'Anyway, after a while I came back to life again – you could say I rose from the dead – but when I woke up I was different. The sun hurt my eyes and burnt my skin. I developed a taste for offal, red meat, blood sausages, that kind of thing.'

'Tasty,' said Jones. 'I don't mind a plate of steak and kidney pie myself.'

'And then I started killing people.'

She turned her gaze to the corporal, who returned it calmly with his grey-blue eyes. She had tried to deny the truth to herself for so long, it felt good to confess it at last, to get everything out in the open. And even though she barely knew Llewelyn, somehow she felt she could trust him completely.

'At first I didn't understand what had happened to me. I knew that I wasn't a werewolf. I didn't change into a wolf under the full moon. I didn't get hairy, or anything like that. But something was different. I wasn't fully human anymore. Mihai, the Romanian boy who lives with me, seems to understand. He calls me a *nosferatu*. It's the Romanian word for devil. The other word he uses is *vampir*.'

'A vampire?' said Jones. 'I once had a girlfriend who was a bit of a goth. She used to dress up in black and paint her lips crimson. I reckon she'd be jealous. So is this why you wear dark glasses all the time?'

She nodded.

'And this change, when you go a bit nuts, it happens to you every full moon?'

'That seems to be how it works. Last night was the third time.' She didn't mention the fact that she'd felt the bloodlust on other occasions too, and that once or twice her fangs had even appeared during broad daylight.

'That goth girl I knew got a bit edgy once a month,' remarked Jones, 'but nothing like this.' His eyes crinkled and Liz could see faint amusement playing on his face. 'Should I carry some garlic around to protect myself from you, then?'

'Garlic doesn't work. Neither do crosses or holy symbols. I've tried them. And I don't sleep in a coffin either. You shouldn't believe everything you see on TV.'

The line of vehicles had started moving forward as the sentries waved them through the checkpoint. Kevin tooted his horn for her to return to the car. But before she could move, Jones grabbed her arm.

His voice turned serious again. 'I may not believe everything I see on TV, but I do believe what I see with my own eyes. Last night, I saw you grow sharp teeth. I saw you move faster than anyone could possibly move. I watched you run through a raging fire unscathed. And I saw you slaughter about a dozen werewolves and drink their blood.' He folded his arms across his broad chest.

'So, what? Are you going to shoot me now?' Her eyes shifted to the SA80 assault rifle he carried wherever he went.

'I haven't decided yet. No need to be hasty. But I'll tell you the truth. My men aren't happy, especially the Dogman. They want you dead.'

'And what do you want?'

He grinned at her again. 'What I want right now, Liz, is a cooked breakfast and a nice, hot bath.'

Chapter Three

Stoke Park, Buckinghamshire, waning moon

Daylight was already beginning to creep in through the east-facing windows of Stoke Park, but Doctor Helen Eastgate had not slept. A pink flush filled the sky, but Helen dreaded looking at it. The bright, cheerful sunrise seemed altogether at odds with the events she had witnessed overnight.

A city destroyed. And not just any city, but a great world city, perhaps the greatest. London, England. As a young woman, she had travelled from the other side of the globe to make it her home. Now it was gone, and she would never again see its winding medieval lanes and neoclassical facades, its Georgian terraces, grand Victorian railway stations and modern glass skyscrapers. She knew too that she would never return to her old home in Australia, never see her parents or her little sister or her old school friends. She ought to be in tears, and yet she was still too shocked to cry.

She wondered if the rose-tinted clouds drifting gently across the sky could be entirely natural, or whether they harboured a deadly cargo of radioactive fallout. The clouds looked innocent enough, but were they just a little too bright, too vivid? Helen was a molecular geneticist, not a nuclear scientist, and had no knowledge of such matters, but she felt a sudden urge to pull the blinds closed and shut out those brilliant colours. Her fear was primal and irrational, the same response anyone must have to a calamity so huge it could not be grasped by the human mind.

Her thoughts and feelings were numb, and she wasn't sure what she was doing here in this office, except that Chanita Allen, the leader of the emergency camp, and perhaps also now Helen's closest friend, had asked her to sit with her as she received reports from a long retinue of military commanders, emergency workers and medical specialists.

Unlike Helen, whose train of thought kept wandering aimlessly, unable to focus on the immediate problem, Chanita was listening calmly, asking questions, and making notes. She appeared entirely unruffled, as if she had been training for this event all her adult life, almost as if she relished the magnitude of the disaster facing them. Even though the catastrophe had nearly claimed her own life, Chanita showed no signs of fright, just of determination and, as ever, her hallmark compassion. The milky whites of her eyes seemed to glow like the rising sun as she listened carefully to her advisers.

One of the army officers, Lieutenant Colonel Sharman, a red-headed man with a thick moustache, was briefing her on the national security situation. 'It's very difficult to be certain of anything at present, ma'am, but as far as we can tell, Britain is now completely cut off from the rest of the world. The destruction of London and other cities has caused total administrative collapse. We still have no official word from the government, assuming that any kind of organized central control still exists. All of the communication networks are down, the military and police command structure is gone, and it's just people on the ground making their own decisions. I think it's fair to say that there has been a complete breakdown of law and order, not to mention security.'

Chanita's warm Caribbean voice flowed as smooth as honey across the reports of chaos. 'Why are the communications down?'

'It's one of the effects of the EMP, the electromagnetic pulse,' explained Colonel Sharman. 'Thermonuclear explosions of the magnitude we saw yesterday produce a large burst of electromagnetic radiation. A high altitude detonation can generate a destructive effect across a very wide area. Given what we know about last night's attacks, we should work on the assumption that the entire country has been affected.'

'Affected in what way?'

'An EMP generates extreme voltages in any exposed electrical system. The larger the system, the more vulnerable it is. Comms networks and power grids are particularly prone to its effects. Our experts say that transformers and pylons in the electricity distribution network will probably have burned out across most of England. Without power, cell phone towers stop working. Telecom lines go down too.'

'And how long will it take before they can be repaired?'

'A long time. If the transformers burn out, fires can spread to electricity substations and power plants, so even if the power lines could be repaired it might take years to rebuild all the necessary infrastructure. It would be a huge engineering project even under normal circumstances. Now, with no government and the dangerous security situation, I don't think we can count on the electricity supply coming back in the foreseeable future.'

Chanita seemed undaunted by his answer. 'Then our choice is simple. We will have to learn to live without it.'

Helen had a question she wanted to ask. It didn't seem an important one, all things considered, but her intellectual curiosity always needed to be satisfied. 'Colonel Sharman, our Land Rover wasn't affected by the EMP last night. We were driving very close to the blast, and yet none of the electronics in the vehicle failed. Why was that?'

The lieutenant colonel turned to address her. 'Our tech guys tell us that the metal frame of a vehicle acts as something called a Faraday cage, protecting it from the electromagnetic field. Plus, smaller electrical devices aren't as vulnerable as large networks like the power grid. A lot of our onsite equipment should still be operational if we can find a way to power it.'

Helen nodded. 'So radios should still work? Can we get news from the outside world that way?'

'Yes, ma'am, but there's very little news being broadcast right now. Most stations are off the air, and nobody really seems to know what's happening.'

'Thank you, Colonel,' said Chanita. 'What can you tell us about the security situation on the ground?'

The officer's face, already stern, turned grim. 'In a word, dangerous. Werewolves are running wild out there. We've received reports of armed groups of insurgents too. When the system began to collapse, prisons were abandoned and the prisoners released. There are a lot of dangerous people roaming freely, and we have no way of telling who's who.'

'But you can use dogs to sniff out werewolves?' said Helen.

'Yes, ma'am. But murderers and rapists, they're not so easy to detect.'

'We cannot refuse entry to survivors because of the risk that they may be criminals,' said Chanita. 'As long as people need our help, we must allow them to come to the camp. We will deal with security within the fence as needed. I trust I can delegate that task to you, Colonel?'

'Yes, ma'am.'

'Then that will be all, Colonel Sharman. Thank you for your report.'

The colonel saluted and left the office, just as if he had been dismissed by a senior army officer, not a former hospital nurse. Helen was amazed that the military were willing to accept Chanita as their commander. She had been placed in her position by Colonel Griffin, the officer in overall charge of the evacuation camps, but there was more to it than that. Chanita exuded a natural authority, a fluency of command. Helen had witnessed that quality before, in her meetings with the Prime Minister. She wondered what had happened to the PM, and whether she had survived the nuclear attack. Colonel Sharman had said that the government had fallen, but it was obvious that all news was extremely uncertain. Helen hoped that the woman she had come to regard as a friend was somewhere safe.

A thought occurred to her, then. Who, but the Prime Minister herself would have had the authority to order the nuclear strike? But surely … no, she couldn't believe that the PM would ever have done such a thing. She refused to believe it.

An aid worker from one of the humanitarian groups operating at the camp began briefing Chanita next. Unsurprisingly, his news was just as bleak. His demeanour was downbeat, almost defeated. He sounded like he had already given up. 'The camp is filled well beyond its capacity,' he told Chanita. 'It was only ever intended as a staging post for evacuees from London before moving them on to other parts of the country. Now there's nowhere for people to go. We have no option other than to accommodate them here. But how can we?'

'What do you see as the greatest priorities?' Chanita asked him, her voice level and calm.

'Everything. We have no electricity, no heating, insufficient food. Without electrical power, the water pumps can't work, so we have no drinking water and no sanitation. It's just hopeless.' He threw up his arms in despair.

Chanita turned to the man's assistant, a young woman standing at his side. 'How can we solve these problems?'

The young woman seemed nervous, unsure what to say, perhaps not certain if she should even say anything, standing next to her boss.

Chanita's soft accent cajoled a response. 'Please, speak your mind. Nothing is off limits in this room. I need to hear all ideas and suggestions.'

'Ma'am,' began the woman, with a sideways glance at her superior, 'we can overcome these problems if we use the tools available. The electricity lines are down, but we have generators, and plenty of diesel to power them. We have solar panels too, and propane heaters to heat the buildings. We can pump clean water from the lake if we rig up a pipeline.'

'Excellent,' said Chanita. 'I would like you to begin the necessary work immediately.'

'Me, ma'am? I don't really have the authority.'

'Neither did I until a few weeks ago,' said Chanita. 'But it was given to me by Colonel Griffin. And now I give you the authority you need. You are in charge of the operation, and you will have whatever resources you require.'

The woman nodded, seeming to grow in confidence at Chanita's words. 'Yes, ma'am. I'll start right away.' She shot a look of pity at her former boss, whose shoulders had slumped and was already shuffling away.

Another soldier knocked and entered then, and for the first time that morning, Helen thought she saw a hint of apprehension creep across Chanita's features. She looked to the new arrival anxiously. 'Captain Rafferty? You have news?'

The captain saluted. 'Ma'am, you asked me to make enquiries about Colonel Griffin.'

'Yes?' said Chanita.

'I cannot confirm his whereabouts. Except that … ,'

'Do not hold anything back from me, Captain.'

Helen studied her friend's face closely. She knew that Chanita and Colonel Griffin enjoyed a much closer relationship than their professional dealings required. Chanita had never confided in her, but her feelings for Griffin were obvious.

'The Colonel's helicopter took off from the southern camp immediately before the attack yesterday evening,' said Captain Rafferty. 'His intention was to return here.'

'Here? To the western camp?'

'Yes ma'am. But he never arrived. His flight plan would have taken him directly across London. There have been no reports from him or his pilot since the nuclear attack.'

Chanita's expression had turned sombre, and suddenly revealed the exhaustion that Helen had already been feeling for hours. 'I see. Thank you, Captain Rafferty.' She held up her hands to stop her next adviser in their tracks. 'Enough,' she said wearily. 'I will sleep now.'

Chapter Four

Norbury Park, Surrey, waning moon

Colonel Michael Griffin woke to pale daylight and the sound of birdsong. The quick high-pitched chirping of a wren, the staccato song of a chaffinch, the low haunting calls of woodpigeons. A cool wind brushed his face, and when he opened his eyes he saw tree canopies above. He was lying on his back in a forest clearing. He had no idea how he had come to be there.

For a moment he felt disorientated, out of place. He was reminded of his boyhood spent in the English countryside, long days playing alone, surrounded by nature. He lay still, listening to the sounds and looking up at the sky. Heavy clouds drifted overhead. The light wind stirred the bare branches of the oaks and quietly rustled the dead brown leaves of beeches. A strange grey dust was falling, like dry and dirty rain, and the sky held an other-worldly yellow tinge that boded ill.

Then memory hit him. His helicopter, a battlefield AW159 Wildcat, had crashed in the night, not long after taking off from the southern evacuation camp at Gatwick Airport. He'd been on an urgent mission, returning to the western camp at Stoke Park in Buckinghamshire. After receiving a secure transmission informing him of the Prime Minister's death, he'd been consumed by just one thought – Chanita. Her sweet melodic voice, her smooth dark skin, her long black hair. He had to get back to her and make sure she was safe. He must not leave her at this critical moment.

He had boarded the helicopter at dusk, climbing into its cockpit as its engines whined into life and its rotors began to spin. The journey should not have taken long. The distance from Gatwick to Stoke Park was just forty miles as the crow flew, and the Wildcat flew much faster than any crow. It was a twin-turbine military aircraft capable of speeds approaching 200 mph. His pilot and co-pilot were experienced, combat-tested veterans. But the journey had been brought to an abrupt and unexpected halt.

He remembered the sudden loss of power as the EMP from the explosions struck. The engines cutting out. The cockpit lights blinking off. The red glare through the windows. The helicopter had been skirting London and was right on the edge of the blast zone, close enough for the EMP to knock out their power. He had watched as the nuclear explosions engulfed the city, spreading a carpet of fire and destruction as far as the eye could see. He had known immediately what they were. No conventional weapon was capable of such terrible and vast destruction.

The mushroom clouds had unfolded slowly above the devastation, boiling and churning in the superheated air, glowing bright orange from the reflected flames below. The nearest cloud had been so close, he could almost have reached out to touch it. It had been as thick as mud, an almost solid structure, rising solemn and sinister in the darkening sky.

The pilot had struggled with the controls, aiming to guide the crippled helicopter to a safe landing, but then the shockwave of the blast had hit them and the craft had rolled and tumbled through the sky like a child's toy in a hurricane.

That was the last he remembered. The helicopter must have crashed in woodland somewhere to the south of London in the Surrey hills. He looked around the tangled wreckage of the craft, its metal frame twisted, yet mostly intact. The helicopter lay on its side, its rotor blades snapped off, its main door missing. The square of sky he had seen had been framed by the open doorway, now turned to face upward. He was still strapped into his seat, the safety belt pressing tightly across his chest. The glass windows of the helicopter were shattered, and smoke from the fuselage drifted through the air. But it could have been a lot worse. They might easily have gone up in flames, engulfed in a fireball, just as London itself had been.

He swept his gaze around the broken shell of the cockpit. He was alone in the rear of the helicopter, but the pilot and co-pilot were still strapped into their armoured front seats. He leaned forward and gently shook the shoulder of the pilot. The man's head slumped down, lolling lifelessly inside his protective helmet. Griffin reached toward the co-pilot in his seat, but a sudden pain in his thigh made him flinch and gasp.

He looked down and saw that his leg was impaled on a section of the broken fuselage, a twisted metal shard protruding from his thigh. His trousers were stained red over a large area. He stayed still and called out, seeking to rouse the co-pilot, if he was still alive. But the man remained motionless.

The Colonel turned his attention to his injury. His leg was impossible to move. He had been speared by the metal rod to some depth. With his medical training, he knew that to try and free himself might easily prove fatal.

If the rod had penetrated the femoral artery, then any attempt to remove it might cause him to bleed out. He could see that he had already lost a significant amount of blood.

Carefully he reached his fingers beneath his leg and explored whether the metal had passed all the way through. With some relief he concluded that it had not. Tentatively he tried to wiggle his toes, testing whether his spine had been damaged. The sudden spike in pain almost made him pass out, but at least he still had feeling and movement. It was important now to remain still and calm, to prevent further tissue damage, minimize blood loss, and to protect against spinal injury.

The correct procedure was to stay exactly where he was and await rescue. The crash site would surely be located quickly from the helicopter's last known radar position, and an army rescue team should already have been dispatched. They would be searching for him now, sweeping the woodland for wreckage and survivors. He had only to sit and wait and very soon he would be safe.

He thought again of Chanita, who he had last seen at the western evacuation camp a couple of weeks ago. He hoped that no harm had come to her. These were dangerous times, and with the Prime Minister dead, a power vacuum would open up. Anything could happen. He had to reach her as soon as possible.

The image of London burning returned to him in a flash then, and a cold dread gripped him. A whole city annihilated. It didn't seem possible. And yet he had seen it for himself at close quarters. The enormity of what had happened suddenly overwhelmed him, and his confidence of imminent rescue began to give way to questions and doubts. He glanced again at the two men in the front seats. He knew they were both dead, and was glad he could not see their faces.

Chanita, he thought. He pictured her face instead, concentrating on recalling every detail. He imagined her voice, her smell, her touch. The memory was powerful, and helped him forget the calamity that had unfolded.

Over his head the trees swayed gently and the birds continued to sing. The sky was lightening, as the world turned and the sun rose. If he closed his eyes, he could believe that help was on its way. If he tried really hard, he could almost convince himself that nothing bad had happened.

Chapter Five

Virginia Water, Surrey, waning moon

James Beaumont walked alone in the forest. His naked body shivered a little in the fresh morning air, but there was nothing he could do about that. He had nowhere to shelter, and no fire to keep him warm. His clothes were torn to rags and left far behind, and he had no sheets, blankets or cloth to cover his nakedness. During the night he had worn a cloak of thick fur. It had kept him warm as he ran through the trees on all fours, his tail twitching behind him, his canine teeth dripping with blood, his yellow eyes turned to the moon.

The forest was a good place for a wolf to live, but not for a human. Now his fur coat was gone, replaced by smooth, pale skin. His sharp teeth and claws were no longer the deadly weapons that he had used to kill. And most importantly of all, the moon was no longer his mistress. In the dead of night he had set himself against its dark authority, and had overthrown its power to control him. Now he was master of his own body, and could choose to be wolf or human at will.

The blood of his victims still covered his naked body, however, and he felt shame. He came to a narrow stream, gushing quickly between the trees, and he knelt in its icy water, splashing away the blood that stained his skin, and saying a short prayer of thanks to God. He shivered even more after rising clean from the water, but felt glad that he had washed away all signs of his sin.

He had no way of drying himself, no way of driving away the chilly touch of the stream. Instead he walked briskly on his bare feet, picking a path through the tall, bare trunks and the densely packed brambles and bushes that lined the forest floor.

Where was he exactly? He couldn't be sure. He had left Melanie, Sarah and Ben at Virginia Water to the west of London, and run away from the city and into the woodland, rivers and heaths of Surrey. All night he had run as a wolf, across grasslands, rolling chalk downs and ancient forest. He had shunned villages, farms and any places of habitation, afraid of coming across people, for fear of killing them. Instead he had killed deer, cattle and other animals, slaughtering them unthinkingly, butchering them in the name of the moon. He had been wild and frenzied, and had thought only of blood and flesh, of tooth and claw, of life and death.

Now he had regained control. But it was too late. He was lost.

Still, he knew where he wanted to go. He needed to find the others again. Melanie, Sarah and Ben. They were his family now and he had sworn to protect them. He had promised to lay down his own life for them if necessary. But first he had to find them.

He stumbled through a patch of nettles that stung his bare feet and ankles, and came to the edge of the trees. Across a patch of rough grass, he glimpsed a hedge, neatly trimmed. And beyond that a house, standing proud in its own land, the only house for miles around. The building was old, something like a manor house, built from oak frames and weathered bricks. Its windows were small and of leaded glass, and its roof was crenelated and turreted, a little like a castle. A thin column of smoke twisted upward from one of its tall chimneys.

James crouched low, out of view of the windows, ignoring the prickly bushes that scratched his arms and legs. To search for his friends he needed clothes. He could survive easily enough in the forest in wolf form, but to go where humans walked, he must walk like them, and dress like them. And he would find clothes inside this house.

But he would not steal. Stealing was a sin. The moon had made him sin in all kinds of ways, and God had taken first his friend Samuel and then his parents from him as punishment. He would sin no more. Instead he would find the owner of this house and ask for clothing. If they refused, then he would leave. Unless …

If wicked people lived in the house, then perhaps he would punish them. Wicked people deserved to suffer. And he was God's avenging angel, bringing justice to the world. If wicked people lived here, he would find them and destroy them. He felt the hairs on his arms begin to thicken and stiffen at the thought. His heart beat stronger, pumping wolf blood through his veins. His gums began to ache, as the hunger for meat made his sharp teeth push through.

No. With great effort, he forced himself back to calmness, quietening the rage that had flared up so quickly and almost consumed him. He had no need for rage. Anger was his enemy, as much as the moon had been. He must learn to control his emotions, or he would become enslaved to them. He would take the form of a wolf only when he wished to. He studied the backs of his hands and saw that the stiff bristles had turned back into fine golden hairs. His gums stopped aching. His heart grew still. The beast was caged again.

He stood up and ran to the hedge that bounded the house and its garden. He followed it until he came to a wooden gate. It was not locked. He entered the garden, closing the gate carefully behind him.

The garden of the house was huge, even bigger than Melanie and Sarah's house in Richmond. The lawn that surrounded the house was well tended, bisected by straight-cut hedges, the borders planted with spring-flowering bulbs. Whoever lived here cared for their garden more than Melanie and Sarah had done. He crossed the neat expanse of the lawn self-consciously, aware of his nakedness. When he reached the back door of the house, he knocked loudly.

He waited, but no one came. He knocked again. There was still no answer.

He approached the nearest window and peered through. The room beyond looked well-furnished and lived-in, but there was no one inside, and no fire in the hearth. He moved along the edge of the house, looking through each of the leaded windows, but every one showed the same. He circled the house in its entirety, but it was empty.

'Hello!' he shouted at the top of his voice. 'Is there anyone home?'

No answer came.

He stepped back from the house, his feet crunching on the gravel driveway, and saw a tendril of smoke still rising from one chimney. Perhaps the owner was upstairs. Perhaps they were afraid of him.

He looked down once more at his own nakedness and felt shame again. He should go away and leave the owner of the house in peace. He had no wish to frighten anyone. And yet wherever he went the story might be the same. People would look upon him and fear him. He knew that people could become hostile when frightened. And besides, he needed clothing and shelter. He glanced again at the smoking chimney and returned to the front door.

Gingerly, he turned the handle. It opened.

The door swung wide open. 'Hello!' he called again, but there was still no reply.

The house was warm and he slipped inside gladly. The room he had entered was a long hallway, with panelled walls and many doors leading from it, some open, some closed. He paused for a moment, then crept quietly to the winding wooden staircase that led up. He emerged a moment later on an upstairs landing, the floorboards creaking with every step. More doors led off the landing, presumably to bedrooms. He stopped and listened, but could hear nothing.

He pushed open the first door and looked inside. The room was sparsely furnished, with just a narrow unmade bed and some painted wardrobes. A cracked china basin stood in one corner. Through the windows he could see the lawn, shrubs and hedges of the garden, and beyond it the forest he had come from.

There might be clothes in the wardrobes, but he would not take them without permission. He turned back to the landing and saw an old woman standing there. She must have been about eighty years old, her hair grey and her face lined. She stood perfectly straight however, without a stoop. In her hands she held a shotgun. It was aimed at James.

Chapter Six

Gatwick Airport, West Sussex, waning moon

Liz could never have imagined that when the world ended she would find herself moving into a Hilton Hotel complete with a bar, restaurant, tea- and coffee-making facilities, and a fully-equipped fitness room. Nevertheless, here she was. The walls of the hotel room felt solid enough (though rather hollow when she rapped her knuckles against them), the carpet deep and soft, and the king-size bed wide and firmly upholstered, so she guessed it was real and not a dream.

'Is nice room,' said Mihai. 'Is very comfy bed.' He slung his travelling bag onto the floor and stretched out across the vast expanse of the bed.

'Not bad,' agreed Kevin, regarding the room's plush decor with suspicion. 'Not bad at all.'

The lights in the room didn't work, however. Nor did the complimentary Wi-Fi, or the kettle. In fact, neither did the TV, the air-conditioning, the mini-bar nor even the elevator. The electrical power was down everywhere, and no one seemed to have any idea when it might be restored. According to one rumour, the nuclear explosions had caused the transformers to burn out at the electricity substations. There was no natural gas in the pipelines either, and no running water. Corporal Jones would have to wait for his cooked breakfast and his hot bath. He might have to wait a very long time.

Her conversation with him at the gate hadn't gone exactly as she'd hoped. But what had she expected? For him to give her a big hug and tell her everything was going to be okay? That being a vampire was no big deal?

Yeah. That was exactly what she'd been expecting. Llewelyn's reaction had felt like a slap to the face. She was obviously going to have to adjust her expectations. One thing she knew – she couldn't allow anyone to kill her now. Too many people depended on her for their safety.

After arriving at the airport, they'd been met by emergency workers and had their needs assessed. Owing to Samantha's late-stage pregnancy, Liz's group had been allocated a family suite in the hotel next to the airport's south terminal. The Hilton was certainly convenient and well appointed. Just a few minutes' walk from the check-in desks, it would have been ideal if they'd been planning to jet off on a flight to the sun. But no planes were flying anywhere now. It was hard to believe that any modern technology would ever work again.

Liz led Samantha into the room. Her baby was due in a few weeks, and she was suffering from high blood pressure, leg cramps and back pain. Pre-eclampsia, the doctor had called it. A very serious condition. Samantha had been told to stay in bed and avoid stress. The walk up three flights of stairs had left her ready to drop. Liz dreaded to think what effect Dean's death might have on her.

'Come and sit down,' said Liz, helping her to a seat where she sat exhausted, holding Lily firmly by the hand.

In turn, Lily clutched her toy elephant tightly against her chest.

Kevin was prowling around the hotel room, looking inside the desk drawers, lifting the paintings on the walls to examine behind them. 'This place seems okay, I suppose, even if the bastards at the gate did steal my gun.'

The soldiers at the checkpoint had carried out a thorough search of everyone before letting them enter the camp. They had confiscated Kevin's newly acquired assault rifle, despite his loud and foul-mouthed protests.

'No weapons inside the evacuation centre,' said one of the soldiers. 'Sign here and you can collect it when it's time for you to leave.'

'Bastards,' Kevin had hissed under his breath. 'I didn't even get a chance to use it.'

'I'm glad you didn't,' Liz told him. 'Anyway, we ought to be safe enough inside the camp.'

'Huh,' said Kevin. 'Maybe.'

But when they tried to take her own gun from her, she refused to let it go. Dean had given her the Glock pistol and taught her how to use it, and although she had yet to fire it in anger, there was no way she would let anyone take it from her. 'I'm a police officer,' she protested angrily. 'You can't take my weapon away.'

She showed them her warrant card, and no doubt it helped that she was still kitted out in her full police uniform, complete with stab-proof vest.

'All right, ma'am,' agreed the sergeant at the gate eventually. 'Just be sure to keep the gun on you at all times.'

'I won't let it out of my sight,' she promised.

The last thing the soldiers had done before allowing them inside was to bring the sniffer dogs over to check them out. Liz had stood stock still as the two dogs snuffled around her feet, lingering noticeably longer over her than any of the others. She remembered how Rock, the Dogman's German shepherd dog, had been confused at first by her scent. It had taken him a good while to decide that he really didn't like the smell of her. Unlike werewolves, it seemed that vampires didn't carry a very strong scent. Eventually the dogs had moved away and the soldiers waved them through.

Corporal Jones and the other Welsh Guards had been sent to join the military camp in tents close to the airport runways, and Liz's group had been directed to the Hilton. She wasn't sorry to see the back of the soldiers, especially after what Llewelyn had told her about them wanting her dead. But somehow she felt she'd be seeing them again soon.

The hotel suite was a large room with an en-suite bathroom, a king-size bed, twin beds and a crib. It was intended to accommodate a family with two children and an infant. But Liz's group comprised six adults, three teenagers, a boy of ten and a little girl. Eleven in total.

They all crowded into the room now. The Singh family consisted of Vijay and Aasha, their parents and grandmother, plus Drake Cooper who was Aasha's boyfriend and seemed to have become part of the family unit.

Vijay's grandmother was elderly and frail, and Liz tried to help her sit down, but the old woman had a fierce independence and brushed her aside with thin bony fingers. 'I can manage perfectly well,' she said. 'If I need help, then mark my words, I will ask for it quickly enough.'

Mr Singh caught Liz's eye. 'Thanks for all your help,' he said. 'My mother-in-law doesn't mean to sound ungrateful. It's just that we've all had such a terrible shock.'

Liz couldn't argue with that. Everyone here had endured unimaginable trauma in the past twenty-four hours. They'd seen their homes turned into dust by a nuclear explosion, narrowly escaped from a raging firestorm, and in some cases lost loved ones in a battle against a pack of werewolves. And now they had been thrown among strangers in overcrowded conditions. They would have to make the best of it.

'This place is ace,' said Drake Cooper cheerfully. 'I've never stayed in a hotel before. I was expecting a tent or something.'

Liz gave him a smile. That was the right attitude. If they were going to come through this ordeal, they would have to remain positive. A good mental outlook was as important to surviving a disaster situation as the physical needs of shelter, food, water and security. Without it, you might simply give up and die. And Drake looked like a tough kid, with his ripped jeans and closely cropped hair. Growing up on the wrong side of town had obviously taught him to appreciate what little he had.

Her greatest worry, apart from Samantha, was Vijay. The boy had spent several days locked in a garage without food or water, and looked in a dreadful state. He had always been thin and small for his age. Now he seemed to have shrunk even further. His eyes were glassy, and he stood alone, saying nothing. In fact, all he had said since being rescued was, 'Rose.'

Rose Hallibury, a girl from Vijay's school, had vanished a month earlier, after her parents and younger brother were killed by werewolves. No one had seen her since.

He was muttering her name now. 'Rose. Must find Rose.'

Liz took him by the arm and led him to sit on one of the smaller beds. 'Try to rest,' she told him, pulling the sheets back so that he could lie down. 'Don't worry about Rose. I'm sure she's safe.'

He let her lower him into the bed and draw the sheets back over him. His eyes closed as soon as his head hit the pillow, and he grew silent, breathing softly.

Liz watched him for a moment. She would need to keep a close eye on him in the days ahead. She would need to keep an eye on everyone in this room. She had always dreamed of having a large family one day. Now she had ten people to take care of, and a baby on the way.

Be careful what you wish for, Liz. A family of eleven was a lot to manage, especially for a part-time police officer, part-time vampire.

Chapter Seven

World's End, Buckinghamshire, waning moon

Rose Hallibury lay quietly on the hard ground, wrapped in the soft, warm folds of her sleeping bag. The dark green fabric of the tent curved over her head, but faint sunlight peeped in around the zipped-up tent door, and she knew that it was daytime. Her dog, Nutmeg, slept at her side, her small head tucked tightly against her mistress' body, her long wet nose nestled in the crook of Rose's arm. The others – Chris, Seth and Ryan – slept soundly too, filling the cramped space of the tent with soft snoring noises and heavy breathing. She lay still, listening to the familiar, comforting sounds, noticing the birdsong from outside, and the gentle roar of the wind across the hilltop where they had set up camp.

The air inside the tent was thick with the pungent odours of man sweat. She was just a lone girl, sharing a small tent with three adult men that she hardly knew. She wondered if she ought to be afraid of them. Yet she didn't feel at all threatened. Chris was a skinny beanpole, more boy than man, bookish and nerdy, peering anxiously and earnestly at everything he saw. Seth, with his long, floppy hair, lopsided smile and thick glasses was one of the most placid people she had ever met. And even the latest addition to the group, Ryan, despite his cropped hair, the muscles that rippled beneath his tight T-shirt, and the tattoo on his bulging bicep, had shown her nothing but the deepest kindness and concern. She knew that she could trust these men just as much as she trusted Nutmeg. And now that her family were all dead, and civilization had fallen, she needed to trust them with her life.

She and the others had walked right through the night, beneath a velvet sky and twinkling stars, not stopping to sleep until gone midnight. They had hardly said a word to each other, and yet they had seemed united in purpose, wanting to put as much distance as possible between themselves and the ruined city that had once been London. Whenever she had turned to look behind her, the towering forms of the mushroom clouds had cast a shadow in the darkness, blotting out the constellations in the sky, almost as if they were devouring the stars. She had seen the others turn their heads in the same direction, and shudder. They had not spoken of the destruction she had foreseen in her visions, and that they had witnessed unfolding together.

This was the first morning in a long time that she had woken from sleep without screaming. For so long now she had been plagued by dreadful nightmares. They had shown her the fires engulfing London, soldiers in gas masks firing their rifles into crowds of civilians, tanks and military vehicles laying waste to the city. Worse, they had foretold the death of her parents, and of her own little brother Oscar slumped in his wheelchair. They had shown her that everyone she loved would die. The evil headmaster, Mr Canning, had been her guide to the nightmares, leading her unwillingly through the visions with his blood-soaked hands, eager to show her more horrors. But the dreams had also shown her how to save Vijay, the boy she cared for most in the world. They had guided her away from him, out of the city to safety. And her final vision, so powerful that it had come to her in broad daylight, had shown Vijay safe and well, escaping from the fire that had nearly claimed his life.

Now the dreams had gone and she was free.

She sat up and unzipped the tent. Nutmeg woke and licked her face tenderly. Sunlight streamed through the open tent door and a gentle breeze entered, bringing with it the strange new smells of the countryside. They promised change, and a new beginning. She had been living in a daze for so long, ever since the nightmares had begun, since children and teachers had first started disappearing from her school, and the men calling themselves the Wolf Brothers had attacked her at the kennels where she worked at weekends. Now she felt suddenly wide awake, more aware than she had been for ages. The world outside was fresh and inviting and she was eager to see more of it.

The others struggled awake as the sunlight fell on them, yawning and groaning and rolling over in their sleeping bags.

'Come on,' she said to them. 'It's time to get up.'

She crawled out of the tent, followed closely by Nutmeg, and drank in her new surroundings. On leaving London behind, they had joined the ancient path known as the Ridgeway and were following its winding route across hilltops, through dense woodland and across open fields. All around was greenery – more countryside than Rose had ever known growing up in the capital city. And the sky was huge, filled with scudding white clouds. The dark mushroom clouds from the explosions had dispersed, and there was nothing to indicate the disaster that had unfolded just twelve hours ago. It was almost as if it had never happened.

Rose ran from the tent, across the open field, stretching her arms out like a plane. She felt reborn. She felt joy. Tears sprang from her eyes in the early morning cold, and the wind blew her hair across her face in a bright coppery curtain. Nutmeg ran at her feet, barking happily.

When she returned to the tent, the other three were staring at her open-mouthed.

'Are you okay?' asked Ryan.

'It's probably shock,' said Chris.

'Perhaps you need to sit down,' suggested Seth.

'No,' she said. 'I'm just happy to be alive.'

'But what about your nightmares?' asked Chris. 'Normally you wake up screaming.'

'I didn't have one. They've stopped.'

The three men nodded slowly, taking in the news.

'Let's eat,' she said.

Ryan broke out some rations and they sat near the tent to have breakfast. The food was simple, just slightly stale bread and some soft cheese, but it tasted better than anything she'd eaten for months. She sipped apple juice from a carton, feeling the sharp acidic flavour hit the back of her mouth. Everything felt good, even the cold wind blowing at her face. She grinned at the other guys as they watched her cautiously, exchanging glances, saying nothing.

'Are you sure you're okay?' asked Seth again.

She beamed at him and nodded.

Ryan pulled out his phone and sat looking at it, frowning. He held it up, then frowned again. 'There's no signal,' he said at last. 'I had one last night.'

'It's the EMP,' said Chris, his mouth full of food.

'What?'

'The EMP. The electromagnetic pulse from the bombs.'

'What's an EMP?' asked Rose.

'I just told you,' said Chris irritably. 'Weren't you

listening?'

'My battery was nearly dead anyway,' said Ryan. 'Yeah, that's it. It's gone.'

A hush fell over the guys as they digested the loss of the phone.

'You may as well throw it away,' said Chris. 'That phone's useless now. Worse than useless. It's dead weight.'

'Should we bury it?' said Seth, his voice hushed.

'Don't be daft.' Ryan put it back in his rucksack. 'So what next?' he asked.

'We carry on with the plan,' said Chris. 'We keep walking west along the Ridgeway to Hereford. When we get there, we'll be safe.'

'Why?' asked Rose. She realized that she'd been following Chris' plan to walk to Hereford for weeks, and had never questioned it. She hadn't questioned anything. Her head had been so full of terror and foreboding that she hadn't been able to think clearly at all. Now she had woken from her trance, her mind was clear and sharp.

Chris frowned at her question. 'I've explained all this dozens of times. Why doesn't anyone ever listen to what I say? We're going to Hereford because it's the wilderness. We need to get far away from towns and cities, to escape from the werewolves.'

'We haven't actually seen a single werewolf since we left London,' said Ryan. 'Maybe we're safe already?'

'No,' said Chris, shaking his head vigorously. 'The werewolves will spread out across the country. They have weapons now, too. They're more dangerous than ever. We have to get as far away from population centres as possible.'

'And that's Hereford?'

'The county of Herefordshire is right on the western edge of England, and is one of the most sparsely populated in Britain,' lectured Chris. 'The only city in the county is Hereford itself, and even that's tiny. It's really just a small market town. Now that the apocalypse is here, it'll be one of the safest places in Britain.'

Rose considered the plan. She couldn't think of any reason not to go along with it. After all, she had no home, no family. Hereford was as good a place as any. It sounded nice, actually. Growing up in the inner city, she had often dreamed of living in the countryside one day. 'How long will it take to get there?' she asked.

Chris' forehead creased as he did the calculation. 'The distance from here to Hereford must be about a hundred miles. If we can walk eight miles a day, it will take us two weeks.'

'Eight miles a day?' scoffed Ryan. 'That's nothing. We can easily do a lot more than that.'

'Maybe a week then,' said Chris hopefully. 'Then we'll be safe.'

'In that case,' said Rose, standing up, 'what are we waiting for? Let's get going.'

Chapter Eight

Stoke Park, Buckinghamshire, waning moon

The journey out of London had been almost unbearable for Sarah Margolis. She couldn't possibly have managed it without the comfort of her sister Melanie's hand to hold hers. Her memories of the walk were hazy, almost non-existent. She had stared intently at her feet the whole time, guided by Melanie, not once daring to look up, in case she caught another person's gaze. Even so, she knew that others were watching her. That thought had come close to paralyzing her.

Anthropophobia. Fear of other people. Some might doubt that the condition even existed, but for Sarah it was a frighteningly real part of every day. On leaving London, that fear had very nearly swallowed her whole.

She hadn't even been aware of the bombs falling until much later when Melanie had explained it to her. Even now she could scarcely believe it. Her phobia had so totally overwhelmed her that she had somehow failed to notice the annihilation of her own city.

Not only that, but James was gone. The boy who had slowly won her trust over a period of several months, who she had finally found the courage to accept into her life, had transformed into a raging monster beneath the full moon, and run away into the forest. By all accounts he had almost killed Melanie before going.

Sarah recalled nothing of it.

They had arrived late at night at an emergency camp of some kind and been processed by soldiers on arrival. She had seen bright lights, heard men's voices shouting, shuddered as the crowds had jostled her. That much, she remembered. Everything else, she tried to block out. *The bombs. James. The endless sea of people.* Now, beneath the dark, safe canopy of the tent, she curled into a ball, and wished it all away.

Melanie was in the tent with her, and had not left her for a moment. Melanie had tried several times to talk, but Sarah had said nothing back. She wasn't ready to talk, not by a long way, not even to her twin sister. She wondered if she would ever talk to anyone again.

At times like this it was impossible to believe that they really were sisters, let alone twins. Melanie, so beautiful and slim, dressed now in skin-tight black jeans that matched her long black hair, and a red leather jacket, flamboyant and bright against her perfect pale skin. Confident too, with a sharp tongue that flashed quickly, often drawing blood with sarcastic and cruel remarks. Sarah, by contrast, had never been thin, or pretty, or confident. She'd been a shy, introverted and bookish girl, and had matured into an awkward, self-effacing and repressed woman. She was a competent nurse and an attentive carer, and had spent her adult life nursing Grandpa during his final years. But she was not always kind and selfless. The darkness within her had grown quietly over the years, nurtured by solitude, and sometimes bursting forth through shocking actions. She knew that Melanie was secretly frightened of her. Sarah was sometimes frightened of herself.

Melanie's boyfriend, Ben Harvey, hadn't tried to talk to Sarah since arriving at the camp, and for that she was thankful. Ben was sensitive to other people's needs, in the way that Melanie was not. He knew that she would talk when she was ready. For now, he gave her the space she needed to heal.

He was fiddling with a wind-up radio, working his way through the frequencies, trying to find a signal. So far the only station he had managed to pick up was the BBC. It wasn't one of the usual stations though, and Sarah hadn't recognized the voice of the newsreader. She presumed it was the BBC, but how could you know for certain?

Trust no one. That was the only safe course of action now. *People are dangerous. It is rational to fear them.*

Ben turned the dial and a voice cut suddenly through the waves of static. 'This is the British Broadcasting Corporation. A nuclear attack has taken place against London and other British cities, including Manchester, Birmingham, Leeds, Liverpool, Sheffield, Glasgow, Southampton and Bristol. Millions are feared dead. Eyewitness reports state that a starburst of eight or nine warheads exploded above London at around 9 pm last night, and that the city has been almost completely destroyed.'

When Sarah had been a little girl, Grandpa had often spoken to her of his wartime memories. The image that had most captured her imagination was of him with his family, huddled next to a radio in the evening to catch the latest news from around the world. His youthful days had been overshadowed by rations, gas masks, air raid sirens and bomb shelters, yet he had talked about them as happy times. He had even shown her the old radio, still in working condition, and stored in the dusty attic in their house in Richmond upon Thames. It had been a huge valve radio, with a polished wooden cabinet. Ben's radio was nothing like that, a bright yellow plastic device with a built-in LED flashlight, but Sarah felt a kinship with her dead Grandpa as she listened to the voice that broke through the background crackles of the airwaves.

'There has been no official confirmation of who was responsible for launching the attack, but it is believed that the missiles came from the UK's own Trident II nuclear missile system and were launched from a *Vanguard*-class submarine belonging to the Royal Navy. Only the serving prime minister has the authority to initiate the launch of a Trident missile, except in the circumstance of the prime minister's death, in which case responsibility is delegated to the chief of the defence staff, acting with the authority of the monarch.'

Grandpa's war had lasted for six long years, and yet it seemed that Sarah's war had already finished, for surely nothing could follow an all-out nuclear attack. It had been easy, really. Nothing to it. Over in a flash. Yet who had won? Could any side truly win a war like this? She didn't even understand who the sides were.

'There are reports that the prime minister is dead, but this remains unconfirmed, and no government statement has yet been issued. In the absence of any central government, power has temporarily been devolved to regional and local administrations.'

The voice of the newsreader fell silent for a few seconds, then began again on a loop. 'This is the British Broadcasting Corporation. A nuclear attack has taken place …'

Ben switched the radio off. 'Jesus Christ, how could anyone have done such a thing?'

Melanie shrugged. 'Who knows? We don't even know who really did it. The government? The werewolves? Hell, it might have been the Russians for all we know.'

Ben grunted in acknowledgement. 'Anything's possible, I suppose.'

'Well,' said Melanie. 'One thing's for sure. We're on our own now, and God help us.'

'We're not entirely alone, though,' said Ben. 'There must be tens of thousands of people in this camp, and the army seems to have it running well.'

'You think so?' said Melanie. 'After what just happened, I think it would be very stupid to trust the army. Millions of people died last night, and whoever did it might not have finished yet. You know, they might just be warming up.'

'I don't see how we have any choice. We have to stay here, at least until outside help comes.'

'Where from?' asked Melanie scornfully. 'It may never come.'

They fell silent and Sarah guessed they were looking at her. She curled up tighter, keeping her eyes firmly shut. She wished Ben would turn the radio on again. The newsreader's voice had been soothing, even as he reeled off his litany of disaster. London, Manchester, Birmingham, Leeds, …

It was hard to understand what the words meant. Dead cities. Dead people. Sarah tried to feel compassion for everyone who had died, but it was impossible. They were just numbers. And in any case, it was better that they were dead, than alive and looking at her, jostling her, closing in around her …

People are dangerous. It is rational to fear them.

Another panic attack was coming, and she willed herself to breathe calmly. If everyone was dead, it would be so much easier. If everyone was dead and silent, she might be able to live a normal life.

'Sarah …' said Melanie.

Sarah clamped her hands over her ears.

'Oh, for Christ's sake,' said Melanie.

'Ssh.' The soothing sound was Ben's voice. 'Let her be. She just needs some time to get over the shock. We all need time to process it.'

'Time?' said Melanie. 'I don't need time. What I need is some fresh air. A chilled bottle of Prosecco would be even better. I'll go look for some.'

The tent door opened and light rushed in as Melanie crawled outside. Sarah screwed her eyes tight to block it out. A few seconds later the darkness returned, soft and reassuring, and she heard the sound of Ben zipping the door back up. She lay there on the ground, eyes firmly closed, breathing slowly, trying to find a way to cope.

After a while the radio came back on. 'This is the British Broadcasting Corporation. A nuclear attack has taken place …'

Chapter Nine

Pindar Bunker, Whitehall, Central London, waning moon

The Prime Minister surveyed her dingy domain with gloom. She had governed a nation once, now all she had was this. A dusty concrete chamber, spartan and sunless, buried deep beneath a city of ghosts. It might have been a mausoleum or a crypt, yet this was not the afterlife. Her heart still pounded steadily within her chest, her breast continued to rise and fall, so she was not dead. She had been lucky to escape the devastation with nothing more than a small gash across her forehead, the result of stumbling clumsily and falling against a desk when all the lights went out.

And yet the city above her was destroyed. The bombs had fallen, just as General Ney had promised. She had heard their thunderous roar and felt the terrifying quake as the underground bunker rumbled and shook. But somehow she had survived.

The building was designed specifically to withstand a nuclear explosion, yet even so it seemed like a miracle. Everything within the complex appeared to be in full working order, exactly as its designers had intended. The lights had shut off after the bombs had exploded, and she had been left in utter darkness. But after a minute of icy terror, believing that she would be left this way forever – a fate perhaps worse than death – they had flickered back to life. The power was still on, so the generators must be running. The air conditioning too was operating, and she knew that it would recycle air for as long as she needed.

She had clean water, and enough food to feed a hundred people for three months. It was all available for her use alone. She was the only survivor in the Pindar bunker. The bodies of General Ney, who had shot himself dead after ordering the nuclear attack, and the three men that he had murdered in cold blood still lay where they had fallen. She couldn't bring herself to touch them, or even to look at them, although she knew that if she were to spend any amount of time in this place, she would have to move the bodies somewhere. Perhaps she could drag them into a storage room and lock the door. The corpses would no doubt putrefy, but there was nowhere for her to bury them. She would have to hope the smell did not come to permeate the entire bunker in the days ahead.

Already she was thinking of survival. That must count for something. Her determination had not faltered. Yet even if she lived, there was nowhere for her to go. She was entombed beneath a mound of rubble, with little prospect of rescue. Still, she was glad to be alive, and she would not give up, no matter how slender the chance of ever seeing daylight again. If she did, this place would certainly become her sarcophagus.

She had not yet moved from the communications centre of the bunker, the room where General Ney had told her of his insane plot to destroy the city. Where else might she go in this grim dungeon? It seemed like the best place to be, despite the presence of the dead men. If she continued to ignore them, they would surely take no notice of her.

I could think of worse people to share my bunker with.

The Leader of the Opposition, for example. Not to mention half of her own party. Spineless lizards, the lot of them.

She powered up the main computer which had shut down when the power briefly failed. Amazingly it booted up without a hitch. She logged in and found an email awaiting her. How could that be possible? Was she still connected to the outside world? Fresh hope rushed through her at the prospect.

She opened the message and saw that it had come from General Ney. And yet the man's body lay on the floor beside her. She had watched him blow his own brains out with his service pistol.

From: Chief of the Defence Staff, General Sir Roland Ney (r_ney@mod.gov.uk)

To: The Prime Minister of the United Kingdom of Great Britain and Northern Ireland (pm@secure.gov.uk)

Prime Minister,

As you know, I am dead. However, if you are reading this message, the first phase of my plan has succeeded. You have survived the destruction of London. If you are to continue to survive in the coming days, you must read and follow my instructions very carefully. It is vital that you follow them to the letter, because my plans for you are not yet over.

You may imagine that I am a madman. However, I assure you that I took the step to destroy London and Britain's other major cities reluctantly and only after careful consideration. I regret the loss of life.

Whatever your thoughts on the matter, all that is in the past.

The greatest challenge lies ahead. Now that you are trapped within the Pindar bunker, quite possibly assumed to be dead, the government will take emergency measures and appoint a new leader. The country cannot be without a leader at this crucial time. The most likely candidate is the Home Secretary. I am confident that you will agree with my assessment that neither him nor any of your other ministers are fit for purpose. They are weak, and you are strong. Only you are capable of completing the task of defeating our enemies and restoring order to the country.

Prime Minister, you must leave this place and travel to Northwood command centre where the emergency government is located. Once there, you must take control. I wish you good luck. Your journey there will be hazardous, but I have every confidence that you are capable of making it. To assist you with your task, I have prepared a helpful video.

Your ever-loyal servant,

General Sir Roland Ney, Chief of the Defence Staff (deceased)

The PM read the message in astonishment, then re-read it twice over. Outrageous. No apology for his behaviour, only a statement of regret. And even from beyond the grave the General sought to use her like his puppet, giving her orders that he clearly expected her to obey. She would not do his bidding. She had done her utmost to thwart his plans while he was still alive, and she was damned if she was going to carry out his posthumous commands.

She glared angrily at the dead man, still lying sprawled across the desk opposite, his service pistol by his side. 'You obnoxious, arrogant bastard,' she whispered. 'How dare you!'

Yet even as the words left her mouth, she knew that she would do exactly as he wanted. What other course of action was possible? Obviously she would attempt by any means to leave this bunker and return to the surface. And what might she do then, other than seek to escape from the ruined city and make her way to Northwood and whatever remained of her government? As for the General's comments on her fellow ministers, she could only agree. Of course she was the most able, the one best suited to the task of rebuilding this devastated nation.

She would do it, just as he had commanded, obeying him in every last detail.

'Damn you, General!' she bellowed across the silent comms room.

She clicked the video that the Chief of the Defence Staff had helpfully attached to his email and watched in appalled fascination as the face of General Ney appeared on her screen, and began to speak calmly to her, giving her his instructions.

Chapter Ten

Virginia Water, Surrey, waning moon

The old woman stared at James' naked body with undisguised distaste. She hefted the shotgun easily in her stout arms. 'What are you?' she demanded angrily. 'A werewolf on the run? Or some kind of pervert?'

'Please don't shoot,' begged James. He froze, unsure whether to raise his hands above his head, or to use them to cover his nakedness. He opted to raise them, knowing how ridiculous it must make him appear. 'I mean no harm.'

The woman's gaze was on his face. 'Answer my question. What are you doing in my house?' Although she was old, her voice was strong and clear. She didn't look frightened. On the contrary, she seemed fearless. And well she might, with a gun trained on him.

James' throat had become dry, and he swallowed. 'I came to ask for your help,' he said. 'I just need some clothes.' But he could tell by her expression that she wasn't impressed by this explanation. She was right to be suspicious. The country must be full of criminals and other kinds of wicked men, roaming freely, and looking to take what did not belong to them.

Tell the truth, he thought. *The whole truth, and nothing less.* To lie was a sin, and James was done with sinning.

'I am a werewolf,' he confessed to her. 'Last night I changed into a wolf under the moon and lost all my clothes. I lost my friends too, and now I need to find them. But I can't go anywhere without clothes. That's why I came here. Not to steal anything, but to ask for kindness. To beg. That's all I am, a beggar.'

He stopped, waiting to find out if the shotgun would blast him to smoky oblivion, but the woman didn't move.

'Your friends,' she said eventually, 'are they werewolves too?'

'No. They're human. Ben is a schoolteacher. Sarah is a stay-at-home carer. The other …'

The truth, he reminded himself. *All of it.*

'Melanie works as a prostitute, or at least she used to, before she met me. And she stole money from people too. But she's stopped doing that. I made her promise to become a better person.'

'You did, did you?' He thought he detected a slight sparkle in the woman's eyes. But her voice was still gruff.

'Yes,' he said. 'And I'm sorry for coming into your house. I didn't break in. I knocked on the door first, and called out, but there was no answer. It was very cold outside, so I just came in. I wasn't going to steal anything, honestly. If you can't help me, just say, and I'll go. I didn't mean to frighten you.'

'Young man, I'm not at all frightened. I'm the one holding the gun, in case you'd forgotten. But why should I believe you? Why shouldn't I just blast your head clean off your shoulders?'

'I don't know,' said James. 'If you want to shoot me, go ahead. I would understand entirely. But if you could give me some clothes instead, then I would be very grateful, although I'm afraid I don't have any way to pay you for them.'

'I see. So let me get this straight. You're a werewolf, and one of your friends is a prostitute and a thief, and you want me to give you some clothes with nothing in return. And I simply have to trust you?'

'Yes. But it's your choice. My name is James, by the way. James Beaumont.'

She regarded him a while longer before a smile spread over her face. She lowered the shotgun and propped it against the wall. 'It wasn't loaded anyway. My husband used it for shooting pheasants and rabbits, but I've never fired it. I don't even have any ammunition any more. I'm Joan. Joan Cunningham. Let me see if I can find you some clothes that fit.'

After she'd given him some clothes and let him warm himself by the fireside, she sat down in the chair opposite. She looked him up and down with wry amusement. 'Well, James, I never imagined a werewolf would look quite like you. In fact you remind me of my Ted as a young man, especially wearing his clothes. He was about your height, though not as slim in later years.'

James smiled. Her husband's clothes were old-fashioned, and a bit on the roomy side, but of very good quality. She had given him a tweed jacket and cotton shirt and trousers. She'd offered him a tie too, but he'd politely declined that. 'I feel like a country gentleman,' he told her. 'You are very kind. You're just like the Good Samaritan.'

'I don't know about that, but I do always try to help people whenever I can.'

'Me too,' said James. 'It's the only thing that still makes sense. "Do unto others as you would have them do unto you."'

'You seem very devout, James.'

He nodded eagerly. 'It's how I was raised. By my parents, I mean. When I became a werewolf, I lost my way for a while. I … sinned, in all kinds of different ways. And then when I tried to return to God, He wasn't there for me anymore. Everything I did seemed to go wrong. God was punishing me for my sins. But I think I've found my path again.'

'And what is your path, James?'

He hesitated before replying. *Tell the truth.* 'After I lost my friend Samuel, I resolved never to kill again. I committed myself to repentance. I refrained from hunting for a whole month and grew very weak. But it still wasn't enough. God continued to punish me. My parents were killed, and I almost lost Melanie too. I was confused. It didn't seem to matter what I did, God heaped misery on my shoulders, and refused to answer my prayers.'

'So what did you do?' prompted Joan, when he grew silent and pensive.

'I decided to embrace my werewolf nature, but to use it for good. I rebuilt my strength, then fought to protect my friends and to defend the weak. And I vowed to punish the wicked.' He paused. 'I expect you think that sounds wrong. But I would never kill anyone unless they attacked me first, or tried to harm an innocent person. God still won't answer my prayers, so I have to choose my own destiny, like Sarah said. Protect the weak; punish the wicked. It's not perfect, but it's the best I can do.'

Joan listened, then turned thoughtful. 'But how to tell the wicked from the good, the wheat from the chaff?'

He shrugged. 'Since God does nothing, it's up to me to decide. Father Mulcahy once told me that in some circumstances it's not only justifiable to kill another man in order to prevent greater harm, but is in fact a duty.'

The priest had told him that just before James had killed him and devoured his flesh. But he chose not to mention that to Joan. He had spoken enough truths for one day, and he had no wish to frighten her. Not that she showed any sign of being frightened.

'My husband, Ted, always kept his shotgun by the

bedside. He told me that if anyone ever tried to harm me, he would shoot them first.'

James nodded. 'You should get some ammunition for the gun. And you should keep your doors locked. Anyone could be wandering around out there.'

'You're probably right. And I imagine that not all werewolves are like you.'

'No.' He thought of Leanna, swearing bloody vengeance against him and Melanie and Ben. And of Warg Daddy, his huge bearlike body and yellow eyes glowing in the darkness, blood dripping from his tongue. But then he thought of Samuel, so full of kindness and generosity. Some werewolves were good and others were evil, much like people.

'So where do you think your friends have gone?' asked Joan.

'They intended to travel to one of the evacuation camps outside London.'

'Well, perhaps I can help you there,' she said. 'The nearest camp isn't very far from here. It's at Stoke Park. I can give you a map if you like, so you can find your way.'

'That would be very kind, Joan. If only I could repay you somehow.'

'Don't worry about that, James.' She smiled at him warmly. 'You already have.'

Chapter Eleven

Beneath London

When Mr Canning had been forced to take refuge in the sewers before, he had spent a lot of time talking to rats. The rats, he was ready to admit, were not great raconteurs. They would never win applause for their after-dinner speeches. No one would ever laugh at their witty anecdotes. He had been glad to leave them behind and return to the surface, and to human company.

Now he was back here again, down in the sewers with the rats. He was like the Greek god, Hades, patron deity of the underworld, fated to wander forever among the dank and smelly corridors of London's underbelly.

The bowels of the earth are now my domain. Well, he had once been master of a South London sink school, so this was not so different. He stifled a snort of laughter.

'What are you laughing at now?' growled Leanna from behind.

He turned and offered her a grin. 'Nothing you would

understand, my dear.' He had come to realize that Leanna had no more sense of humour than a rodent. The first time he had lived in the sewers, he had longed desperately for human contact. But now that he had Leanna to make conversation with, he was beginning to think that he might prefer the rats after all.

He had to be realistic though. Leanna may not be a bag of laughs, but she was a highly gifted young woman. A werewolf and a genius too. Almost certainly mad, but that was easy to overlook in one so talented and ambitious. All things considered, Leanna Lloyd might just be his best bet.

At least they both had clothes to wear now, even if they were slightly torn and bloody. And his belly was nice and full, thanks to the previous occupants of the clothing. Oh yes, things were definitely looking up.

'Are you sure we're heading the right way?' Leanna asked him.

'Yes. I already told you. I know these sewers like the back of my hand.'

'These tunnels all look the same to me.'

'That, my dear, is because you are woefully uneducated when it comes to the workings of the underworld. Don't worry. Most people are. Out of sight, out of mind, as they say, and that has never been truer than when it comes to sewerage.'

'Whereas you –'

'Yes, my dear, I am a connoisseur of crap.' He gave her a wink. 'Did you ever imagine that the London sewer network could be so extensive? It is, quite possibly, the greatest infrastructure project of the nineteenth century.'

Leanna said nothing, feigning disinterest, but listening to him with rapt attention nonetheless. His old gift for teaching hadn't deserted him. He felt like a magician, pulling rabbits from a hat, each white rabbit a nugget of knowledge. Or perhaps rabbit poop would be a better metaphor in this case. Whatever. He continued with his lesson.

'The original architect of the network was Sir Joseph Bazalgette. What a wonderful name, don't you think? He constructed more than ten thousand miles of pipes, tunnels and drains. Think of that – ten thousand miles of sewer in a city measuring just ten miles across. The system joins up with the capital's lost rivers, the tributaries of the Thames that were buried underground as the city rose above the plains. We may see some of them on our journey, if we are lucky.'

'Just as long as we get out of this horrible place as soon as possible.'

'Don't worry, you are in good hands. We are in the middle level sewers right now. No doubt the deepest levels are completely flooded. Our route will take us west beneath central London. And then …'

'What?'

'The sewer system won't take us all the way out of the city, only so far. Then we'll have to find another way. But don't worry, I have some ideas about that.'

'You didn't tell me this before.' Leanna's voice was heavy with suspicion.

'Well, I'm telling you now. When we've travelled as far as we can through the sewers, we'll cross over into one of the near-surface railway lines, probably the Piccadilly line, and that will lead us right to the very edge of London. Anyway, I thought you'd be glad to leave the sewer behind.'

'I will.'

'I can't promise you safety, however. I don't know what we'll find when we reach the surface.'

'No.'

They both fell silent for a while, consumed by their own thoughts. For all Canning knew, when they emerged from the sewers they would find themselves in a nightmare world. Fire, devastation, radioactive fallout. Hell might prove to be above ground, not below. He pictured a scorched earth, black clouds boiling overhead. A place of death, all traces of life wiped clean. On his own, Canning would perhaps have been tempted to remain underground with the rats and the perpetual stink of shit. At least it was safe here. But Leanna was desperate to escape from the city.

'So, tell me about your plans,' he said. 'When we eventually reach our destination, what will you do then? You talked of becoming queen.'

'I already am queen,' she snapped. 'Don't ever forget it. I started all this. It was my idea. I brought lycanthropy from Romania and spread it all around the world. I raised and commanded a great army. I came so close to victory, I could taste it.'

'But you were betrayed at the last moment,' he prompted. 'Your commander-in-chief abandoned you.'

Leanna refused to respond to him, and Canning knew he was treading into dangerous territory. He mustn't ever remind her of her failure, or mention the name of the traitor who had deserted her. Warg Daddy's name would push her over the edge. Leanna wasn't half as strong as she believed. She was brittle, and unable to face the truth of her own shortcomings. He had seen school bullies who were just the same. To suggest that she was weak was to invite violent retribution.

'So you plan to rebuild your army?' he asked softly.

'Of course. I will gather all the surviving werewolves together. I will wipe any resistance from my path. And then I will do as I please. This time, I will be unstoppable.'

'Hmm,' he said, noting her constant use of the word "I". He had never before encountered such unbridled megalomania. 'Your plan is to rule the world. I like it. And how do you see me fitting into this picture?'

'You?' she said, as if noticing him for the first time. 'Do you wish to help me, then?'

'I desire only to serve,' he said, bowing low.

He wondered if his flattery was too much, if she might suspect him of mocking her, but it seemed to have the desired effect. 'I shall need a new deputy,' she conceded. 'Someone loyal and capable.'

'And ruthless and cunning too?' Mr Canning grinned in what he hoped was a suitably Machiavellian way. 'Look no further, my dear.'

She nodded slowly in acknowledgement.

He considered the opportunity that Leanna presented. Serving her would certainly offer him a means of advancement, and a ticket out of the ruined city. It was not like he had any better opportunities, and he disliked the idea of going alone. But he would have to watch his back, and strive to contain her worst excesses. He must not thwart her ambitions, but he ought not to feed them either. With every new scheme and victory, she would become more dangerous.

They walked on along the brick tunnel. The water in the central channel was running against them now, showing that they were heading uphill. It would not be too far to go until they reached the end.

'Why do you always wear that eye patch?' Leanna asked suddenly.

'I prefer not to talk about it.'

'Have you always worn it?'

'No.'

'Then what caused you to lose an eye?'

Mr Canning stopped walking. He had no desire to relive the memory of being stabbed in the eye by one of his own Year 10 students, Rose Hallibury, armed with a ball point pen, of all things. Oh, the indignity! 'Perhaps there's nothing wrong with my eye. Perhaps I just wear it to frighten little girls,' he said, leering at her. 'Anyway, while we're discussing our ailments, what caused that scarring on your skin?'

The red blistering across one half of Leanna's face had bothered him ever since he'd first laid eyes on her. It wasn't the ugliness of the affliction that troubled him, but his inability to discover its cause. He had asked around, but no one had been able to tell him. It was a major gap in his knowledge, and Mr Canning detested gaps. When he had been headmaster at Manor Road Secondary School, he had tried his best to instil a love of learning in his young charges. 'Lift your head out of the sand and gaze at the heavens,' he had beseeched them, to no avail. They had been far more interested in their Netflixes and their Snapchats and their Minecrafts. Snivelling, ungrateful wretches. They were probably all dead now. At least, he hoped they were.

Leanna grabbed his shoulder from behind and twisted him around. Her grip was like iron, far stronger than he had ever suspected. She forced him onto his knees and pushed her pockmarked face up close to his. With her spare hand she brushed her long blonde hair to one side to reveal the full extent of the scar tissue that covered one side of her face. Her red lips parted to reveal sharp white teeth. 'Take a good long look,' she said.

He did, through his one eye.

She drew back, allowing the curtain of golden hair to fall back into place.

'Never,' she said, in a voice like the cracking of ice crystals, 'mention my scars again.'

Chapter Twelve

Gatwick Airport, West Sussex

Vijay Singh sat on the edge of his bed, staring silently out of the hotel window. He rocked gently back and forth, seeking comfort in the repetitive movement, studying the world outside his window, yet seeing nothing.

One thought kept looping through his mind. Where was Rose?

He couldn't believe that she was dead. She must have escaped from London. She must be out there somewhere. But where?

He couldn't see much from the hotel window, just a multi-storey car park, almost full of cars.

Could Rose be here in the airport somewhere, along with all the other refugees? He didn't think so. She had last been seen heading west out of London, not south.

Then where was she? She could be anywhere.

'Vijay, come and help me with my knitting.' The voice

of his grandmother cut across his thoughts. 'Come,' she commanded. 'I *wish* to see my favourite grandson.'

He had never been able to resist his grandmother's *wishes*. He slunk over to the chair where she was knitting, and sat on the floor in front of her.

The knitting needles flew in her fingers, their tips moving so quickly he could hardly see them, let alone follow the patterns they made. Knitting was a mystery, as impossible to fathom as what had happened to Rose.

'Enough of this moping,' said his grandmother sternly. 'This girl, Rose, has gone and no amount of miserable staring out of windows will bring her back.'

'What should I do then?'

'Go and find your friend, Drake. He will help to cheer you up.'

'Do you think so?'

'Yes. That is what friends are for.'

He didn't have to go far to find Drake. He and Mihai were coming along the hotel corridor as he left the room. The pair made an odd couple. Drake, tall and muscular, with his fair hair clipped almost to his skull. Mihai, small and skinny, with chestnut eyes and a great mop of messy dark hair that had surely never been near to a pair of scissors.

Drake greeted him excitedly. 'Hey, Vijay, just the man we wanted. Come and see this. It's awesome.'

Mihai beamed at him, as if he had just won a medal. The Romanian boy was only a kid, but he wasn't much shorter than Vijay. He and Drake seemed to have become good friends during the time Vijay had spent gazing out of his window, thinking of Rose. Two whole days must have gone by already since they came to the camp, but Vijay hadn't left his room.

He followed them reluctantly up the stairs of the hotel. The hotel's lifts weren't working now that the electricity had gone. Neither were the lights or the heating. It was funny how quickly you could grow used to it. He had almost forgotten what electricity was.

'You are not gonna believe this,' said Drake as they reached the top floor of the hotel.

'What?' asked Vijay glumly. Unless they had somehow managed to find Rose up here, he couldn't imagine what could be so amazing.

Drake led him along the corridor on the top floor, then through a door marked "Staff only."

Vijay regarded the sign and hesitated. 'We shouldn't be –'

'Yeah, yeah,' said Drake. 'We shouldn't be here. Just come on through before someone sees us.'

On the other side of the door a staircase led up one more level. Drake and Mihai climbed it and pushed out onto the open roof of the hotel.

'Ta da!' said Drake. 'What do you think?'

Vijay stared in amazement. The flat rooftop was no place for hotel guests. There wasn't even a wall or a barrier at the edge. You would literally fall right off if you weren't careful. He hung back reluctantly, staying close to the safety of the stairwell.

'How did you get up here?' he asked. 'Wasn't this door kept locked?'

Mihai nodded eagerly. 'Yeah, door locked. But unlocking no problem.'

Drake beamed at the kid. 'Mihai can pick locks like your gran knits cardigans.'

'You picked the lock?'

'Is very easy,' said Mihai. 'Grandpa Kevin, he teach me how.'

'Come and have a look,' said Drake.

Vijay made his way cautiously across the windy rooftop. He wasn't really afraid of heights, and after a minute he lost his fear of falling. He joined the other two, and sat with them right at the very edge, dangling his feet over the side.

'How far down do you think it is?' he asked.

Drake peered over. 'Dunno. A hundred feet?'

'Is very long way,' agreed Mihai. 'Best don't fall off.'

It was scary, but exciting. From up here, Vijay could see a lot further than from his hotel room. In front of the hotel stood the south terminal, and beyond the terminal building were the runways, and the gates where the planes were parked. He was surprised to see that the planes were still there. They looked like they were just waiting to fly away. But where would they go? Not a single plane had taken off all the time he had been here.

'Look over there,' said Drake, pointing.

The army had set up camp on the grassy fields beyond the runways. Rows of tents were surrounded by military vehicles, including tanks and armoured cars.

'That must be where Corporal Jones and the other Welsh Guards are staying.'

Vijay nodded. He hadn't seen the soldiers since they'd come to the airport. He'd almost forgotten about them, but he guessed they must be on duty, helping to keep the camp safe from werewolves.

'You ever been in a plane?' Drake asked Mihai.

'No. Only car, train and boat. And horse, of course.'

'You've ridden a horse?'

'Small one. More like donkey.'

'If you could fly anywhere, where would you go?'

Mihai thought. 'America,' he said brightly. 'I like to see big skyscrapers. Eat popcorn and watch Dallas Cowboys win Super Bowl.'

Drake chuckled. 'Maybe one day, yeah? What about you, Vijay? Where would you go?'

'There's only one place I want to be, and that's wherever Rose is.'

Drake sighed loudly. 'Mate, you gotta forget about this Rose thing. She could be anywhere.'

'I can't forget about her,' said Vijay. 'She's all that matters.'

'Rose is name of girlfriend?' asked Mihai.

Vijay shifted uncomfortably. He hadn't really talked about Rose with anyone else, apart from Drake. To call her his girlfriend wasn't strictly true. Perhaps it wasn't true at all. Perhaps she had only ever been his girlfriend in his mind. 'It's complicated,' he said, hoping to shut down any further discussion. 'You're just a kid. You wouldn't understand.'

'Rose is hot girl?' persisted Mihai.

'Cheeky,' said Drake. 'But yeah, she is.'

'She's beautiful,' said Vijay, thinking of Rose's pale skin, red hair and green eyes. 'She's just perfect.' He gazed dreamily into the distance, lost again in his imagination.

Drake gave him a rude shove, almost making him fall off the roof. 'Listen, mate, the only way you're ever gonna see her again is if you start paying attention to what's going on right in front of you. You're lost in a dreamworld, yeah? Life's a hundred times more dangerous than it used to be. You gotta keep your wits about you, or you're not gonna make it.'

Vijay nodded. As usual, Drake was right.

'And you should count your blessings,' Drake continued. 'You still got your friends, your family, and a place to live. That's more than a lot of people have, yeah?'

'Yeah,' said Vijay reluctantly.

'My family all dead,' said Mihai. 'Just Liz and Grandpa Kevin now.'

'And my family are all gone,' said Drake. 'No idea where my mum and dad are. But you, Vijay, you've got your mum and dad, your sister, and even your grandmother. You just don't know how lucky you are.'

They were right. He was lucky. And he did need to pull himself together. But … 'At least you have Aasha,' he said to Drake. 'You have a girlfriend.'

'Yeah,' said Drake, 'but to be honest we're not really getting on too well right now. Things between us are kinda awkward.'

'I know that Aasha can be difficult sometimes,' said

Vijay. That was a polite way of putting it. His sister had always been argumentative and stubborn.

'It's not just that. I wonder if the two of us really have that much in common. I wonder if she's worth all the constant fireworks and hassle.'

Mihai looked puzzled. 'But Aasha is hot girl too, yeah?'

Drake laughed. 'I'm beginning to think that they're the worst kind. Aasha, Rose … they're driving us both mad. Anyway, what do you know? You're only ten years old.'

Mihai shrugged. 'Sure, is only ten. Is just little kid. But still, I know this for sure. Aasha, she is very hot girl.'

Chapter Thirteen

Norbury Park, Surrey

The red kites circled slowly overhead, riding effortlessly on the wind, screeching eerily as the light faded. They watched Colonel Griffin from on high as he sat strapped in the mangled helicopter cockpit, staring up at them helplessly. A whole night and day had passed and still no help had come. Now, as evening fell, the Colonel was finally ready to accept the truth that the birds had known all along – that no help was coming, and that if he did not act soon he would join the pilot and co-pilot as food for the carrion eaters. The red kites knew he was dying. They must suspect, and perhaps hope, that his death would come quickly and that they could soon begin their feast.

No food had passed his lips since the day of the crash and he had already drunk his meagre supply of water. The cockpit provided no shelter and little warmth. He had a life-threatening injury, had lost a significant amount of blood, and was at severe risk of hypothermia. He had to get himself out, and quickly, or else the twisted wreckage of the Wildcat would become his tomb.

But how to proceed?

If a major blood vessel was severed, then dislodging the embedded metal spike from his leg could cause a rapid and untreatable loss of blood. He had already lost a dangerous amount, and lack of fluid had not helped. Whatever he did next, he must do it quickly and decisively. By morning it would be too late to do a thing.

He searched around the cockpit for his med kit and found it wedged below his seat. Carefully he reached for it and began to remove the equipment he would need. He began with an injection of morphine and waited a few minutes for the pain relief to take effect. Next he tied a tourniquet above the wound, tightening the strap around his thigh as hard as he dared. Too hard and he risked permanent damage to nerves and circulation. Too soft and he would lose blood rapidly. Severe blood loss was the number-one killer on the battlefield, and a rupture of the femoral artery would be a death sentence if not treated quickly and expertly. Fortunately, he was the best expert he knew.

There was little room in the cockpit. The metal rod that pierced his thigh anchored him in position and allowed very limited space to move. To escape from this trap he would have to twist sideways somehow. Yet even the slightest movement caused searing pain, despite the morphine. He steeled himself for what he must do.

He played out the necessary manoeuvre in his mind, planning exactly how he would do it. Then, carefully but with determination he eased himself back in his seat, moving slowly so as not to further damage the tissue, and grimacing as the pain increased in intensity.

Bad news. Blood gushed from the wound as soon as he began to move. A major vein or artery was bleeding. He applied extra pressure with his fingers as he sought to free himself. The pain was excruciating. He roared in agony, taking breaths in deep gulps. A fresh fountain of blood erupted from his leg as he shifted and turned, gradually drawing clear of the penetrating metal spear. Eventually he was out, but his problems were only just beginning.

A bleed of this magnitude must mean that the femoral artery was damaged. If it was severed he would certainly die. If it was merely damaged, there was still a ghost of a chance. Griffin was no stranger to emergency battlefield medicine, but this would be the first time he had practised it on himself.

He felt a rush of anxiety at the prospect of treating his own wound, but anxiety was one of the normal side-effects of shock and he shrugged it away. He was breathing rapidly too, and his skin felt cold and clammy. More symptoms of severe shock, but that was to be expected given the amount of blood he had already lost.

It was agony to move his leg, but he managed to lift it up and rest it on the helicopter seat, elevating the wound above his heart to reduce the rate of bleeding.

Much would now depend on the severity of the wound. He examined it carefully. The metal shard that had pierced his thigh had done him a favour by opening up the flesh so he could get a clear look at the damage. Sweat formed on his fingertips as he probed the wound and mopped away blood with a surgical sponge. The femoral artery was cut, as he'd suspected, but the cut appeared clean and was not as large as he'd feared.

And yet to operate on himself was insanity. A feeling of hopelessness grew inside him.

Just shock, he told himself. *Keep going. The most insane action now would be to give up.*

He clamped the artery above and below the bleed, gave himself a second morphine boost, and then began the almost impossible process of stitching the wound.

His leg was cold to the touch, and time was very much against him. The severe blood loss had dropped his blood pressure to a critically low level. In due course this would lead to tissue necrosis and eventual organ failure. Already his breath was rapid and strained, and his heart pumped fast and loudly in his chest, fighting a losing battle to keep him alive.

Focus, Griffin.

He began to sew up the artery with practised hands, hands that had carried out the same operation on a thousand men. Hands that did not tremble even now he had to save his own life.

'Especially now,' he muttered aloud, grimacing against the rising pain.

A moment later he opened his eyes and found himself slumped back in his seat. He must have lost consciousness briefly. The twin dose of morphine had reduced the pain substantially, but the suffering was still almost unendurable. That, combined with the low blood pressure, and it was hardly surprising he had fainted. He was sweating profusely and had to fight for every breath. Time was running out. Every second mattered. Every drop of blood was precious. He counted his rapid breaths, using it as a distraction technique to fight the pain and to continue with his task.

He pretended he was sewing a tear in a piece of clothing, not struggling to repair his own flesh. The needle went in, then came back out. In, out. It was a simple task, one that his mother might have done to darn his father's old socks. All it needed was concentration.

Eventually the wound was closed and the bleeding stopped. He removed the clamps and felt pins and needles as the blood flow returned to his leg. That was a good sign. Yet still the operation was not complete. He cleaned and closed the surface wound with more stitches, binding it tightly with surgical gauze.

He blacked out for a second time, and awoke gasping for breath, his heart hammering as it fought to pump depleted blood around his oxygen-hungry body. The bleeding may have stopped, but he had lost a massive amount of blood. He really needed an emergency transfusion of plasma or red blood cells, but that was impossible here. Instead, he rigged up a simple intravenous saline supply into his arm, and lay back in his seat, wrapped in a blanket to try and stay warm.

He felt his eyes grow heavy and this time he had no fight left to resist the passage into darkness. If he survived the night, he would wake again to sunlight and birdsong. If not, he hoped that there would be no pain in his final moments. He tried to picture Chanita, smiling. If he could only see her once again, it would be enough. It would make the agony worth enduring. As he fell unconscious he thought he heard her voice. He wondered if it was real, or if it was just the sound of the red kites calling.

Chapter Fourteen

Gatwick Airport, West Sussex

The knocking on the door was as loud as gunfire. Liz sat bolt upright, jolted from a light sleep, and reached for her wristwatch. Six in the morning. She had only been asleep for a couple of hours. Her body rhythms had shifted, and she was becoming gradually more nocturnal.

The door to the hotel suite banged again and this time a voice cried out. 'Help! Police! Emergency!'

Liz crawled from her makeshift bed – a mattress on the floor – and staggered over to the door, weaving her way past her sleeping companions. The room was filled to capacity, with Samantha and Lily sharing the double bed with old Mrs Singh, Vijay in one of the single beds, and Mihai in the other. The rest of them had found space on the floor, making do with whatever bedding they'd been able to scavenge. It was far from ideal, but Liz wasn't going to complain. They were together, they were warm and dry, and for the moment they seemed safe. At least, they had until now.

She opened the door and found a group of agitated people in the darkened corridor outside. Their flashlights were bright enough to dazzle her and she automatically pulled on her sunglasses, almost without thinking. She was beyond caring whether people found her behaviour odd. 'What is it?' she asked. 'What's happened?'

'A killing,' said a man she recognized as one of her new neighbours, Joe Foster. He was a middle-aged man, an engineer of some kind, with a shock of dark hair, and wire glasses perched on his long nose.

'A woman's been murdered,' said his wife, Pamela, a friendly woman who already seemed to know everyone in the hotel. 'Come quickly.'

Liz followed them along the corridor and down one flight of stairs to the floor below. 'How fortunate for us that you're a police officer,' said Pamela, seeming more excited than appalled by the idea of a woman's murder.

'Not so fortunate for Liz,' said Joe. 'With her being the only police officer around here, it looks like she's going to be given all the police work from now on. Not very fortunate for the dead woman either.'

'Can you tell me exactly what's happened?' asked Liz.

'It's better if we show you.'

They led her to a room almost immediately below Liz's, where a crowd had gathered around the open door, blocking the corridor.

'It's the police,' announced Joe to the group. 'Step aside. Make room for her to see.' His voice commanded authority and they did as he asked. He held the door wide open for Liz to enter.

The room had the same style of furnishing as Liz's own room, but was normal-sized, not a suite. It contained just one double bed and some mattresses spread around the floor. She entered and found half a dozen people inside, clustered around a woman's body lying on one of the mattresses. They cleared a way for her as she approached.

The corpse was covered from head to toe with a white sheet, and Liz drew it back to reveal a slender woman, aged around twenty, with long blonde hair and blue eyes, lying on her back and staring up at the ceiling. Her face looked serene, as if she were just resting, but her skin was unusually pale and her lips were blue. *Pallor mortis*. One of the first indicators of death. Liz kneeled beside the body, checking for a pulse and any signs of breathing, but as she'd anticipated, there were none.

'Is she really dead?' asked Pamela.

'Shush,' said her husband, Joe. 'Let Liz do her job.'

'Who is she?' asked Liz.

'Hannah Matthews. She's my daughter.' Liz looked up and saw a man of around fifty, tall, with the same hair and eye colour as the dead woman. His face was drawn tight and his eyes were ringed red with tears. 'She's been murdered.'

Liz turned to face the crowd of onlookers still crowding around the entrance to the room. 'All right. There's nothing more for you to see here. Please give us some privacy.'

Joe closed the door on them, but stayed behind in the room with his wife. 'We're good friends of Scott,' said Pamela. 'We knew Hannah well. Everyone did. She was a lovely girl.'

'Right,' said Liz. She pulled the white covering away completely and knelt over the body to examine it closely. The dead woman's skin felt cool to the touch, but there was no stiffening of the limbs yet, so she guessed the time of death was within the last few hours. The cause of death didn't take long for her to discover. The woman's neck showed two deep wounds, roughly two inches apart. Her whole neck was badly bruised, as if she'd been strangled or held down while the stab wounds were inflicted. Apart from that, Liz could find no other markings on the body, which was fully clothed.

She studied the two red holes in puzzlement. They didn't look like knife wounds. They were too small and round, more like puncture marks from some kind of sharp spike. She had no way of telling how deep they were, but there was surprisingly little bleeding for a fatal stabbing.

The sharp aroma of blood aroused her own appetite, but she took a deep breath and pushed such thoughts firmly to one side.

'Tell me what happened,' she said. 'Who discovered the body?'

The woman's father, Scott Matthews answered. 'I did. I'm usually the first to wake. I got up to use the bathroom, and when I came back, I noticed that Hannah's neck was bleeding.' He faltered, fresh tears falling as he relived the memory. 'I tried to rouse her, but she was already dead.'

'And who else shares the room?' asked Liz gently, turning her attention to the five other people, sitting on the bed, or clustered around the edge of the room. All of them looked absolutely shocked and petrified.

'These are my two sisters, and their children,' replied Scott. 'We've been living here together for the past week.'

'Did any of you see or hear anything?' Liz asked.

They all silently shook their heads.

Scott was making an obvious effort to recover his poise. 'Like I said, I was the first to wake. The others were all asleep when I discovered that Hannah was dead.'

'Joe and I have the room next door,' explained Pamela. 'I heard Scott cry out, and came in straight away. Scott was kneeling on the floor next to Hannah, trying to rouse her.'

Liz looked from Scott to the others, wondering which one of them might possibly have carried out this murder. In a case like this you didn't usually have to look far. Yet none of these people looked like suspects. Scott, the dead girl's father, was obviously distraught. His three nieces and nephews were just children. And Scott's two sisters looked utterly shocked. But something that Pamela had said was bothering her. 'You said that you came in and found Scott next to the body,' she queried. 'How did you open the door?'

'It was unlocked,' said Pamela. 'I walked straight in.'

'That's right,' said Scott. 'The door locking mechanism doesn't work with the power down, so it isn't possible to lock the door.'

It was the same with Liz's room. The card key system was useless without electricity. 'But didn't you put the chain on the door at night?' she asked.

'It's broken. I complained about it, but the people running this place are far too busy to fix little things like that.'

Liz examined the door and saw that the chain was broken, just as Scott had said. 'So anyone could have entered the room during the night and killed Hannah?'

'I guess so, although I can't understand why I didn't hear anything.'

Liz nodded miserably. Her list of possible suspects had just widened to include everyone in the entire hotel, perhaps even the whole of the evacuation camp. She was only a lowly police constable, working alone. She had no experience of running a murder enquiry. She had no forensic support, no fingerprint database, no backup team, not even a pathologist to establish the precise time and cause of death.

What did she have? Her instincts. Her police training. And a corpse in need of answers.

The others looked at her hopefully. 'What are you going to do now?' asked Joe. 'Take witness statements? Make door to door enquiries?'

'Are you going to start interviewing suspects?' asked Pamela. 'You can use our room to interrogate people, if you like.'

Liz sighed. She glanced down again at the body of the murdered woman. 'Does anyone know if there's a doctor around here?'

Chapter Fifteen

Loudwater, A40, Buckinghamshire

Warg Daddy twisted the throttle and felt his bike leap forward like a hunting lion. Faster he pushed it, then faster still. Its engine rose to a tumultuous roar. The bike hugged the road, belting along the straights, cupping the curves as smoothly as his hand over a woman's body. Its huge tyres rolled over tarmac, crunched on gravel, and skidded across muddy grass in the places where the highway was blocked and he had to duck around the wreckage of cars and trucks.

Faster he urged his bike, as fast as he dared. Even faster, until the burning pain in his head was gone, and the world was a blur, his problems a distant memory, and all he could feel was the roar of the wind, the throbbing of the bike between his legs, and Vixen's fingers curled tight around his waist, as his girl clung on to him desperately for life. The rest of the Wolf Brothers trailed behind him on their own bikes, struggling to keep up.

Why slow down? There were no speed limits any more. No traffic cops. No one to tell him what to do. There would never be any of those things again. Everything he hated about the world had been blown away forever.

But there were no petrol pumps either, no one to repair or service his bike, and no one to clear the roads of abandoned cars. Up ahead the way was blocked in a tangle of steel, glass and plastic. A pile-up of dozens of vehicles, with more trapped behind.

Warg Daddy raised a hand and signalled for the Brothers to stop. They pulled up behind him alongside the line of abandoned vehicles and began to search for fuel. He watched as they scavenged what they could, siphoning off the precious fluid into their thirsty tanks. The roadside filling stations may all be empty, but every car on the road was a potential reservoir of free fuel. Liquid gold was theirs for the taking.

The petrol vapour shimmered in the warm air and Warg Daddy inhaled deeply, enjoying its heady perfume. He'd always loved the smell of gasoline. Some people told him that sniffing oil wasn't wholesome. They said it wrecked your brains. Maybe they were right. But he didn't care. Nothing compared with the deep intoxication of those rich airborne hydrocarbons. And now that he was a werewolf and could smell every nuance, they had become ten times more satisfying. Every sniff was a mind-blowing trip to ecstasy. And anyway, his brains were half-wrecked already. Maybe more than half. Maybe almost entirely gone.

The midday sun glinted brightly off the chrome exhaust pipes of the bikes and the shattered windscreens of the smashed cars. Warg Daddy watched the Brothers go about their work through his darkened Ray-Bans. It wasn't gasoline fumes that made his head hurt, it was sunlight. But since leaving the city behind, the headaches that had tormented him for so long had almost gone. His vision was no longer flecked with red. The relentless growing pressure inside his skull had eased.

Perhaps it was the deafening noise of the warheads that had blown the pain away as they deposited their megaton payloads of destruction across London. Or else the blinding flash of light in his rear-view mirrors as he had sped from the burning city, almost at the last moment, deliciously close to ground zero. Perhaps it had even been the deadly fingers of radiation – gamma rays, alpha particles and neutron beams – invisible even to his super senses, but which had surely reached out and clutched at him with their lethal embrace. Whatever had done it, his mind was clear now, the pain pushed into oblivion.

The road ahead was clear too. He scanned the horizon. Nothing. No movement on the road. No one.

The full extent of his freedom was only just beginning to dawn on him. It wasn't just traffic regulations that had ended. There were no laws of any kind, and no one to enforce them even if there had been. No cops. No judges. No courts or prisons. No rules. No limits. He could do whatever he wanted.

The only law now was the oldest one of all – the strong shall rule the weak. And Warg Daddy was the strongest of the strong.

He was free of Leanna as well. He thought of her, still trapped in central London when the bombs fell. His mind's eye lingered on her long blonde hair and crystal blue eyes, her slender limbs and chiselled cheeks. She had been beautiful, a babe, and had meant something to him once. She had given him the gift of lycanthropy, and he had loved her, served her, worshipped her. Damnit, he had very nearly given his life for her. But those days were over. Leanna was gone. Only the faintest shadow of her cruelty lived on in his mind, and it was fading with every mile he rode. When his journey was over, she would be gone forever, and he would be free at last. He had Vixen now instead. He leaned back against her and felt her soft touch as her hair fell across his face. She wrapped her thin arms around his broad chest, kissing the wolf tattoo on his neck.

She was an angel, Vixen. A dark angel of death. He had watched her slaughtering soldiers, ripping limbs out of sockets with her bare hands, severing body parts with her teeth, supping blood through pale lips. Vixen took lives like other girls took online dating quizzes. She was a worthy partner, a soul mate. They would always be together, bound by blood, bonded by love. He kissed her back, enjoying the sweet taste of her tongue.

The Brothers finished filling their tanks and returned to their bikes, kicking their engines back to eager life, choking the air with delicious toxic fumes. Of the original twelve Brothers, only eight remained. Slasher, Meathook, Bloodbath and the rest. They were hungry for the open road, and so was Warg Daddy. They turned to him, waiting for him to give them his order. Behind him, Vixen hugged him tight, ready to roll.

He was Leader of the Pack and they would ride wherever he said. But he had no destination in mind. A destination marked a journey's end. His journey was only just beginning. He had no plan, no goal, no objective, other than adventure.

Ahead of him the long road beckoned and whatever it brought his way, he was ready. 'Come on,' he said to the Brothers. 'Let's go!'

Chapter Sixteen

Gatwick Airport, West Sussex

A retired doctor lived on the top floor of the hotel, and his name was William Pope. Liz was very pleased to make his acquaintance.

'Call me Bill,' he said, shaking her hand. 'But I'm not a forensic pathologist, just a general practitioner. And I retired more than ten years ago. My real speciality these days is golf.'

'I understand that,' said Liz. 'I just need someone with a medical background to take a look at the body and make an educated guess about the cause and time of death.'

'I can certainly do that,' said Doctor Pope.

She led him down to the room where Hannah's body still lay, and introduced him to the family. Doctor Pope shook hands solemnly with Scott Matthews, the dead woman's father. 'I'm sorry for your loss.'

Scott was bearing up stoically, but the rest of the family were in tears. 'Perhaps you could take them to your room while we examine the body?' suggested Liz to Pamela.

'Oh, right, of course,' said Pamela, looking disappointed at being asked to go. 'Come on then, let's go next door.'

'I'd like to stay here,' said Scott.

Liz waited for the others to leave, then closed the door behind them. She really didn't need an audience for this.

'No doubt you'll need to inform Major Hall of the death,' said Doctor Pope.

'Who's Major Hall?'

'He's the man in charge here. You haven't met him yet?' said Doctor Pope in surprise. 'I'd have thought he'd be very keen to meet a police officer. He's a real stickler for rules and regulations. He likes everything to be done by the book.' He turned to the corpse. 'Goodness me.' He kneeled down slowly, his knees creaking, and began to carefully examine the body. 'Clear signs of *pallor mortis* and *algor mortis*, but the muscles are still relaxed. I would estimate the time of death to be between two and four o'clock in the morning. When was the body discovered?'

'Just before 6am.'

'And what time was the victim last seen alive?'

'About midnight.'

'That sounds about right then.' He peered closely at the holes in the woman's neck. 'Hmm. Very peculiar. Has anyone moved or cleaned the body?'

'Not as far as I know,' said Liz. She looked to the woman's father, Scott, for confirmation.

'No,' he answered emphatically. 'All I did was cover her with the sheet. Why do you ask?'

'Well,' said Doctor Pope, pushing his fingers around the neck wounds, 'these two puncture wounds are not especially deep, but they've managed to pierce the common carotid artery and internal jugular vein. That would normally lead to very extensive bleeding, but there appears to be little evidence of that. Only a little blood is apparent on the victim's clothing, and almost none on the carpet. I can't explain that.'

'Could the murderer have used a cloth or towel to mop up the blood?' asked Liz.

'Possibly. But it's clear that a great deal of blood has been lost, and a double wound of this nature would probably have caused a considerable fountain of blood. I'm sorry,' the doctor added, seeing Mr Matthews' look of distress.

'Are the neck wounds definitely the cause of death?' asked Liz.

'I would say so, yes.'

'What about the murder weapon?'

Doctor Pope turned his attention back to the double puncture wound. 'Some sharp object, roughly cylindrical like a knitting needle, but oval rather than circular. The wounds are clean, so I would imagine a metal weapon, but I couldn't rule out plastic, resin or even bamboo. The two puncture holes are relatively shallow, no more than three centimetres deep, suggesting something not particularly long – perhaps a nail – or else that the murderer applied just enough force to pierce the vein and artery.'

'I've searched the room thoroughly,' said Liz, 'and found nothing like that.' It would have been a different matter if she'd searched her own room, she reflected. Mrs Singh's collection of knitting needles would make potentially lethal weapons.

'I don't know what else I can do to help,' said Doctor Pope, returning awkwardly to standing. 'My main concern now would be the appropriate disposal of the body.' He turned to address Scott Matthews. 'Have you given any consideration to whether you'd like your daughter to be buried or cremated?'

Scott shook his head.

'Well, I think that should be your next priority. There are no facilities for storing a body here. So regardless of the murder investigation, the funeral will need to be carried out within two days at the latest. I trust that won't be a problem, Constable Bailey?'

The doctor was right. Already flies were buzzing around the room, showing great interest in the deceased. Although Liz's police training made her want to preserve the body and the scene of the crime until all evidence had been collected, it was clear that in this new world, the window for evidence collection was closing rapidly. 'All right, doctor,' she said. 'Thank you for your help.'

She left the grieving family and returned to her room upstairs. Kevin met her with a concerned look. 'I saved some breakfast for you, love,' he said. 'Full English. It might be a bit on the cold side now.'

It seemed a miracle that the hotel was still capable of cooking and serving food. But Doctor Pope had told her that although the electricity and gas supplies had failed, the airport still had emergency generators, as well as propane heaters. And there was apparently no shortage of diesel and propane to power them. The camp organizers had managed to keep the fridges and freezers in the kitchens running, and had stockpiles of tinned food too. The mains water supply network had failed because the pumping stations needed to keep the water at pressure had all stopped working. But the army had rigged up rainwater collection systems on the roofs of the terminal buildings, and were pumping emergency water from a nearby reservoir. Life went on.

At least for most people.

'So, who did it?' asked Kevin. 'Did you catch the bastard?'

'Not yet. I'll need to make more enquiries.'

The plate of sausage, beans, bacon and fried potatoes that Kevin had produced was as cold as the corpse she had just left, but Liz devoured the food ravenously, washing it down with a cold cup of coffee. Her work day was only just beginning, and it seemed that her police skills were going to be just as much in demand here as they had been back in London. Perhaps even more so, since she seemed to be the only police officer around.

Mihai, Drake and Vijay were eyeing her eagerly. 'We'll help,' said Drake. 'We can be your deputies.'

'Is right,' agreed Mihai. 'You need our help now.'

Liz shook her head. 'No way. You're going to stay here and help to look after the others.'

'Come on,' said Drake. They don't need us to look after them. We'll be more use helping you, yeah? You got no one else. Anyway, I reckon that if you'd listened to us when we first told you that Mr Canning was a werewolf, you could have arrested him much quicker.'

Liz stared glumly back. Her failure to arrest Mr Canning was perhaps her biggest regret of recent times. Drake was right. If only she'd taken their tip-off more seriously, she could have saved at least one girl from being eaten by the killer headmaster.

And it was true that she could use some assistance. Now that Dean was dead, she had no one else to turn to. Vijay and Drake were almost adults. Drake was already taller than her and was starting to fill out and develop some muscle. Even Vijay looked keen to help, and she was pleased to see some life back in the boy. Perhaps giving him a job to do would help him get over his recent trauma and take his mind off Rose.

She had doubts about Mihai, but the Romanian boy had proved his resourcefulness on more than one occasion. And she suspected that if she didn't find a role for him, he would choose one for himself.

He was studying her closely with his dark eyes. He gave her a wicked grin, as if he knew she'd already made up her mind. 'We all policemen now. We make great team together. So, tell us what to do, boss.'

Chapter Seventeen

The Ridgeway, Oxfordshire

Chris Crohn was happy, and that was a surprise. Chris was rarely happy, and had not been happy for a very long while. In fact he had been deeply unhappy and troubled for as long as he cared to remember.

Being thrown together with strangers in an unfamiliar environment ought to be the worst thing he could have imagined. Normally he hated being in the company of others, as he found almost all other people infuriating. He had always preferred solitary pursuits – tinkering with circuit boards, coding algorithms on his desktop computer, and conjuring digital miracles in the privacy of his small apartment in Manor Road. Few people had ever appreciated the wonder of what he did, and now that his apartment had been turned to dust in a nuclear holocaust he could do those things no more.

He trudged along the rocky path of the Ridgeway, one

foot after another in a steady rhythm, remembering all of the activities he could no longer do. The list was long. Long enough to pass several hours. It ought to have left him profoundly depressed, and yet somehow, with the sun on his face and a light wind rustling his hair, life didn't feel too bad.

A blue sky overhead, fields and trees all around, birds and wild animals going about their business. On a distant hilltop, a wind turbine turned uselessly in the steady breeze. It was kind of ironic, now that all electricity production had ceased. The wind turbine was like Chris himself – obsolete and redundant, and unable to fulfil the job it was intended to perform. What could he ever hope to do in this primitive new world?

The digital age had ended. Computers were history, and even Ryan's smartphone had stopped working. The networks were all down, GPS had been switched off, and the phone's battery had run flat, never to be recharged again. Chris had been thrust back into a new dark age. His skillset was badly in need of upgrading, or rather downgrading, back a thousand years or more. He ought to be profoundly sad. And yet here he was, happy.

The reason was simple. Suddenly, unexpectedly, and without even trying, he had become a leader, and he knew why.

In times of chaos, people looked for certainty. When their world had crumbled to dust, they turned to someone who was not afraid to show them the way. Chris was that person. He was a beacon of rationality, shining in the darkness; a fount of knowledge and wisdom, when all around was ignorance and doubt. It was as if his whole life had prepared him for this fate. He didn't believe in fate, or destiny, or even luck, but he did believe in the law of averages. He had been treated with such little gratitude his entire life, it was about time that his situation changed.

Chris didn't like to lead from the front. Instead, he walked at the back of the group of four – or five if you included the dog, and even Chris was willing to concede that the animal had a certain degree of intelligence, perhaps not much less than Seth or Ryan – watching them as they made their way in a south-westerly direction along the chalk ridge road. It gave him a deep satisfaction to see them heading that way.

They were following this route because he had convinced them that it was their best option. All his life he had done his best to persuade people that he knew best, and time after time, he had been ignored. Even though he devoted more effort than everyone else to preparing his plans, researching his facts, and refining his strategies, the world had taken no notice of him whatsoever. He had lacked the power of persuasion that could bring his ideas to fruition. Now, they were listening to him. They were following his plan. They were going where he wanted.

Yes, his luck certainly had changed. Even though he didn't believe in luck.

They were making excellent progress and were almost halfway to Hereford, well ahead of schedule. They had encountered no one else along the path, neither human nor werewolf, and that was all for the good.

Although Ryan's smartphone had died, removing Chris' ability to connect to the world of knowledge that was the internet, he was finding out all about the Ridgeway from the informative signs that marked its length. He had learned that the Ridgeway dated back to the Bronze Age period, and had been used by travellers for five thousand years. A large number of important archaeological sites were dotted along its route, from stone circles to hill forts and ancient burial chambers. It would have been interesting to stop and visit some of these places, but of course they couldn't afford to do that. But there was one place that he wanted to see more closely – the white horse of Uffington, one of the most famous landmarks, and it was directly on their way.

The white horse was a giant stylised image of a horse,

carved into the white chalk hillside. The figure dated back some three thousand years, and they ought to be passing it the following day, or the day after. Yes, a gigantic white horse was something to look forward to. His enthusiasm redoubled, he hefted the backpack on his shoulders and hurried to catch up with the others.

Rose turned her head as he reached her. 'I remember you now,' she said. 'I knew I'd seen you somewhere before, but I didn't know where. You were the computer nerd at school, weren't you?'

Chris bristled at the comment. 'My job was IT Technical Support. And have you only just remembered me?' He oughtn't to be too surprised, he supposed. In his previous life he had been invisible. He'd been Chris the nerd, who fixed the email and the printer, who ordered more ink cartridges and solved the networking problems. His genius had gone unrecognized for so many years.

'My mind was muddled before,' said Rose. 'The nightmares made me forget everything. Now they're gone, I'm starting to think clearly again.' She skipped ahead, running along the path with Nutmeg dancing in delight at her feet.

Up ahead, Ryan was frowning. Of all the people in the group, Ryan was probably Chris' least favourite. He was all muscle, and Chris didn't trust muscle. The more muscle, the less brains, in his experience. Still, Ryan wasn't entirely stupid. He wasn't as dumb as Seth, for instance.

Ryan waited for Chris to catch up with him, before asking a question. 'What do you think about Rose?'

Chris hadn't given Rose a lot of consideration. He'd been too busy reminiscing about computers. 'I don't know what you mean. Can you be more specific?'

'Well, how does her behaviour seem to you? Since the nuclear attack.'

'I think she's getting better. She's recovering from her PTSD.'

'But her dreams have stopped. What does that mean?'

'It means that she's recovering from her PTSD,' said Chris, annoyed at having to repeat himself. Why didn't people ever listen to what he said? The world was full of idiots.

'Yeah, but if her dreams have stopped, she can't see the future anymore.'

'That's true,' agreed Seth. 'How are we going to know what to do now?'

'What?' Chris glared at the two men, fury building in his chest. How could they be so stupid? 'Rose didn't see the future in her dreams!' he shouted at them. 'They were just nightmares; symptoms of trauma and distress. It's a well-documented psychological phenomenon.'

'She told us that London was going to burn,' said Ryan, 'and it did.'

'It was a prophesy,' said Seth.

'London didn't burn,' protested Chris. 'It was annihilated in a series of thermonuclear explosions.'

'Same thing,' said Ryan obstinately.

'Anyway,' continued Chris, striving to restore some calm and order to the world, 'we don't need prophets and soothsayers. We have a plan. My plan.' A leader ought to demonstrate confidence and assurance. A leader should not lose his rag every time some idiot opened his mouth.

But Ryan wasn't listening. He spoke to Seth instead. 'If Rose's visions have stopped, do you think that means that all the bad stuff has come to an end now?'

Seth shrugged, causing his long brown hair to flop over his eyes. 'Dunno, maybe.'

'Let me tell you this,' said Chris, speaking loudly and clearly so the words would penetrate their thick skulls. 'The bad stuff has certainly not come to an end. You don't need visions or dreams to know that a shedload of bad stuff is waiting for us just around the corner. And if you don't do exactly what I tell you, the bad stuff is going to land right on your head.'

'Is that right?' said Ryan.

'Yes. I'm in charge now,' said Chris, 'and you have to follow me, not Rose's stupid dreams and prophesies. I only agreed to let you join our group because you had a smartphone, and now that doesn't even work.'

'We let Ryan join us,' said Seth, 'because he was the only person who knew the way to Hereford.'

Chris turned to him, unable to keep his frustration at bay. 'We would never have got lost in the first place if it hadn't been for you,' he shouted. 'If you'd done what I told you in the first place, we'd have been in Hereford months ago.'

Seth opened his mouth to say something, but Chris didn't want to hear it. He planted both hands against Seth's chest and shoved him as hard as he could.

Seth toppled backward, tripping over a tuft of grass at the side of the chalk path, and down a grassy bank. His arms circled like windmills as he disappeared over the edge. 'Ow!' he screamed as he landed in a heap at the bottom of the ditch.

Chris gazed on in shock. What had he done? He had completely lost his temper, and with it his authority. What kind of leader hurt his own followers? A few examples from history presented themselves – Stalin, Mao, Pol Pot. He shook his head. He had no desire to become that kind of leader.

He ran down the slope to where Seth lay sprawled in the mud. 'I'm sorry,' he said to his friend. 'I didn't mean to push you. Are you okay?'

Seth tried to sit, but immediately doubled up in agony. 'My ankle!'

Ryan came down the bank and kneeled next to him, examining his foot.

'Don't touch it!' screamed Seth. 'Oh my God, it hurts so much!'

'What's wrong with it?' asked Chris. 'Can you fix it?'

Ryan shook his head from side to side. 'Nope. I think it might be broken.'

Chapter Eighteen

Stoke Park, Buckinghamshire

'May I come in?' asked Chanita, peering around the door to Doctor Helen Eastgate's laboratory.

Helen looked up from her desk. 'Of course. You don't need to ask. Come right in.'

Chanita pushed the door open and entered the lab bearing a tray of bone china tea cups, silver teaspoons and a pot of freshly brewed Earl Grey tea. Civilization might have come crashing to a halt, but at Stoke Park some traditions were still being upheld, at least for the time being.

Helen cleared a corner of her messy desk for the cups and saucers while Chanita closed the door behind her. It had been several days since she'd had a chance to visit Helen, and it was time the two women had a proper talk.

Chanita and Helen had been attempting to travel into London when the missiles had exploded. They had very nearly been caught in the blast. If they had started their journey ten minutes earlier, they would almost certainly have perished.

Since returning from that trip to resume the running of the camp, Chanita had been so busy she had barely found the time to eat, drink or sleep. But she had a good team around her now, and they had taken on a huge chunk of the workload. Now at last she had found time to come and visit Helen. Seeing her friend's lined and drawn face, she realized that her visit was well overdue.

'So how are you feeling?' she asked Helen, pouring the tea carefully into the two cups. The slow sound of the golden liquid made a refreshing and soothing change from the hubbub of the camp's hectic command centre.

'Good,' said Helen.

Chanita studied her face closely. Helen looked far from good. She seemed close to despair. Her long blonde hair was uncombed and tangled, possibly not even washed for days. Her youthful features seemed to have aged, and her eyes looked heavy and tired. Helen's laboratory, which had never been tidy, was now positively chaotic, with books and paper spilling over every surface, and test tubes and glass slides scattered randomly amongst microscopes and bottles of coloured liquid.

'Helen, if you don't mind me saying, you don't look yourself to me.'

Helen said nothing, but reached for a cup and took a sip of the tea. Her fingers quivered and the cup shook gently in her hand. She quickly replaced it on its saucer, spilling some of the hot liquid over the desk. She made no effort to mop it up.

'What's the matter?' asked Chanita.

'Do you even need to ask?' Helen gestured at the mess in the room. 'What's the point of this? What am I doing here?'

Chanita knew what Helen was referring to. A week or so earlier, Helen had been filled with optimism after discovering that Chanita possessed natural immunity to lycanthropy, and that her immune system produced antibodies against the disease. She had hoped to use the discovery to develop a cure or a vaccine. They had planned to return together to Helen's laboratory at the Biomedical Institute of Imperial College, London, to synthesize antibodies from Chanita's blood. Together they could have found a way to defeat lycanthropy. But now those plans lay in ruins.

Chanita took Helen's hand and held it tight. She could feel a continuing tremble in Helen's fingers.

'It's not only the facilities in London that have been destroyed,' said Helen. 'I had colleagues in Manchester I could have worked with. But Manchester is gone too. Not to mention Birmingham, Liverpool, Glasgow … All those people, dead. And now there's no chance of taking my work forward.' She snatched her hand angrily from Chanita's grasp, sending her cup of tea flying across the room. 'Shit!' Helen threw her hands to her face and began to sob.

'Helen, I –'

Helen leapt to her feet and stumbled away out of Chanita's reach. Her movements seemed jerky, almost clumsy.

'Helen, what's –'

'There's just no point to anything anymore,' said Helen. 'I came so close. After all the tests I ran, I finally discovered someone with natural immunity to the disease – you. I really thought I was on the brink of developing a cure, or at least a vaccine. And then –'

'There's still hope, Helen.'

'No. There isn't. It's impossible to clone antibodies without the most advanced lab facilities. We can't do it here, not with all the will in the world. It's over, Chanita. Forget it. The only way we're going to be able to stamp out this disease now is by killing every last werewolf. It's up to the army to do it. I can't help.'

'There must be something you can do,' said Chanita. 'There's always a way. Remember what I said to you on the day we first met? We have to keep doing the job we've been assigned. With patience and persistence we can make a difference. Look at me – a month ago I was just a nurse. Now I'm running a camp, responsible for thousands of people.'

'That's all very well. You're very inspiring, it's true. But look at this – ' Helen reached across a worktop and picked up a test tube containing a red liquid – 'Do you know what this is? It's a sample of your blood. In here is the key to eradicating the disease. But what can I do with it? Nothing!'

She turned to place the tube back on her worktop, but it slipped from her grasp and smashed to pieces on the tiled floor. The blood seeped slowly across the tiles, spreading slivers of glass.

Helen slumped, wordlessly, her shoulders shaking with loud sobs.

Chanita had never seen her friend cry before. She had never seen her act this way, so full of despair and hopelessness. She crossed the room and wrapped her arms around her, comforting her in shared silence.

Eventually Helen's tears dried up. She fished a handkerchief from her trouser pocket and blew her nose loudly. 'What use was that blood anyway, if I can't get access to a lab?'

Chanita watched her clumsy, uncoordinated movements as she folded the handkerchief away and bent over to start mopping up the spilled blood. 'What is wrong with you?' she asked gently. 'Never mind all this business about finding a cure. What's happened to you?'

Helen looked up, her eyes still red with tears. 'You mean the shaking? The clumsiness? I can't hide it anymore, can I?'

'What is it?'

'Huntington's disease.'

Now Chanita understood. Huntington's was a genetic disorder that slowly and progressively destroyed the nervous system. She had seen the symptoms often enough in Helen, but had dismissed them as carelessness or clumsiness. Trembling fingers and slow, jerky movements were one of the more obvious first signs of the disease. The condition would steadily progress until she was no longer able to walk or even stand unaided.

'I'm so sorry, Helen.' She could think of nothing more to say. As a nurse she knew that the disease was incurable and untreatable. Helen might have only another ten years to live.

Helen sat on the floor amid the debris, looking utterly defeated. 'It's over. You go back to running the camp. There's nothing more you can do for me.'

Chanita looked down at her friend. It broke her heart to see her in such a pitiful state. She had completely given up hope, not even caring that the blood from the test tube was soaking into her white lab coat.

'The blood –' said Chanita.

'Never mind about that,' said Helen. 'I'll clean it up.'

'The blood –' An idea was taking shape in Chanita's mind. She was no doctor or scientist, only a humble nurse. And yet …

'What about the blood?' asked Helen.

'What would happen if you simply took a sample of my blood and injected it directly into someone else's bloodstream? Would the antibodies be passed on? Could you use it as a cure?'

Helen stared at her. 'I …' Suddenly she was a scientist again, a glimmer of optimism flashing in her blue eyes. 'Direct intravenous infusion? It's possible that the antibodies from your blood could be passed on. The blood group … it would have to be compatible.'

'I'm O Negative,' said Chanita quickly. 'My blood can be given to anyone.'

Helen sat up. Her eyes stared into the distance,

unfocussed, thinking. After a moment she reached out a hand and Chanita hauled her back onto her feet. 'We can try it. There's a chance.'

Never mind if there was a cure. For Chanita, seeing Helen find hope again was more than enough.

'But to test a cure,' said Helen, 'we'd need to get hold of a live werewolf.'

Chanita held onto her hand and smiled. 'I'll see if I can find you one.'

Chapter Nineteen

M40 Motorway, Oxfordshire

Warg Daddy pulled up before the next motorway junction, right in the middle of the carriageway, at the very brow of a hill. The tarmac stretched out for mile after empty mile, both ahead and behind. He had encountered no other moving traffic for miles now. The road was his, and his alone.

The Brothers pulled to a halt beside him, brakes screeching, rubber burning, all wrapped in black leather, white wolves riding on their backs. They scanned the horizon, seeing what he had already seen, asking themselves the question he was asking himself.

Only Slasher had the courage to voice it aloud. 'Which way next?'

Warg Daddy was in no rush to answer. He was happy to enjoy the view over the rolling hillsides, the warm sunshine on his face. The fields to either side of the road were studded with spring flowers, welcoming the warmth of the new season. Baby lambs wandered through the grass, their legs wobbling as they followed their mothers. Birds tweeted in the hedgerows. Warg Daddy felt a sudden rush of … happiness? Was this what he had been seeking all along? He lifted the visor of his crash helmet to see better.

His vision was clear now that he had left Leanna and all her troubles behind. She had been the cause of the pain that had drilled into his skull like an unrelenting jackhammer, day after day. He understood that now. She had made him her slave, rewarding him with nothing but suffering. Now she was gone. The skies stretched out from distant horizon to blue infinity, and the roads were free of jams. He could do whatever he willed, go wherever he chose. But how to choose? When you had no destination in mind, one road was as good as another. Too much choice made it impossible to decide.

'North?' suggested Slasher.

'I say we continue west,' said Bloodbath.

'What say you, Meathook?' asked Warg Daddy.

'We should go south. South is best.'

Behind him Vixen shifted noiselessly in her seat. Whatever her opinion on the matter, she kept her counsel to herself. She was a quiet one, Vixen, speaking only when asked. In any case, it was for Warg Daddy to make the decision. He was Leader of the Pack and they would follow where he led.

He lifted his Ray-Bans cautiously, but the bright sun burned his eyes and he dropped them back into place. No matter. Even with his sunglasses on he could see further than any of the Brothers. His senses of hearing and smell were keener too, not that there was anything much to hear or smell right now over the roar of the bikes and their smoky exhausts. And he was used to leading. It was as natural to him as breathing.

But for some reason it was hard to make a choice.

His thinking wasn't coming as easily as it should. He

shook his head, struggling to free himself from the traces of brain fog that still lurked inside his skull. The mists swirled in the corners of his mind, wrapping grey tendrils around his thoughts. He pulled off his helmet and rubbed the smooth baldness of his crown until the mists receded a little. North, south, east or west? The choice seemed overwhelmingly difficult.

He rubbed at his head some more, working his thumb into the skin until clarity eventually came. Now he saw clearly, and the choice wasn't as hard as he'd imagined.

The truth was, it made no difference which way they rode. Choices only mattered if you had a plan, and Warg Daddy was done with plans. He'd had enough of Leanna's relentless planning and scheming. Strategies, objectives, goals and deliverables. Where had all that got them? They had raised a generation of werewolves, built a Wolf Army, led it into battle, and almost defeated the British Army. They had tasted victory, and stood at the very cusp of triumph. Together they might have taken over the entire world. So, yeah, maybe planning had its uses. But the price was too great. It had robbed him of his will to live.

He reached deep into his pocket and drew out an old coin. The coin was tarnished, its two faces faded and grimy but still just legible. With a flick of his thumb he flipped it high into the blue sky, up towards the clouds. The coin spun, once, twice, many times, until falling back to earth. He caught it on the back of his hairy hand and covered it with his palm.

The Brothers gathered round to see, as if he were a sideshow conjuror performing a cheap magic trick. Their fate hung in the balance. Whatever the coin revealed, their destiny would be fixed. He slid his palm away to reveal the coin, lying heads up. 'We go west,' he announced, as if it had been his choice after all. The Brothers nodded sagely, affirming his decision. But there would be no more decisions. From now on, there would only be fortune. He had given himself up to chance, and with it, the freedom and adventure it would bring.

Chapter Twenty

Norbury Park, Surrey

Colonel Griffin spent another night in the helicopter, this time wrapped in a thermal blanket, but still shivering from the cold. Now that March had come, the days were growing noticeably longer, but there was a deep chill at night, and frost in the morning. He knew that to survive this coming day he would need to address the critical needs of water, food and shelter, not to mention dealing with his medical care. As soon as the sun rose above the treeline he made his first attempt to escape the wreckage of the aircraft.

The effects of the morphine had worn off, and now all movement was sheer agony. His leg was useless, just a heavy weight that he must drag with him, trying to move it as little as possible. The helicopter lay on its side, making it impossible to open the nearest door. The open doorway on the other side of the cockpit was lifted up to face the sky, requiring a climb of some six feet or so. In his current state, it may just as well have been a mile high.

He gritted his teeth and pulled himself out of his seat, clambering into the front of the cockpit over the body of the dead pilot. There was no dignity in his escape, and he slithered across the pilot's body, oblivious to the touch of dead flesh. He yelled with every breath, fighting the pain, afraid of passing out yet again. The windscreen had been entirely shattered in the crash, and he hauled himself out over the jagged teeth of glass at the front of the helicopter. Somehow he made it out of the mangled cockpit and lowered himself to the ground.

The forest floor was cold and frost-hard under the shade of the trees, but the dark leaf mould that covered it was soft and crumbly. He scooped up a handful and breathed in its old, earthy smell. It was good to be back in the open air, free at last from the metal cage that had almost trapped him forever.

After a short rest, the sound of trickling water through the trees was enough to spur him on. He hauled himself along on his back, dragging his mangled leg along the ground, trying to protect the wound from dirt and further damage. He hadn't investigated his injury since carrying out his rudimentary operation, and he suspected that the leg was fractured in at least one place. But that could wait. First he needed to quench his thirst.

It took an age to reach the running brook, but he made it eventually. He leaned down into the shallow ditch and scooped up welcome handfuls of pure, freezing water. It stung his throat as he swallowed, but he was grateful nonetheless. He drank until he was satisfied, then refilled his water bottle.

Looking back at the helicopter, the spot where he had crash-landed seemed to him like a miniature paradise on earth, a tiny undiscovered Eden hidden deep within the English woodland. Trees, early wildflowers, birds and forest creatures called it their home. He lay on his back resting, watching the sun slowly climb in the sky. The frost melted away as he listened to the birds, saw the early morning wind stir the trees, and felt the weak sun begin to warm his face. It would be sweet to lie here all day, among the yellow daffodils and wild crocuses, thinking of nothing. But that was the path to a quick death. Reluctantly he turned from the stream and began to drag himself back to the wreckage of the helicopter.

The clothing he had worn for the short flight was too thin. He needed warmth. The pilot and co-pilot were dressed in standard army issue one-piece flight suits, made from fire-resistant material. The suits were lightweight, breathable and comfortable. Not only were they fire-resistant, but their thermal properties would also provide excellent insulation against the cold. How he was going to find the strength to strip a suit from one of the men he didn't know, but it was clear that he must find a way somehow.

By the time he had covered the short distance back to the helicopter he was exhausted and took another long rest. There was no hurry. He had all the time in the world. He closed his eyes and dozed in the gentle sunshine.

When he opened his eyes again the sun was high in the sky. He had no idea how it could have moved that far. One thing was certain. He had to get on with his task. He cried out in agony as he hauled himself back up across the nose of the helicopter and into the cockpit. His leg needed more attention, but he had to solve his problems in the right order. Another night in the cold would surely kill him if he didn't find warmth.

The pilot was about his size, and he managed to unbuckle him from his seat. Once he had done that, the body of the dead man slumped forward. He had no strength to drag the pilot from the cockpit. Instead, he set about unzipping and unfastening his flight suit, one step at a time. Shoulders, sleeves, torso, legs, feet. The job became harder the closer he came to completing it. He had no idea how long it took to undress the man. Time seemed to have taken on an elastic quality. Hours could pass without him seeming to achieve a thing. But eventually it was done. He pulled the flight suit on over his own clothing, crying out every single time he touched his damaged thigh.

The next item on his agenda was food. It was already late afternoon and he hadn't eaten for nearly two days. He had lost nearly half of his blood and was desperately weak. He had to get something inside him before nightfall.

The pilot had a bag tucked beneath his seat and Griffin pulled it out with a small sense of victory. Opening it, he felt like a child unwrapping presents on Christmas morning. Protein bars. Energy drinks. The temptation was to consume the entire contents in one meal, but he knew he had to ration what little he had found. He ate one of the protein bars and drank half of one drink, then stored the rest away for later. Finally, he crawled back out of the helicopter to refill his water bottle from the running stream.

He had still not checked his wound, and already darkness had crept across the sky. But at least he had warm clothing, a little food, and he was still alive. Now he was utterly exhausted and he knew that sleep would come to him immediately.

It was the end of the third day.

Chapter Twenty-One

Gatwick Airport, West Sussex

The second murder came a couple of days later, and once again Joe and Pamela brought Liz the news, rousing her from a fitful slumber in the early hours of the morning. 'It's another young woman,' Pamela told her, ashen-faced. 'Over in the main terminal building this time.'

Liz checked her watch. It was 4:30 am. She'd only just managed to fall asleep. 'Okay, I'm coming.'

Drake jumped out of bed too, and shook Vijay and Mihai awake. 'We're ready to come with you,' he told her.

'Run and fetch Doctor Pope from upstairs, then. Tell him it's another body.'

Liz dressed quickly, slid the holster containing the Glock around her waist, and followed them all downstairs, out of the hotel and through a covered walkway that led to the airport building itself. The airport hotels had limited capacity, and the bulk of the refugees had been assigned a place in one of the two airport terminals. The south terminal was closest to Liz, and this was where Joe led them now.

The night was still cold and dark, and Liz glanced nervously around. It was dangerous to be outside during the hours of darkness, especially with a killer on the loose. There were reports of werewolves being spotted beyond the airport fence, but she knew that if any were out there now, she would probably be able to smell them before they came too close. Besides, she had the gun by her side, and wouldn't hesitate to use it.

She'd reluctantly drawn a blank with the murder of Hannah Matthews. The truth was that with the door unlocked, anyone might have gained access to the room. None of the other members of Hannah's family had seen or heard a thing, nor had any of the people Liz had questioned in the hotel building. The murdered woman had not been sexually molested, and nothing had been stolen from her. It appeared to be a motiveless crime. Moreover, Liz's tools for gathering evidence were extremely limited. She had basically nothing to go on apart from the mysterious method of the murder itself.

The puncture wounds and bruising around Hannah's throat were deeply disturbing. No murder weapon had been found, but the size and depth of the two holes, and the lack of blood in the vicinity of the crime scene suggested alarming possibilities to Liz. Was a werewolf at loose within the hotel? Or worse, another vampire? She had surreptitiously sniffed each person she had interviewed, but had detected no trace of wolf.

Following Doctor Pope's advice, Scott Matthews had buried his daughter in a small grassy patch of land amongst trees, situated some distance from the hotel. A large number of people had attended the funeral, and a Church of England priest had conducted the ceremony. Liz had watched with mixed feelings of sadness, guilt and trepidation. A killer was still on the loose, and she was nowhere nearer to discovering their identity.

She hurried into the south terminal now, quizzing Joe and Pamela for as much information about the latest murder as possible.

'The victim was a woman in her early twenties. I don't know her name,' said Pamela. 'But a friend of mine came to tell us. She knew that we'd had a similar crime at the hotel. I said I'd bring you to investigate, since there's no official police force in the airport.'

'Similar in what way?' asked Liz, dreading the answer.

'Same manner of death,' confirmed Pamela. 'Two holes in the throat.'

Liz groaned inwardly and adjusted her dark glasses as she entered the south terminal. It was a huge building, many times larger than the hotel. The departure lounge was one vast open space, with a mezzanine level overlooking the main floor. A large glass roof was supported by pillars. It was dark inside, but bright lights flickered where people held up flashlights or candles. The smallest sounds echoed off the hard surfaces, forming a continuous undercurrent of noise like the whispering of the wind in trees.

'Over there,' said Drake, pointing to the place where a large group of people had gathered.

Liz pushed her way through to the front of the crowd, followed closely by the others. The murdered woman lay in a sleeping bag, still tightly zipped up.

Liz showed her warrant card to the onlookers, and the doctor lowered himself to the floor to begin his examination.

An elderly couple had discovered the body, and they were keen to tell their story. 'The poor, poor girl,' said the wife. 'We only met her a day or two ago. We didn't know her very well at all.'

'Was it you who discovered the body?'

'No. It was my husband, Frank.'

'I don't sleep very well any more,' began the woman's

husband. 'Especially not in a noisy place like this. Just when I'm almost falling asleep, someone coughs or a baby cries, and I'm back to square one.'

'Can you tell me what you saw?' asked Liz.

'Well, I was just getting up to use the bathroom –'

'Frank needs to use the bathroom a lot in the night these days,' interrupted his wife.

'Yes,' said Frank irritably. 'And I noticed a dark figure crouching over Chelsea.'

'Chelsea is the name of the deceased?'

'That's right. We don't know her surname. She never told us. She was a quiet girl. She kept herself to herself. I don't think she had any family. At least, we never saw her with anyone.'

'So you saw a dark figure,' prompted Liz.

'Yes. Leaning over the body on all fours. I didn't see their face. It was too dark, and I didn't have my glasses on.'

'A man or a woman?'

'I couldn't possibly say.'

'Big or small?'

'I'm not sure.'

'So, what happened?' asked Liz.

'Well, I started to get to my feet, and suddenly this person was making a bolt for it. He – or she – was very fast. I saw them running away, and then they vanished.'

'Vanished?'

'Well, ran out of the door, I suppose,' said Frank. 'That must have been what happened.'

'Frank isn't sure about that,' said the man's wife. 'He thinks they might have turned invisible and disappeared into thin air.'

'No, no,' said Frank crossly. 'That's not what I said. It's just how it looked at the time. I wasn't wearing my glasses. I didn't really believe that's what happened.'

'Into thin air,' repeated the woman, ignoring him. 'Like a ghost.'

'Well,' said Doctor Pope, 'whoever did this was no ghost. The murder looks very much like the previous one. Two puncture wounds, same depth and separation as before. Once again, a massive loss of blood but very little blood to be found on the victim's clothing or in the immediate vicinity. I must say, it's very mysterious.'

'All right,' said Liz. 'Let's start interviewing everyone who was sleeping nearby. Someone must have seen or heard something.'

With the help of the three boys, she managed to speak to over a hundred people, but none could shed any further light on the murder. No one had seen the mysterious crouching figure, apart from Frank, and now even he was starting to have doubts about what he saw. 'It might just have been a trick of the light,' he told Liz at the end of the morning. 'Perhaps I didn't really see anyone at all. It was too dark to be certain.'

She sighed in frustration. A second murder, still no clues, and she hadn't even managed to grab breakfast yet. Her hunger seemed to be boundless these days. She needed to get something inside her, so that she could think. 'Can you please go and find me something to eat?' she said to Drake and Vijay.

'What kind of thing?' asked Vijay.

'Liz likes meat,' said Mihai. 'Any kind, she don't care. Sausage, bacon, pork chops, barbeque chicken. Let's go looking.'

They ran off together in search of food.

Just then she caught sight of Corporal Jones striding towards her from the other side of the terminal building, two of his men beside him. She recognized Evans and the Dogman, together with his dog, Rock.

They were really the last people she wanted to meet right now, but there was no escaping them. The dog bared its teeth at her as it drew near, growling quietly. The Dogman held it tightly on a lead. 'Down boy. Easy.'

Jones was his usual cheery self. 'Liz, we thought we

might find you here. We heard a rumour about a murder. Thought that might be your kind of thing.'

'Well, there's nothing much for you to see,' she said. Doctor Pope had finished his examination over an hour earlier, and Liz had authorized the removal of the body. In such a crowded environment it didn't seem healthy to leave a corpse lying around. The dead woman, Chelsea, had no relatives, and so there seemed no reason not to bury the body later on today. Liz had seen all she needed to. It wasn't like she could run any forensics.

'I heard this wasn't the first murder,' said Jones.

'It's the second case that's been reported to me.'

Rock was still straining on its leash and the Dogman allowed the dog to come closer to her. 'We heard the victim had bite marks on her neck,' he said.

'Two puncture wounds,' corrected Liz. 'Too deep for human teeth. The doctor says they might have been made by a sharp needle or a similar weapon.'

'Or perhaps by a creature that wasn't entirely human,' suggested the Dogman.

Liz ignored him.

'Have you reported the death to Major Hall yet?' asked Llewelyn. 'He has a zero-tolerance policy for any kind of criminal activity, or any rule-breaking, no matter how minor. He'll certainly want to hear about this.'

'No. I don't know where to find him.'

Llewelyn grinned and inclined his head behind her. 'Maybe not, but I think he knows where to find you.'

Liz turned and saw another group of soldiers marching her way. Unlike Jones and his men, who wore green berets that matched their camouflage uniforms, the new arrivals wore maroon berets.

'Parachute Regiment,' muttered Jones, with a mixture of admiration and contempt. 'They think they're the bees' knees.'

The Welshman had mentioned the paras to Liz before. Despite his grumblings about them, she was certain she detected a strong element of hero worship in his comments.

Major Hall and his associates strode briskly over to them. Llewelyn and his men immediately jumped to attention and saluted the commanding officer. Major Hall stood with his hands clasped behind his back. 'At ease, men,' he said.

He offered no handshake for Liz, but instead stood silently surveying her. She returned his stare. Major Hall was very tall and broad-chested. He was aged around forty, wore aviator-style sunglasses that almost completely hid his eyes, and had hair shorn so short it was impossible to tell its colour. He stood at least an inch above his fellow officers and men, and was so heavily built he made them look puny by comparison.

'I've heard reports of a suspicious death,' he told Liz. 'Are you the investigating officer?'

Liz was glad she was still wearing her police uniform. It gave her an immediate authority. 'Police Constable Liz Bailey. Since nobody seems to be operating in an official capacity here, I was asked to investigate. The woman was murdered. I'm taking witness statements.'

Major Hall didn't query her right to be conducting the investigation. 'I understand that the cause of death was … unusual.'

'Wounding to the neck,' said Liz uncomfortably.

'And this is the second such death?'

'That's right.'

'What's your working theory? Do you have any suspects yet?'

'I'm following up a number of leads,' she lied.

The Major offered her a faint smile. 'I'll leave the investigation in your capable hands. Let me know when you've found the guilty party. I'll arrange for his execution myself.' He turned on his heel to leave.

'Wait, what?' said Liz.

The Major spun back to face her. 'You heard me,

Constable Bailey. Execution. I'll tolerate no criminal behaviour of any kind under my command. None whatsoever. And murder is punishable by death, in my opinion. An eye for an eye. A tooth for a tooth.'

Liz grew suddenly hot under her heavy uniform. She drew herself up to her full height, almost level with Major Hall's wide chest. 'With respect, sir, your opinion is irrelevant. People have rights. Just because the country is in a state of emergency, it doesn't mean that the rule of law no longer holds. When I find out who did this, they will have to be given a fair trial, and punished appropriately.'

The faint smile on the Major's face had been replaced with an ugly, threatening scowl. 'The rule of law that holds within this camp is whatever I decide. I keep the peace here. These people are under my protection, and I will not permit them to be harmed.' He turned and gestured toward the glass doors and windows along the edge of the terminal building. 'The area surrounding this airport is lawless territory. Do you have any idea how dangerous it is out there? The government has fallen. Military command has been devolved down to field commanders like myself. The police force, as you know, is non-existent, apart from you, apparently. And lycanthropes are roaming wild beyond the fence. If it were not for the vigilance and bravery of my men, those animals would already have overrun this camp. I will not allow anyone to threaten the security of this facility from within.'

He turned away from her, then turned back. 'And Constable Bailey, allow me to let you into a little secret. Just between the two of us. I absolutely hate lycanthropes. I have a personal grudge against them. I have lost good friends and colleagues to them. Let me be entirely clear, so that there is no possibility of any misunderstanding between us. If your investigation leads you to even suspect anyone inside this camp of being lycanthropic, you will report them to me, and I will execute that individual myself. I am not a judge in a court of law, and I do not require evidence beyond reasonable doubt. Is that clear?'

He marched away without waiting for a response, his men following in his wake.

'Well, he seemed pretty clear about that,' remarked Jones. 'I like a man who knows his own mind.'

'I don't believe it!' said Liz. 'The arrogance of the man. He has no right to execute anyone, whatever he might think.'

'I think he makes a good point,' said the Dogman, staring hard at Liz as if he suspected her of being the murderer herself. Perhaps he did. 'This wasn't the work of a human killer. Anyone can see that.'

Rock growled quietly at his side, hackles raised, not taking his eyes from Liz.

She recalled that Rock had instantly gone berserk in the presence of a family of werewolves, even though they were in human form. If there was a werewolf hiding somewhere in the camp, surely they would have been detected? Rock certainly wasn't the only dog on patrol here.

The other soldier, Evans, kept his gaze on Liz too, and his hand on his rifle, as if expecting her to suddenly grow long teeth and leap at somebody's throat.

Only Llewelyn seemed relaxed. 'They're ruthless bastards, the paras,' he remarked thoughtfully, gazing in the direction of the exit that Major Hall and his men had taken. 'Always have been. Always will be. But they never fail to get the job done.'

Chapter Twenty-Two

Beneath London

There was a rumble up ahead in the tunnel. 'What's that?' Leanna asked, fearing the worst. She had come to loathe these cold, dark sewers almost as much as she loathed her companion.

'Water,' muttered Canning, his brow crinkled in concentration.

It was already deeper here, the dark water rising above her waist, and flowing faster too. Despite Leanna's strength, the water pushed against her like a physical barrier, doing its best to stop her moving forward. If she lost her footing on the slippery floor, she might easily be swept away by the current. 'Are you sure this way is safe?' she asked Canning.

'Just keep close to me,' he answered. 'Don't wander off.'

He motioned at the side passages, leading off to left and right. They were lower than the main passageway, almost entirely submerged beneath oily liquid, and Leanna had no intention of wandering down any of them. This place was a maze. Already she had lost all sense of how they had come to be here, or in what direction they were headed. If she lost Canning now, she might never find him again.

He continued to push on, wading through the shallower water at the side of the tunnel, and Leanna followed, fearing to get left behind.

'They are beautiful, though, aren't they?' he said, stopping briefly to shine his light at the ceiling.

He meant the sewers, she guessed. She was willing to concede that they had a certain atmospheric quality. The black and gold bricks glistened brightly under the beam of the flashlights. The tunnel curved and soared overhead, almost like the roof of a cathedral, and the gurgling green waters bubbled around them like a subterranean lake.

'Beautiful, yet treacherous,' said Canning, casting a glance back at her.

'It's getting deeper,' she said.

'Yes.'

Was he trying to drown her? She wondered if he had led her here deliberately, hoping to lose her amid this vast network of twisting and branching passageways, each one very much like the others. If so, she would tear him to pieces.

Up ahead, he stopped and held up a hand, listening intently. 'This way. Quickly!'

The waters were rising, inch by inch, and flowing ever faster. She pushed after him, her sense of dread increasing with every step. The air space above her head was growing smaller as the waters rose. Soon it would be gone.

Up ahead, the light from his flashlight suddenly vanished. She shone her own light at the place he had been and saw an iron ladder screwed to the wall. Its top disappeared up a dark chimney.

He had betrayed her! She should have known. What

had she learned? Never to trust! And yet she had allowed this one-eyed charlatan to lure her into this death trap. 'Canning!' she shrieked.

The water was almost at the ceiling now, and she splashed forward, her feet barely meeting the floor. She swallowed a mouthful of foul liquid, and then another. She struck out with her hands and dropped her flashlight into the water. It went out.

Now there was nothing but darkness and the flooding tide, and the sound of her own voice screaming and coughing.

A hand closed around her wrist.

She tried to fight it off, but she could not fight both hand and water. She dipped beneath the surface and swallowed another mouthful. Her lungs began to burn. And then the hand was pulling her up, drawing her out of the flood and onto the rungs of the ladder. She gripped the cold iron hard, panting as her breath slowly returned to normal.

The flashlight clicked back on. 'Are you all right, my dear?' said Canning. 'I thought I had lost you there for a moment.'

'You bastard, you tried to drown me.'

His lips curled down in disappointment. 'My dear, I just saved your life. And for the second time too. First I saved you from the explosions, now from drowning. I was hoping for some praise. If we are to work together as a team, you really are going to have to learn to trust me.' He pocketed the light and began to climb the narrow chimney.

Leanna followed. Below her, the waters surged and boiled.

At the top, he grabbed her arm and hauled her into a higher-level passageway. The ceiling was lower here, and she had to crouch, but it was dry.

He switched his light back on. 'The lower levels have completely flooded,' he said. 'We need to get to the surface.'

Leanna cast a glance back at the tunnel she had so narrowly escaped from, and saw the vile water continuing to rise. She needed no further persuading.

Soon a flight of steps appeared, and the path led steeply upward. A glimmer of light was visible at the far end. A short distance further, and another iron ladder led up to an open manhole. The bright light of day shone down, like the light of heaven itself. Canning switched off his flashlight and climbed the ladder. Leanna followed.

She emerged from the sewers to a scene of almost complete destruction. This must once have been a street of houses, but they were nothing more than charred bricks now, all colours turned to grey. A firestorm had swept through, burning everything in its path, leaving only swirling dust and debris in its wake. On the horizon, black clouds of smoke billowed where the inferno still raged, and hot wind blew her hair as the fire drew in oxygen to feed its flames.

'Where are we?' she asked.

'Somewhere in West London, maybe close to Ealing. It's hard to tell. All the landmarks have gone. There's nothing left at all.'

She climbed atop a mound of rubble and stared into the distance, turning slowly to look in every direction. Wherever she looked, the streets and buildings had been reduced to mounds of grey waste. Nothing moved out there but swirling smoke and glowing fires. A pale sun tried to break through, but it was weak and colourless in the low, leaden sky. The city was dead, just as she had suspected.

She was glad to be out of the stinking sewers at last, out in the open air, with the sky above her and the wind in her face. It was a harsh wind, that smelled of soot and death, but its taste was to her liking. She would ride that hot wind as far as it would take her, bringing death to her enemies.

Canning seemed disconcerted by the extent of the

destruction. 'What if it is all like this? Everywhere? What if the whole world has been destroyed?'

'Then we will rebuild it. The past is gone, and this is the age of the werewolf. We have nothing to fear from destruction.' She reached down and scooped up a handful of dust, throwing it into the air and letting the wind take it. 'I am the burning wind now,' she declared exultantly. 'I am the fire that sweeps all aside. Soon my enemies will be dust, just like this.'

She jumped down and landed gracefully at Canning's side. 'Come on! What are you waiting for?'

They set off together, following the line of a railway track. The parallel lines of steel were still intact, leading them into the distance and into the future. This track was her path to freedom, and she would have run along it, if it were not for Canning, and his huffing and puffing. 'Where will this take us?' she asked him.

Canning looked around. 'I think this line will take us to Uxbridge, or the place where Uxbridge once stood. From there, we ought to leave London not far from Windsor.'

'Excellent. Then I'll make Windsor my base.'

It could not have been better. If she were to rule as queen, she would need a throne. And what better place to find a throne than in a royal castle?

Chapter Twenty-Three

Stoke Park, Buckinghamshire

James walked at a steady pace, keeping away from the main roads and towns as far as was possible. Once, he had to cross the six lanes of a strangely empty motorway, and sometimes he had no choice but to sneak through quiet villages and even small towns. But he planned his route carefully, snaking along the bank of the River Thames for part of the journey, and taking diversions away from larger towns, through woodland and across pasture where sheep, cows and horses grazed. He waited until night before approaching built-up areas. It took longer that way, but he had no wish to meet anyone as he travelled.

He stopped once to kill and eat a sheep, and to take shelter in a barn, then again to spend the night hidden in a dense thicket. He took wolf form when darkness fell, so that his thick coat of fur would keep him warm until morning.

He met no one on his travels and soon grew used to being alone. He thought of his friend, Samuel as he walked. He had known Samuel for only a brief time before he had been cruelly snatched away, but it had been the happiest time of his life. When Samuel died he had raged at God, and at the cold-hearted moon, furious at the senseless injustice. But perhaps he had been too quick to judge, for even in his darkest hour, when Samuel had just been killed, God had sent him Melanie, and given him the chance to save her life. In turn he had been rewarded with her friendship, and that of her sister, Sarah, and Ben too. He had even enjoyed the company of Grandpa, even though the old man had not recognized him from one day to the next. And now Joan had helped him, when she might just as easily have turned him away. So even though God remained silent, He was always there, watching James and helping him. All James had to do was keep his faith and trust in God, and one day he would be reconciled. One day too, he knew he would be reunited with Samuel.

God offered him no guidance now, and he no longer had even the cold light of the moon to lead him, but with the help of Joan's map, it didn't take very long to reach the camp. He arrived there just as the afternoon light was fading and the air began to grow cool. He wondered what to do. Should he spend another night outside, curled up warm beneath the trees? Or should he try to enter the camp in human form, and start to search for the others?

According to Joan, Stoke Park had been a country house hotel, and was now being used by the army to house people who had left London and had nowhere else to go. There would probably be hundreds of refugees there, maybe even thousands. It could take a long time to find three people amongst so many. And there would be soldiers there too. It would be dangerous. He remembered the dogs at the army checkpoint on the way out of London. The dogs had been sniffing for werewolves. It would be terrible to be shot by soldiers just as he arrived at the camp where his friends were staying. In any case it was growing too dark to see well and he decided to spend the night alone, and to carry out some reconnaissance first thing in the morning.

He found a small patch of trees near a gurgling brook, carefully removed and folded the clothes that Joan had given him, and turned himself into a wolf, ready to sleep. The stars twinkled above him, bright jewels in a black sky. He noticed how dark the night sky had become these past few days, and how bright the stars burned. So many more were visible since the electric lights had all gone out. It was an amazing sight. He wondered if God was sending humanity a message of hope. Like the rainbow after the Great Flood, it was a promise that God would never again send bombs to destroy the world.

He awoke, hours later, startled by noise and by lights. It was still pitch dark where he lay, and this was not daylight that shone through the trees, nor even the light of the moon or the stars. The white beams of light sliced through the blackness like knives. They were flashlights. The noises that broke the silence were of men shouting orders, and of dogs barking.

Still in wolf form, he sprang to his paws and spun around, seeking a way to escape.

The lights were closing in on him, and he heard men crashing through the undergrowth. The dogs were loose, and were coming straight for him. They had already picked up his scent.

There was no time to think. He abandoned his belongings and dashed away through the ferns and nettles, deeper into the ghostly trees, picked out in white by the lights of the soldiers. He knew he could easily outrun the men, but the dogs might catch him, and if he slowed to fight them, he could end up getting shot.

Frantic barking filled the night as the dogs closed on his trail. The boots of the men crashed through the woods, and they shouted to each other and to the dogs. A bullet whickered over his head and embedded itself in the trunk of a tree.

He veered left suddenly, trying to throw his pursuers off his track, plunging into a shallow stream and running along it for some distance, hoping to hide his scent. The dogs followed, but slower, and the sound of their barking grew less. He bounded up the opposite bank of the stream and made a dash for open country, but suddenly a bright light shone directly in his face. He skidded to a halt and saw a military vehicle right ahead, its searchlight trained on him.

'Take aim!' shouted a voice, and more lights turned his way – flashlights fixed to men's rifles.

James threw his paws protectively over his face and curled into a ball. He could try to fight these men, maybe even kill some of them before they could shoot, but he was just as likely to end up dead. Besides, they were just soldiers, doing their job of guarding the camp. He wished them no harm.

'Shoot to kill!' came the order.

'Stop!' he growled. 'Please don't shoot!'

No reply came, but the soldiers hesitated. Their guns did not fire.

'I surrender!' he bellowed, and willed himself to assume human shape. The change began slowly, the thick sandy fur slowly drawing back into his skin, his muscular arms and legs gradually weakening. As the change took hold he could see the doubts growing in the soldiers' eyes. He willed it to proceed faster, and soon his long snout was remaking itself into the nose, mouth and jaw of a human face.

'Hold your fire!' he heard, as more men emerged from the trees and surrounded him. 'Restrain the dogs.'

By the time he was fully human again, the dogs were back on their leashes, barking furiously in frustration. A soldier approached, an officer by the look of him, and shone a bright light directly into James' eyes. 'This one will do,' he said. He lifted his rifle butt and brought it crashing into James' face. 'Tie him tightly and put him in the back of the truck.'

Chapter Twenty-Four

Stoke Park, Buckinghamshire, quarter moon

Melanie Margolis was growing quietly mad. Okay, not so quietly. She had shouted at Sarah and yelled at Ben, despite promising herself that she would never row with either of them again. That promise hadn't lasted long, just a handful of days. She hated herself for that, and had taken herself out for a long walk, leaving Ben to watch over Sarah in the tent.

It wasn't surprising she had lost her temper. Patience had never been Melanie's strong point, and what little she had was running extremely thin. The city of tents that made up the emergency camp was cramped, smelly and noisy. The food here was dreary and unimaginative, and the bathroom facilities were absolutely disgusting. There were a few electricity generators running, belching out noxious diesel fumes, but they were only for essential services. There was basically no electricity, no lighting, no heating, and precious little clean water. When night fell it was pitch black. People were going to bed at sunset and rising with the sun, just like they must have done in the middle ages. Melanie was used to doing the exact opposite – rising in the evening and stumbling back into bed at dawn. She had always been the last to leave any party.

The soldiers and humanitarian workers all appeared very diligent and hard at work, but were far too busy, or just plain ignorant, to answer any of her questions. *How long are we going to be here? Who's in charge? How do I report a missing person?* No one knew, or cared.

Only a few facts were certain. London was gone. The government had fallen. James was missing. And it was up to Melanie to make the best of it.

She wasn't too worried about herself, or Ben. They could both take care of themselves, and of each other. She had prepared well for the situation, packing enough toiletries and skincare products to make up for the woeful lack of anything decent in the camp. She had brought only one change of clothing, but her choice of leather jacket and boots had been a good one, warm and waterproof. At least she didn't look ridiculous like Ben dressed in Grandpa's old clothes. And to be fair, life at the camp wasn't as bad as she had feared. They were safe, and the tents, though uncomfortable, were weatherproof. The food, though interminably dull, was nutritious enough, and she could hardly expect Michelin-starred menus in what was little more than a soup kitchen.

She was more worried about Sarah. Before leaving London, her sister had not been out of the house in such a long time, that she simply couldn't cope. Living in the camp was an impossibility for her. She had been like a zombie for the first couple of days, not eating, not speaking, barely even conscious of her surroundings. She still wouldn't leave the tent, but at least she was accepting food now, and saying a few words. But one thing was obvious to Melanie, even if Ben refused to admit it. Sarah could not stay here in the camp. However dangerous it might be beyond the fence, if Sarah was going to have any chance of recovering from her trauma, they were going to have to leave and find somewhere far away from human civilization, or what passed for it these days.

Besides, there was another pressing reason to leave the camp. James. That was why she was so mad now, out pacing the camp alone. She had tried to raise the matter with Ben, but it had been hopeless.

'We have to go and look for him,' she'd argued. 'James is all alone, out there somewhere in the wilds. Anything could have happened to him.'

'But we can't go and look for him,' said Ben in that maddeningly reasonable way he had of speaking to her.

'Why the hell not?'

'We can't leave the camp. It's far too dangerous.'

'That's precisely why we have to find him. He might be hurt or injured.'

'Melanie, he almost killed you last time we saw him.'

'That's because he was a wolf. You know he's perfectly safe when he's human.'

'Okay, yes, but my point is that James is quite capable of looking after himself. He will just have to come and find us. Anyway, the soldiers probably won't even allow you to leave.'

That had been the final straw. 'Won't allow me to leave?' she had repeated incredulously. 'Let those damn grunts at the gate try to stop me.'

She had made her way from the tent, stalking through the vast sea of unwashed homeless wretches that populated the rest of the camp, pausing briefly to admire the main headquarters building and peer nosily through the windows. It had been a grand hotel once, and Melanie had stayed here, back in the days when all was well with the world, and a woman with Melanie's qualities could expect to be wined and dined at the best hotels and restaurants. What was the name of the man who had brought her here? She couldn't recall. Most of her clients had left little lasting impression on her. But she remembered the food. Dining in the sumptuous orangery, on Guinea fowl and Jerusalem artichoke. Her mouth began to water at the memory. Now look at the place. Overrun with soldiers and emergency staff, scurrying about, leaving dirty coffee mugs on the polished table tops.

She sighed. The world had changed, and wasn't ever going back to the way it had been. In any case, she had changed too. She was no longer that woman. A harlot, James had called her, on learning the nature of her "job."

'Wow, how Biblical,' she had retorted. 'Factually incorrect too. I never accepted money from any of those men in payment for sex. I only stole from them afterwards.'

It was hardly something to boast about, now she came to think of it. Anyway, she was a harlot no more. Nor a thief. Now she had Ben.

Ben Harvey. What had that poor man ever done to deserve a woman like her?

She could have kicked herself at the way she had treated him. And poor Sarah too. Once again her fiery tongue had got the better of her. Never mind. She would make it up to them later.

She turned her back on the eighteenth-century mansion house and set off along the curving path that swept past what had once been a 27-hole golf course and was now a refugee camp. No golf would ever be played here again, and that was just fine with Melanie. She had always loathed golf.

She followed the road, crossing the bridge over the ornamental lake and arrived at the camp exit. A tall metal gate barred the road next to the lodge buildings, and it had been reinforced with sheets of solid steel. A dozen or so soldiers dressed in full combat gear stood on guard, their armoured vehicles parked on the nearby grass. They watched her warily as she marched up the road toward them, her boots clicking on the tarmac at a steady, relentless pace.

Two soldiers stepped forward to intercept her as she sought a way past the sealed gate. Their assault rifles twitched in their arms.

Melanie treated them to a dazzling smile and a toss of her long hair. 'Would you open the gate for me, please? I would like to leave the camp.'

'I'm sorry ma'am, that won't be possible.' The soldier's voice was cold, impervious to her charm.

'Won't be possible?' she asked innocently. 'Whyever not?'

'Orders.'

'Well soldier, can't you bend the rules just this once? I promise not to tell a soul.'

'Sorry. No.'

She tried again, this time injecting as much scorn as she could muster into her voice. 'Just stand aside and let me through. Or shall I raise a complaint with your commanding officer? I could make a lot of trouble for you.'

The man didn't seem remotely daunted by her changed tone of voice. 'Our orders are that no civilians may leave the camp at present. Under any circumstances.'

She studied the soldier more closely. He was an ugly brute, with big jug ears and a nose that looked like it had once been broken. His name was sewn onto the front of his uniform. Mackenzie. 'Am I a prisoner here, Private Mackenzie?' she asked.

'Sergeant Mackenzie,' he corrected her. 'And no, you are not a prisoner. Nevertheless, it isn't possible for you to leave. Not until the security situation changes, or I receive fresh orders.'

'I see. Then tell me, Sergeant Mackenzie, how far are you willing to go to obey your orders? Are you prepared to shoot a woman?'

The sergeant chuckled unpleasantly. 'Lady, I'm nearly a head taller than you, even in your heels. I'm double your weight. And I have extensive combat training. I don't think I'm going to have to shoot you to stop you leaving this camp.'

Melanie stepped right up to him and poked a manicured finger in his chest. 'You don't frighten me,' she said. 'I've handled bigger men than you before.'

The sergeant stared at her in astonishment, then broke into a grin. 'I'm sure you have. But this time I promise you that your luck's run out.' He nodded at his comrades and two of the other soldiers grabbed Melanie's arms and began to drag her away from the gate.

'Get off me!' she screamed. 'Let me go!'

'Melanie?'

She turned and saw Ben standing on the road. The soldiers stopped.

'What do you think you're doing?' Ben shouted at them. 'Let her go!'

Sergeant Mackenzie nodded once more and the soldiers released her.

'What are you doing here, Ben?' asked Melanie furiously. 'Did you leave Sarah on her own?'

'I had no choice. I had to come and look for you.' He took her hand. 'Come on. They're obviously not going to let you out of the gate. Come back to the tent with me and Sarah. We'll have to find another way to help James.'

She brightened 'You're going to help me find him, then?'

'Yes. We'll find a way, I promise. But not like this.'

She kissed him. 'I knew you'd agree with me in the end.'

She walked back to the tent arm in arm with him, their earlier arguments forgotten. That was what made Ben so wonderful. He never bore a grudge.

But when they reached the tent, Melanie's stomach turned a somersault. 'Oh my God! Where is Sarah?' Her sister was gone.

Chapter Twenty-Five

Norbury Park, Surrey, quarter moon

Colonel Griffin had spent the last night sheltering in the lee of the broken helicopter. He had lacked the energy and the will to crawl back inside the cockpit, but that had been pure folly. Even in its battered state, the cockpit would have provided some shelter from the elements. He was lucky that it hadn't rained overnight. If it had, he would have woken drenched and frozen, with likely hypothermia. He must not make that mistake again.

The birds woke him with their dawn songs, the light turning from grey to a pale yellow as he nibbled another of his protein bars and finished the last of the energy drinks. He watched a rabbit scamper from the bushes as he breakfasted, and took a moment to contemplate the yellow primroses clustered near the base of a tree. Spring was not far away now. His favourite time of year. As a boy he had known all the names of the flowers, and could tell the trees by their leaves and fruits. He had forgotten some. His life had steadily filled with other concerns. Perhaps now he would have time to return to those simple, far-off days.

Today was the beginning of the fifth day since the crash. It scarcely seemed possible. He had done so little during that time. Had he miscounted? He could hardly trust his own memory. He reached out and took hold of a thin stick lying nearby. It was about two feet long. He snapped it into five roughly equal lengths. Five days. Five whole days since the cataclysm. It would be many more days before he could walk. He lined the sticks in a row beside the helicopter and set about examining his leg.

He should really have changed the dressing yesterday, but somehow he hadn't managed to find the time. Now, as he unwrapped his thigh, he realized his mistake. The wound needed thorough daily cleaning if he were to avoid infection. And an infection out here in the forest would be fatal. But at least there was very little fresh bleeding. The repairs to the damaged artery had held. Just as long as he managed to avoid any strenuous activity, the primary wound should heal, in time.

He examined his damaged leg further. The upper half was still severely bruised. He felt carefully along it, and didn't like what he found. The leg was twisted slightly, about halfway along the thigh. It was highly likely that he had suffered a fracture of the femoral shaft, the bone that ran from hip to knee. It would be impossible to repair the broken bone without surgery. And if the bone could not heal, he would probably never walk on it again. He could do nothing about that now. Instead, he cleaned the wound and rebound it carefully, resting his foot on a rock to lift it up. It was important to raise the leg as much as possible to reduce the swelling.

He rested for a while, then drank more water and refilled his bottles from the stream. When he felt strong enough he began the laborious job of dragging himself back over to the helicopter. This time he would search it thoroughly and take anything that was useful.

It took him over an hour to complete the task, but at the end he was pleased. His haul consisted of a second ration pack, another med kit, and an emergency pack containing a two-man tent, blanket, and torches. There was also a flare launcher, some fishing hooks, a knife and water purification tablets. He doubted he would need the water tablets as the stream was as pure as the fast-running brook where he had played as a boy. The flare launcher he put aside for later. The tent he managed to set up with relative ease. It was a sturdy four-season model with a fully waterproof membrane. He had used similar tents when training inside the Arctic Circle. It ought to withstand the Surrey climate well enough.

The protein bars and energy drinks would stop him from going hungry for a couple more days. But his leg would take far longer than that to heal. He had two options available to him: find food, or get help.

He knew enough about woodland plants to identify those that were edible – fungi, leaves, roots, shoots, and water plants. He might find acorns too, and tree bark. It was the wrong time of year for fruits, but there was plenty of fresh growth in the woodland during springtime. If he was serious about lasting longer than a few days, however, he would need to trap animals. He knew how to make snares for small mammals and birds, and he could use his fishing hooks to catch trout and other fish in the stream. Snails, worms and slugs were nutritious, and could be caught with nothing more than a keen eye. He had survived in the wild before and could do it again.

That night he waited until darkness fell, then unpacked the flare gun. It was a single-shot disposable gun and he would have only one chance. It seemed unlikely that he would manage to attract the attention of rescuers, and yet he had to try. He was not in the wilderness, but perhaps just a few miles from the nearest settlement. For all he knew, there might be a major road or even a town just out of view. He would try, at least.

He waited until it was fully dark, then fired the gun into the sky. The flare rose up and burst directly overhead, revealing his exact location to anyone who might be watching. It burned brightly, but all too briefly, falling back to earth and fading to blackness once more. If anyone was out there, he hoped they had been looking in the right direction at the right time.

He sat up waiting for a couple of hours, wrapped in a blanket, but no answering flare came, and no more light or sound disturbed his solitude. Eventually he gave up and crawled into his tent for the night.

When he awoke the next morning, he broke off a sixth stick and placed it next to the other five. It was the beginning of the sixth day since the world had ended.

Chapter Twenty-Six

Stoke Park, Buckinghamshire, quarter moon

The camp was vast and sprawling, and Melanie went from tent to tent, shouting out her sister's name at the top of her voice. 'Sarah! Sarah!'

Ben walked at her side, calling and searching, working up and down the rows of tents, hoping for a glimpse of Sarah's mousy brown hair amid the chaos.

Melanie detested this place and its occupants already. Everywhere she went, unhelpful faces stared back. The stink of rubbish and rotting food filled the air, mingling with the choking smoke from bonfires. People sat outside their tents, doing nothing while Melanie rushed between them, tripping on the guy ropes in her urgency to find out where her sister had gone.

What on earth could have caused Sarah to leave the tent? It was inconceivable that she would have gone out of her own accord. She had been in a state of total shock since leaving London. She must have been abducted. But no one nearby had noticed any kind of disturbance. No one had heard a woman scream.

Someone must have seen what happened.

Yet no one had.

'Sarah! Where are you?' More eyes swivelled in Melanie's direction as she shouted. Blank, indifferent faces. She desperately wanted to give these people a good shaking. Better still, a hard slap. One of them must know where Sarah was. Even if they didn't, they could volunteer to help. Yet they seemed to know nothing and care less.

It was Melanie's fault, of course. Predictably, she had shouted at Ben when she'd first discovered the empty tent, putting the blame on him, but that was unfair, as always. Ben would never have left Sarah alone if he hadn't needed to come searching for her.

All Melanie's problems were her own fault, she knew that. She had promised James she would change her ways and become less selfish, but that was turning out to be far harder than she'd expected. Now she was paying the price.

Learn the lesson, Melanie. How many times did she have to be taught it?

'Over there,' said Ben, pointing.

Melanie looked and saw a gathering at the very edge of the city of tents. People were milling around a small convoy of military vehicles. She had no idea what was going on.

'Let's go and check it out,' said Ben.

Reluctantly, she followed. It didn't look a very likely place to find Sarah, but something must be happening there. She didn't have any better ideas.

A small crowd was gathered around an army truck and a couple of Land Rovers. Soldiers were holding them back, but the people were angry, shouting at the soldiers, demanding something. Melanie knew there was a general mistrust of the army following the nuclear strike. Rumours were circulating that the government had conspired with the military in ordering the attack, and that the army was now tightening its control over the surviving population, gathering them into camps and holding them prisoner. Melanie could quite believe it after her failed attempt to leave through the gates. There was certainly a lot of tension between army and civilians, and those tensions seemed to be spilling over now.

Ben dragged her by the hand through the jostling crowd, using his height and strength to muscle people out of his way.

When they reached the front, Melanie threw her hand to her mouth in shock. 'Ohmigod! It's James!'

The boy was crouched down in the middle of the circle, stripped naked and bound with thick ropes. His hands were strapped behind his back, and more ropes tied his ankles together. He was kneeling in the mud, and as he lifted his head, she saw that he had been badly beaten. His face was a bloody mess, and his torso showed signs of severe bruising. One of the soldiers grabbed his hair and forced him roughly back to the ground.

'Werewolf!' the crowd was jeering and shouting. 'Kill him!' They pushed forward, hungry for blood and vengeance. Only the ring of soldiers with their rifles raised stood between them and James.

'Stand back,' shouted their commanding officer, a man with a bristling ginger moustache. 'This creature is our prisoner. He poses no danger to you. You have my word.'

The mob bellowed back, telling the officer just how much they valued his promise.

'Those monsters killed my family!' shouted one man.

'They murdered my husband!'

'We'll rip him to pieces!'

The commanding officer raised his rifle into the air and fired off three shots in quick succession. A hush fell over the baying mob.

'This facility is operating under the rule of martial law. I am Lieutenant Colonel Sharman, and I am in command of security within the boundaries of the camp. I will not tolerate any attempt to disrupt the peace.'

The officer swept his gaze over the crowd. 'This creature has been captured by my men to be used for experiments under the supervision of our medical director. I guarantee that he will be kept securely caged at all times, and that there is no risk to any civilians. Does anyone have a problem with that?'

'I do,' said Melanie.

Ben grabbed at her but she broke free of his grasp and took a step forward.

The colonel walked over to her, the gun still in his hands. 'And you are?'

'My name is Melanie Margolis. You can't treat the boy like this. He's not an animal.'

'No,' said the colonel sharply. 'You're right. He's a lycanthrope. Many people here would say that he is worse than any animal. If they had their way he would be dead already. My men are here to protect him.'

Melanie opened her mouth to speak, but a blonde-haired woman in a white coat was pushing her way through the soldiers toward James. She bent down at his side and lifted his chin to study his bruised and bludgeoned face. James looked mournfully up at her, and then across at Melanie. He turned away as if he did not know her.

'Bring him to the lab,' said the new woman, standing up.

'What are you going to do to him?' called Melanie.

The woman hesitated, then came over to her. Her long blonde hair blew across her face, and she brushed it aside, revealing bright blue eyes. She spoke to Melanie in a soft Australian accent. 'I'm Doctor Helen Eastgate. You have some concerns about his treatment?'

Melanie nodded. 'You bet. Do you want to hear a list?'

'There's no need for your concern. I'm going to try to cure him.'

'Cure him? How? You can't just use him as a human

guinea pig.'

'He's not human. But I'm going to try to restore his humanity.'

'It's all right,' cried James. 'I want to be cured.'

'There,' said Doctor Eastgate, curtly. 'It seems we're all in agreement.' She turned to walk away.

Before Melanie could say anything else, another figure stepped out of the crowd and tugged at the doctor's arm. Melanie caught a glimpse of a woman with mousy brown hair. Her voice was barely audible above the murmurings of the mob. 'Please, let me come with you. I want to help you run your experiments.'

Melanie's eyes opened wide. It was Sarah.

Chapter Twenty-Seven

Gatwick Airport, West Sussex

A third murder had taken place in recent days. As before, the victim had been another young woman, and the manner of the killing had been identical to the two previous cases. This time, Liz had come close to making a breakthrough.

She'd arrested a man who'd been seen leaving the crime scene in the dead of night, and interviewed him under caution, after reading him his rights. 'You do not have to say anything,' she told him. 'But, it may harm your defence if you do not mention when questioned something which you later rely on in court.'

'Eh?' said the guy, astonished. 'Rely on in court?'

'Well, that's what I'm supposed to say,' said Liz defensively.

Drake, Vijay and Mihai had wanted to sit in on the interview, but she'd shooed them away, bringing in Kevin instead, who seemed to think his role was to act as bad cop. He rolled up his shirt sleeves and paced the interview room menacingly, putting both the suspect and Liz on edge. 'We know you done it,' he told the guy, banging his fists down on the table. 'We know you're a werewolf. You'd better confess, or we'll hand you over to Major Hall for interrogation. He'll kick your arse, good and proper.'

The suspect looked suitably scared by the display of aggression, but resolutely clammed up and refused to say anything more.

'We will *not* hand anyone over to Major Hall,' said Liz. 'This is a police investigation. And this man is not a werewolf.'

She didn't offer to explain how she knew that. Not even Kevin knew that she could smell werewolves herself, if she sniffed them up close.

'That's right. I'm not,' agreed the man. 'Give me some fruit or vegetables to eat, and I'll prove it.'

'What were you doing, then, creeping away from a murder scene?' demanded Kevin. 'It doesn't look good, does it?'

'I'm saying nothing. I want to see a lawyer.'

'No,' said Liz. If there was one good thing about the new world order, it was that there were no more lawyers to disrupt her investigation.

'All right then,' said their suspect. 'I admit it. I nicked the girl's iPhone. I know I shouldn't have. But she was already dead, I never touched her, I swear.' He produced the stolen iPhone from an inside pocket and tossed it onto the table with a clatter. 'The bloody phone's dead too. I wish I'd never bothered.'

Liz released him without charge. Despite the efforts and enthusiasm of Kevin and her young assistants, plus the help of her neighbours, Joe and Pamela Foster, and Bill Pope, the doctor, she still had nothing to go on, other than a firm conviction that a werewolf, or more likely a vampire, was to blame.

Corporal Jones and the Welsh Guards made another

appearance and gave her their opinion. 'My boys think you're the killer,' said Llewelyn, matter-of-factly. 'I say no, but I think the burden of proof's on you, Liz.'

At least Kevin was keeping an open mind. 'Who do you think it is, then?' he asked her after they'd released their one and only suspect.

'I don't know, Dad, but I don't think it's a werewolf. Werewolves always rip their victims to pieces. It might be a vampire. I don't currently have a better explanation.'

Kevin nodded. 'I reckon you're right. A serial killer with sharp teeth and a taste for blood. Sounds exactly like a vampire to me.'

The idea horrified Liz. She was doing her best to come to terms with being a vampire herself. Armed with dark glasses and sunblock, she had learned to manage her aversion to sunlight. Her razor-sharp fangs appeared only under the influence of full moonlight, or whenever she became really angry, and she had mostly managed to avoid losing her temper. The rest of the time her teeth retracted conveniently and invisibly into her gums. Even her desperate hunger for meat, offal, and ideally blood, was manageable, at least for as long as the camp's meat supplies held up.

But if they ran out of meat, she didn't know what might happen. The bloodlust might overwhelm her completely, just as it already had on previous occasions, when she had killed and drunk blood beneath the light of the silver moon. If that happened, she would become no better than the mysterious serial killer.

Kevin noticed the look of anguish on her face and hurried to qualify his conclusion. 'I'm not saying that all vampires are evil,' he said. 'Some of them might be perfectly nice, just like you. After all, you only ever slaughter the bad guys, don't you?'

Slaughter. Kevin had never been very sensitive with his choice of words. But in this case it was accurate enough.

And who exactly were the bad guys anyway? What right

did she have to judge good and bad? She was no judge, merely a lowly servant of the law. Her duty was to follow the evidence, and to protect all members of the public from harm, without fear or favour. That duty still existed, even now that the police force and all the institutions of civilization had so very clearly collapsed. In fact it was more important than ever. Even if she was just a lone enforcer taking justice into her own hands, someone had to uphold the values that held civilization together. Someone had to protect the weak and the vulnerable. And that person was Liz, whatever she was: police officer or vigilante, human or vampire.

'Do you reckon Major Hall really will shoot the guy who did it?' asked Kevin. 'He certainly hates werewolves. Not surprising really. It's his job.'

'Yeah,' said Liz. 'He definitely does seem to hate them. He's a bit of a zealot. I would never hand anyone over to him for a fair trial.'

Even if she did solve the case, there was little chance of protecting the culprit from rough justice. The mob would see to that. Prison wasn't a realistic option. She'd heard a rumour that after the fall of the government, all of the prisons had been cleared out as people fled for safety. In some cases the prisoners had been released by their guards. In other cases, the army had carried out mass executions. Like all rumours these days, it was impossible to know for sure.

One thing she did know was that if she didn't catch the murderer soon, the Welsh Guards were likely to come looking for her. Llewelyn might still have an open mind, but the others had already decided on her guilt. Perhaps her best option was to leave now, before she was shot by the guardsmen, or executed by Major Hall, or lynched by an angry mob.

Except that she couldn't. She needed to stay for Samantha's sake. She had sworn to Dean to look after her if anything ever happened to him, and she was going to make good on her promise.

Samantha was almost entirely bed-bound these days. Her cramps, insomnia, back pain, and headaches were worse than ever. Doctor Pope had become a regular visitor, treating her with kindness, and clearly pleased to be dealing with a living patient instead of the corpses that Liz usually brought him. The baby was due in the next couple of weeks. The worst would be over soon.

Or would it?

The camp's food supplies wouldn't last forever, and neither would its water, medicines, and other essentials. Refugees were still arriving at the camp each day, although their numbers had dwindled greatly since the beginning of the month. Those who came now told tales of being pursued by werewolves, some armed with weapons. The number of survivors still out there must be growing smaller by the day. Major Hall hadn't been exaggerating when he'd described the land beyond the camp's defences as lawless territory.

What really concerned Liz was the lack of long-term planning. Major Hall seemed interested only in holding back the werewolf threat. Most people she spoke to were convinced that if they could survive inside the camp for long enough, outside help would come. But Liz wasn't so sure.

Chapter Twenty-Eight

M4 Motorway, Berkshire, crescent moon

The car was only a tiny slow-moving dot on the horizon when Warg Daddy first picked it out, but immediately he knew what it was. His vision was perfect, far better than 20/20, even with his eyes hidden behind his Ray-Bans. Long before the Brothers even suspected the car's existence, he had opened the throttle of his bike and was burning up the road, closing the distance rapidly on his prey.

They hadn't come across a moving vehicle in days. This one was being driven timidly, its owner carefully seeking a safe path between the burned-out wrecks that littered the highway, some still smoking, others long since abandoned. But there would be no safe path.

Warg Daddy lusted for a kill. Butchery and savagery had freed him of his pain before, but now, ever so slowly, the headache was returning. At first it had been the mere ghost of discomfort, no more troublesome than the wraith of Leanna, still haunting the darkest corners of his mind. But it was creeping back slowly, threading its hot, acid tendrils through his brain, poisoning his mind, scalding his neurons, and shading his thoughts ever darker.

No matter. He had borne its torment before and he knew its cure.

Violence. Destruction. Murder.

His bike ate up the miles, closing quickly on the lone car up ahead. Already it was taking on form, turning from a coloured dot into a three-dimensional shape. The name of that shape was Toyota Prius. Its colour was blue. Its fate was oblivion. Warg Daddy accelerated harder, hungry for horror, greedy for gore, desperate for devastation.

Behind him the Brothers revved their bikes, struggling to match his pace. He watched them in his mirrors, black shapes, like bats swooping down from the sky.

Valkyries. That's what his old mate, Wombat would have said. *Valkyries riding out to bring back the souls of the slain.* Wombat was always saying shit like that. Warg Daddy had mocked him at the time. Now a strange sadness visited him as he remembered the fallen Brother. Wombat had been a fool, no doubt, but he had been a loyal fool, one of the very first of the Brothers. Leanna had killed him, stealing his life in order to set an example to the others. Or maybe just for pleasure. You never knew with Leanna.

Well, we shall be like valkyries then. Daughters of Odin, creatures of fate, selecting those who might live, and those who would be slain in battle, and taking them back to the halls of Valhalla to prepare for Ragnarok. Wombat had been obsessed with tales of Norse gods and Viking warriors. Perhaps that's where he was now, drinking mead with dead heroes, and preparing for the end of the world. It was a comforting thought.

Prepare well, my old friend. The end of the world was coming soon, as unstoppable as a juggernaut.

The Prius was close now, and seemed to have noticed them. It was taking evasive action. Its driver had speeded up, swerving around the crashed cars, desperate to escape his fate.

But no one can avoid fate. However fast you ran, wherever you tried to hide, whatever deals you might strike with the Devil, fate was always one step ahead of you, patiently waiting your arrival.

Warg Daddy arrived now, and suddenly the Prius was trapped like a rat in a maze. A wall of wrecked cars blocked the road ahead and the driver had no choice but to stop.

Warg Daddy braked too, stopping just behind the car. The Brothers joined him moments later, engines roaring, leather jackets standing shoulder to shoulder, blocking all chance of escape. They were ready to seize their victim and drag him kicking and screaming from his car.

Warg Daddy raised one hand. 'Wait.'

A minute passed, and then another. The Brothers grew restless, but Warg Daddy was in no hurry. Fate was never impatient.

Eventually the driver emerged from his car. A short man, heavy with fat, sweat on his brow, wet patches under his armpits, literally quaking in his boots. This was a man who had looked into the future and didn't like what he saw. This was a man whose future prospects looked very poor indeed.

He turned his head to Warg Daddy, blinking in the sunlight. Raw terror filled his eyes. 'What do you want from me?'

Warg Daddy looked on, saying nothing.

'Take my food,' said Prius Man. 'Take my car. Take everything. Just, please, let me live.' He glanced around helplessly, searching for something, hoping for anything that might yet save him from his doom.

Warg Daddy watched, silent, waiting.

Slasher and Meathook dismounted and approached the man. They seized him by his sweaty collar and dragged him over to Warg Daddy.

'Please,' begged Prius Man. 'Don't kill me.'

Slasher pushed him to his knees and Meathook kicked him onto his side, then gave him another good kicking, because Meathook was like that. Warg Daddy motioned for him to stop.

Prius Man lay on the road, looking up, beseeching Warg Daddy for his life.

Warg Daddy rubbed his head. The pain was rising higher, like a black tide. As the sun grew higher and brighter, the ache inside grew stronger and darker. Leanna's voice was growing louder too, rattling around like echoes inside his skull, whispering, telling him what he could and couldn't do. Sometimes, in the dead of night, after Vixen had left his arms, and he was alone with his thoughts, he could almost make out Leanna's words. Soon, he feared, the phantom Leanna would begin to command him, giving orders that must be obeyed. He worried that he might follow her instructions, simply to make her shut up.

Prius Man was blubbering now. 'Please. I don't want to die.'

Warg Daddy stooped down, bringing his gaze level with his victim's snivelling features. He cupped the man's chin in his huge palm. 'Die?' he queried. 'Who said you were going to die?'

The man looked up, hope flooding his face. 'You're not going to kill me? I just saw you and I assumed …' His words trailed off as he caught the look in Warg Daddy's eyes.

'It is not for me to decide your fate,' declared Warg Daddy. 'Only the gods can do that, and I am not a god, merely a messenger.'

Prius Man stared at him, hope alternating with despair as he struggled to discern meaning in Warg Daddy's pronouncement.

Warg Daddy turned to address the Brothers. They were staring at him too, puzzled. Meathook, Bloodbath, Slasher,

Vixen. He was leader of the Pack, and they were waiting for his explanation. 'We answer only to fortune,' he told them. 'We are servants of blind chance. We will not take this man's life unless the gods tell us to.'

Everyone was looking at him, blank incomprehension still on their faces.

He sighed. Words would not serve him here. He must lead through action, and instruct his followers with a demonstration. He reached into his pocket and drew out the tarnished coin, resting it in his palm. It had been gold once, or perhaps bronze, and glittered dimly under the noonday sun. He wiped it with his palm, but the grime would not shift. No matter.

'Heads you win, tails you lose,' he told Prius Man.

He flicked his forearm, and the coin rose spinning into the air. They watched it as it spun, from life to death and back to life, ever spinning, ever changing. He caught it neatly as it landed, and looked to see what fate had chosen.

He paused, giving the moment the sense of occasion it deserved. After all, a man's life hung in the balance. These things should not be rushed. When the suspense had grown to fever pitch, he announced the outcome.

'Tails,' he said, shaking his head sadly. 'You lose.'

Chapter Twenty-Nine

Stoke Park, Buckinghamshire, crescent moon

When Sarah had first seen James brought to the camp he had been naked, but he was wearing clothes now. She couldn't stop herself from smiling when she saw the way he was dressed. His clothes were old man's clothes, almost like Grandpa's. Corduroy trousers, a cotton shirt and a tweed jacket.

'Where on earth did you find these?' she asked him.

'A kind lady called Joan gave them to me. They belonged to her husband, Ted.'

'Well, you look very distinguished, like you're going to a shooting party at a country house.'

He smiled at her sadly. 'I don't feel distinguished.' His eye was still red and swollen and his nose had been broken when the soldiers beat him. They had kicked him in the ribs too, and he sat hunched on the floor, his wrists and ankles tightly bound. Worst of all was the metal cage they had locked him in. Sarah could hardly bear to see him this way, but Colonel Sharman had insisted on it.

She still couldn't say what had led her to James, other than sheer chance. When Melanie had stormed out of the tent and Ben had gone to find her, Sarah had decided to take the opportunity to venture out. She had read enough psychology books over the years to know that the only way to overcome a phobia was to face it down. Desensitisation, the therapists called it. Exposure therapy. She knew also that if she did not overcome her fear of other people, she would not be able to survive, now that the world had changed so much.

She had only intended to take a quick peek through the open door of the tent, to begin to expose herself to the outside world in a short, controlled dose, perhaps just for a few seconds. That was what the psychologists recommended. Gradual, slow exposure. But after a minute, nothing terrible had happened, and she had plucked up the courage to step all the way outside. There were people all around the tent, but none of them looked her way. They seemed consumed by their own worries. She wondered if they were all secretly scared too. Perhaps everyone was afraid of something, not just her. The thought gave her courage.

It occurred to her then that other people might not be her real problem. After all, she had never been afraid of Grandpa, and had grown to accept James, and Ben too. Perhaps the root of her phobia lay elsewhere.

What if it is Melanie I am truly afraid of?

Her sister could be so overbearingly confident, it was intimidating to be around her. She adopted such an attitude of invulnerability, that Sarah felt insubstantial by comparison. And Melanie had no patience. She was forever throwing barbed comments Sarah's way, each one like an arrow or a poisoned dart piercing her skin. With Melanie gone, she felt suddenly braver than she had done for a long time. She left the safety of the tent behind and began to tiptoe through the camp.

She kept her eyes firmly on the ground so she wouldn't have to make eye contact with any of the strangers. There were ropes everywhere, and cooking utensils, and all kinds of rubbish, so it was sensible for her to look at her feet. Besides, she had no idea where she was going, so she had no need to look up. It didn't matter which way she went.

If I have a panic attack, I just need to close my eyes and breathe deeply.

But no panic attack came.

One footstep she took, and then another, and still nothing awful happened. No one tried to speak to her. No one even seemed to notice she was there.

I am invisible. I can walk anywhere, and no one can see me.

The thought strengthened her resolve, and after a while she found herself at the very edge of the tents, all the people behind her. She walked on across the empty field, the wind blowing gently at her hair, the bright sun warming her face. Sensations she had not felt for so long.

Is this how it feels to be alive?

Suddenly an army convoy was approaching, noisy and overwhelming. She froze in her tracks, closed her eyes and waited for it to pass, but instead it drew to a halt and soldiers poured out of the vehicles. Sarah almost shut down in panic.

Breathe deeply.

She stood still and hugged herself tight, her eyes screwed shut, willing the men to leave her alone. But their voices grew louder and were soon joined by others. Something bad was happening, and she was at its centre. Her heart began to thud so loudly she could no longer hear what was being said. People gathered around her, pressing against her, and she moved to the front of the crowd to escape from their reach. Angry shouts began. Loud noises. She clamped her hands to her ears, but then three deafening gunshots rang out.

She opened her eyes and could hardly believe what she

saw.

James.

He was cowering on the ground in a pitiful state. She wanted to rush over to him and hug him close, but soldiers barred her way. More people arrived and there was more shouting. Then suddenly a woman in a white coat, a doctor, was in front of her, saying she was going to experiment on James.

Sarah reached out and clutched at the doctor's sleeve. 'Please,' she begged. 'Let me help.'

Everything had happened in a whirl. The woman, Doctor Helen Eastgate, had tried to shake her off, but she had persisted. Seeing James there, in such desperate need, had pushed all fear from her mind.

'I'm not a doctor, or even a trained nurse,' she had explained to Doctor Eastgate. 'But I know a lot about medicine, and I have years of practical experience.'

Somehow she had convinced the doctor to take her on as a lab assistant.

'Well, I could use some help,' Helen had said eventually, after quizzing Sarah on her medical knowledge. 'Welcome to the team.'

Sarah hadn't said a word to Helen about knowing James. She knew instinctively that she had to keep that secret.

'Don't tell anyone that you know me,' she whispered to him now. 'If the doctor finds out, she'll send me away.'

'Okay.'

'I'm going to find a way to get you out of here.'

How, she didn't know. But she was here in the lab, and she had gained Helen's trust. She would find a way to free James.

Sarah had never had a proper job before. She still didn't really know what this one was. But that didn't matter. As long as she was close to James. And remarkably, she had quickly grown used to being in the doctor's presence. Helen Eastgate had a relaxed manner that quickly put her at ease. Being away from Melanie probably helped too.

'We're going to run a series of experiments,' Helen explained to her. 'I've already identified a donor who possesses natural immunity to lycanthropy. My hope is that we can use her blood to undo the damaging effects of the virus in the test subject.'

'A cure, you mean?'

'That's my ultimate goal. We'll be injecting small amounts of the donor's blood into the patient's bloodstream, to see if the antibodies can reverse the genetic changes that have made him lycanthropic.'

'Where did you find the … test subject?' asked Sarah.

'The soldiers picked him up outside the fence,' said Helen. 'It looks like they had to beat him to subdue him, but he's not badly hurt. The injuries are just superficial. I've applied some first aid to fix his wounds.'

Sarah tried not to let her gaze linger over James' injuries. 'Is this the first time you've tried the cure?' she asked.

'Yes.' Helen flashed her a smile. 'We're making history here, Sarah.'

'And are you confident it will work?'

'I actually have no idea,' admitted Helen. 'But there's only one way to find out.'

An armed soldier unlocked the cage and stood on guard while Sarah helped to prepare James for the first test. As Helen had instructed her, she bound his fingers securely with tape so that he wouldn't be able to scratch her, and fixed a mask over his face to stop him biting. Then she rolled up his sleeve and held his arm.

James didn't struggle as Helen administered the first injection.

As soon as it was done, the soldier locked the cage again.

'Might the antibodies harm him in some way?' asked Sarah, doing her best to conceal her horror at the prospect.

Helen must have detected some concern in her voice, because she answered, 'Sarah, it's only natural to feel pity for this man. I can't help but feel some myself. But although he may look fully human, believe me, I've seen what these creatures are truly like. They feel no kindness, no empathy, no compassion. All humanity is gone. You must always remind yourself that this is no longer a man, but a cold-blooded predator with only the outward appearance of a human being.'

'But could the injection kill him?'

'It's possible,' said Helen. 'If that happens, I'll ask Colonel Sharman to find us a new test subject.'

Chapter Thirty

Iver Heath, West London, crescent moon

As soon as he left London, Mr Canning's world turned green again.

Behind him lay a hellish wasteland, blackened and ruined, where nothing lived. Ahead of him was lush vegetation – fields and trees, hedgerows and flowers. Birds sang in the sky, and in the distance he glimpsed sheep suckling their lambs. He had always been fond of the English countryside. Now it seemed nothing less than a promised land, overflowing with milk and honey.

'You see?' said Leanna triumphantly. 'Not everything has been destroyed.'

He nodded, struck dumb with relief.

'Which way to Windsor?' she asked.

Canning looked about. 'That way. It ought to be around ten miles from here. We can easily make it before sundown.'

'Then come on!'

They set off down a country path that wound between the trees, all disconcertingly normal. Canning was still getting used to the sun in the sky, instead of a stone roof above his head. The world seemed to have grown much larger during the time he had spent underground.

'What will you do when we get there?' he asked Leanna. She had still not shared any details of her grand scheme with him. He could have told her that ruling the world was merely an objective, not a plan. But he decided to keep that thought to himself.

'Wait and see.'

Was this how it would be, then? Mutual mistrust? Was that really a sound basis for teamwork?

'Am I your fool?' he asked her sharply. 'Do you keep me merely for your amusement? Shall I dress like a jester and perform tricks to entertain you? Or do you expect me to contribute something to our partnership?'

She smiled at him, and perhaps for the first time since meeting her, he imagined he saw genuine warmth. 'Don't worry. You have demonstrated your loyalty to me by saving my life.'

Ah, recognition of his heroic action at last. Well, it was about time.

She continued, 'I will give you plenty of opportunity to use your skills and talents to the full. But be patient.'

Her smile faltered and she sniffed the air.

Canning smelled it too. 'Werewolves.'

The werewolves crept out of the undergrowth where they had been hiding all around. A group of perhaps a dozen, both men and women, in human form of course, dressed in camouflaged combat uniforms. They were armed with a variety of weapons – blades and guns; pistols and rifles.

Canning felt foolish. He and Leanna had been crashing through the undergrowth, talking openly, as if the world belonged to them. No wonder they had been caught by surprise.

One of the newcomers was obviously their leader. He stepped forward from the ring that had encircled Canning and Leanna, an assault rifle in his hands. 'Well, well. What do we have here?'

Leanna marched up to him and put her hands on her hips. 'Do you know me?' she demanded.

He smiled thinly. 'I know who you are. Leanna. I served in the Wolf Army under Warg Daddy. We all did.'

He gestured at the others, who grunted their acknowledgement. But their guns were raised. Their faces were hostile.

Canning studied them carefully. Four men, eight women, plus their leader. Unlucky thirteen.

'My name is Nathan. We fought for you once, and were proud to serve the Wolf Army. We would have lain down our lives for you. But the Wolf Army is no more. You and Warg Daddy abandoned us and left us to die. We serve ourselves now, and no other.'

Leanna stood her ground. 'I did not abandon you. Warg Daddy betrayed me. He betrayed all of us. Join me again. I will build a new Wolf Army.'

'No.' Nathan gripped his assault rifle with both hands. 'Those days are gone. It's dog eat dog now. And we're top dogs in this neck of the woods.'

Canning picked out the weakest individual in the group, a young woman armed only with a hunting knife, and shifted toward her. Her gaze was fixed on Nathan, and she held the knife loosely. He could take her easily. But she was only one of many. The other twelve mostly had guns. He hoped Leanna would play this cool.

She raised her voice in anger. 'I am no dog! I am your queen. Now kneel before me!'

Canning swallowed nervously. That had not been cool. But it had created an opening. The others were all focussed on Leanna now. No one was watching him.

Nathan laughed cruelly and aimed his rifle at her head. 'That's not going to happen, Leanna. I was planning to just shoot you, but since you like ordering people about, I think it might be more fun if you kneeled down and begged for your life.'

An unearthly shriek erupted from Leanna's lips.

Canning moved fast, barrelling toward his chosen target, grabbing her arm and plucking the knife from her grasp. He twisted her around and used her body as a human shield. One of the men opened fire at him with a semi-automatic, and Canning charged him down, using the woman's body to absorb a stream of bullets. He landed heavily on his assailant and plunged the hunting knife into his throat with both hands, pinning his lifeless body to the ground.

Leanna had launched herself at Nathan, using Canning's surprise attack to grab hold of the barrel of his gun and swing it away from her. The assault rifle opened up, dealing a deadly spray of lead in the general direction of Nathan's neighbours. Screams and shouts rent the air.

Canning seized the semi-automatic and opened fire, rolling into a rough patch of bushes as shots were returned. He might have only one eye, but it was keen and precise. Already half of the combatants were down.

Meanwhile Leanna had entered a berserk frenzy, sinking her teeth into Nathan's neck, while simultaneously raking the clearing with bullets from the assault rifle. Blood and screams filled the air. Leanna spun a deadly dance, shooting wildly in all directions, seeming without care for her own safety. Or Canning's, for that matter.

From his hiding place amid the brambles and scrub, Canning continued to fire. The enemy shooters were poorly trained, opening fire with a hailstorm of bullets and quickly having to stop to reload their weapons. He picked them off one by one.

Nathan's body sank to the ground and Leanna snatched the rifle from his dead hands. She closed on the remaining werewolves, gunning them down mercilessly until only one remained.

The last survivor, a scrawny man armed with a pistol, threw down his weapon and put his hands in the air. 'Please, have mercy!'

Leanna strode up to him, kicked the weapon aside and pushed the barrel of her gun into his face, knocking him onto his back. The man gibbered in terror, his eyes screwed shut. Leanna dropped her gun, fell astride his chest and gripped his head tightly between her hands. 'What is your name?' she demanded.

The man opened his eyes cautiously. 'Aaron.'

'And where are you from, Aaron?'

'Windsor. We're all living in Windsor now, inside the castle.'

'How many are you?'

'Close to a hundred.'

'And you are all from the Wolf Army?'

'Yes.'

Leanna scowled. 'Warg Daddy did not train you well.' She cast her gaze around the dozen corpses that littered the glade. 'You were not worthy opponents.'

'No.'

'Stand up!' she ordered.

Aaron rose shakily to his feet. 'Please don't kill me,' he begged.

'Return to Windsor,' Leanna ordered him. 'Tell your friends to prepare themselves for my arrival. Together, we will build a new Wolf Army, under the leadership of General Canning. He will teach you how to fight, and how to win battles. You will no longer bring shame on yourselves, as you did today.'

Canning's eyes opened wide at the mention of his name and his new title. He was still reeling from having almost been killed.

'Tell them to welcome me in victory,' continued Leanna, 'or else to flee like rats. Any who defy my authority will be slaughtered. But for those who prove their loyalty, I promise they will be rewarded.'

Chapter Thirty-One

Gatwick Airport, West Sussex

'So, let me get this straight,' said Vijay. 'You're telling me that Liz is a vampire?'

He and the other two boys were up on the hotel rooftop again. It was a good place to meet and talk. No one else knew how to get up here. It was their secret hiding place. And besides, Vijay liked it here. From this height he could see for miles. He liked to sit here and stare into the distance, wondering where Rose might be.

'A vampire, yeah,' said Drake. 'Try to pay attention, Vijay.'

Drake and Mihai must think he was extremely gullible to fall for this latest prank. He studied the two boys suspiciously, but they seemed sincere, especially the Romanian boy, and Vijay didn't think he was the kind to tell tall tales. Not unless he really believed in them.

'Is *nosferatu*, yes,' said Mihai. 'Is *vampir*.' The kid was certainly very insistent. His English wasn't up to much, but he seemed to know his Romanian folklore. If Mihai could be believed, central Europe must have been absolutely crawling with werewolves, vampires and other kinds of shape-shifters and monsters for centuries past. It was surprising that more people hadn't reported them to the authorities. Although, according to Mihai, they had.

'Everyone know about *vampir*,' said Mihai. 'Is in books. Is on TV. Is very famous.'

'And you believe that Liz is one?' Vijay asked Drake.

'Yeah, trust me. It's legit. You ain't seen what happens to her when she changes. She's, I dunno, like a whirlwind, running through flames, kicking arse. Her eyes light up all bright and shiny and she has sharp fangs and everything.'

Vijay studied the others through narrowed eyes, waiting for them to crack into fits of laughter, but their faces remained straight. 'You're not just winding me up?'

'No, seriously. You must have noticed how pale her skin has become?'

'I thought that was just the sunblock she wears.'

'And her blood red lips?'

'Lipstick.'

Drake scowled. 'You've seen the amount of meat she eats. I mean, everyone likes to munch on a bacon sarnie, yeah? But Liz can't get enough of the stuff. She'll eat the bacon and leave the bread on the plate.'

It was true that Liz seemed very partial to all kinds of meat, especially the most stomach-churning kinds. But Kevin was exactly the same. Vijay had watched the man put away a whole plate of liver once. Disgusting. It probably just ran in the family. 'That doesn't prove she's a vampire,' he said. 'Since when did vampires eat meat anyway? They don't do that on TV. I thought they just drank blood.'

'Mate, she'd drink blood if she could, but they don't have none of that down at the canteen, do they? Look, you believe in werewolves, yeah? So just believe in vampires too. I dunno what your problem is.'

Vijay stared out across the distant tarmac of the runway, and beyond that at the fence that kept them all safe. Drake made a valid point. There was no doubting that werewolves were real. They were out there, right now. And if werewolves were real, why not vampires too?

He waited one last moment to see if Drake and Mihai would crack. If this was a wind-up, he would kill them both. 'Okay, I believe you,' he said. 'So both werewolves and vampires came from Romania originally?'

'Yes,' said Mihai. 'In Romania, werewolf is called *vârcolac*. Vampire is *vampir*. Is many other monsters in Romania too. *Strigoi, moroi …*'

'Don't ask him to explain them all,' said Drake hurriedly. 'They're like, way too complicated for anyone to understand. The country's just stuffed with bloody monsters.'

'And we think that all these creatures are really victims of a disease?' said Vijay. 'Lycanthropy.'

'Right,' said Drake. 'At least I do, anyway. Mihai still thinks they're demons, or something.'

The boy shrugged. 'Maybe disease turns people into demons.'

Vijay stopped to think over the implications. 'So, does this mean that Liz is dangerous? Ought we to report her to the people in charge? Like Major Hall?'

'No!' said Drake, immediately. 'Of course not, you idiot! Major Hall would have her shot by firing squad.'

'Liz not dangerous,' said Mihai, shaking his head vigorously. 'Not very.'

'Well, maybe just a little bit,' admitted Drake. 'Actually, yeah, now you mention it, she is really dangerous. But not to her friends.'

'But we don't think she's the killer?'

'Defo not.'

Vijay breathed a sigh of relief. He liked Liz a lot. It was hard not to. He still liked her, even now he knew she was a vampire. As a Sikh, he had been taught to accept all people, regardless of race, colour, religion, or sexuality. He knew that in troubled times, tolerance of others was more important than ever.

'So why are you telling me all this?' he asked.

Drake looked at him as if he was an idiot. 'Isn't it obvious?'

'No,' said Vijay crossly. 'That's why I asked.'

'The murderer must be another vampire, yeah?'

'That's just one possible theory.'

'Now you're starting to sound like Aasha,' moaned Drake. 'She always tells me I'm wrong, even when she knows I'm right.'

Vijay had nothing to counter that. That was exactly how Aasha was.

'So,' said Drake, 'let's use our brains. What do we know about vampires that could be useful?'

'They like to drink blood?' suggested Vijay.

'Right. So that explains the wounds on the neck of the victims. And it also explains why there wasn't much blood on their bodies, or on their clothes.'

'Because the vampire drank it all?'

'Yeah,' said Drake. 'What else do we know?'

'They'll just carry on killing,' said Vijay.

'Right, yeah. Good point.'

The thought was sobering. This was no ordinary serial killer they were dealing with, although that would have been bad enough. This murderer had abilities that went far beyond the human, and they would never stop killing, because for them, killing meant life.

'*Vampir* can turn into bat,' said Mihai.

Drake stared at him. 'You reckon?'

'Yes,' said Mihai eagerly. 'Is how killer vanished into thin air.'

Drake seemed to be taking the idea seriously. 'That's what that guy Frank said, wasn't it? The murderer just disappeared.'

'You can't believe that,' said Vijay. 'People can't really

turn into bats. That's just impossible!'

'No, you're probably right. But maybe vampires are very good at hiding.'

Vijay snorted. Liz had never demonstrated any amazing ability to hide. Unless of course she had been hiding so well he hadn't even known she was there. He looked over his shoulder now, just in case. But there was no one else on the rooftop with them, vampire or otherwise.

'Maybe *vampir* turn invisible,' suggested Mihai.

'No,' said Vijay. This discussion was turning silly. He'd agreed to vampires, but there was no way he was going to believe in invisible vampires, or people who turned into bats. 'That old guy probably just couldn't see very well. He told us he wasn't wearing his glasses. He didn't even have a description of the murderer, or anything. I wonder if he was making the whole thing up.'

Drake shook his head. 'We must keep an open mind. And we gotta use all our clues.'

Mihai nodded. 'Use all clues. Yes.'

'The big question,' continued Drake, 'is how we gonna use all this info to catch the vampire?'

'Catch the vampire?' echoed Vijay.

'Catch it.'

The boys regarded each other nervously for a moment.

'Is easy,' said Mihai at last. 'To catch *vampir*, just set trap.'

Chapter Thirty-Two

Norbury Park, Surrey, new moon

The number of sticks on the forest floor grew ever larger. Griffin dragged himself from his tent to count them. Fourteen.

That did not necessarily mean that fourteen days had passed, however. It was not that simple, not now that the fever had come.

He tried to place a new stick each morning, but some days he forgot. It was hard to focus on the task, even though it was truly not a difficult one. Some mornings he woke, then slept, then woke again. Some days he could not be sure if he had woken at all, or if the feverish dreams that invaded his sleep were with him still.

He could not be certain, even now, that he was truly awake.

It was the infection in his leg that had brought the fever. The wound had become infected on the seventh day, or perhaps the eighth. He had unwrapped it to be greeted by the early smell of decay. He had cleaned the open sore thoroughly with antiseptic and bound it as well as he could. But the infection progressed quickly.

He had treated a case of gangrene once, long ago in a faraway country. A hot, desert country. He couldn't quite recall its name. Gas gangrene, a nasty business. The patient's toes had already turned black and cold when Griffin first saw him. He should have been brought in earlier, and it was too late to treat the infected tissue. The man's foot was already dead. There had been no other option than to amputate the foot and lower leg. The patient had survived, thanks to good modern medical care. Without it there would have been no chance.

Griffin's own leg was turning bad. He had known that infection was a risk, and had done his best to prevent it. But he could only do so much here, alone, in the middle of a forest. Despite fastidious cleaning and binding, some kind of bacteria had invaded the wound. The symptoms were clear enough. Swelling, inflammation, a discharge of yellow fluid. And the smell, of course. The smell of death.

Death. The word stirred another memory. Ah yes, his dead companions, the pilot and co-pilot who had brought him on this mission, and done their best to save the helicopter from crashing. Brave men. They hadn't deserved to be left to rot inside the mangled frame of the helicopter, or to be feasted on by the red kites. He had somehow found the strength to pull them from their seats and bury them in shallow graves, one lying next to the other, brothers in arms. He had managed to do that for them, at least. He remembered saying a prayer at their graveside, a few stumbling words of comfort.

'He that believeth in me, though he were dead, yet shall he live.'

But who had he really been trying to convince by those words? The dead men, or himself?

He hauled himself across to the babbling stream and splashed cold water over his face to see if it would help. It did. He leaned forward to immerse his face fully in the icy water and held it there for as long as he could bear. It had the desired effect. He was properly awake now. Wide awake, and that was how he had to stay. He wouldn't make it if he kept lapsing into the dreamworld.

He must choose life, or else death would choose him.

His leg was numb where the broken bone had damaged the nerves. It felt cold. The bone would never heal, he knew that much. The femoral shaft must have snapped right in two. He could feel the break with his fingers. The nerve damage might be permanent too. And the infection? If it spread beyond his leg, he would die. There was no doubt about it.

If there was a bonus, it was that the numbness had dulled the pain. Just as well, since he had used up all the morphine. His leg no longer burned, although now his head burned fiery hot instead, like the flare he had fired into the black night sky. No one had answered that flare. His cry for help had gone unheeded. He scanned the morning sky now, looking for the tell-tale vapour trails of overflying aircraft, and listening for the sound of helicopters. Nothing. Not one sign of life in fourteen days. He hadn't even heard the distant engines of cars or other vehicles. The only sounds were the calls of the birds and the gentle rustling of the trees.

Had the world ended? Was he all alone, the very last person on earth? From what he had seen so far, it seemed quite possible.

He was no stranger to solitude. As a boy he had spent long hours of every day alone with nature, and had loved every moment. Another memory floated into his mind, this one of a deer, in a forest just like this, many years ago. It was a fallow deer, a young buck, its antlers magnificent. He had approached it warily, expecting it to flee at any moment. Yet it did not move, but remained crouched in the thicket, its legs folded beneath its body. He had walked closer, moving slowly and quietly. The deer knew he was there, but did not run. Eventually he came within six feet of the creature.

It was beautiful. Its coat was red-brown, with white spotting along its flanks, and a white throat. The deer lay with one leg out to the side. He moved closer to take a look. The animal tried to rise to its legs, but the one leg buckled, sending it back to the ground. It groaned loudly.

Its leg was broken, he realized. 'Don't move, I'll get help,' he told the animal, and ran back to the house to tell his father.

On hearing his story, his father had reached for his rifle. 'We can't save it, Michael. We can only put it out of its misery.'

He had begged his father not to do it, to show mercy and compassion, to somehow find a way to save the deer.

His father had explained it to him. 'The leg cannot be saved. Without it the poor creature will die a slow and painful death. This rifle will bring compassion. Death will be a mercy.'

He hadn't left his father to do it alone, but had gone with him. 'Please, is there no other way?' he had asked, a hundred times. His father shook his head, patiently.

In the end, death had come quickly. A single shot to the back of the head. 'The deer felt nothing,' his father assured him. 'We did the right thing. It was better this way.'

He had almost forgotten that deer. It had been so long ago.

A broken leg. Death. He had been unwilling to accept it, no matter how many times his father had told him it must be done.

That experience had propelled him to study medicine and eventually to become a doctor. A chance event had changed the course of his life.

Life is nothing but chance, my friend. Just one crazy dice roll after another.

Someone had said that to him once. He hadn't believed

it at the time. He didn't believe it now.

I would always have become a doctor, deer or no deer. Chance had nothing to do with it.

He looked up and saw a small deer staring silently at him through the trees. A roe deer, not a fallow deer. A doe, not a buck. A real live animal, not a phantom from his past. It stared at him briefly, then bounded away in a flash.

He had been unable to save the deer of his childhood, but he was damned if he was going to allow a broken leg to end his own life.

'There's no one around here to dig my grave,' he muttered. 'And dead men don't bury themselves.'

To die with no one to say a word over his grave, that would never do. In any case, he had already made his choice, and had chosen life.

Death was for other men.

Chapter Thirty-Three

Stoke Park, Buckinghamshire

James shifted in the confined space of his cage, seeking comfort, but finding none. His arms were still tied behind his back, even though he was within the cage, and they ached terribly. The cage stood in one corner of the doctor's laboratory and he had not been allowed out of it since his capture. This was his entire world now, and he had nowhere else to go, nothing to do, and no one to talk to, except Sarah when no one else was around to listen.

That was not often. Usually the doctor spent long hours at work in the lab, and often a soldier would come and watch over him. The soldier never spoke to him, except to give orders. 'Stand up!' 'Lie down!' 'Do what the doctor says!'

He always obeyed without question. He didn't want to cause any trouble.

He had watched the doctor closely, noting the single-mindedness with which she went about her work. She was always reading papers, or examining samples under a microscope, or else staring intently at something, thinking hard. She never seemed to stop. But he had also noticed the way her fingers trembled, sometimes her whole hand shaking. He had seen her stumble as she rose from her chair, and the clumsy way she bumped into furniture, or knocked over objects on her workspace. Her papers were covered in coffee stains, or were misfiled, or lay in great heaps, ready to topple over onto the floor. She spent a lot of time hunting for misplaced items, and cursing her own untidiness.

Sometimes she hummed absent-mindedly, or muttered words and phrases to herself in her slightly clipped Australian accent.

She rarely bothered to say anything to him.

He would have liked to help her, by alerting her whenever a stray piece of paper fluttered to the floor, or telling her where she had left the safety glasses she was searching for. He would have liked to question her about the cure, and how it might affect him. But some instinct warned him to stay quiet and not to draw attention to himself.

And so he said nothing.

He understood why Sarah couldn't speak to him openly, and why they had to pretend that they didn't know each other. If the doctor discovered their secret, surely Sarah would be sent away. That was the very last thing he wanted to happen. He didn't really mind not being able to talk to her, just as long as he could see her and be near her, and know that she was safe.

The doctor wasn't as cold and cruel as she had first seemed, either. She had been afraid of him, that was all. Now, by being obedient and well-behaved, he was starting to win her over. She no longer regarded him with open fear and hostility. Sometimes, her voice sounded almost kind.

Her name was Helen, but he didn't dare call her that.

She wandered over to the cage and studied him now, some thought animating her features.

James said nothing, just sat quietly, watching her tuck stray golden hairs behind her ear.

'How do you feel?' she asked him eventually.

He didn't understand the question. 'Sad. Lonely. Confused,' he said.

She shook her head dismissively. 'I meant, how do you feel physically? Do you feel any different since I began giving you this treatment?'

He thought about it hard before answering. He had been thinking about it every day since Helen had started the programme of injections. He hoped that the cure would work, and that he would become human once again. He really wanted to change. But he didn't feel anything yet.

'No, I don't think so.'

'Do you understand what this treatment is for?'

'I think I do. I've been listening to what you tell Sarah, your assistant. You're hoping that the injections you're giving me will spread antibodies through my bloodstream, and destroy the virus.'

She nodded. 'If it works, the genetic changes that the virus caused will be reversed and you'll become human again.'

'Do you think it will work?'

'I haven't seen indications of any changes yet.'

'I hope it does work.'

'Do you?' she asked, sounding surprised

'Yes. For one thing, I'd like to be able to eat normal food again.'

'Right. You must be getting very hungry.'

She had offered him a plate of cooked food when he'd first arrived, but he had politely declined, explaining that he could only eat raw meat, preferably from live prey.

'I am hungry,' said James. 'Very hungry.'

'There isn't much I can do about that,' said the doctor. 'I can't give you the kind of food you want. I'm sorry.'

'No.' He hadn't really expected her to bring him live animals to eat. He knew that people found the idea of him killing and eating live prey disgusting, even though they were happy enough to eat animals that other people had killed. He had felt the same once, when he'd been human.

Still, it didn't seem fair to starve him. Even animals got fed. Even laboratory rats. But he kept the thought to himself.

'Is there anything else you need?'.It was the first real sign of kindness she had shown him.

'I wonder if you might bring me a blanket?' he asked. 'I don't need it for warmth. I don't really feel the cold. But it would be … comforting.'

'I'll see what I can do.'

'And you could call me James, if you like.'

'What?' Her voice had become hard again.

'I know you might not want to call me by my name,' he added hastily. 'You prefer to call me the patient, or the test subject. I know why you do that. It's in case something goes wrong, and the experiments … don't work out.'

'It's not that,' said the doctor crisply. 'You're not the only lycanthrope I've known. The first one was a student. She came to the university where I worked, and asked if she could study with me. I knew at once that there was something wrong with her, but against my better judgement I trusted her. That was a big mistake. When I discovered the truth about her, she tried to kill me. She very nearly succeeded, and I could tell how much she enjoyed it.'

'I'm sorry about that.'

'I won't ever make the same mistake again,' said the doctor. 'So, the reason I call you the test subject is to remind myself that despite your harmless appearance and your good behaviour, underneath you are still a cold-blooded, flesh-eating monster.'

She turned away and left him then, alone in his cage in the darkened laboratory.

Chapter Thirty-Four

Gatwick Airport, West Sussex, crescent moon

'So, let's work this out. Logically, yeah?'

Vijay nodded. Drake was on a roll and when he was like this, it was best to let him get on with it. Interrupting him would just make him cross.

The three of them – Vijay, Drake and Mihai – were up on the rooftop again, a good place for blue sky thinking. They were spending a lot of time up here now, weather permitting. Back in the hotel room was no place to be, what with his grandmother's knitting, Kevin's complaining, Aasha's moods, Samantha's pregnancy, and Liz being generally grumpy about not being able to catch the murderer. Outdoors was off-limits to civilians, and if the soldiers caught you sneaking around outside, they would give you a hard time, even though the boys were supposed to be police deputies now.

Besides, there was nowhere better to work out a plan

like this. A top secret plan. One so secret, they couldn't even tell Liz about it. Especially not Liz.

'Let's use our knowledge and pool our brainpower. We're a team, yeah? We can do this.'

Mihai was clearly feeling the team spirit. 'Is team, yeah, let's do it. So, what we gonna do, boss?'

Drake told him. 'To catch a vampire, we need to exploit its weaknesses, right?'

'Right,' said Vijay. 'Logical.'

So far, so good. With Drake's determination to devise a plan, and Mihai's inside knowledge of vampire lore, Vijay was moderately optimistic that they had a chance of coming up with a solution. Hopefully it wouldn't be a risky one. The less it involved him, the better.

'Well, what are they?'

'Sunlight,' suggested Vijay.

'Good one. Except that Liz doesn't really have a major problem managing that, does she?'

'No, I suppose not. Nothing that factor 30 can't handle.'

'What else?'

'Stick through heart,' said Mihai.

'Yeah, a classic solution. A wooden stake through the heart. A nice sharp one, I guess. Let's chalk that one up. What about garlic? Holy symbols?'

Mihai shook his head. 'Did not work on Liz.'

'You already tried them?' asked Drake with some surprise.

'Sure.' Mihai showed them the silver cross that he wore around his neck. He mimed pressing it to Liz's forehead.

'Did she mind?'

'Not so much.'

'And the garlic?'

'She pull face, that's all.'

'What about coffins?' asked Drake. 'Do vampires need to sleep in coffins during the day?'

'In Romania, always,' said Mihai. 'In England, not so

much.'

'I've never seen Liz climbing out of a coffin,' said Vijay. 'Or anything that resembles one. She just sleeps on a mattress like anyone else.'

'Suppose so.'

'Are we a hundred per cent certain that Liz is a real vampire?' he asked. He still couldn't completely convince himself that this wasn't some elaborate prank.

'Yes,' said Drake and Mihai together.

They sat thinking for a bit longer. Vijay watched as the clouds drifted across the flat landscape. Watching clouds was a good way to get creative. There was something restful about the way they moved. These clouds were dark and heavy and kind of ominous. They looked ready to shed some serious rainfall.

'Running water?' he suggested. He had heard somewhere that vampires couldn't cross rivers or streams.

'There ain't really a lot of water going spare around here,' said Drake. 'Running or any other kind.'

'I suppose not. Then what about fire?'

'Nah. Liz is completely immune to it. I've seen her run into a sheet of flames and out the other side. Not a mark on her.'

Vijay was pretty much out of ideas already. Trapping a vampire wasn't half as easy as it sounded, despite Drake's confidence and Mihai's assurances. The way the Romanian kid talked, it was if he'd grown up hunting for werewolves, vampires and other monsters back in his home country. But there must be some solution to the problem. They couldn't be the first people to have ever tried to trap a vampire. 'Any other ideas, Mihai?' he asked.

'Cut off head. Is always good way to kill *vampir*.'

'Yeah?' said Drake, raising one eyebrow. 'Maybe we'll save that for last resort. If we can't kill it any other way.'

'Wait,' said Vijay. 'Kill the vampire? I thought we were just trying to catch it.'

'We'll do whatever it takes, yeah?' said Drake

ominously. 'Ain't no one else gonna save the world, right?'

'Yeah. I suppose.' Vijay's nerves were starting to fail him. The discussion wasn't going in the direction he'd hoped. Between them they had absolutely no idea how to catch a vampire, and now the stakes were being raised higher. Not that he wanted to think about stakes. 'Listen, why don't we just talk to Liz about this?'

'Seriously? Come on, if Liz gets a sniff that we're planning to do something dangerous, she'll be on the warpath. We'll be grounded, for sure.'

'And are we? Planning to do something dangerous, I mean?'

'Nah, mate. Just catching a vampire, is all.'

Vijay gazed out over the rooftop to the terminal building opposite. The answer was out there, surely, floating through the air like the clouds, just out of his grasp. Cutting off heads, and stakes through the heart weren't the way to go. There had to be something much less dangerous. They were thinking about this in entirely the wrong way. After all, they didn't really need to kill the vampire, or even catch it. They just needed to observe it going about its business, so they could find out who it was. And for that they needed …

'We need to offer it a victim.'

'A sacrifice?' asked Drake.

'No, not a sacrifice. More like bait. No one's going to get killed. It doesn't even have to be a real person. We could stuff a sleeping bag with clothes and leave it for the vampire to find. Then we could hide and watch it so that we can uncover its identity.'

Drake mulled it over. 'It's probably the best idea so far. Vampires ain't stupid, though. A real person would be better.'

'But who could we possibly use? You're not suggesting one of us?'

'Nah. That would be well risky, mate. In any case, the vampire seems to prefer women, or girls.'

'Hot girls,' suggested Mihai.

'Who then?'

They looked at each other.

'Is easy,' said Mihai. 'Is very obvious.'

Vijay shook his head in disbelief. 'Kid, you cannot be serious.'

Chapter Thirty-Five

Gatwick Airport, West Sussex, waxing moon

The murder count was stuck at three, but Liz wasn't fooling herself that it would stay that way for long. A vampire wouldn't ever stop killing. It was in their nature to kill. No one knew that better than she did.

Now she faced a dilemma. Until the killer struck again, she had no leads to follow. The bodies were all buried; the clues, few as they were, all gone. Her only hope of catching the perpetrator was to wait for a fourth body to turn up. It was hardly an enticing prospect.

Drake, Vijay and Mihai had their hopes pinned on another victim being found soon. They were as keen as her to solve the case, but for them, this was all just a game. They might think they were adults, but they were too young to really understand the impact of a murder on the victim's family. She was regretting allowing them to get involved in the case.

Kevin had enjoyed his brief role helping her interview

suspects, but he was obviously relieved that things had quietened down in recent days. He'd suggested more than once that the serial killings might have run their course and that the murderer had retired. 'I reckon you should leave things be,' he advised her. 'Don't go stirring things up. This murder business ain't really your job, love.'

'Of course it's my job, Dad. I'm a police officer.'

He showed her his stern face, the one he wore when he was convinced she was wrong about something. 'Are you? I don't see no one paying you or nothing.'

She had known he wouldn't get it. What had her father ever understood about vocation, or responsibility? 'For you, it's always about the money, isn't it?'

His expression didn't change. 'If I was only interested in money, I would never have taken a job as a truck driver.'

'Listen, it's like this. Someone has to keep everyone safe. Major Hall is doing that on the outside, keeping the werewolves from killing everyone in the camp. But it's just as important on the inside. If it wasn't a vampire killing people, it would be some other crime. Crime doesn't go away just because worse things are happening in the world.'

'No, but millions of people are dead already. These murders are just a few more.'

'They're not numbers, Dad. They're people. Every life matters.'

'Your life matters too, love. It matters more than any. Just saying.'

'Listen, I won't put myself in any danger,' she promised him. But she knew as she said it that it was untrue. Danger lay on all sides, whatever course of action she took – even if she did nothing.

She ran through her options.

Option one. She solved the murder case, uncovered the identity of the serial-killing vampire, and made an arrest. That was a good option; the best. But then what? Major

Hall would carry out his threat and execute the killer. Suddenly the existence of vampires would become public knowledge. The mob would start baying for blood. Next it would be open season on vampires. Not good.

Option two. She failed to solve the crime. More gruesome murders followed. Time ran out. The Dogman, or Evans, or perhaps even Llewelyn himself, would decide to take things into their own hands. She would end up with a bullet to the head. Not good. Not good at all.

Option three. She couldn't actually think of any other ways this might go. Not good.

The best plan right now was probably not to think about it. If she didn't think, she didn't need to worry. Besides, she had plenty of other things to be worried about. Samantha was a good place to start. Her due date was only a week away.

Doctor Pope was now visiting her every day, checking her blood pressure and offering words of advice. And for once, Samantha seemed to be following them. She was allowing others to look after her, while she rested and kept her feet up.

Liz was hoping for an easy birth. If things became complicated, there were precious few medical facilities available at the airport. Remarkably, despite all the early problems with the pregnancy, and all the stress of losing Dean and evacuating London, so far nothing terrible had happened. Samantha had reached a state of calm, looking forward to the birth of her baby to avoid looking back to the death of her husband. There was a lesson for Liz there – look forward, toward a brighter future. Don't look back. Don't worry about what might go wrong.

Old Mrs Singh was certainly ready for the birth. She had already turned out a full wardrobe of clothes for the baby, and her knitting showed no signs of stopping. 'Here,' she showed Liz. 'Booties for the baby.' The woollen boots were pale pink.

'So you think it's going to be a girl?' asked Liz.

'Girl, boy. Both spell trouble,' said Mrs Singh.

'I think it's a boy,' said Samantha. 'It kicks so hard. Come and feel. It's kicking now.'

She allowed Liz to position her hands against her huge belly. Her skin was stretched tight like a drum. Liz felt the kicks coming from inside, like a creature struggling desperately to escape. 'I feel it,' she said. 'Those are strong kicks. Maybe it is a boy.'

Mrs Singh peered at her from her chair. 'Girls kick just as hard,' she said. 'Harder.' She looked in Aasha's direction. 'They never stop kicking.'

Aasha was watching the changing shape of Samantha's belly with an expression of pure horror. 'That's gross,' she said.

Samantha smiled. 'Do you want to feel it?'

Aasha shook her head quickly. 'Yuck, no way. Well … okay, yes.' She kneeled down next to the bed and let Samantha move her hands. 'Oh, wow. I felt it. That is so weird.'

'It's almost ready,' said Samantha. 'Any day now.'

'Any day,' agreed Liz.

Chapter Thirty-Six

Stoke Park, Buckinghamshire, waxing moon

Chanita was officially the camp's medical director, and she still tried to make time for a tour of the onsite hospital most days. The makeshift facility was being run under military command, and felt more like a field hospital in a war zone than the civilian establishments she was used to. But there was no doubting the dedication and professionalism of the staff, both civil and military. And yet they were fighting a losing battle against disease. Every day, more and more patients were being diagnosed with some new problem.

The teenage boy she had visited on her rounds today was clearly severely ill.

'What's wrong with him?' she asked the doctor in charge.

The boy was feverish and drifting in and out of consciousness. His skin was covered with a rash made up of large, flat blotches. His eyes were inflamed and he started to cough loudly as Chanita looked on.

'Measles,' said the doctor. 'Sadly, it's becoming all too common. People of this age are particularly vulnerable if they haven't been vaccinated.'

'What can you do for him?'

'There's no cure for measles. We have to let it run its course. Nine times out of ten, the patient recovers, but in the most serious cases, it can be fatal.'

Chanita knew that well. She had seen measles cases before, when she'd worked at the emergency department of King's College Hospital. She knew the horrible complications that could result from the infection. Fits, fevers, infections of lung, liver or brain. Measles was a deadly disease. Before vaccination, it had claimed millions of lives every year.

The boy's coughing grew louder and he began to cough up dark red spots of blood. It looked like a serious infection had already taken hold.

'We're using antibiotics to combat the bacterial infection,' continued the doctor, 'but the truth is we're running very short of all kinds of medicines, and we have no new supplies coming in.'

Chanita led the doctor out of earshot of the patients. 'I'm afraid that I have no good news on that front. We haven't been able to make any contact with the government. We don't know for certain that any centralized administration still exists. The regional governments are crumbling. Lieutenant Colonel Sharman tells me that beyond this base, it's anarchy. We're basically on our own for the time being.'

The news reports from other countries were just as bleak. Stories of chaos, fighting and martial law followed one after another, relentlessly. In recent days the news was becoming scarcer as one by one, countries turned "grey", with reporting simply ceasing.

The doctor shook his head. 'We can't go on this way. We're seeing a surge in all manner of infections. I have patients coming in with conditions I can barely treat. TB, pneumonia, norovirus, food poisoning, parasites, even scurvy. The conditions in the camp simply aren't sanitary. We have no fresh food, there's no hot water, and insufficient access to clean water.'

'Everyone's doing their best to fix the problems,' said Chanita defensively. 'They're working flat out.'

The doctor wasn't done yet, though. 'Tell me about it. I've hardly slept for almost twenty-four hours myself. But the fact remains we're in crisis. If nothing changes, soon we'll have no antibiotics, no anaesthetics, no blood. We'll be back in the Dark Ages. And someone told me that we only have enough tinned food for another week. Is that right?'

Chanita stared back at him helplessly. The list of problems he had reeled off were the problems she struggled each day to fix, with dwindling hope of success. 'We all just have to make the best of what we've got, doctor. What else can we do?'

He sighed. 'I know that. I'm sorry. Lack of sleep is making me lose my temper.'

'We'll get through this somehow,' she told him. 'We have to.'

On the way back to her office, she dropped in on Captain Rafferty. 'Any news of Colonel Griffin?' she asked hopefully.

'No, ma'am. Sorry.' The young captain's face was grim.

She knew what he was thinking. Why was she still asking for news of Griffin? He was long since dead. Any fool could see that. But she refused to give up hope. Without hope, she was lost.

She returned to her desk and sat there for a while, staring at the mounds of reports, each one representing some fresh difficulty, or informing her of yet another failure. The paper on the desk was piling up, just as outside the problems were mounting, just as the troubles weighing on her mind grew heavier with each passing day. She stared at them, not knowing what to do next.

A knock on her door roused her from her daze. Helen Eastgate. The doctor's bright blonde hair always brought a smile to Chanita's face. 'Come on in, Helen. I could use some cheering up. Tell me what progress you're making.'

Helen's tests on the captured werewolf, injecting him with antibodies from Chanita's own blood, had been running for some time now, and always gave her a glimmer of hope when she thought about them. If a cure could be found, it would change everything. It would give everyone fresh hope that all their problems could be overcome.

But it was obvious from Helen's face that the news she brought wasn't good. 'I've finished running my experiments on the lycanthrope.'

'And?'

'The tests are all negative. The antibodies have had no effect at all. The werewolf is still a werewolf.'

It felt as if the last support was failing, that the floor beneath Chanita was finally collapsing. 'Nothing?' she whispered.

'The virus has already delivered its genetic modifications to the host's cells, and there's no way of reversing them.'

'So a cure is simply impossible?'

Helen nodded.

Chanita felt tears running down her face before she even knew she was going to cry. She dabbed at them with a tissue, but there was no chance of stopping the flow. Instead she let them run freely. 'It's all too much.' The burden she had been given was simply too heavy. 'I can't do it anymore.'

Helen wrapped her arms around her. 'Don't give up. There's always hope. That's what you told me, remember?'

'I do. Patience and persistence, that's what I said.'

'That's right.'

'I'll do my best. But I just wish that Michael could be here.' She continued to sob against Helen's shoulder. If

Michael Griffin were with her, she knew that she could face anything.

Chapter Thirty-Seven

The Ridgeway, Oxfordshire, waxing moon

The confidence that Rose had found since the end of her nightmares was slowly ebbing away. The newfound lightness that had filled her limbs when she was walking across the open country had turned to a heavy slowness that seemed to drag her down now that they were unable to continue their journey. Since Seth had broken his ankle, her energy and enthusiasm had steadily drained away. Meanwhile the moon had grown almost full again.

It wasn't Seth's fault that he had broken his ankle, of course. Chris was to blame. Chris often seemed to be responsible for the problems they encountered.

But blaming Chris wouldn't help Seth's ankle to heal.

Instead, she turned in on herself. The enforced wait was giving her plenty of time to think. Too much time. Her thoughts spiralled back to everything she had lost. Her home, her parents, her brother, and Vijay. And now she had even lost her dreams.

She hadn't realized it at the time, but she had grown to depend on her visions, almost like a drug. They had been terrifying, but they had brought their own logic and given her a solid reassurance, even though it had been built on fear. Now her third eye had closed and the future was once again a dark place, unknowable and terrifying.

Ignorance brought its own kind of fear. Even though her journey was at a temporary halt, she felt that she was stumbling through a valley of shadows, her eyes closed, her hands clasped over her ears. All certainty was gone. For all she knew, even though she was going nowhere, she might be stepping towards a precipice – a figurative one at least. Perhaps a monster lumbered after her, teeth gnashing, tendrils and claws reaching out for her, gaining on her minute by minute. She could not know. Her visions were gone, and in their place, instead of finding the peace and calm she had hoped for, she was confronted with a new kind of nightmare. The nightmare of not knowing.

It was enough to make her scream.

It wasn't just her. The others were being driven mad by the enforced stop too. They bickered constantly. She was worried that soon a fight would break out. Ryan or Chris might go off on their own, leaving her behind with Seth. If that happened, she might have to abandon Seth herself, simply to survive. She wouldn't allow it to come to that.

'We have to start moving again,' she announced to the others one morning. 'Even if we only walk a very short distance, we have to try to do a little each day.'

'I can't,' moaned Seth. 'My ankle is still all black and swollen. It hurts if I put any weight on it. It hurts even if I don't.'

'You have to learn to tolerate it, Seth,' said Chris. 'Otherwise you won't be able to survive in the wilderness. Pain and hardship are the new normal. We all have to toughen up.'

'Yeah?' said Seth crossly. 'That's easy for you to say.

Perhaps I should break your ankle too, to help you toughen up.'

'That's good, Seth,' said Chris encouragingly. 'Start to fight back. Don't just lie down and take it.'

'When I'm better, I promise you I won't take any more from you.'

Rose looked to Ryan for support. Ryan was the sensible one. He had bound Seth's broken ankle with a bandage from their first-aid kit. He had quickly become the group's resident medic and go-to survival expert. He shook his head at Rose's suggestion. 'The ankle will take another six to eight weeks to heal. Walking on it now would simply fracture the bone all over again. Better to keep it still and rest up.'

'Good idea,' said Seth. 'Leave me in peace.'

'But we've already been resting for weeks,' protested Rose. 'We can't stay here any longer. It's not safe to stay in one place, and we have to move on to find more food.'

'I agree with Rose,' said Chris. 'We can't simply wait for Seth's ankle to get better. The fracture can't be that serious, or else the bone would probably be sticking out through the skin.'

'Aargh,' said Seth, wincing. 'Don't say that.'

'Any broken bone is serious,' said Ryan. 'Especially now that we don't have access to an X-ray or a doctor. Seth might not be able to walk for a long time. He might never walk again.'

Seth looked like he was going to faint. 'Stop saying things like that! None of you have any idea what it's like lying here all day, every day, in complete agony, with nothing to do.'

'Then let's at least try to move,' said Rose. 'What if we tie a splint to your leg to stop it moving? You could lean on Ryan and Chris.'

'No way. It hurts too much.'

'Well, what if we make a stretcher out of sticks and fabric? Then you don't have to walk at all. Ryan and Chris could carry you. We only need to travel a short distance each day.'

'That's not such a bad idea,' said Ryan. 'I reckon we could manage that.'

'Let's do it, then,' said Rose.

'What do you say, Seth?'

'Do I have a choice?'

'No,' said Chris.

'I thought this was a democracy.'

'It is, and you're outvoted. That's how democracy works.'

Chapter Thirty-Eight

Gatwick Airport, West Sussex, waxing moon

Someone was going to be murdered, and the way things looked to Drake, odds-on it was going to be him.

'You must think I'm stupid,' said Aasha, tossing her black hair angrily. She had that look in her eye that made him worry for his personal safety. He had brought her up onto the hotel rooftop to make sure that their discussion stayed well out of Liz's earshot. Now he was having doubts about the wisdom of that. It was a long way down to the ground, and no safety barrier to prevent him from toppling over the edge. Especially if someone pushed him.

He was glad that Vijay and Mihai were up here with him. Although, of course, it was Mihai who had talked them into this crazy idea in the first place.

'No, no, I don't think you're stupid,' he said to Aasha. 'Really.'

'Well, someone on this rooftop is totally stupid,' she

informed him, her hands on her hips, her eyes blazing with fire, 'and if it's not me, who do you think it is?' She took a step forward and jabbed at him with her finger, forcing him closer to the edge of the roof.

He glanced behind him. It really was a long way down. He could picture one way this confrontation might go – with him down there, and Aasha looking down from the rooftop, still shouting at him, even though he was dead. But it was too late to back out now. He ducked away from the roof edge, skirting back toward the centre.

Right on cue, Vijay stepped into the fray. 'Drake, I can't believe you even suggested such a ridiculous thing. What is wrong with you?'

Aasha turned to Vijay with some surprise. 'You don't think I should do it? I thought you were in on this stupid idea too.'

'No. Of course not. You're my sister. I would never allow you to do this.'

Drake watched Aasha closely. He could almost see the cogs turning inside her head.

'You wouldn't allow me?' she demanded, her hands back on her hips, fixing Vijay with a gaze that held just as much indignation as the one she had used on Drake.

'I meant –'

'You have absolutely no say in what I choose to do.'

'I know that,' said Vijay. 'I didn't mean it like that. I meant that I wouldn't allow Drake to tell you what to do.

Aasha snorted. 'As if that was ever going to happen.'

'So you won't do it, then? You won't do what Drake suggested?'

'Why? Don't you think I'm up to it?' she asked. 'Just because you have no guts, it doesn't mean I don't.'

This was exactly how they had planned it would go. It was like they were reading lines from a script. Aasha was also reading from the script they had prepared for her, even though she didn't know it.

The only way to persuade Aasha to do something was

to suggest to her that she couldn't.

'I ain't saying it would be easy,' said Drake. 'Cos it wouldn't.'

'Is not safe either,' said Mihai. 'Is very dangerous.'

Aasha stared at him, as if she hadn't noticed him before. 'What did the kid say?'

'Name is not kid,' protested Mihai.

'He said it might be risky,' said Drake. 'But it really wouldn't be.' He glared crossly at Mihai. They had discussed this plan carefully. They were pretty confident that the risk to Aasha would be minimal. They weren't gonna let the vampire get anywhere close to her.

'Why did the kid say it, then?' asked Aasha. 'Does he know something you haven't told me?'

Drake exchanged glances with Vijay. There was a lot they hadn't told Aasha, but they had agreed not to mention the word "vampire" to her. As far as they knew, Aasha had no idea that Liz was a vampire, or that the murderer might be one too. As far as they knew, Aasha didn't even know that vampires existed, and they wanted to keep it that way.

'The kid don't know nothing,' said Drake quickly.

'Name is Mihai,' said Mihai indignantly.

'You don't need to tell me that it would be risky,' said Aasha. 'I already know that. The idea is totally insane. You're asking me to act as bait to catch a serial killer.'

'Not bait exactly,' said Drake. There was a better word for it than bait. He looked to Vijay. Vijay was good with words.

'More like a lure,' said Vijay. 'A decoy, that's it.'

Aasha threw back her long black hair. 'Don't you think it's sexist to use a girl as a decoy?'

Drake hadn't anticipated this particular objection. He looked to Vijay for guidance.

'Yeah, it is sexist. That's so typical of Drake to suggest it. A boy would be just as good. Especially since it's so dangerous. In fact it would be better if Drake did it.'

Drake swallowed. Vijay had gone wildly off script.

Another picture formed in his mind – himself with two small puncture holes in his neck, his skin pale and cold, his blood mysteriously drained from his lifeless corpse.

Aasha laughed contemptuously. 'Drake? What self-respecting serial killer is going to want to murder him?'

'Cheers,' said Drake.

'The point is,' said Aasha, 'that you've assumed that the murderer would choose me, just because I'm a girl. Just because the first three victims were women. But we don't know if the killer is a man or a woman, or how they choose their victims, or even why they kill them in the first place. Do we?'

'Uh …' said Drake. He could feel his cheeks turning pink.

A look of suspicion grew on Aasha's face. 'Do we?'

Drake looked to Vijay for rescue. The wheels were beginning to fall off the plan.

'Do we?' demanded Aasha more forcefully.

'Uh …' said Vijay.

She folded her arms across her chest. 'All right, tell me everything you know. Tell me whatever it is you're hiding.'

Vijay told her.

Drake watched Aasha's face grow steadily darker. Eventually she exploded in a fit of rage. 'A vampire? This is even more stupid than everything you said already.' She fell silent for a moment, thinking. 'So not only were you planning to use me to catch a serial killer, you intended to trick me into being live bait for a vampire!'

'It wasn't a trick,' protested Drake.

Aasha marched toward him, and he ducked away again.

She reached out and grabbed his arm. 'Why didn't you tell me that vampires are real?'

'Because I thought …' He trailed off. Why hadn't he, exactly? 'I didn't think you'd believe me. Vijay didn't at first. I thought you'd probably just laugh at me.'

'You were scared that I'd think you were a moron?'

'I guess.'

'But not afraid that I might get bitten by a vampire?'

'I –'

'Shut up,' said Aasha. 'I've heard enough. Lying in wait for a vampire attack has got to be one of the worst ideas you've ever had.' She raised a hand to stop him interrupting. 'This is how we're going to do it.'

Once she had explained her idea to him, it seemed simple and obvious. 'Why didn't we think of that ourselves?' he asked Vijay.

Vijay shrugged. 'We were totally dumb.'

Drake nodded in agreement. It was the only possible explanation.

'So,' said Mihai. 'Plan is this. No bait for *vampir*. Just hide in dark and wait for *vampir* to come creeping.'

'That's right.'

'Okay. Then what?'

'Then nothing. We just need to see who the vampire is. Then we can report them to Liz.'

'What if *vampir* sees us?'

'Then,' said Aasha, 'we'll find out just how brave you boys really are.'

Chapter Thirty-Nine

Stoke Park, Buckinghamshire, waxing moon

Helen's attempt to find a cure for the disease may have failed, but she had not given up all hope. Although her experiments had shown that the antibodies in Chanita's blood had no effect on the test subject, who was already a fully-turned lycanthrope, there was still a possibility that she might be able to use Chanita's natural immunity to develop an antitoxin.

The basic principle of an antitoxin was simple. Take a blood sample from a donor – in this case, Chanita – containing antibodies capable of resisting a particular disease – in this case, lycanthropy – and inject it into a healthy patient. The antibodies from the donor should now provide the patient with immunity from infection by the disease. Antitoxins had been used for over a hundred years to treat acute infectious diseases.

Helen's lab equipment might be primitive, her working conditions cramped and basic, and all the odds stacked against her, but all she needed was the patience and persistence that Chanita so often talked about. Plus some luck. She could really use a healthy dose of good luck right now.

'Here you go,' she said, passing another glass slide to Sarah. 'More blood cells for you to count.'

'No problem,' said Sarah, sliding the sample under her microscope.

Sarah had settled into her job of lab assistant very well. Despite Helen's severe misgivings about taking on the odd, awkward woman who had tugged at her sleeve and begged so passionately to let her help, her doubts had proved to be unfounded. Sarah had a natural aptitude for the work. She was steadily growing in confidence, and had become a highly capable and diligent helper. She showed no fear of the test subject, James, and she had learned very quickly to perform the tasks that Helen asked her to do. She seemed to have boundless patience, even for the most mundane activities. Counting blood cells was probably Helen's least favourite job, especially now that Huntington's was making it harder for her to do it accurately. In fact, now that Helen's fingers could no longer be relied upon to remain steady, Sarah had become an indispensable helper.

'What kind of blood is this?' asked Sarah, when she'd completed the count.

'It's actually a sample of my own blood that's been treated with a dose of immune antibodies from Chanita. I allowed some time for the antibodies to multiply, then added a drop of infected blood from James.' She stopped, surprising herself that she had used her patient's name. She mustn't allow her guard to drop. But it was difficult, when the young man was so gentle and unassuming. So … human.

'So you're testing to see if you can make a sample of your own blood immune from the virus?'

'Right,' said Helen. Sarah was always quick to grasp the

nature of the work. 'Normally the virus would take hold very quickly and overwhelm the immune system of the blood sample. What I'm hoping is that in this case, the blood that has had the antibodies added to it will have succeeded in fighting off the infection.'

'So is your plan to produce a vaccine?'

Helen gave a nervous laugh. 'Not a vaccine, but an antitoxin. Don't worry about the difference – it's just a medical detail. That's my hope. I wouldn't call it a plan. Not yet.' She studied the latest batch of results with a mounting sense of excitement.

'Good news?' asked Sarah.

'Definitely. These tests have worked exactly as I'd hoped. The antibodies from Chanita have made my blood sample completely immune from infection. We've run ten separate tests now, and each one has been successful.'

'Great. So what next?'

'Good question. All we've done so far is make small samples of my blood immune to the disease. There's still a huge question about whether we can actually confer immunity to a living person.'

'So, what? Do you need a volunteer?'

'I guess so.'

'Look no further.'

Helen shook her head. 'I'm not sure you understand the implications, Sarah. To test the procedure, I would need to inject the antibodies into your bloodstream, wait for them to spread throughout your entire body, and then inject you with contaminated blood from James. It's the only way to be sure the antitoxin works.'

'Sure. I already understood that. So what are we waiting for?'

'I'm not sure that this is ethical. If it fails, you would become lycanthropic.'

'Well, I'm giving you my informed consent. Anyway, you had no ethical qualms about running experiments on James.'

Helen blanched a little at Sarah's accusatory tone. 'That's different.'

'Why?'

'Because he's –'

'Not human? Do you still believe that?'

Helen shifted awkwardly. She had been having doubts for some time about the way she was treating James. At first, she had found his presence repulsive. She had been glad of the metal cage that held him, the ropes and ties that bound his wrists and ankles, and of the presence of an armed guard whenever they needed to take a sample of his blood. But the armed guard had not been needed. James had complied fully with all requests, willingly offering up his blood for her tests, showing polite interest in her work, and generally behaving impeccably, despite the inhumane conditions he was subjected to. He was nothing like Leanna Lloyd. Unlike Leanna, his eyes were alive and kind, not dead and cold. It was hard to believe that he was a werewolf, and if it wasn't for the evidence that only the microscope revealed, she would have had trouble believing he was lycanthropic.

She actually felt shame about the way she had treated him. She had dismissed the armed guard some while back, and agreed to untie James' arms and legs, allowing him to move freely within his cage. She had given him the blanket he had asked for. In return, he had politely thanked her, even though she still refused to bring him live animals to eat. His behaviour had thrown her into confusion. Perhaps she was wrong to assume that the disease turned everyone into an evil monster.

'Don't try to make me feel guilty, Sarah. These creatures are dangerous, however they might appear. You don't know them as well as I do. They don't have any feelings or emotions. Any semblance of humanity is just an act.'

'You can't still believe that, Helen. You must know that James is kind and gentle.'

He was watching them now, from his cage. As always he was sitting in silence, his legs crossed, his arms folded neatly in his lap. His long straggly hair framed the fine bone structure of his face, which was now half-hidden by a bushy beard. He was a picture of calmness and tranquillity, only the slight movement of his head showing that he was a living person, and not a statue.

'Yes.' She had no choice but to admit it. James was completely not like Leanna Lloyd. She had known that something was wrong with Leanna within minutes of first meeting her. James had been in the cage for weeks now, and had never shown any sign of the fiendish behaviour she had accused him of.

'I was justified in treating James like this,' said Helen. 'I was trying to find a cure for him.' But she knew she was convincing no one. 'I was just doing my best to help,' she finished lamely.

'Then let me help too,' said Sarah. 'Test the antitoxin on me.'

Chapter Forty

Gatwick Airport, West Sussex, full moon

The full moon became visible once the sun had set, and Liz felt that familiar tingle in her gums. She drew the curtains tightly shut against its cold light, and began to pace around the hotel suite, overflowing with nervous energy.

'Sit down, love,' said Kevin. 'You're driving us all crazy.'

Major Hall had ordered a full lockdown of the terminal buildings and all of the airport hotels, and imposed a strict curfew between dusk and daybreak. 'Anyone found out of their room will be shot without warning,' he had informed them, seeming almost to relish the prospect. 'We are preparing for a full-scale assault on our defences by lycanthropes during the hours of darkness. All military personnel will be involved in the defence of the camp. We will not permit a single one of those animals to breach the perimeter fence.'

Jones and the Welsh Guards were involved in the operation too. Liz had run into Llewelyn that afternoon and found the Welshman unusually subdued. 'Griffiths is getting worse,' he told her. 'His wound is infected and they're running low on antibiotics. And they have no blood supplies either. The medics think he might not make it.'

'I'm sorry to hear that,' said Liz. Griffiths had been shot and injured the night they'd left London. She had thought he was making a good recovery. 'Good luck,' she wished him. 'For tonight, I mean. Stay safe.'

'Thanks. And you make sure you stay safely indoors.'

'Don't worry, I will.'

Nothing could possibly induce her to step outside tonight. She was determined to keep as far away from the moonlight as possible. Even so, she could feel the pull of the moon as it rose above the horizon. Her heart rate rose and her breathing steadily quickened as the moon rose higher. The hairs on her skin became hyper-sensitive, and her teeth and fingernails ached with the desire for violence.

'Damn it!' she shouted, punching her fist against the thin wall of the hotel room. 'I won't let it take me!'

The others cowered back, giving her as much space as they could. As far as Liz knew, only Mihai and Kevin were aware that she was a vampire, but from the way the others behaved, she guessed they had all been warned what to expect. That was probably for the best. She couldn't handle anyone asking questions about her behaviour.

As long as she stayed away from the window and the moonlight didn't touch her, her felt sure she'd be okay. She reminded herself that she had harnessed her vampire powers for good in the past. She had rescued Vijay and his friends from rioters the first time she had turned; then saved Kevin from gangsters; and finally used her strength to fight off a pack of werewolves threatening Mihai and Lily. *Use your power now*, whispered a voice, very much like her own. *Give yourself up to the light.*

'No!' she bellowed, kicking the furniture with her foot.

It had felt good to be a vampire. That feeling of infinite power. The speed. The agility. The energy flowing from tip to toe. *Let it happen*, whispered the seductive voice. *It's only natural.*

She pulled the Glock from her holster and thrust it toward Kevin. 'Here. Take it. If I change, or if I try to harm anyone, if I even look like I'm going to do something, shoot me.'

He shook his head. 'I ain't gonna do that, love. Not in a million years.'

'Take it!' she screeched, forcing the gun into his hand. 'Promise me you'll kill me.'

'No,' said Kevin again. 'No way.'

Anger flooded her senses at his refusal. Her fangs burst through her gums throwing a quick spatter of blood across his face. She opened her mouth wide and leaned in close to him. 'Promise me!' she roared.

Kevin's face turned white. The gun was in his hands now and pointing in her direction. His fingers trembled wildly. 'Okay,' he mumbled. 'I promise.'

With enormous effort she forced herself away from him and felt her teeth slowly retract. 'Okay,' she said. 'I'm sorry. I didn't mean to scare you.'

Vijay's grandmother rose from her chair and took her by the hand. She seemed entirely unafraid of Liz. 'After my husband died I used to feel great anger too,' she said. 'I learned to find calm through breathing. Try it. Breathe slowly through your nose. In, then out. In, then out. It helps if you sit down.'

Liz did as instructed, sitting on the floor and breathing deeply in and out in time with the old lady.

'You see?' said Mrs Singh triumphantly. 'It works.'

Very slowly the hours passed. No one slept that night, apart from Lily, who curled up in Samantha's arms and snored softly. From time to time, Liz rose to her feet again, pacing the room, before allowing Mrs Singh to calm her down again.

Outside the night was punctuated with the noise of fighting. Single shots; sustained fire from machine guns and assault rifles; sometimes even distant explosions.

Once, Kevin parted the curtains to look out, and a sliver of moonlight found its way inside. Liz pushed herself away from it, and yelled at Kevin to draw the curtains back.

'I only wanted to see what was happening,' he said sheepishly. 'Looks like Major Hall and his men are doing their best to keep the enemy at bay.'

Liz too, kept the voice in her head from tempting her into savagery. It was her inner voice that was her real enemy, not the moonlight. If she could silence the voice, she might find her true self again. She might learn to control the power that lived within her.

Mrs Singh and her breathing exercises kept her calm. Once, she even recovered enough humanity to think of Llewelyn Jones and his men, and hope that no harm had come to them. Even the Dogman didn't deserve to die, however loudly he might argue that Liz herself ought to.

When daybreak came, she was completely calm, and utterly exhausted. Kevin returned the gun to her with a look of relief. The sunlight filtered weakly through the curtains, banishing all memory of the moon, and she lay her head on her pillow. She was asleep within seconds.

Chapter Forty-One

Pindar Bunker, Whitehall, Central London, waning moon

The cold, calm features of General Ney appeared on the Prime Minister's computer screen in the Pindar bunker, his iron grey hair shorn brutally short, his bushy eyebrows joined together in a monobrow. His peaked cap was fixed rigidly in position, and his dark blue uniform immaculately pressed as always. He was looking good, for a dead man. The only colour on the screen came from the General's brightly striped medals ranged across his barrel chest, and the gold sashes and shoulder epaulettes that decorated his dark uniform.

The PM had watched the video hundreds of times already. After all, the General's relentlessly booming voice had been her only source of human contact since becoming entombed in this place. She knew his script by heart, but it wouldn't hurt to listen to his instructions one last time before she attempted to carry them out.

'Prime Minister,' bellowed the General through the speakers, 'your first task will be to escape from the Defence Crisis Management Centre, known by its codename Pindar. I suspect that you shall be very glad to leave it behind after all this time.'

The man was certainly right about that. Cooped up in this claustrophobic hole in the ground, she had been driven almost as mad as the General himself. She had been here for well over a month now, ever since moving here at the start of the evacuation operation, when the General had deemed it unsafe for her to continue living above ground. The last four weeks had been spent entirely alone, if you discounted the presence of four dead bodies. She had eventually found the strength to drag the corpses from the comms centre and down the corridor into a storeroom, which she had locked carefully. She was by no means superstitious, but the prospect of spending a month alone in an underground bunker with a room full of cadavers had frayed even her nerves.

On screen, the General continued his briefing. 'The Pindar bunker was constructed during the Cold War and was designed to withstand a nuclear attack by an enemy power. The main part of the three-storey building is located deep beneath the Ministry of Defence on Whitehall. The complex has three entrances, the first in the Ministry of Defence building itself, the second beneath Number Ten, Downing Street, and the third at the BT telecommunications tower. The latter two entrances are reached via access tunnels from the central part of the bunker.'

The General's brows knotted fiercely as he continued. 'But on no account should you attempt to leave the complex for at least one month following the nuclear explosions.'

The PM had been filled with dismay on first hearing this. A whole month in this mausoleum had seemed like an eternity. She had carefully marked the hours and days –

sometimes even the minutes and seconds – as they had slowly passed. She had wondered at times if her sanity would survive intact as she waited for the month to end.

'The attack that I launched against London consisted of three Trident II missiles, each equipped with three nuclear warheads. Each of these nine warheads had a yield of one hundred kilotons and was set to detonate at a height of two thousand metres. The total destructive force was approximately equal to seventy times that of the bomb dropped over Hiroshima, more than enough to kill all lycanthropes within a radius of fourteen miles.'

The PM grimaced in disgust. 'Not to mention any people unfortunate enough to have remained within the city,' she told him.

'The shockwave and the heat burst from the blasts will almost certainly have eradicated anyone who was not fortunate to have been below ground in a bunker or sealed basement, or within a fortified structure. Within a one-mile radius of each strike, all buildings will have been flattened. Furthermore the heat bursts will have ignited large-scale firestorms that will have swept across large parts of the city. No one could survive such a fire. But the detonation altitude of two thousand metres was carefully calculated to prevent the fireballs produced by the airbursts from actually touching the ground. The effect of this was to greatly limit the radioactive fallout from the blasts. After one month has elapsed, radiation levels within the city should have returned to normal background readings, and all fires ought to have burned themselves out, or else been doused by rainfall. It will be safe for you to begin your journey.'

And I have followed your instructions to the letter, General. I have been patient, and I have prepared for my great escape.

'The safest way out of London will be underground. I suggest that you leave the Pindar facility via its Whitehall entrance. Stay below ground and join the Q-Whitehall tunnel system which contains the secure link that connects

Pindar and Whitehall to the national telecommunications system. Follow the tunnel north where it eventually connects to a shaft leading to the underground railway station at Charing Cross. From here you will be able to follow the Bakerloo Line to the station at Baker Street. Here, change to the Metropolitan Line, which will take you all the way to Northwood station. You will then only have a short journey above ground to reach Northwood Headquarters.'

You make it sound so easy, General, almost as if the trains might still be running.

'Needless to say, you will be entirely alone as you make this trip. All communications with the outside world will have been lost.' On screen, General Ney saluted her. 'Prime Minister, as you know, I have every confidence in your ability to undertake this mission successfully, and to lead the country to a bright new future. I wish you luck on your journey.'

Wow, thanks, General. I will miss your wise words.

She clicked on the video to close it down, then logged out of the computer, still conscious of security. Old habits died hard, it seemed. But it was time for her to learn new skills and develop new ways of thinking. She didn't fool herself that the journey would be as simple as the General made it sound.

She had carefully collected the weapons of the three soldiers who had been so callously murdered by General Ney. Her armoury consisted of two assault rifles and the service pistol that the General had taken from his brigadier. It was the gun that he had used to carry out his executions.

The assault rifles frightened her. She couldn't imagine herself carrying one with her as she made her escape. They were too technical, and there was too much that might go wrong. The service pistol was more her style. She weighed it in her hand. It was heavy, but not too heavy to carry. She had never used a gun, but the basic principle was simple enough to grasp. Aim it. Pull the trigger.

How many bullets did it contain? The General had used six to kill the brigadier and the two infantrymen who had remained in the bunker as her protection force. He had fired one round to warn her off, and another to take his own life. Eight used in total. But she had no idea how many there had been in the first place. She considered taking the gun apart to see how many rounds remained, but worried that she might not be able to put it back together. She would have to pray that enough bullets remained if ever she needed to use them.

She placed the gun carefully in its holster and strapped it around her waist. She lifted the rucksack of supplies that she had packed and strapped it to her back. Kitted out with warm, waterproof clothing, sturdy shoes, and enough food and water to last a week, she felt warily cautious. She had no idea what to expect in the tunnels that lay beyond the bunker, but she was more than ready to find out. After so many weeks trapped inside this grim prison, she was ready for anything.

Chapter Forty-Two

Stoke Park, Buckinghamshire, waning moon

Disease was beginning to spread through the camp like wildfire. Medical supplies were critically low, food was being rationed, and with little rainfall to replenish the lake, Chanita's advisers had warned her that even their source of drinking water might soon come under threat.

'What are we going to do about it?' she asked, but no one had any easy answers for her.

She had given up querying Captain Rafferty about the whereabouts of Colonel Griffin. If any news came, she knew that she would be the first to be informed. She still clung to a small flame of hope. He couldn't have been killed. He had to be alive, somewhere.

The only person with any good news for her this morning was Lieutenant Colonel Sharman. 'We were braced for a full onslaught last night. But remarkably there was relatively little werewolf activity, even under the full moon. I don't fully understand why. Anyway, I'm pleased to report that we fought off all attacks without sustaining a single casualty.'

She nodded. 'Good work, Colonel. Excellent.' It was all she was good for these days. Empty words, and an easy smile. Perhaps that was her job now. Nothing more than a figurehead. Someone to give the appearance of confidence, even as the ship went down in flames around her. Still, if that was what her role required, she would do it. She walked the hospital ward once more, dispensing platitudes, talking to the doctors and the nurses, offering kind words to the patients. Her presence seemed to lift their spirits, if only for a short time.

She noticed how thin they were looking in recent days, staff and patients alike. The stockpiles of food in the camp were all gone now. She was sending Colonel Sharman and his men ever further beyond the camp boundaries on missions to gather food and medicines, but each day they seemed to bring back less than the day before. And sometimes not all the men returned. It was dangerous out there, even for well-armed and combat-trained soldiers.

Chanita had long since given up on any hopes for rescue. Not only had central government failed, now the regions were falling too. Communications with the other evacuation camps had ceased. To continue to survive, they would have to fend for themselves.

She badly needed cheering up. She had been so preoccupied she hadn't been to visit Helen Eastgate for ages. She decided to go and see her now.

Helen seemed in surprisingly good humour this morning. 'Chanita, hi! Come on in. Let me introduce you to my new lab assistant, Sarah.'

Chanita entered the bustling lab and offered her hand in greeting. 'Nice to meet you, Sarah.'

She had heard about Helen's assistant but had been too busy to meet her. The new woman appeared very shy. She nodded meekly and accepted Chanita's handshake timidly, her gaze lowered.

Chanita turned instead to regard the metal cage that took up one quarter of the room. 'This must be your test werewolf.' She stopped, stunned by recognition. 'James? James Beaumont?'

He stood up from the floor and nodded. 'Chanita.'

She had first met James when she had been a nurse at King's College Hospital in London. He had been one of the early bite victims, bitten by a man, if she remembered correctly. No one had known then about the true nature of the infection. James had been treated in intensive care, and then discharged. She remembered him as a quiet, well-spoken boy who had always been very polite.

Helen and Sarah both looked nonplussed. 'I had no idea you knew James,' said Helen.

'I had no idea you were using him for your experiments.'

'I'm not anymore. I've been working on something else.'

'What?'

'It's quite exciting, actually,' said Helen. 'I've succeeded in passing on your natural immunity to Sarah.'

Chanita blinked in astonishment. 'You've developed an antitoxin?'

'Exactly. I simply injected some of your blood into Sarah. Her immune system assimilated the new blood cells and began to manufacture fresh copies of the antibodies. Now she has the same immunity as you.'

'But you can't be certain,' said Chanita anxiously. 'You'll need to test it.'

'I already have.'

'I see.' Chanita vividly recalled how Helen had run the same test on her, by injecting her with a drop of contaminated blood from a werewolf. She had suffered an allergic reaction to the infection, her temperature rising, and a fever taking hold. It had been one of the longest nights of her life. But she had come through unharmed.

The test had proved her natural immunity.

'Sarah's reaction was far less severe than yours,' said Helen. 'The antitoxin gave her almost total immunity to the effects of lycanthropy.'

Chanita suddenly needed to sit down. She took a seat and began to think through the implications of what Helen had told her. 'So could you give the antitoxin to everyone in the camp? You could roll out a programme and make everyone immune to the condition!'

'In principle, yes. But it's not that easy. We'll have to take blood from either you or Sarah and inject it into a small number of volunteers. It will take a couple of weeks for the immunity to take effect and for the treated volunteers to start producing their own antibodies. Then they can become donors themselves. But to treat thousands of people, it's going to take many months, maybe even years.'

'But you could do it?'

'Yes.'

'Then what are we waiting for? I'll give you all the support you need and make it a top priority.'

Helen and Sarah exchanged glances.

'What?' demanded Chanita.

'Do you think the camp can survive that long?' asked Helen.

'It has to. I won't allow these people to die.'

'But they already are. Sarah and I were discussing this earlier with James.'

'With James?'

'Yes. The way we see it, the biggest threat to survival now isn't lycanthropy. It's all the other diseases. Measles. Pneumonia. Common diseases that we can no longer treat.'

'The medical staff are doing the best they can,' protested Chanita.

'Of course. But what if there was another way? A way to make those diseases go away?'

'I don't understand.'

'It was James himself who finally convinced me,' said Helen. 'It wasn't what he said, but how he behaved. I've worked with other lycanthropes before and I thought I knew what they were like. But James has made me think again. He does seem to be very different from the others. He's gentle, caring … even compassionate. I now believe that he's fully human, emotionally speaking. He's perhaps even more humane than most humans.'

Helen had taken on an eagerness that Chanita had seen in her before, whenever she was convinced that an idea would work. Yet Chanita felt a coldness grip her stomach. She dreaded what Helen might say next.

'When I first started my experiments on the virus that transmits lycanthropy,' continued Helen, 'I discovered that turning its victims into werewolves is only one of its effects. It makes them stronger and more capable, even when in human form. It develops their senses, and sometimes makes them more intelligent. At the same time it eradicates other diseases.'

'Eradicates them?' asked Chanita, frowning.

'Totally. It's basically a universal cure. Pneumonia, HIV, diphtheria …' She paused. 'Even Huntington's. One thing I learned from reading Professor Wiseman's notes was that the werewolves he studied in Romania were always healthy and appeared to be immune to common illnesses. They even made seemingly-miraculous recoveries from physical injuries. They displayed an ability to regenerate.'

Chanita was staring at Helen now. 'But –'

'My fear is that by rolling out an immunization programme, we'll be protecting people from becoming werewolves, but condemning them to death from ordinary infectious diseases. One of the lycanthropes I knew was a student of mine. She talked of perfecting the human race. At the time I thought she was mad. Now I see that she may have been right, or at least in part.'

Chanita spoke as sternly as she could. 'Stop! This is madness. If I understand what you are saying, you are talking about turning people into werewolves. Have you completely lost your mind?'

'No, I don't think so.' Helen turned to James. 'James, you explain.'

James had been watching the exchange intently. Now he spoke softly to Chanita. 'You're right that some werewolves are monsters. I know the student who studied with Helen. Her name is Leanna. She was one of the original werewolves to bring the condition from Romania. She's absolutely evil. And at first, I thought I was too. I admit that I killed people. I hated myself for that. I wanted to die. But Sarah taught me that it didn't have to be that way.'

'Sarah?'

'Yes. I've known Sarah for a long time, since before we came to the camp. We've been through a lot together. But we had to keep our friendship a secret from Helen.'

'It's true,' said Sarah. 'I helped James come to terms with being a werewolf. And in turn he helped me overcome my own … problems. You must understand that James has broken free from the change that affects other werewolves. The moon doesn't control him anymore.'

'I don't understand,' said Chanita. 'What on earth do you mean?'

'Show her,' said Sarah.

James nodded. He unbuttoned his shirt and dropped it to the floor, then removed his shoes and socks. A look of intense concentration came over his face. His brow furrowed and his lips parted. Chanita noticed a change in his eyes, a glint of yellow, and a darkening as the pupils dilated. Slowly, his skin began to ripple and a fine layer of golden hairs appeared over his face, chest and arms. He stripped off the rest of his clothing to reveal a body entirely covered with thickening fur. His skin was moving more, as his arms and legs grew strong and thick and his chest broadened. His neck elongated and his head changed shape, becoming longer and more dog-like.

Chanita stared, dumbed into silence. James' body stretched, and he dropped to all fours as a tail sprouted behind him. She watched in amazement as nails and teeth pushed through, and his eyes became large and bright.

Finally it was done. He sat back on the floor of his cage, his front paws stretched out before him, panting lightly with his long tongue hanging out.

'You see?' he said. 'I can change between wolf and human form whenever I want. I'm completely in control.'

Chapter Forty-Three

Uffington, Oxfordshire, waning moon

Rose stood at the top of the scarp, staring down at the white chalk horse carved into the hillside below. The horse was enormous, hundreds of feet long, made from shallow cuts in the grassy hillside to expose the white chalk beneath, almost like the markings on a football pitch. It was hard to make sense of its shape from close quarters. The flowing lines rose and fell with the sweep of the land, but she thought she could make out the body of the horse, its legs and head. That round spot just before her must be its eye, that pair of short parallel lines its mouth. She supposed it must be possible to see the whole picture from one of the hills opposite, or from the valley below. It was incredible to think that this work of art had been made thousands of years earlier, with only primitive tools.

This place had a peculiarly ancient feel, bare and windswept. From her high viewpoint she could see a low, round hill with a flat top immediately below the horse. According to a nearby sign, the small hill was named Dragon Hill and was supposedly the place where St George had slain the dragon. Ahead of her, the Ridgeway continued up to a much larger hill that had once been an Iron Age fort. There was no sign of the original wooden structure of the fort, but tall earthen ramparts and a deep ditch had been dug all around the hilltop as fortification and were still clearly visible. She wondered what it had been like to live in this strange place, so many thousands of years ago. In this desolate landscape, empty of all signs of modernity, it was easy to imagine the distant past reaching out to her.

She turned back to see Ryan and Chris carrying Seth along the chalky path. Ryan was making the work look easy, but Chris was clearly out of breath. But they had made good progress and it was time to stop. Perhaps the old hillfort would be a good place to make camp for the night. She pointed up to it and led them up the last few yards of the track.

'Oh my God, be more careful!' yelled Seth as they lowered him to the ground.

'Quit moaning,' said Chris. 'We only carried you half a mile today. It'll take forever at this rate. The least you could do is show some gratitude.'

Seth opened his mouth to retort, but Rose cut him off. They had argued far too much already. 'We've almost run out of food. I think there's a village about a mile or so in that direction. Why don't we go and see if we can find something to eat?'

'But what about me?' said Seth. 'You can't just leave me here on my own.'

'I'll stay with him,' said Chris. 'You and Ryan can go.'

'Sounds good to me,' said Ryan, stretching out his arms. 'Chris, see if you can manage to put the tent up while we're gone.'

Rose and Ryan set off along a path that led down the

hillside, Nutmeg running ahead, keen to find rabbits. The track was straight and narrow, but just wide enough for two to walk abreast. The wind blew at their backs, chasing ever-changing patterns in the long grass at each side.

'You can see for miles from here,' said Ryan. 'I love being out in the countryside, don't you?'

'I'm not sure,' said Rose. 'I think I'm a city girl at heart. I miss home. I miss my family.'

'Sure,' said Ryan. 'I understand. I never really had much of a family myself, so I guess there's not too much to miss. But perhaps that makes me better prepared than most to deal with what's happened. You can't pine for home comforts if you never had a proper home.'

'I guess so.'

'My mum died when I was small and I never knew my father,' he explained. 'I spent my time moving between foster parents and children's homes.'

'I'm sorry,' said Rose. She had grown up in such a close-knit family, with her mum and dad, and her brother, Oscar, that she couldn't imagine the life that Ryan described.

'No need to be,' he said. 'My childhood was happy enough. I can't complain.'

After half an hour of walking they came to the village of Uffington.

Ryan put out a hand to stop her, then raised a finger to his lips.

It was wise to be cautious. They hadn't met a single person in many days, and had no idea what was happening in the world. The few small villages and settlements they had encountered on their journey had all been strangely empty, but who knew what they might find here?

Ryan went ahead, walking up the middle of the single-track road. They passed a few houses, but saw no indications that anyone was home. There were no cars in front of the houses, no smoke rising from chimneys, no twitching curtains or faces in windows.

'Where is everyone?' whispered Rose.

They carried along until they came to a junction that seemed to mark the centre of the village. The houses here were older – thatched cottages with roses growing up their walls – a chocolate-box image of English life. Their footsteps rang loudly in the silent street.

A little further along they came to a pub. 'If we're going to find food or people, this will be the place,' said Ryan. 'I'll go first. You stay safely back.'

The pub looked very traditional, with hanging baskets displaying daffodils and other flowering plants, and a sign advertising bed & breakfast accommodation. Rose peered through the windows into the dark interior, but the bar appeared to be empty. She followed Ryan as he pushed open the door and went inside.

The entrance was low and even Rose had to stoop to avoid banging her ahead on the wooden beam. The interior of the pub was dim, and she paused on the threshold waiting for her eyes to adjust to the gloom. The bar room was deserted, but there were signs of a fight. Tables had been tipped over and chairs smashed. Broken glasses and bottles lay on the floor and there was a powerful stench of stale beer. There was another nastier smell beneath it. She covered her mouth.

Nutmeg sniffed the spilled beer and then ran over to the bar, her nostrils flaring wide as she frantically thrust her nose up against it, snuffling desperately.

Ryan looked behind the bar to see what Nutmeg could smell. 'Oh, shit,' he said. 'Don't come any closer.'

But Rose wanted to see for herself. She joined him at the bar and peered over the top. Two corpses lay on the floor, a middle-aged man and woman. Their throats had been ripped open, and the man was missing one arm. Their faces were crawling with flies.

'Killed by werewolves?' whispered Rose.

Ryan nodded. 'Looks that way. Judging by the smell, they must have been dead for some time.'

'They won't mind us looking for food, then,' said Rose. She led Ryan through a door marked *Staff only*, and found herself in a small kitchen. There were two more corpses in here, a younger man and a teenage girl. They had also been savaged and were showing signs of decomposition. Nutmeg went up to them and began to sniff.

'I think I'm going to be sick,' said Ryan. 'Let's go.'

'No,' said Rose. 'We mustn't leave empty-handed.'

The food in the fridges and freezers had spoiled and smelled putrid, but the kitchen was well stocked with tinned and packaged foods, and bottled drinks. They filled up some cardboard boxes with supplies and set off back toward the white horse, glad to be out in the fresh air again.

Ryan threw her a sideways glance as they walked. 'That was brave. Weren't you afraid in there?'

Rose shook her head. 'What was there to be afraid of? Those people were dead. They couldn't hurt us.'

'Yeah, I know,' said Ryan. 'Still. It creeped me out. I'm glad you were with me.'

It took them longer to make the journey back. The road sloped upward this time and the wind blew hard in their faces. The boxes were heavy too, or at least Rose found hers heavy. Ryan was carrying two and didn't seem to have a problem with them.

There was something Rose wanted to say to him, a worry that had played on her mind for some time. 'You know, we're only going to survive if we stick together. Safety in numbers. The opposite of what Chris says. Each one of us has a different set of skills. Promise me that we'll stay together.'

Ryan looked at her with surprise. 'Of course. I wasn't planning on running away. In fact, I don't know what I would have done if I hadn't met you guys. I've been on my own for a long time. It's good to have some company.'

She gave him a smile. 'When I first met Chris and Seth, I'd lost everything. My home, my family, my friends. I think I'd lost my mind. They honestly saved my life.'

Ryan nodded. 'Chris is a smart guy, even though he can be … awkward at times. And Seth …'

'Seth makes Chris tolerable,' said Rose.

'Exactly.'

They both smiled.

When they reached the top of the hill, they discovered that Chris and Seth had been joined by a group of half a dozen strangers. They were sitting cross-legged in a circle and appeared to be drinking cans of beer. One of them was playing a flute. Chris' face registered outrage and indignation.

'Our numbers seem to have grown even more,' said Ryan.

One of the newcomers, a girl with long purple hair, stood up and waved to them. 'Hey, you must be Rose and Ryan. Awesome. Your friends told us all about you. Come on over. It's time to get this party started!'

Chapter Forty-Four

Pindar Bunker, Whitehall, Central London, waning moon

With a huge effort, the Prime Minister heaved aside the sealed metal door that led from the Pindar bunker. It was dark beyond, and cool, damp air greeted her, laden with the scent of mildew and decay. She wrinkled her nose. She had been hoping for fresh air after spending so long inside the airtight bunker, but this smelled awful. She was gripped by a sudden fear. Perhaps the General's careful plan would fail at the first hurdle. If the exit was blocked under rubble, she might find no way out.

She trained the steady beam of her flashlight around the dank cellar. Water dripped from the ceiling and a dark pool of oily liquid stretched out across the floor, but it was no more than an inch deep. She dipped the toe of her boot into the blackness and stepped bravely forward, dismayed to feel cold wetness spread immediately around her feet.

So much for waterproof footwear.

She waded across the cellar and up a short flight of stairs, away from the water and into another basement. She must be deep beneath the Ministry of Defence building in Whitehall. Here a door marked "Q-Whitehall" led off to one side. It was just as the General had described. She opened the door and found herself inside a low tunnel, perhaps seven feet in diameter. Her flashlight showed her a curved roof supported by thick steel and concrete bulwarks. A large number of cables snaked along its walls. Overhead lights were fixed at intervals, but they were not working. The tunnel floor was of rough, broken concrete and clearly not designed for pedestrian access, except perhaps for the repair and laying of cables.

'Follow the tunnel north,' the General had told her. A simple enough instruction, but which way was that? Trusting her instinct, she took the left branch of the tunnel and began to make her way along it, the sound of gravel crunching beneath her boots. For once in her life she was glad she was so short. Any taller and she would have had to bend double. Every thirty feet or so, even narrower tunnels branched off like dark mouths, carrying cables in all directions.

After what seemed like an age she came to the tunnel's end. A borehole plunged down into the bowels of the earth, taking cables to the deep level telecoms system that spanned London. And at the very end was a metal door labelled "Trafalgar Square Station."

She frowned briefly in puzzlement before recalling that Trafalgar Square was the original name for Charing Cross station. The General had not let her down.

She pushed open the door and was assaulted with an even harsher smell of cold, wet clay. A drip-drip sound echoed from below. Slowly she descended into the darkness, her boots ringing loudly off the metal stairs. She had only gone a few feet before she stopped in dismay. The entire stairwell below her was flooded.

She stopped to gather her thoughts. The Bakerloo line at Charing Cross was one of the deep underground lines, sunk to a depth of sixty feet so that it could cross beneath the River Thames. If the tunnel had been breached, then water from the river would have flooded into it, filling the entire deep railway network with water. There was no way through.

So much for your plan, General. Your blasted bombs have brought it to a quick end.

There was nothing to do except turn around and go back up the stairs. She returned to the Q-Whitehall tunnel and set off back along its length. When she reached the door leading back into the Ministry of Defence basement, she continued on past it, following the tunnel south. She was following her own gut now, free of General's Ney's controlling instructions, tracing a route deep beneath Whitehall, heading toward the Treasury Building on King Charles Street. She wondered if it would connect to one of the near-surface underground stations, or perhaps lead back up into one of the government buildings, if any were still standing.

Dirt and dust trickled from the roof as she walked, and in places her feet splashed through puddles, but eventually she reached a steeply sloping stair leading up. She followed it up through several landings before she reached a sealed door. The door resisted her, but she pushed and pushed and eventually it gave way, spilling her out into blinding sunlight. She fell to her knees and stared out, blinking and shielding her eyes, trying to make sense of her surroundings.

She was in London, or a ruined version of the once-great capital. All around stood crumbling facades of famous buildings. Westminster Abbey, the gothic church that had stood for nearly a thousand years, and in which every British monarch since William the Conqueror had been crowned, had collapsed in on itself. The Palace of Westminster, once the home of the House of Commons and the House of Lords was now a smoke-blackened ruin. Incredibly, the Elizabeth Tower, known more commonly as Big Ben, still rose above the charred landscape, strangely defiant amidst the destruction. Water lapped at the base of the tower. Somehow the river must have burst its banks. The central arches of Westminster Bridge had collapsed too, and on the south bank of the river, the huge circular wheel of the London Eye had toppled and fallen into the water. It lay on one side, half submerged, its glass capsules broken and flooded.

Behind her, only the stump of a building remained, a few white columns and arches visible above a mountain of fallen masonry. From its location opposite the Houses of Parliament she deduced that this must once have been the Foreign and Commonwealth Office, the Grade 1 listed building that had been one of the jewels of Whitehall. It was a miracle that the exit from the tunnel hadn't caved in, or been buried beneath the mounds of rubble.

The Prime Minister shuddered. If she needed proof that the world she had known was utterly gone, it was here all around her. She allowed herself a final look, committing the desolate scene to memory, then turned away from it, heading west along the edge of St James' Park.

London had fallen, but her country needed her. Perhaps more than ever.

Chapter Forty-Five

Uffington, Oxfordshire, waning moon

Chris was furious, angrier than he'd been for a very long time. Angier even than when he'd shoved Seth down the hill and broken his ankle. Almost as angry as the time he'd been forced to take the job as tech support guy at Manor Road school, after being rejected for every other job he'd applied for. But he knew that he had to keep his anger in check. Look what had happened before. If he hadn't lost his temper with Seth, he would be in Hereford now, not stuck on a hilltop with this latest bunch of morons.

The idiots had arrived while Rose and Ryan had been away on their food-hunting mission. They had simply wandered up the hillside as if they were out for a Sunday afternoon picnic, and Chris had known as soon as he'd seen them that they were trouble. But he'd had no way to escape. They had joined him and Seth, and sat down on the grass, all friendly and eager to talk. Chris detested people who talked so much, especially when it was obvious that they had nothing intelligent to say.

They were discussing the white horse now, and as Chris had suspected, they knew nothing.

'You can't actually see the horse from here, can you?' said one of the guys, a loud-mouthed freak called Josh. He wore a zip-up top, sweatpants, white training shoes, a baseball cap screwed on sideways, and had studs in each ear.

'Yeah,' said his girlfriend, Brittany, who had purple hair and heavy eye makeup. 'Like, what's the point of it, then?'

Josh seemed to think he knew the answer. 'I expect it's like those animal drawings in the desert in South America. What's that place called? The pictures are so big you can only see them from the sky. Like they were made to be seen from UFOs or something.' He looked to Chris for confirmation.

'You mean the Nazca Lines in Peru,' offered Chris grudgingly.

'Yeah, that's it. Exactly,' said Josh. 'I guess this is the same. See that flat-topped hill down there, near the horse? That must be a landing pad for UFOs. Like, mind blown.' He took a swig of his beer and offered a can to Chris. 'Sure you don't want some of this?'

'No. I don't drink beer.'

'You smoke weed, then? Don't suppose you have any on you, by any chance?'

'No.'

'Us neither. All our shit's gone. But it's not all bad. We've still got plenty of beer.'

He passed a can to Seth, who pulled it open and took a swig. 'Thanks,' said Seth.

Chris scowled at him.

One of the other newcomers pulled out a flute and began to play a breathy, high-pitched tune. Brittany swayed along in time to the music. The three other strangers sat in silence, drinking beer and throwing surly looks Chris' way.

Josh had introduced them on arrival, but Chris had already forgotten their names. What did it matter? They were nobodies. Hopefully they would leave soon, and he would never have to see their stupid faces again.

'So who do you reckon drew the horse, Chris?' said Josh. 'Aliens?'

'People,' said Chris. 'There's no such thing as UFOs. And you don't need to be able to see the horse from the sky in order to draw it.'

'How else could you do it?'

'You could draw a small version first, then scale it up, just like architects do when they design buildings.'

A hush fell over the group while Josh digested Chris' insight. The flute player paused and the temperature seemed to fall a few degrees. Josh's eyes narrowed. 'Dude, you don't know it all. Don't start thinking you're smarter than us. Because you're not.'

Brittany threw her beer can on the ground and pulled the ring off another. 'So, tell us, Chris, if you know everything, what caused the apocalypse? Where did all the werewolves come from?'

'It's a contagious disease,' said Chris. 'Scientists believe that it originated in central Europe, probably Romania.'

Brittany smiled at him, victory in her eyes. 'See? You're not so clever after all. That's what they want you to think.'

'Who?'

'The government,' said Brittany. 'It was the government that caused it.'

'Which government?'

Josh took over. 'That's not important, Chris. Governments are all the same. USA, Russia, Britain, China. It could have been any one of them. Perhaps it was all of them working together. It may not even have been the government, just some corporate arseholes. Makes no difference. When you start looking at everything that's fucked up with the world, who do you find at the bottom of the rabbit hole? Old, white men. Rich, corporate dudes.

Anyway, whoever did it, they're totally fucked now. They got what was coming to them.'

'Yeah,' said Brittany. 'Now nature's back in the driving seat. Look around. The forests are growing again. It was bound to happen. You can't unbalance the universe as much as we did and not expect it to fight back.'

Chris looked around, but couldn't see the forests she was talking about. There wasn't a single tree on the hilltop. But he did see Rose and Ryan returning with some supplies.

'Are those your friends?' asked Brittany. She stood up and called to Rose and Ryan, beckoning them over. 'They look like fun,' she said to Chris. 'More fun than you.'

Rose and Ryan approached cautiously, carrying the boxes of food and drink.

Josh's mouth widened into a grin. 'Food, that's awesome. Let's share it. You can share our beer. I'm Josh. This is Brittany.' He didn't bother to introduce the others. The flute player began his mournful playing again.

Rose looked the newcomers over warily. 'Where are you heading? Are you planning to stay the night here?'

'We're going to Glastonbury,' said Brittany. 'You know? The festival? Although, obviously, there's no festival now.'

'There will be once we get there,' said Josh, laughing. 'Glastonbury, here we come!'

'Hey,' said Brittany. 'Why don't you come with us? The more the merrier! We can help to carry your friend, Seth. That sounds good, yeah?'

'No,' said Chris, desperately. 'We're not going to Glastonbury. We're going to Hereford.'

'Hereford,' repeated Josh. 'I've been there. It's a bit of a boring place. Just cows and stuff. You know? Agriculture. Why do you want to go there?'

'Yeah,' said Brittany. 'Forget that. Come to Glastonbury instead.'

'I don't know,' said Rose.

'Well, it's the same route most of the way,' said Josh. 'No need to make a decision right now. We can travel together for a while, either way.' He pulled more cans of beer out of his rucksack and passed them around. 'Let's just have some fun while we can.'

Chapter Forty-Six

Norbury Park, Surrey, waning moon

The infection was gone at last, and Griffin's leg was as good as it would ever be. He had removed the dressing now that the skin had healed. The scar tissue would harden over time, and perhaps eventually fade, but it would never be pretty. Neither would the swelling where the bone had fractured. But the redness had receded and the feeling had returned.

Not that it felt good.

It was still unbelievably painful to put pressure on his leg. Standing was agony. Walking was simply impossible.

His goal now was to build up his strength. Although he was desperate to start looking for Chanita, he knew that to proceed recklessly would guarantee that he never reached her. He was no good to her dead.

Life in his own little corner of paradise was slowly getting better. He was getting the hang of hunting and foraging, and growing to like the taste of what he found.

And the weather was gradually improving too. The Vernal Equinox had passed and it was getting light early. The birds sang noisily in the trees, the blackthorn and cherries were in full blossom, there were buds on the hawthorn, and the trees and hedges were in leaf.

Warm, sunny days, and no shortage of bugs for me to chew.

No, he was in no hurry to leave the forest glade. He had long since given up counting the days since the crash. What did it matter? He was going nowhere. It was wiser to stay put. There was still a faint chance that rescue would come, although that seemed distinctly unlikely. More pertinently, he was safe here, and if he moved away from the crash site he risked getting lost.

You are lost already, Griffin.

All right, technically he was lost, but he had a rough idea of his location. If he ventured away from here, he might head in the wrong direction and miss his destination entirely.

But that is a weak excuse.

His navigation skills were good. He could use the sun to determine the points of the compass, and he was in southern England not a desert. It would be impossible to travel very far before encountering a road or a town, or some landmark that would allow him to pin down his position.

But I cannot walk.

Then make a pair of goddamn crutches!

These were all mere excuses, and he should take no notice of them. The fact was, there was no longer a compelling reason to stay here any longer. It was time to begin his journey.

He searched the clearing for some sturdy branches and spent the rest of the morning fashioning them into crutches with the help of his knife and rope. Hauling himself upright was excruciating, but he managed it after a few attempts and stood on his one good leg, his weight balanced on the crutches.

The thought of Chanita waiting for him in the western camp gave him strength.

He took one clumsy step, then another. Before too long he was striding around the clearing, swinging his leg and his crutches like a pro.

Carrying his tent and equipment would pose an extra challenge.

He packed everything up, drank once more from the stream and refilled his bottles ready for the long journey. The pack on his back was heavy, and already his leg was aching from all the practising. He would be sure to take it easy and not set himself any daily target. In any case, he had no way of measuring distance, and no clear idea how far he would have to walk. The journey would take as long as necessary.

One thing he knew. The first step would be the hardest.

He was wrong about that. The first step was easy. But after half an hour, the sweat was pouring down his back and the wooden crutches were rubbing the skin from under his arms. It was hard going, trudging through the forest, ducking under low branches, pushing through thickets, and avoiding the roots that snaked across the forest floor. He leaned against a gnarled oak tree to rest and drink water.

It was tempting to sit down, but he knew how hard it would be to get back on his feet again.

Go on. Just a short rest. You've earned it. Take the weight off your leg.

He could stop here if he wanted. He could set up his camp for the night in this sheltered spot, knowing that he had at least begun his journey.

No need to overdo it, Griffin. Just a little walking every day.

But that would be pathetic. Chanita's face loomed in his mind's eye, smiling at him sardonically. 'Yeah, don't push yourself, Colonel. It's not like I'm in any kind of hurry to see you after all this time.'

'Sarcasm, huh?' he told her, grinning. 'You think I've just been sitting about all this time with my feet up? I've had one or two little problems to deal with.'

'Yeah, yeah,' her honeyed voice drizzled in his ear, 'we've all got problems to deal with. Don't think that special rules apply to you, even if you are the best-looking doctor I've ever met.'

He gripped his crutches and stumbled off again, heading in the direction he figured was north-west. It didn't take him long to reach the edge of the forest. A gentle meadow spread out before him. In the distance he could see the edge of a town.

Civilization. It had been just a couple of hours' walk away. Life might be going on as normal, just a short walk across the field. But somehow he didn't think it would. What could "normal" possibly mean now that London had been obliterated? Economic collapse, werewolves hunting the survivors, criminal gangs at large? He changed his path to route him well away from the distant town. He had managed well enough on his own for weeks, and he had no intention of risking meeting other people now.

There was only one person in the whole world he wanted to see.

'I'm waiting for you, Colonel.' Her rich, melodic voice in his head was a soothing balm. 'I'm not going anywhere without you.'

'I'm coming for you, girl,' he said aloud. 'I'm on my way and nothing's going to stop me.'

Chapter Forty-Seven

Uffington, Oxfordshire, waning moon

The long snaking road stretched out before Warg Daddy, beckoning him on. Where it led, nobody knew, but he would follow it always, mile after endless mile. For the road was his, and he was the road.

It wound its way between rolling hill and deep forest, from burned-out village to abandoned farmstead. Sometimes bending, sometimes straight; rising, falling; forever changing. But it never stopped. The road went on and on, for the road was everything, and there was nothing but the road.

This was the best part of the day for riding. Twilight, when the glaring rays of the sun had faded, and the night was folding over the land, bringing peace and tranquillity to his thoughts. The only sound now was the steady roar of his engine, throbbing between his legs. There were no worries, no choices, only the road. He took the next bend in a lazy arc, keeping to the centre line. The road was his now, his alone, and he would follow it, right until its very end, all the way to destiny.

Destiny. It was the place we were all heading, whether we knew it or not. Some fooled themselves, thinking they could choose their own path. Warg Daddy knew better. There were no choices, only one path, only fate.

The shimmering light of the moon kissed the tarmac, turning it silver, lighting his way as he wound down through wooded valleys and up over bare escarpments. No artificial lights glowed in the night anymore, except the beam of his bike's headlamp. Life was so much simpler now, and that was how he liked it. No more decisions for him to make.

Decisions. They had been his downfall. If he had never had to make any, he might have been happy. Although, he reminded himself, there had never truly been any choices. Choice was an illusion. There had only been fate, sheer chance, driving him on to destiny.

He swung around the bend and brought his bike to a sudden halt. Up there on the next hill was a horse. Huge, white, magical in the moonlight, it was carved into the hillside like a dream. Was it real? Was he imagining it? It seemed to glow brighter as he looked.

The Brothers brought their bikes up beside him and followed his gaze.

'Hey, look,' said Meathook. 'That sure is one fuck of a big horse.'

'Yeah.' Slasher nodded in agreement. 'One giant motherfucker.'

So it was real then, not just a figment of his imagination. That was good. It was always good to know what was real, and what was false. These days, he could no longer be sure. He could no longer trust the voices in his head, for they were not always his.

He knew who the voices belonged to, though. Ghosts.

Dead souls wandered through the corridors of his mind, rattling chains and whispering in his mind's ear.

Sometimes truths, sometimes lies. Sometimes promises, sometimes threats. Always whispering, especially at night.

'Look!' said Meathook. 'A fire.'

Warg Daddy looked. A small, sputtering camp fire burned on the hilltop above the horse.

People. Prey. He could see them from here. A group of men and women, some sitting, some dancing around the camp fire.

They were there for the taking. An easy kill. A narrow path led up the hillside and Warg Daddy traced it with his eyes. The path led right up to the camp. It was an invitation to slaughter.

Slasher licked his lips. 'Shall we go?'

Warg Daddy hardly heard him. The ghosts had returned, more insistent than ever. Wombat, the fallen Brother, always so loyal, always with his head in a book. Wombat knew everything. Tales of the Norse gods, songs of the Valkyrie, the legend of Ragnarok.

'The twilight of the gods,' muttered Warg Daddy to himself. It had been Wombat's favourite subject, almost the very last thing he'd talked about, just before Warg Daddy had led him to his death, that fateful night on Clapham Common.

'Ragnarok: the falling of the world, when the great battle will unfold,' intoned Warg Daddy, invoking Wombat's own pronouncement. Had that already happened, or was it still to come? There had been a battle of sorts, although Warg Daddy had fled at the final moment from his role as commander-in-chief of the Wolf Army. Perhaps the great battle lay in the future. Maybe he would be forced to take up arms again. 'Then the old gods will die and the world will be born anew.'

Meathook's face creased in puzzlement. 'Warg Daddy? What?'

A second ghost rattled his chains in the dusty attic that was Warg Daddy's imagination. Snakebite. The ghost of Snakebite was mean and unforgiving, filled with a desire for vengeance and retribution. His face was a putrid mass of rotting flesh, with just one eye remaining to stare angrily at Warg Daddy. He clanked his chains noisily, filling Warg Daddy with fear. 'I'm sorry,' said Warg Daddy. 'I'm sorry I killed you.' For it had been he who blasted Snakebite's brains out of the back of his skull with his combat shotgun. Had that been his decision? Or had it merely been fate? Could he honestly put all the blame on chance? 'It was just bad luck, Snake. Just an unlucky draw of the cards.'

Slasher snapped his fingers in front of his face. 'Warg Daddy? What's wrong? Snap out of it!'

But now the third ghost had arrived, the one he feared the most. Leanna. She slid through the cracks in his skull like a wraith, clothed in ice, her hands blackened with cold. She wore a pale hood, silken, almost translucent. It covered her face, but she turned toward him now, slipping the cloth from her head. 'No,' he mumbled. But he couldn't stop her. She pulled the hood fully away, so he could see. 'No,' he cried again. The hideous scarring on her cheek was worse than ever, crawling across her face like leprosy. Her ice blue eyes burned into his. 'Traitor!' she shrieked. 'Back-stabber! Viper!'

Warg Daddy bowed his head. He was all those things, and worse.

Choices. He could not deny them. He had made them. They had been his.

He would not make any more.

Vixen shook him gently from behind. 'Warg Daddy? What shall we do? Shall we go up the hill? There are people there. Shall we feed on them?'

They were staring at him. Slasher, Meathook, Bloodbath. All the Brothers, waiting for his choice.

'You have to decide,' said Vixen.

That was all he had to do. He was Leader of The Pack. His job was to make choices. But he would not. 'No,' he bellowed. Instead, he pulled the tarnished coin from his pocket. It was only a small, rusty piece of metal, and yet it held his future. His fate would be decided by its spin. He flipped it into the night, not even bothering to watch as the moonlight caught its faces. Dark, light, dark, light. Why watch? The gods had already made their decision. All that was left was for him to find out.

The coin came to rest on the back of his hand. It was done. He glanced back up at the hilltop where the fire burned bright above the white horse, then looked down to discover his destiny. 'Drive on,' he said.

Chapter Forty-Eight

Stoke Park, Buckinghamshire

Chanita could scarcely believe the decision she had made. It felt like madness, but she knew that it was the only way. It had taken a long and heated debate with Helen, lasting well into the night, to convince her that this was right.

It wasn't just James demonstrating his ability to change from human to wolf and back again that had finally persuaded her. It wasn't even his calm demeanour and the fact that she had known and liked him when she had treated him in hospital, back in London.

It was simply that she had no better options.

The camp had run out of medicines, and disease was now rampant. There was little the doctors could do to stop its spread. The people in the camp were weakened by hunger, and by the insanitary, crowded conditions, which made a breeding ground for infections of all kinds. If she did not act, the camp would surely fall.

The next morning, she called a crisis meeting of the camp's military and civilian leaders to discuss the situation.

The first to speak was Lieutenant Colonel Sharman. The military leader acknowledged Chanita and the others in the room with a curt nod. His face was tight, and his eyes clearly wore the strain of the past weeks. 'As you already know, my men are struggling to locate new sources of food and other essential supplies, especially medicines. Each day we are being forced to venture further and further afield, and almost every day we come under attack from armed werewolves. At first it was difficult for me to grasp why the enemy did not simply launch attacks on the camp itself. Despite our heavy military presence, it is not easy for us to secure such a large perimeter, and it would have been relatively easy for the werewolves to make incursions into the camp under cover of night. On the night of the full moon especially, I feared an all-out assault, but none came.

'Now I understand their strategy. It's a scorched earth policy. They're burning hospitals, medical centres and other locations where medicines are stored, and also destroying sources of food like warehouses so we can't easily reach fresh supplies. Instead of attacking us here, where we have a strategic advantage, they're forcing us to travel ever further, and picking us off one by one. We thought we were safe inside the camp because they didn't try to invade us, but all this time they've been conducting siege warfare. Now the reality is clear – we cannot continue to sustain the population within the camp.'

Grim-faced, the colonel returned to his seat.

One of the civilian leaders rose to speak. 'What are you saying, Colonel? That we must leave the camp? If the camp breaks up, many people will die. They will have no food, no medical treatment, no protection from the werewolves. Are you saying we should simply abandon them to their fate?'

The colonel rose. 'No, that is not what I am saying. But

something must change. We cannot continue as we have been. You know yourself that by keeping the people here, we are condemning them to a slow death, either from malnutrition, or disease, or ultimately, when we are too weakened to resist, slaughter at the hands of our enemy.'

He paused and cleared his throat. 'There is a way out. Those of you who know their military history will be aware that sieges usually end in a negotiation and surrender. It makes no difference whether it's a medieval siege of a castle, or a modern hostage situation. Negotiation is the only solution, and is what we must turn to, before it is too late.' He threw a look in Chanita's direction. 'Colonel Griffin would have understood that. Any commanding officer would.'

An uproar erupted in the meeting – 'How can we negotiate with monsters?' – 'They seek only to kill and eat us!'

The colonel shook his head. 'There is always a bargaining chip, if we have the courage to look for it.'

More outcries greeted this statement – 'You mean that some of us must be sacrificed to save the rest!' – 'Outrageous!'

Chanita brought the meeting to silence. 'There is another way forward, that does not involve surrender.'

She stopped, aware of the immense burden resting on her shoulders. She wished that Colonel Griffin could be at her side. She needed him now more than ever. His courage and conviction would surely carry the meeting with him. She did not possess half his persuasive powers, but she took comfort from the fact that he had left her in charge, confident that she had the capability to do the job. She must not fail him now.

'Lieutenant Colonel Sharman is correct in his assessment. If we continue as we are, many of us will die of disease or starvation. If we surrender the camp, many of us may be killed by our enemy. We no longer have medicines. But a miracle cure is available to us. A walking miracle. I would like to introduce you to James Beaumont.'

The door to the room opened, and James entered, uncaged and unbound, and led by Helen with Sarah following.

'James is a lycanthrope,' announced Chanita, 'and his blood provides a way to cure all those in the camp who are sick.'

A gasp rose up from her audience and people began to cower back, or step forward, guns raised. Chanita called out for them to stop. 'James poses no threat to us. He is different to the other lycanthropes. He possesses the ability to control his form, choosing wolf or human at will. He has learned to live on animals, and does not eat human flesh.'

The people in the room seemed only partially reassured.

Chanita beckoned for Helen to lead James up to where she stood. 'Doctor Helen Eastgate will now outline her proposal. Helen?'

She sat and listened as Helen explained the plan to a sceptical meeting. It was simple enough to grasp. Inject micro-doses of lycanthropic blood into those who were sick, sufficiently diluted to avoid the usual effects of anaphylactic shock. The patients treated with James' blood would become lycanthropic like him, but they would live, and they would share his ability to control their urges.

One of the doctors walked out before Helen even finished speaking. 'I would rather let my patients die than turn them into werewolves!' he shouted. Several others joined him and left the room.

But Chanita was undaunted. She still had her strongest card to play. James.

When Helen had finished speaking and answering questions, James took the stage. And, as he had done for her, he turned himself into wolf form for all to see.

Most of the people in the room fell back in panic as a wolf appeared in their midst. Once again some of the soldiers took aim with their guns.

Chanita went to James and kneeled at his side, rubbing his fur with her hand. 'Watch!' She placed her fingers inside his mouth, while James sat calmly, his pink tongue lolling out, saliva drooling. Helen and Sarah took it in turns to do the same as her.

A few of the other people in the room were brave enough to approach James and touch him for themselves. Eventually Colonel Sharman himself came up and allowed James to lick his hand.

'This is our future,' Chanita told the meeting. 'It may not be the future we would have chosen, but it is the only one available to us. The alternative is death.'

Chapter Forty-Nine

London, quarter moon

London was a ravaged city, a haunted landscape populated with skeletal buildings and the dust of the dead. Wherever the Prime Minister roamed, she found fresh devastation. It had been a shock as she first began walking, with Big Ben behind her. Every step brought her a new image of destruction.

One of her greatest shocks had been to come face to face with Buckingham Palace, the London home of the British monarchy. It had never been her favourite landmark, but it was one of the most famous. Now the eighteenth-century structure was half collapsed, exposing its many elaborately-furnished rooms to the wind and the rain. Glimpses of gold and marble interiors were visible as she peered through the iron gates that still stood before it, even though the rest of the surrounding fence lay in mangled ruins.

So much had been lost. She wondered if it could ever

be repaired. Centuries of building, of progress and civilization all gone. Might it be rebuilt one day? Or would it turn into a shrine to the past, to be reclaimed by nature? She thought of those ancient ruins of the Incas in the jungles of South America, and of the abandoned cities around Chernobyl within the radioactive exclusion zone. The General had promised her that the radioactive fallout from the bombs would be minimal, but she had only his word for that. For all she knew she was soaking up a fatal dose right now. She could do nothing about that, except keep going forward.

In places she discovered charred bodies, burned to a crisp, unrecognizable. Twisted metal frames that had perhaps once been cars littered the roadways. Fire-blackened facades of buildings teetered over her, looking as though a strong gust of wind would bring them crashing down. And covering it all was a thick layer of dust, turning everything grey.

In parts of the city, black columns of smoke still rose, even though it had been more than a month since the fires had first taken hold. Perhaps they would be like fires in a coal mine, continuing to burn slowly for years.

After a while she stopped seeing the details of the destruction. Most of it was impossible to identify in any case. She had lost track of which road she was on, could not even tell if she was still following a road. The mounds of debris spread out everywhere.

When night came she broke into her rations, then removed her boots and wrapped herself in layers of warm clothing to shelter in the lee of a broken wall. She fell asleep dreaming of the sounds of traffic, and of voices and music, of the hustle and bustle of a city she had once loved.

She awoke with a start, her heart pumping, her ears straining for the noise that had woken her. There it was again, a real sound, not a dream. A human voice.

She was on her feet in a moment. She looked around

the empty street, scanning the jagged walls and fallen masonry, searching for movement. Soon two figures came into view, a man and a woman, scrabbling over the mounds of rubble, talking to each other.

They stopped when they saw her and grew wary. Both wore dirty clothes, and had long unkempt hair, the man thickly bearded, tinged with grey.

'Hey!' called Greybeard. 'What are you doing here? This is our patch.' He came toward her, unfriendly, threatening.

The PM struggled to pull her boots on.

'What you got in there?' asked his companion, a woman with red hair braided into dreadlocks. She pointing to the PM's rucksack. 'Whatever you got, it's ours now.'

Greybeard reached out for it.

The PM snatched it from his grasp.

'Hey,' said Dreadlocks suddenly. 'I don't fucking believe it. It's her! She did this!'

'What?' said Greybeard. 'Who?'

'Don't you recognize her? It's the fucking Prime Minister!'

'You've got to be kidding me.'

They both stared at her, incredulity on their faces. 'You're right,' said Greybeard at last.

A second later, Dreadlocks was screeching at the top of her voice. 'I always knew you politicians were the scum of the earth, but I never thought you would stoop so low as to bomb your own people.'

'I didn't,' said the PM. 'I promise you I had nothing to do with this. In fact I tried to prevent it. You must believe me.'

'Believe you? I never believed a single word you've ever said. Politicians are all liars, but you're the worst. And you're a mass murderer too. You're the biggest mass murderer in all of history.'

'Look how short she is,' said Greybeard. 'She's nothing. A nobody. No better than anyone else. Whatever gave her the right to boss everyone around?'

'Democracy,' said the PM. 'The people chose me as their leader.'

Greybeard spat on the ground. 'Bullshit.'

'Listen to me,' began the PM. 'I tried to –'

'Shut it! I don't want to hear.' Greybeard came forward, fists clenched. 'You murdered millions of people. Well now it's your turn to die.'

The PM reached for her holster and pulled out the pistol. She held it steady, aimed at the man's head. 'Don't move any closer. Step back.'

He stopped, thwarted, but Dreadlocks was too furious to hold back. She ran forward, scooping up a broken brick as she closed.

The roar of the pistol was deafening, and it jerked in the PM's hand, almost flying from her fingers.

Dreadlocks fell back, a bullet hole in her head, a look of surprise on her face.

Greybeard paused for a second, then lunged forward, mad with rage.

The gun rang out a second time, and this time the PM was ready for the recoil. She held her arm steady, ready to shoot a third time if necessary.

But her attackers lay still, their eyes closed, their voices silenced.

They were my people. I was responsible for them.

But she wouldn't accept the blame for everyone's mistakes.

She replaced the gun in her holster and slung her rucksack over her shoulder. Two more bullets gone. She could only hope that enough remained.

Chapter Fifty

Uffington, Oxfordshire

Rose watched in dismay as Josh wriggled out of the small tent he shared with Brittany, and rose to his feet, bleary eyed, his hair in wild tufts.

He yawned. 'Oh, wow, what time is this? You guys never heard of sleep?'

She and the others had risen at dawn and packed their gear in silence, hoping to break camp early to leave Josh, Brittany and their friends behind. But Josh must have heard Ryan and Chris creeping past the tent with Seth on the stretcher.

'We wanted to make an early start,' said Rose.

'Yeah, nice one,' said Josh. 'Good thinking. The early bird and all that. Just wait for us to get our shit together.' He kicked at the guy ropes of the tent the others shared, making it collapse on top of them. 'Come on, get your arses out of there! It's time to go.'

'How are we going to get away from these guys?'

whispered Ryan to Rose.

'I don't know,' she whispered back.

In any case, she thought, even if they had managed to make a dawn getaway, their chances of outrunning the newcomers had never been very high, with Seth and his broken ankle to slow them down.

The others crawled out from under the tent, shooting black looks at everyone, Josh included. They had stayed up until late, drinking, singing and dancing.

'Is this for real?' said Brittany, peering out from her tent, her eye shadow smudged over her cheeks. 'We only just, like, went to bed.'

'There's really no need for you to come with us,' said Rose. 'Why don't we travel separately? It's not like we're even going to the same place.'

Josh frowned. 'Well, we still haven't decided that for sure, have we? If you don't want to come to Glastonbury with us, maybe we'll come and join you in Hereford instead. That could be cool.'

'Okay then,' said Rose reluctantly. 'We'll wait over here.' She led Ryan and Chris a short distance away, and they carefully lowered Seth to the ground. 'What are we going to do?' she whispered.

'Just tell them straight,' said Ryan. 'Just say we don't want them to come with us.'

'Yeah,' said Chris. 'I can tell them. I don't mind if they hate me for it. I'm used to people hating me.'

'Is it really such a big deal if they come?' asked Seth. 'Why don't we let them? They could help take turns at carrying my stretcher. We could travel much faster if we stick together.'

'That's a good point,' said Ryan.

'No,' said Rose. 'I don't trust them. We're better off without them. Chris, you tell them.'

The others had packed up their gear and were slouching about looking grumpy. 'Okay, we're ready,' said Josh. Let's go.'

Chris stepped forward. 'Actually, we've decided we don't want you to come with us. We'd rather travel alone.'

An ugly sneer appeared on Josh's face. 'Oh yeah? And what if we decide to come anyway? Are you going to run off with your guy Seth on a stretcher? I don't think so.'

Brittany tugged at his elbow. 'Come on, Josh. We don't need these fuckers. Let's just go.'

'No!' He shook her away. 'No one tells me where to get off. This is the end of the fucking world, in case no one else has noticed. We all need to stay together. No one gets left behind.'

Brittany bit her lower lip. 'We're not going to get left behind, babes. We'll leave them behind.'

Josh raised his hand and slapped her across the cheek. 'I said no! We all stay together.'

Brittany stumbled away from him, hugging herself tight, her dark eyes filling with tears, shooting daggers first at him, and then at Chris. Finally she turned her wrath on Rose. 'What do you say, you skinny bitch? You're the one who tells these guys what to do, aren't you? Are you just going to turn your back on us?'

Rose shook her head, not knowing what to say. Everything about these people gave her the creeps. What frightened her most was the uncertainty. She had never seen them in her dreams. She had no idea what to expect from them. But she didn't need dreams or visions to tell her they were dangerous. Nutmeg cowered at her side, frightened by the shouting and the violence. Rose patted the dog on the back of her neck to calm her down. In turn, Nutmeg licked her hand, helping to calm her too.

It was Seth who broke the deadlock, appealing for peace from his stretcher. 'Please, I can't stand this bickering. Let's just agree to be friends. Josh is right, we're safer in numbers.'

'No,' mumbled Chris. 'I keep telling you that we're not.'

But for once, Seth was adamant. 'Well, you're wrong.'

Josh's rage seemed to vanish and he beamed broadly at Seth. 'Well said, Seth. You are most definitely two mental steps ahead of everyone else here, and I include myself when I say that. Guys, let's do what Seth says. Be grateful, not hateful, yeah?' He gestured to Brittany, who was nursing her slapped cheek. 'Sorry I hit you, babes. I just lost it for a sec. Come on, let me kiss it better. And you should apologize to Rose here.'

'Apologize?' said Brittany, as he kissed her face.

'Yeah, babes. You were well out of order, calling her a skinny bitch and all that. What were you thinking, babes? Say you're sorry. Do it now.'

Brittany hesitated, biting her lip again, but Josh twisted her head until she was facing Rose. 'Sure, yeah, sorry if I offended you,' she said reluctantly.

Josh broke out in a big grin. 'Good. We're all friends again. That's how it's going to be from now on. No more conflict, just peace and love. Glastonbury, here we come! So, who's going to carry Seth first?'

Chapter Fifty-One

Gatwick Airport, West Sussex, crescent moon

There had been no more killings since the full moon, and now it was time for a birth. Liz chased the men from the room, and then the women gathered around Samantha, preparing for her baby to be born at last.

Nine months it had taken to make a baby.

Nine months ago, Dean had still been alive. He and Samantha had been living happily in Battersea in South London, planning for a future together with their baby. The Beast of Clapham Common had yet to make its first appearance, and the Ripper murders had not begun. And Liz had still been human.

Nine months ago, Liz had not even met any of the women in this room, apart from Samantha herself. Now they were family.

The men had been glad to leave the hotel suite before

anything got underway. Kevin in particular had been enthusiastic to make his escape. Mr Singh and the boys had joined him.

Vijay's mother and Aasha appeared nervous, but old Mrs Singh was in her element, giving orders to the other women, and offering words of wisdom to Samantha. 'Fetch clean water,' she told her daughter. 'Go and find more towels,' she instructed Aasha. 'You,' she said to Liz, 'bring that nice doctor from upstairs.'

They all dashed off on their errands, leaving Samantha in the care of Mrs Singh. 'Breathe deeply in and out,' the old woman said. 'One … two … three …'

Liz was relieved that someone was taking charge. She had worried that as a police officer, everyone would assume that she knew what to do. They often did, and sometimes in the most ridiculous situations. How many times had she had to explain to people that her job was to arrest criminals, not to search for lost dogs, break up a late-night fight between noisy tom cats, or to find out why their pizza delivery guy was thirty minutes late?

She would much rather be out arresting criminals than helping with the birth of a baby. But this was personal, not part of her job.

She was glad to find Doctor Pope ready on standby, his bag already packed in anticipation of Samantha's labour. 'This is a very punctual baby,' he said. 'Not even one day early or late. Let's hope that bodes well for a smooth birth.'

Samantha was in full flow when Liz returned with the doctor, groaning in agony and uttering a string of swear words that Liz had never heard her say before.

'Keep moving around,' Mrs Singh was saying to her. 'Walk, squat, lean against the wall, or just sway back and forth. It will help you cope with the pain. The worst place you can be right now is lying in the bed like a great big elephant.'

Liz had never seen an elephant lying in a bed, but Mrs

Singh's advice seemed to be helping.

'Scream and shout if you want to,' she encouraged Samantha. 'Do whatever you like.'

Samantha was happy to oblige.

Doctor Pope regarded the two women with some amusement. 'It seems like everything is in order here. With any luck I won't be needed.'

'We will need a doctor if something goes wrong,' declared Mrs Singh. 'Otherwise let nature take its course.'

'Sounds good to me,' said the doctor.

The baby seemed in no particular hurry to arrive, and labour went on for hours. 'Nothing to worry about,' said Mrs Singh, as Samantha gasped in pain every time a new contraction came. 'This is all perfectly normal.'

'That's right,' said Doctor Pope.

Aasha looked horrified. 'This is normal?'

'Absolutely.'

'Then I am so never having a baby.'

Lily was watching from the sidelines, anxious but curious. Aasha took the little girl's hand. 'Your baby brother or sister will be here soon, don't worry.'

Mrs Singh pointed at Liz. 'You, go fetch a fresh bowl of clean water.'

When Liz returned, the birth had moved on to the next stage and Samantha was screaming loudly. Aasha was looking sick. The other women were crowded around.

A strong scent of blood flooded Liz's nostrils, almost knocking her back with its intensity. Her heart accelerated and her breath began to come in quick gasps. Her mouth filled with saliva and her vampire teeth twisted through her gums.

She knew she had to leave, and immediately. The smell of the blood was too intoxicating for her to bear. It was driving her wild with bloodlust. She thrust the bowl of water into Aasha's hands. 'Take this.'

'What?' said Aasha. 'Me?' The girl looked almost ready to panic. 'I can't!'

But Liz was the one who needed to get out. She couldn't stay a moment longer in the presence of such a strong reek of blood. 'Do it!' she said firmly.

This time Aasha obeyed. She took hold of the bowl as Liz dashed from the room.

Liz closed the door behind her and leaned back against it in the corridor, panting deeply. Gradually her heart rate returned to normal and her breath slowed. She felt her teeth retract. She stood there for a while, knowing she could not go back inside, but not wanting to leave either. Eventually, Samantha's cries came to an abrupt end, and a new sound greeted her. The crying of a newborn baby.

Chapter Fifty-Two

London, new moon

The PM's journey through the wreckage and the ruins was far slower than she had planned. Huge areas of the city had been reduced to rubble. Even where buildings still stood, they were mere shells. Walls and windows and roofs were missing, leaving just bare structures hulking over dust-strewn streets, like houses of cards that had been shaken. There were no straight lines in this city. Everything was bent or twisted out of kilter. Everything had turned to grey. Wherever she went, the terrain was strewn with personal items. Books, papers, clothing, furniture, children's toys. People's possessions exposed for all to see.

It would have been easier and a lot quicker if she could have followed the simple underground route that the General had mapped out. But at least her trek above ground had given her the chance to view the destruction of the city at first hand. Without seeing it for herself, it would have remained an abstract idea, a fact not fully understood, perhaps not even accepted. She knew now without a shadow of doubt that London was gone forever, and that whatever the future held, it would be entirely different from the past. The survivors of this calamity would have to build a new civilization, from scratch if necessary.

After many days of struggle she emerged onto the open fields of Hampstead Heath, and made her way up to the viewpoint on Parliament Hill. From here she could see for miles. She turned and spent several minutes taking in the view.

A large part of London had been completely flooded. All along the river embankments, in Docklands, Greenwich, and a long way to the south, the water spread out in a gigantic lake, almost a mile wide in places. She guessed that the flood defences of the Thames Barrier had been destroyed. Or else the explosion had produced a surge so large it had spilled over the low-lying land to each side of the river. London had been a floodplain once, and now it was again.

The world had seemed so solid and safe before. Western civilization had taken so many centuries to build. Who knew it had been forever teetering just a few short weeks away from total meltdown?

Incongruously, many of the tallest buildings still stood intact, rising up from the water like a drowned city. She recognized the famous shapes of Big Ben, the Gherkin, the Shard. They must have survived the shockwaves from the airbursts, and been saved from the firestorms by the water. By contrast, many of the buildings on higher ground had been laid waste by fire.

The oldest part of London, the City of London itself, stood proud on the three ancient hills of Ludgate, Cornhill and Tower Hill, forming a small island within the flooded city, on which St Paul's Cathedral was remarkably well preserved. Well, it had stood for three centuries and survived the blitz of 1940, so that seemed fitting.

As for the more modern suburbs, they were either flooded or burned to the ground. The vast sprawl of roads and buildings which had taken two thousand years to slowly creep across the surface of the land had vanished, and in its wake the physical geography of London was revealed. From the PM's high vantage point on the Heath, the land dipped steadily toward the low-lying valley floor of what had been eastern and southern London. A few isolated peaks such as Primrose Hill and Crouch Hill stood on higher ground, and the distant rise of Biggin Hill was just visible far to the south.

Behind her, on the higher ground to the north, the dead slept peacefully in Highgate Cemetery, watched over by stone angels. Beyond that lay a grey, dusty wasteland of ruined houses and crumbling tower blocks. That was the direction of Northwood HQ, but the route there looked impassable.

She turned instead to the west. The land dipped lower again in that direction, and there were green areas, untouched by the firestorms, and many buildings still intact. The way looked safer and more inviting, and she set off down the hillside, her vision fixed on the far horizon.

Chapter Fifty-Three

Windsor Castle, Berkshire, new moon

Mr Canning gazed out over the massive crenellations of Windsor Castle's Round Tower. From the top of the tower's two hundred steps he could see for literally miles.

Behind him, to the east, lay the blackened ruins of London, only a few of its famous landmarks still standing amid a sea of wreckage and rubble. Where the Thames had burst its banks, was nothing but floodland.

To his south, the green acres of Windsor Great Park stretched out as far as his keen one eye could see. On the distant rise of Snow Hill, he picked out the huge statue of the copper horse, a representation of the mad king, George III, dressed as a Roman emperor on horseback. Leanna, it seemed, was reviving a tradition of deranged monarchs. Canning gleefully saluted the dead king. 'We are all mad now,' he muttered.

He turned his attention west, where the town of

Windsor was burning merrily to the ground, greedy flames filling the evening sky with smoke, and turning the sunset a deep blood red. 'Burn it!' Leanna had declared. 'It spoils the view from my bedroom window.' And Canning had happily obliged. The occupants of the burning houses had been moved on, massacred or brought into the castle to be used as food or sport, depending on Leanna's whim. They were being held in the castle's Lower Ward, spread out below him.

He had never pictured himself as a general, but he was steadily growing into the role. It was true that he had no military training, but he had studied military history and knew the theory of warfare well enough. How else could he have risen to the top of the teaching profession?

He did not fool himself that this great fortress would offer any protection against a modern invading army. The Norman motte on which the Round Tower was constructed had provided stout defence against Saxon rebels during the time of William the Conqueror, but it would be useless against an aerial assault by strike fighters. Its thick stone ramparts would offer little resistance to high explosives, and the iron portcullis in its gatehouse would be easily breached by a Challenger tank. Canning knew that these medieval fortifications were all for show, simply a part of Leanna's play-acting fantasy. But still. He would rather be inside its gates than out there, amid the burning streets.

His fighting forces were limited. Aaron, the single werewolf that Leanna had spared from her slaughter to send as messenger to the surviving werewolves, had exaggerated the number of werewolves who had taken refuge inside the castle. They were somewhat fewer than a hundred. Of those, some ten or so had refused to submit to Leanna's rule. Their heads now adorned the tower's battlements. Around sixty remained, and they were armed only with a mix of assault rifles, semi-automatic pistols, shotguns and sniper rifles. They lacked any kind of armoured vehicle or heavy weaponry. They were weak, and he could not yet lead them into battle.

Canning turned finally to peer out over the northern edge of the tower. Beyond the burning houses of Windsor and Eton, the view in this direction was mundane. Roads, a distant motorway, railway tracks, then tower blocks and densely packed houses, all lined up in neat rows. The urban sprawl that had leaked out from London. And yet this dreary vista concealed a danger. Beyond the suburban settlements, further than even he could see, lay their enemy. Thousands of humans, packed into the camp at Stoke Park, protected by trained and well-armed soldiers. He knew that his Wolf Army stood no chance in a full-scale battle against such a foe. Leanna was pressing him to go on the offensive, but that would be suicidal. Even under a full moon, the werewolves could not do battle against armoured fighting vehicles.

No. For now, they must content themselves with skirmishes and ambushes. He would pick his enemies off one by one as they ventured out of the safety of their camp. His forces would grow as news of Leanna's return spread among the surviving werewolves. They would come to her, drawn by hunger, greed, or lust for glory. He would train them in the arts of fighting, and instil an iron discipline. And they would gather real weapons. Tanks, armoured cars, anti-aircraft guns, rocket launchers. Why stop at that? Somewhere, there were bigger weapons still. Helicopters, combat aircraft, frigates, destroyers.

Oh yes. Why stop at General Canning when he could be Air Chief Marshal Canning and Admiral Canning too?

High above him, the Royal Standard snapped in the wind. The flag was traditionally flown only when the ruling monarch was in residence at the castle. Well she was here now, a mad queen maybe, but a ruthless genius, determined to rule at all costs. And he had pinned his future prospects on her success. What did that make him? He preferred not to think about it. He had made his choice.

'Better to serve a mad queen than to hide in a sewer with only rats and spiders for friends,' he told the crows that fluttered around the top of the tower.

Not that he had any friends now. Leanna was no friend, merely an ally of convenience. A general must walk alone. Well, he was used to that. It had been no different when he had been headmaster. Friends, he could scarcely remember a time when he had last had one. Enemies, on the other hand, he had never been short of. But now he had the means to vanquish them. One by one they would fall. And then … yes, one day, he might dispose of his final enemy, the mad queen herself. Then he could claim her throne. King Canning. It had a certain ring to it, did it not?

But until that time he would be unswervingly loyal.

He leaned out over the battlements and shouted across the courtyard of the Lower Ward. 'God save the Queen! Long live our noble Queen!'

Chapter Fifty-Four

Gatwick Airport, West Sussex, crescent moon

'Cheers, mate,' said Kevin, raising the bottle of Fullers London Pride to his mouth. He swigged back the ale, just nicely at room temperature, and belched magnificently. Was this happiness? It was as near as damn as he'd come to it in a good while. Sitting on the open grass on a sunny afternoon in April in the company of a crate of beer and some mates. If there was a better life, he had never seen it.

The Welsh Guards were a decent bunch of blokes, even though he could only understand half of what they said and couldn't pronounce any of their first names. 'Call me Clue-Ellin,' Llewelyn had said, but Kevin couldn't. Jones was easier.

No matter. The language of beer was universal.

'That's not a bad ale,' said Corporal Jones, smacking his lips. 'Not quite as smooth as a pint of Cardiff Dark, but still quite tasty. You Londoners obviously know a thing or two about beer.'

'Cardiff Dark? Never tried that one,' said Kevin. 'Maybe one day.'

'Maybe,' said Jones. 'There's always a chance, I suppose. There might still be a few barrels knocking around somewhere back in Wales. I doubt they're still brewing it, though.'

'Yeah, right,' said Kevin. Gloom was always lurking just under the surface, even on a day like today. 'What happens when all the beer runs out, you reckon?'

Jones shook his head sadly. 'That really will be the end of the world.'

The other two, Evans and the lance corporal, nodded in agreement. Hughes was the lance corporal's name, but the others called him the Dogman, on account of his dog, which followed him everywhere. Kevin could call him the Dogman too, if that's what the man liked. It was easier on the tongue than his first name, which was completely unpronounceable. The dog, Rock, was with them now, lying on the grass, one eye closed, the other open, watching them like a hawk. A one-eyed hawk. Kevin had no love for dogs, but he had missed the company of honest working men. There were far too many women and children in his life these days.

He wasn't quite ready to call the Welsh Guards his friends. Not yet. Sharing a beer was one thing. Becoming a friend, that took a lot more time and effort, and even when you thought you'd reached that point, friendship could turn out to be a fragile thing. Kevin's life story was littered with broken friendships. Broken noses too, on a few occasions. He could scarcely remember having a real friend, only enemies who had not yet declared themselves. Gary the butcher was perhaps the closest he'd ever come to true honest-to-goodness friendship, and Gary was a dead man now. Then again, better a dead friend than a living enemy.

He raised the bottle to his lips again. London Pride. It sounded a whole lot more appetizing than Cardiff Dark. He couldn't say he'd be sorry if he never got to try any of that particular brew, however much the Welshmen might sing its praises.

'I wonder how that baby's coming along,' said Jones.

'Dunno.'

The birth of a baby was no place for a man to be, and Kevin had been the first to make a quick exit from the hotel room as soon as Samantha showed signs of going into labour. When his own wife had given birth to Liz, he'd been happily down the pub, downing pints like God intended, and he had no desire to get close-up to that kind of thing now. It wasn't that he was squeamish. Growing up the son of a butcher, blood and guts didn't bother him in the slightest. Women's matters on the other hand … they were called that for a reason.

This was the first time he'd paid a visit to the Welsh Guards since coming to the camp. Now he was here, he wondered what had taken him so long. Too much of a loner, he supposed. Mind you, the Welsh Guards looked to be keeping themselves to themselves too, not mingling much with the men from other regiments and battalions.

The army had set up a field of tents between the two runways, with vehicles parked all around. As far as Kevin could make out, the paras were in charge of the operation, and groups of soldiers from the various other regiments had been roped in to do the grunt work. It was the same when he'd served in the army in Northern Ireland during the Troubles. Squaddies like him had done the jobs no one else wanted. Manning checkpoints in the middle of the night, dealing with rioters and petrol bombers, marching up and down the Bogside district or the Falls Road, having stones thrown at him by the local Protestants or Catholics. *Welcome to the British Army, son.*

It had been the same forever. Men like Kevin always got the worst jobs, and no one ever thanked them for it.

The more shit a man shovels, the less anyone wants to shake his hand. That was a fine saying. He ought to scribble it down somewhere, or at least try to remember it. Whenever he needed words, he could never find the right ones.

'How is your mate, Griffiths?' he asked Jones. The soldier had been shot getting them out of London, and was obviously still in the care of the doctors, since he wasn't here now.

It had been the wrong question to ask. Jones shook his head grimly. 'Not so good. Not so good at all.'

'Doesn't look like he's going to make it,' said the Dogman bitterly.

'I'm sorry to hear that.'

'In fact,' said the Dogman, flaring into anger, 'things are quickly turning to shit around here.'

'Not now, Hughes,' warned Jones.

'Why shouldn't I say what's on my mind?' said the Dogman. He turned to Kevin. 'Don't think you can buy our friendship with a crate of beer. We know what your daughter is.'

Kevin glared at him. So here was the enemy, declaring himself for all to see. Another broken friendship, and a very short-lived one at that. A few years back Kevin would have been on his feet already, throwing punches at the Dogman's ugly face. He'd like to see that face turn purple and black. Another broken nose to add to the list. Kevin knew that he could take the lance corporal easily, despite the man being younger and heavier than him. But he sat where he was. Experience must have taught him something. Or maybe Liz had done that.

'You're wrong about Liz,' he said steadily. 'She ain't no killer. At least,' he corrected himself, she ain't never killed no one who didn't deserve it.'

'So you say,' said the Dogman.

'So I say,' said Kevin. Maybe he would give the lance corporal a bit of a kicking after all. Someone certainly should. But first he would give talking a chance. 'Anyway,' he said, 'there ain't been no more killings for weeks now. Looks to me like the mysterious killer has gone away.'

It seemed like a slim hope, but that was the only kind of hope Kevin knew.

'You reckon the killer's gone?' sneered the Dogman. 'That's because you don't know what's really happening.'

'Hughes,' warned Corporal Jones, 'that's enough.'

The Dogman fell silent.

'Tell me what I don't know,' said Kevin. 'Let's hear it.'

'It's nothing more than rumours,' said Jones. 'We don't have any facts. The Dogman shouldn't have said anything.'

'Come on. If you know something about these murders, you gotta tell me.'

Corporal Jones sighed. 'So, what we hear through our army contacts is that people have been going missing from the camp. Mostly women and children. They simply disappear and are never seen again. There's no actual proof of this. The people going missing often don't have any family, so no one can say for certain that they've disappeared. These are just rumours.'

Kevin leaned forward excitedly. For once, talking seemed to have produced better results than punching. 'Just rumours, huh? You believe they're true?'

Jones regarded him through half-lidded eyes. 'And what if I do?'

'Then Liz needs to go looking for them. If she's gonna catch the murderer, she needs to find these missing people, or uncover what happened to them. And you boys need to help.'

'Why's that, then, Kevin?' asked Jones.

Kevin scratched his nose, thinking. This Welshman was a tough nut to crack. 'The way I see it, we all got the same interests. Liz needs to solve this case to prove her innocence. You need her to solve it, so that you can trust her again. Right?'

'I guess so. So how can we help?'

'If Liz is gonna catch a serial killer, things might get

hairy.'

'Hairy,' agreed Jones. 'They might well do. Yes.'

Kevin nodded. Luck was with him for once. The corporal seemed open to suggestions, and Kevin knew exactly what to suggest. 'When life gets hairy, it helps if you have a tool to clean up hairs.'

Jones frowned. 'A tool? You mean –'

'A gun, like,' said Kevin, just to make sure there was no misunderstanding. 'Just a small one,' he added quickly. There was no point pushing his luck too far. 'Just big enough to take down a vampire.'

Chapter Fifty-Five

Stoke Park, Buckinghamshire

Helen could no longer be certain where the idea had originated. Had it come from her, or from Sarah, or from James? Whoever had first proposed the idea, Chanita had become its champion, pushing forward its implementation, despite objections on all sides.

Sometimes even James himself seemed to be having second thoughts. 'Are you sure we're doing the right thing?' he asked Helen.

'Don't tell me you're having doubts.'

'It's just that … do you think I really am human?'

'Yes,' said Helen firmly. 'In fact, I can safely say that you taught me what it means to be human.'

She had been badly in need of that lesson. After her near-death experience at Leanna's hands, she had lost sight of the truth for a while – that it was wrong to prejudge people by their class, or race, or even because they had an affliction that was difficult to control. James had proved beyond doubt that lycanthropy didn't necessarily turn everyone into a depraved killer. If he could control his impulses, then others could too, especially with his help.

'Remember that the variant of the virus we're administering comes from you, and it should have the same effect on others as it has on you,' she reminded him. 'And we won't simply be releasing the patients without supervision. On the contrary, they'll be very closely watched.'

She wondered at times if she had crossed an ethical line. Professor Wiseman certainly had, when he began to capture werewolves and run experiments on them as if they were laboratory test animals. He had convinced himself that he was acting for the greater good, and had paid the price with his own life. But this was different. Helen wasn't injecting her patients against their will. They were fully briefed on the risks of the treatment and gave their informed consent.

She had even begun to think again about treating herself. If the treatment programme went well, then she could use the cure to overcome her own Huntington's. She began to hope tentatively for a future in which she would not be condemned to walk with a stick or use a wheelchair. She began to yearn for a full life, not one cut short by sickness.

She realized that optimism had crept back into her life. Whether or not she chose to cure herself, she accepted that she would likely never return to Australia, and she was resigned to that. She had even found herself becoming contented with the British weather. On a fine spring morning like this one, there was much to be said for a mild maritime climate. All in all, Helen felt more positive than she had in a long time. She was finally living her dream to cure disease, doing more practical good in a few short weeks than she had achieved in all her years of academic research at the university.

But it wasn't easy to persuade everyone in the camp to accept Chanita's solution. Many refused to. Even some of the sick patients themselves chose to face death from their illnesses instead of being offered a cure by lycanthropy. All around the camp there was disquiet. 'How does this make us different to the werewolves who killed and maimed our friends and families?' asked one man.

The only answer they had was James himself.

Chanita and Helen were taking him around the camp, encouraging as many people as possible to meet him. They enlisted his friends, Sarah, Melanie and Ben, to vouch for his good behaviour, describing how he had risked his own life to save a boy from another werewolf. The message was simple: 'James is different. Just look at him.'

'You must be desperate if you have to use me as a character witness,' Melanie whispered to Helen, when no one was listening.

'Well, I guess we are,' she admitted.

At every gathering, Chanita delivered the same sobering warning: 'The alternative is sickness and death.' That argument was enough to convince most people.

Still, the security situation inside the camp was tense. Lieutenant Colonel Sharman called off the missions to find medical supplies. If the plan worked, medicine would no longer be needed. Instead, his men patrolled inside the camp, suppressing unrest and putting troublemakers behind bars.

Helen was busy, with Sarah's help, administering the micro-doses of blood to those most badly in need of it. Chanita was adamant on that point. Lycanthropy was to be used only as a cure of last resort, for those who were most seriously ill. Although some healthy volunteers stepped forward, asking to be changed, Helen sent them away. As Chanita put it, 'This is a necessary evil, not a lifestyle choice.'

They still didn't know for sure what the long-term effects would be.

The controlled micro-doses successfully avoided the worst side effects of the virus, and those who were injected with James' blood made good recoveries from whatever illnesses they had. It seemed that there was nothing that couldn't be cured by lycanthropy. Helen was monitoring the patients carefully, and they appeared to be making good progress. They could eat normal food, and none of the usual symptoms of lycanthropy had taken hold. None had yellow eyes, or a desire to eat human flesh, or even the light sensitivity that was the usual distinctive hallmark of early-stage lycanthropy.

'It seems almost too good to be true,' said Helen.

'The real test will be when the full moon rises,' James said.

It was not so many days away.

In the meantime, Chanita agreed to allow James out of the camp at night, so that he could hunt. He found plenty of game out there, mostly rabbits, hares and deer. He brought back some of the animals he killed so that their meat could be cooked and shared among the refugees in the camp.

Ten days before the full moon, the first of the treated patients complained of a dislike of bright light. More followed, but Helen was not too worried. 'I've been fully expecting some minor side effects,' she told Chanita. 'In fact, I'm surprised it took this long.'

Chanita nodded. 'I'll ask Colonel Sharman's men to keep a close eye on the patients. If there's any sign of trouble ...'

'But none of them have shown any violent tendencies,' said Helen.

'Yet.'

'And they're all still eating normal food.'

'Yes, that's very encouraging.'

Two days later, one of the patients was sick after eating a bowl of vegetable soup.

'I really just want to eat meat,' said the woman. 'I

forced down the soup, but it felt like my body simply rejected it.'

'I'll bring you some meat instead,' said Helen.

'Raw?' the woman asked hopefully.

Helen asked Colonel Sharman to keep an armed guard close to her at all times. She raised her concerns with Chanita later that day.

'I can't say that this worries me,' Chanita said. 'When we treated the bite patients back in the hospital in London, we had to strap them down at all times. They were extremely violent, right from the initial infection. These patients are nothing like that.'

'Even so,' said Helen. 'We need to watch them.'

'They are being watched.'

As the full moon drew closer, more symptoms began to develop. Light sensitivity among the patients became more common. Some developed the yellow sheen and mucous covering that Chanita was familiar with, and that Professor Wiseman had documented. Several refused to eat fruit and vegetables. But none had become aggressive. And all of them had recovered from whatever illness had been afflicting them.

'None of this should surprise us,' said Chanita. 'James shares the same symptoms, and more besides.'

'But what's our long-term game plan?' Helen asked her.

'Long term? My long-term plan is to make it through to the end of today,' said Chanita, looking exhausted. 'Seriously, long term sounds like a luxury. Half of the patients would already be dead by now from measles or pneumonia if we hadn't acted. Anyway, it's not the patients I'm most concerned about. We've succeeded in stopping the spread of infectious disease, but we still don't have enough food coming in. The rationing is leaving people hungry and angry. It's not the patients who are becoming restless and violent, but ordinary people. Colonel Sharman is having to work hard to keep trouble to a minimum. And my current biggest concern is whether the enemy will attack the camp when the full moon comes next week. So long term? Forget that. We'll take matters one day at a time.'

'And what if things go seriously wrong with the patients?'

Chanita returned her question with a level gaze. 'Colonel Sharman has his orders.'

Chapter Fifty-Six

Gatwick Airport, West Sussex, waxing moon

Drake felt Aasha shaking him roughly awake in the middle of the night. 'Eh?' he groaned. 'Whassat?'

'It's time,' she whispered, dragging him out from under his sheet.

They'd agreed to get up at two o'clock in the morning to go vampire hunting. He had only just managed to get off to sleep, if you could call it sleeping. It was more like a brief blink in and out of oblivion, between semi-permanent rounds of exhaustion. It was impossible to sleep properly now the baby was born. Midnight feed. Three o'clock feed. Six o'clock feed. The madness never stopped.

He grabbed the wooden stake he'd sharpened in readiness, and struggled to his feet. Then he slipped out of the hotel room as quietly as he could, so as not to wake any of the others.

'Don't wake the baby,' warned Aasha.

'Don't wake the baby? Are you crazy? That's like saying, don't sting the wasp.'

Were all babies like this? No wonder parents were so totally messed up.

'Promise me,' he said to Aasha as he stumbled down the darkened corridor, 'that if we stay together, we'll never have one of those.'

'A baby?' she asked, looking worryingly interested by the possibility.

'Yeah.'

'Totally,' she said. 'Unless of course I change my mind.'

They made their way downstairs to the hotel lobby where Vijay and Mihai were already waiting. They looked as bad as Drake felt, Vijay's eyes red and half open, Mihai's shoulders slumped. 'I didn't sleep a wink,' said Vijay. 'That baby just doesn't stop crying.'

'You boys are like babies,' said Aasha. 'Stop whingeing. Imagine how tired Samantha must feel.'

'Is easy to imagine,' said Mihai. He pointed to his bloodshot eyes. 'Is just like this.'

Aasha's eyes were shining brightly in the dimness of the hotel lobby. She didn't look the least bit tired, but seemed massively excited by the prospect of creeping around the airport at night. She gave Drake a quick kiss on the lips, which was something she hadn't done for a while. 'You should have just told me that you were trying to catch a vampire, right from the beginning,' she said. 'This is the most fun I've had since we came here.'

'Fun, oh yeah. I forgot about that part,' said Drake. 'You'd better keep reminding me.'

'Don't forget that it's dangerous,' whispered Vijay. 'This vampire is a cold-blooded killer. You saw what happened to Liz on the night of the full moon. She came really close to ripping someone's throat out.'

'Cheers,' said Drake. 'Now my happiness is complete.'

The mood of the group changed once they left the relative safety of the hotel. Outside the air was crisp, almost sharp. Although it was April and the days were growing warmer and sunnier, there was still frost on the ground some mornings. Drake felt his senses heightened as the cold brought him back to life, banishing all thoughts of babies and sleep. The vampire was out here somewhere. Maybe it was stalking its next victim even now.

He tightened his grip on the wooden stake. He was the only one who'd thought of bringing one. It would have been better if they were all armed with some kind of weapon, but it was too late for that now. In any case, the others weren't really up to fighting. If things turned nasty, Vijay would be more hindrance than help. Mihai was a tough kid, but only ten years old. Aasha never took any crap from anyone, but she was just a girl. In an emergency, Drake couldn't trust any of them to step up. He would have to do it himself.

'Come on, then,' he said, moving to the front. 'Let's go.'

The plan was simple enough. Sneak inside the terminal building, split up and take positions around the building. Then wait and watch. If the vampire came hunting for another victim, they wouldn't try to catch it, but would raise the alarm and try to get a good look. If they could identify the vampire, Liz could make an arrest later.

It had seemed like a good idea when they'd talked about it up on the rooftop in the light of day. Now, with the blackness of night pressing in on all sides, he wondered if they were making a big mistake. It was too late to turn back though. Mihai had already slipped away, creeping off on his own into the darkness. The kid had balls, there was no question about that. And if he could do it, so could Drake.

Aasha gave him another kiss and crept away in another direction. Now it was just him and Vijay.

'You gonna be all right, mate?' he asked his friend.

Vijay nodded.

'Why don't you just stay here near the entrance?' Drake

suggested. 'I'll go and take a look around inside.'

Vijay nodded gratefully, and Drake slipped inside, walking stealthily through the terminal building. A few lights glimmered in the darkness, turning to shine on him as he walked. Other people were staying awake, probably doing the same as him. Keeping watch over friends and neighbours. Watching for danger. That was sensible. In that case, the chances that the vampire would show were slim. And yet it had killed on three occasions already. It would be sure to kill again. If the vampire tried to kill someone tonight, Drake would surely spot it.

He crossed the central floor area, past the check-in zones, stepping carefully between sleeping families, and climbed up the escalators to security. There were not so many people sleeping up on this level. He passed a café and a restaurant, both closed now, and wandered into the security lanes, where passengers had once queued to have their hand baggage searched. He had only ever flown once, on a cheap holiday to the Costa del Sol with his mum and one of her boyfriends. He had memories of sun, sea and sunburn. He had tried a beer for the first time, and hadn't much liked it. But that wasn't the point, was it? The point was fooling yourself that the beer tasted good, that life was on the up, and that things could only continue to get better. He had been fooling himself his whole life, he supposed.

No one was going on holiday anywhere now. They probably never would again, and this entire airport was nothing more than a human warehouse, and not a very comfortable one at that.

There were no windows on this level. In the enclosed darkness he could just make out the hulking shapes of the metal X-ray machines. There was no one around and the big space felt creepy.

He was about to turn round and go back down to the lower level when he heard a sound.

Chapter Fifty-Seven

Drake ducked down behind one of the silent X-ray machines. He stilled his breathing as much as he could, and listened hard.

All he could hear was the thud-thud-thud of his own heart, but he knew he had heard a sound. His heart felt like it was pushing its way up and out through his throat. The blood pumping in his ears was almost deafening.

But despite the din from his own body, he heard the sound again.

Scratch.

That single sound in the dark, silent space felt ominous. That was not the creaking of the building. It was not the quiet sound of a mouse. He didn't know what it was.

Scratch.

His heart was galloping so wildly, he could hardly bear to stay still, yet he forced himself to sit with his back glued to the metal of the X-ray scanner. The machine was huge, easily big enough to shield him from view if someone was there in the security hall.

Why was he thinking "if"? Of course there was someone there. The temptation to peek was strong, but he resisted it. All he had to do was stay out of sight and very soon the –

Scratch.

It was even closer this time. An unmistakably inhuman noise, even scarier because it was so quiet and stealthy.

Was this the vampire coming for him? Was he going to be the next victim? Another mysterious murder? Now he felt stupid that he had told Vijay to stay near the entrance. Whose idea had it been to split up in the first place? That was a rookie mistake. If the vampire knew he was here, on his own, he was as good as dead. He could try shouting for help, but that might simply secure his fate good and proper. No, just stay still and be silent, that was the best policy. But get ready to run. Get ready to run like mad.

He clutched the wooden stake tightly. If the vampire came near, he would lunge at it and stick it through the heart. He had done a bit of knife fighting in the past, so he knew how to do it. He just hoped the wooden point would be sharp enough.

A black shape glided through the thick darkness toward him.

He yelped in fright, his arms frozen at his side, not even able to think, the wooden stake useless in his hand.

So much for fight or flight. His arms and legs wouldn't move. All he could do now was gibber with terror.

The shape slid closer, unhurried, unafraid.

'Who is it?' blurted Drake. 'I know there's someone there.'

Were those the stupidest last words ever?

The black thing came right up to him and pushed against his arm. He shrieked. The feel of it was horrible. Thick, smooth fur, rubbing against his skin, tickling the hairs that stood tall all over his arms. It pressed against him, then turned its head. Two green eyes stared into his face. They were huge.

He screamed and leapt to his feet, holding the wooden stake ready to strike.

The green eyes looked up at him, puzzled. He looked down at them and realized that their owner must be about a foot tall.

Meow.

It was a black cat.

'Bloody hell,' gasped Drake. 'You scared me to death.'

The cat licked its paws calmly, its eyes still fixed on him. It meowed again.

He sank back to his feet in relief. His legs and arms were shaking now. The cat turned and rubbed itself against him again, mewing hopefully.

'Are you hungry? I bet you are.' The animal felt thin and bony. It must be living here in the terminal building, scavenging for leftover food. By the looks of it, it hadn't found much. 'I know how you feel,' said Drake. 'Life could have been kinder, yeah?'

The cat allowed him to stroke its back. It paced back and forth, purring gently, its green eyes lighting its movement, pressing its warmth against him. Slowly, his heart returned to something like normal speed.

Suddenly the cat stopped and arched its back. Its purring came to a halt and instead it hissed.

A cold feeling of dread crept up Drake's spine. He couldn't hear anything, yet somehow he sensed another presence. He laid a warning hand on the cat's head and raised a finger to his lips. He had no idea if the cat understood his meaning, but it stayed quiet, not moving an inch.

Drake strained to listen. He was almost certain he could hear the soft tread of footsteps.

Every hair on the cat's back stood to attention. The animal padded forward silently, stepped across Drake's outstretched legs and slipped around the corner of the X-ray machine. Drake watched it go in fear.

The footsteps came to a halt and the silence deepened so much he could imagine that time itself had stopped. He could almost hear the echoes of the silence. For a long minute nothing happened. Eventually he could stand it no longer. He slid along the floor, the way the cat had gone, until he reached the corner of the scanning machine. He held his breath and poked his head around it.

A figure was standing in the middle of the hall, its limbs frozen mid-movement in a strange, unnatural position, like a statue. Only its head was moving, slowly turning through the darkness, left to right, right to left, like a searchlight sweeping the room. Its eyes glowed yellow.

Drake ducked back.

The footsteps started again, treading softly across the floor. Which way were they heading? It was impossible to tell for sure, but they seemed to be drawing closer. Drake looked left and right, but there was no obvious way of escape. If the vampire caught him here, he'd have nowhere to run.

The footsteps continued on their slow, hesitant path. That was no normal walking. That was the sound of someone creeping quietly, stealing stealthily like a thief. Or a killer. Or a vampire. And they were definitely coming nearer. Oh yes.

He clutched the wooden stake so hard it felt like it might snap. If the vampire reached him, would he have the courage to stick the stake in its chest? Could he kill someone? A vampire? He would find out soon. The footsteps were very close now, just a few yards away.

A sharp hiss cut through the air and the steps came to an abrupt halt.

Drake waited a moment, but couldn't stand the suspense. If he was going to die, he at least wanted to know how. He stuck his head out to see what was happening.

The vampire had paused just the other side of the

scanner, and the cat was arching its back again, hissing even louder than before. It showed its teeth and scratched at the floor with its claws. The hissing grew louder and then the cat was spitting at its foe, hairs bristling, ready to attack.

The vampire watched the cat, a slow malevolent grin spreading across its face. It was a para, one of Major Hall's men. Drake was sure of it.

Then the para spun on his heel and marched out of the security hall, leaving Drake and the cat alone again.

Chapter Fifty-Eight

Overton Hill, Wiltshire, waxing moon

They had nearly come to the end of the Ridgeway, and Chris was growing increasingly apprehensive. Just as Ryan had promised, the old road had led them west, away from the urban hinterland around London, to the green fields and forests of the countryside.

They had passed many ancient sites on their route, including the prehistoric stone circle of Avebury. Chris had marvelled at the huge stones planted in the ground like the teeth of some gigantic dinosaur. Josh and his friends had thrown empty beer cans at them, and the guy with the flute had climbed on top of one of the stones, performing a drunken dance beneath the stars.

Now they were approaching Overton Hill, the very end of the old chalk road, and it would be time to turn north and travel on to the promised land of Hereford. But Josh and the new guys were still insisting on going to Glastonbury.

Chris thought that he could depend on Rose and Ryan to back him up, but Seth was another matter. Seth had become a turncoat, a traitor. His ankle was still no better, and he actually seemed to enjoy being carried everywhere like a maharaja in his palanquin. He even treated the new guys as his best friends, laughing at their jokes and encouraging them to talk about their stupid ideas.

'I can't imagine a world without the internet,' he was telling them now. 'Except that, wow, this is it.'

'I know,' said Josh, who was leaning on a stout walking stick fashioned from a branch he had picked up en-route. 'Crazy, right? But you know what? It's because of the internet that we're so well prepared for survival. Did you ever watch those videos showing you how to survive by, you know, drinking your own urine?'

'Ugh, gross,' said Seth. 'But yeah, I watched so many zombie shows on Netflix, I reckon I could survive anything now.'

'Totally. We must remain alert at all times, and be combat-ready,' said Josh, adopting a karate-style pose with his stick. 'Keep a clear mind, and always have an escape route planned.'

Chris snorted in derision. These people knew nothing about survival. They had come to the wilderness with no proper equipment, no food, no knowledge even of how to light a fire, how to cook, how to hunt. They had barely been able to open a tin can. Chris had shown them how to make sparks using a flint he had found on the Ridgeway. He had taught them how to light a fire from dry kindling. Without him to show them what to do, and Rose and Ryan to go on food missions, they would probably be dead already.

Seth was the worst of all, the most inept survivalist Chris knew. Clueless and dumb, he was so ignorant he didn't even know how stupid he was. Yet ironically he had somehow managed to develop the looks of a rugged pioneer. Without a razor to tend to his facial hair, his goatee beard had grown thick and matted. His hair was now so long it permanently covered his eyes. He looked like a low-rent Thor who had lost his Stormbreaker hammer and forgotten to keep up his strength training.

'Glastonbury, here we come,' said Seth as they reached the top of the hill. 'Can we see it from here?'

Chris laughed mirthlessly. Glastonbury was still miles away. But there was no point explaining that to Seth. He had entirely lost his grip on reality.

Josh turned to him. 'You got something you want to say, Chris?'

'I just think we should go to Hereford.'

'Well,' said Josh, 'that is where you are wrong. 'Do you want me to explain why?'

Chris didn't. But he suspected he had no choice.

'Hereford is boring. Whereas, Glastonbury, apart from being the location of the world's greatest music festival, is also the site of King Arthur's grave and the Holy Grail.'

'Wow,' said Seth. 'Like, amazeballs.'

'Incredible,' said Chris. 'You do realize that there won't actually be a music festival when you get there? And that King Arthur and the Holy Grail are pure myth?'

Josh came over to him and prodded him in the chest with his finger. 'And you do realize that no one enjoys your smart-arse comments? And that you look ridiculous dressed in those old clothes you're wearing? None of which seem to actually fit you, by the way.'

Chris looked down at his clothes in surprise. The old coat and boots had been given to him by a vicar at a church where they'd stayed in London. He'd picked up the various other items at homeless shelters on the way out of the city. Josh was the first person to criticize his dress sense since the world had ended. Seth's outfit was the same mix of cast-offs and hand-me-downs, but Josh didn't seem to have a problem with the way Seth dressed.

Seth laughed. 'You should have seen Chris the night we escaped from the hospital,' he said. 'He was wearing hospital pyjamas and slippers, and a white coat he took from one of the dead doctors.'

'Wait. What?' Josh grew suddenly still. Chris could see him processing the new information. 'You two escaped from a hospital? Which one?'

'Don't tell him, Seth,' warned Chris.

But Seth took no notice. 'The quarantine hospital in London, where they kept all the werewolves. We escaped with them on the night of the full moon.'

'You two were locked in the quarantine hospital?' said Josh. 'With the other werewolves?'

'Yeah,' said Seth. 'That was a real bummer, like, totally craptacular.'

'But you two aren't actually werewolves, are you? It was all just a big mistake, yeah?'

'The soldiers gave us a good going over with their sniffer dogs,' said Seth, laughing again. 'And the dogs decided that Chris was a werewolf. So the soldiers locked us up.'

Chris felt the blood draining from his face. 'Shut up, Seth. Stop talking.'

But it was already too late. 'Put him down,' commanded Josh to the guys who were carrying Seth.

'Why? What?' asked Seth, bewildered. 'What for?'

'You idiot, Seth,' said Chris. 'Now they think we're werewolves.'

'Duh,' said Seth. 'Come on, Josh. Is this for real? Did you think we were waiting until the full moon to come so that we could eat you?'

Josh grinned. 'That wouldn't be cool, would it?'

'No.'

'Right. So I don't think we'll risk it.' He lifted his walking stick high and cracked it hard against Chris' forehead.

Chris wobbled for a moment, and actually thought he saw stars. Then the ground rushed up to meet his face and all the stars went out.

Chapter Fifty-Nine

Rose watched in horror as Chris collapsed to the ground, blood streaming from a gash in his head. She ran to him and kneeled down, examining the wound. It didn't look deep, but Chris had been completely knocked out by the blow from Josh's stick.

Nutmeg barked and leapt forward, hurling herself at Josh, her jaws parted, ready to bite.

'Nutmeg, no!' called Rose, but it was too late.

Josh brought the wooden walking stick down and swept the dog to one side. She tumbled onto the grass and Josh delivered a sharp kick to her belly. She rolled over, whining.

Rose ran to her and cradled her in her arms.

'Hey!' shouted Ryan furiously. 'What the hell do you think you're doing?'

Josh raised the heavy stick again and stood ready with it. 'Stand back, Ryan, unless you want a taste of this yourself.'

Ryan's fists were clenched tight and he advanced on Josh. He was as tall as Josh and more muscular. 'You think you can take me?'

Josh snarled. 'Give it a try.' His friends had picked up sticks and rocks and were bunched behind him, looking mean.

'No, Ryan,' called Rose. 'Enough, already. Don't you get hurt too.' Nutmeg whimpered in her arms, quivering gently as Rose held her tight.

'Listen to Rose, Ryan,' said Josh. 'No need for you to get the same treatment as Chris.'

Ryan stood his ground, his fists balled. 'You drop that stick now!'

'No way. Not while you're giving me that angry look. And not while there are two werewolves right here.'

'You must be even stupider than I thought if you believe that Chris and Seth really are werewolves,' said Ryan.

Josh lifted his branch higher. 'Choose your words more carefully, Ryan. Or someone else is going to get a face full of this.' He spoke to Brittany. 'Babes, put your foot on Seth's ankle, yeah?'

'What?' said Seth. 'No!'

But Brittany seemed happy to oblige. She placed her foot against the broken joint and pushed down.

Seth screamed.

'That's enough for now, babes,' said Josh. To Ryan, he said, 'Or shall I tell her to do it again?'

'No.'

Chris was coming round again after losing consciousness. 'What? Who?' He blinked. 'Why?'

Rose laid a hand on his arm. 'Just lie still.'

'Tie him up,' said Josh to one of his friends. The guy pulled out some rope and began to bind Chris' hands behind his back. Chris was too dazed to resist. When it was done, Josh relaxed a little. 'That's better. Now we can talk.'

'You have got to be insane,' said Ryan. 'Chris and Seth are not werewolves.'

'How can you prove it?' asked Josh.

'Prove it? That is such a dumb question.'

'Brittany? The ankle again, please, babes.'

Seth's screams drowned out Ryan's protests.

'Let's get this totally out in the open,' said Josh, 'so there won't be any more misunderstandings. Chris stays tied up until the next full moon. If he doesn't turn into a big bad wolf, then happy days. Everyone walks. Apart from Seth, that is.' He giggled. 'Until then, any hassle from you, and Seth gets his ankle twisted again. Maybe we'll have some fun with Chris too. The bastard deserves a good kicking, werewolf or not.'

'Please, why don't you just let us go?' begged Rose.

Josh shook his head. 'You must really think I'm stupid. You might come after us. You know we're travelling to Glastonbury. The full moon isn't far away now, so we don't have long to wait. In the meantime, I suggest that you and Ryan go and find some more food. If you don't return, or if you try any funny stuff, I'll let Brittany play with Seth some more.'

Chapter Sixty

Gatwick Airport, West Sussex, waxing moon

Liz was now almost completely nocturnal. It made perfect sense. Sunlight hurt her eyes and burned her skin, and if she was going to catch a killer, her best chance was during the hours of darkness. Besides, since Samantha's baby had been born – a boy, called Leo – it hardly made any difference what time of day or night she tried to get some sleep.

She was returning to the hotel room just after sunrise when she spotted Drake, Vijay, Mihai and Aasha slinking back too. Where could they possibly have been at this time?

'Hey!' she called.

They jumped guiltily at the sound of her voice, telling her more than any words would have done.

'All right,' she said, catching up with them. 'Tell me where you've been and what you've been up to.'

A sudden hissing noise made her start.

She looked down and saw a black cat entwined around Drake's legs. The animal had its teeth bared and its back arched. It hissed again and spat in her direction, before running up the stairs.

'Oh,' said Drake. 'I don't think Shadow likes you very much.'

'Shadow?'

'My cat.'

Liz waited for an explanation.

'It's not really my cat,' said Drake. 'But we're kind of friends.'

'Looks like Shadow doesn't want to be your friend, Liz,' said Aasha.

'No.' Shadow wasn't the first cat to hiss at her. Cats seemed much better than dogs at recognizing vampires, and there was no doubt that they hated her on sight.

'That's exactly what Shadow did when it saw the para,' said Drake.

'Huh? What para?'

The kids shuffled their feet and looked at each other awkwardly.

'Right,' said Liz. 'Come and tell me exactly what you've been up to.'

The sat together on an outdoor table round the back of the hotel. The sun had hardly risen, and wasn't strong enough to cause Liz any bother, even with her sunglasses off. The kids avoided her gaze, unwilling to tell her what they'd been doing.

It was Aasha who broke the silence. 'So, the boys had this, like totally stupid idea.'

'How stupid?' asked Liz dubiously.

'You wouldn't believe. But don't worry, I talked them out of it. Instead we went vampire hunting.'

'You did what?'

'Not hunting, really,' blurted Vijay. 'Just looking. More like watching. Just casually.'

Liz made her voice as stern as she could. 'Do you have

any idea how dangerous that might have been?'

Drake exchanged glances with Vijay. 'Yeah, we do now.'

'But we found *vampir*,' said Mihai. 'So is all good.'

Liz stared at the boy. 'No,' she said slowly. 'That is not all good. Now tell me exactly what happened.'

Drake told her his story. 'So that's how I found Shadow,' he concluded. 'And when I saw how Shadow behaved with you, that just proved it.'

'Proved what, exactly?'

'That the para I saw was the vampire. The cat did exactly the same when it saw him.'

'It's not proof, Drake,' she told him. 'That's not the kind of proof that would stand up in a court of law.'

'No, but –'

'There are all kinds of possible explanations for what you saw. The soldier you saw wasn't necessarily looking for a victim. He might simply have been on patrol, checking for danger. He might have been looking for the vampire himself.'

'He wasn't,' insisted Drake. 'When he heard Shadow, he was worried that someone had seen him. Shadow hated him. There's no other word to describe it.'

'Maybe. Did you get a clear view of him?'

'It was dark. But I'm sure that he was one of the commanders working under Major Hall.'

'Would you recognize him if you saw him again?'

'I'm not sure.'

'Okay,' said Liz. 'Well, we've got a possible lead, so well done. But promise me that you'll never do anything like that again without telling me first.'

'Promise,' said Vijay.

Liz glared at the others in turn. Aasha was the last one to promise.

When they returned to the hotel room, Kevin was keen to have a word with her. 'You got a minute, love? I might have some info.'

She took him back downstairs to the outdoor table. She was too tired to stop the kids trooping downstairs to join them. After all, they were supposed to be helping her solve the investigation.

'So what is it?' she asked.

'I been talking to Jones and the boys.'

'Oh. Great. Did they threaten to kill me again?'

'No. Well, not in so many words. But they told me that people have been going missing.'

'Missing?'

'Yeah. Just disappearing. Women and children mainly.'

This was the first that Liz had heard about vanishing people. But if the killer had changed tactics, it would explain why there had been no bodies discovered since before the last full moon. 'Dad, are you thinking what I think you're thinking?'

'If you're thinking these missing people are lying dead somewhere with bite marks on their necks, then yeah.'

'You think the killer's been hiding the bodies?'

'Sounds that way to me.'

'The para!' said Drake. 'You gotta make an arrest!'

'But we don't know which one,' said Vijay.

'One of the paras is the vampire?' said Kevin, raising his eyebrows.

Mihai raised a hand. 'I saw para go into building.'

'When?' asked Liz. 'What building?'

'Was yesterday. I see him from rooftop. Is big building like shed, but next to runway.'

'You mean a hangar?'

'Why would he be going in there?' asked Kevin.

'Any number of reasons,' said Liz. 'You all have to stop jumping to conclusions. This is not how the police work. We need evidence.'

'But we should defo check it out, yeah?' said Drake. 'How else are we gonna find any evidence?'

Chapter Sixty-One

The hangar was huge and grey, just like all the others at the airport. Liz regarded its double doors suspiciously. 'Are you certain this is the right one?' she asked Mihai.

'Is this one, yes,' confirmed the Romanian boy. 'But para not go in through this door. He use small door in side.'

She and the others followed him around to the side of the building. They had all come – Kevin, Mihai, Vijay, Drake and Aasha. She couldn't complain about her team being under-resourced. Lacking in equipment perhaps, inadequately trained and shockingly unprofessional, but not short of numbers, nor enthusiasm. Well, you just had to make the best of what you had.

She slid her hand over the holster containing the Glock. The cold steel felt reassuringly solid to the touch. She'd been carrying the gun around for months now, and one of these days she was surely going to use it. Hopefully not today. But it was good knowing it was there.

Mihai led them to the small side door and turned the handle. The door was locked and secured with a heavy padlock.

'What we gonna do?' asked Drake, kicking the metal door in frustration.

'This ain't a problem,' said Kevin. 'I can get this open in a jiffy.'

Liz turned to him. 'You know how to pick locks? Where did you learn to do that?'

He opened his mouth to speak but Liz held up a hand.

'Stop! On second thoughts, I don't want to know. But are you certain you can unlock it?'

'A simple padlock? Even the kid could unlock this,' said Kevin.

'Sure,' said Mihai. 'Is no big deal.'

'Don't tell me,' said Liz to her father through gritted teeth, 'that you've taught Mihai how to pick locks?'

'Course I did,' said Kevin. 'It's a valuable life skill. Especially these days.'

Liz nodded, beaten by Kevin's logic. 'Go on then, Mihai. Let's see what you can do.'

He brought out a set of tools and began to work on the lock. Liz looked over her shoulder anxiously, but for the moment there was no one around. She turned back to watch the boy. She had to admit, Mihai had dexterous fingers and seemed to have a knack for lock picking. Kevin offered the boy encouraging noises, but never once had to make any suggestions. In less than a minute the door was open.

'Right,' said Liz. 'Now don't all rush inside. We have no idea what to expect. Stay close behind me.'

She pulled the door open and entered quietly.

The hangar looked smaller inside than out. But that was an optical illusion caused by the enormous aircraft that were stored here. They seemed to completely fill the space, the tips of their wings almost touching the curving walls of the building. Each of the huge fuselages must have measured well over a hundred feet in length, with a wingspan to match. They loomed high above her.

The building was dim and she drew out a flashlight and began to shine it around. The light threw spotlights on the glossy surface of the planes, picking out the Union Jack logo of British Airways, but it was too weak to penetrate into the furthest depths of the hangar.

The others followed close behind, adding their own lights. Kevin was the last to enter. He closed the door with a clang, and the sound reverberated around the massive space like thunder, bouncing off the metal walls and smooth concrete floor. If anyone else was in here, they would certainly know they were no longer alone. Perhaps it was safer that way. Liz had no desire to stumble upon an unwary vampire feeding on its prey. Especially not with the kids in tow. She felt her fingers slide once again over the Glock.

'Look,' said Kevin, shining his light into the far recesses of the building. 'What's that over there?'

Liz followed the beam of his light and swallowed hard. It was too far to see clearly under the feeble beam of light, but she didn't like what she saw. 'Wait here,' she said, but as soon as she started to walk she heard the others following in her wake.

'Jesus,' said Drake. 'Is that what I think it is?'

Liz was pretty sure that what she was seeing was exactly what Drake thought it was. But she kept her mind open until she was right up close. Eventually there was no room for doubt, only for horror.

'I think we've found our missing persons,' said Kevin grimly.

He shone his light up toward the roof of the hangar. Hanging on long metal wires suspended from the ceiling were bodies. They were upside down, like bats, the metal wires tied around their feet. Their arms hung down in lifeless slumber. Their faces were pale.

There were not one or two corpses here, or even three.

'There must be thirty or forty bodies up there,' said Kevin.

Liz stepped forward to examine the nearest. The cadaver was cold and rigid to the touch. She reached up to the victim's neck, and her fingers found two holes, spaced two inches apart. The corpse began to swing gently and a cloud of flies rose into the air.

'Why hang them from the ceiling?' asked Aasha.

'To feed, and to drain their blood,' said Liz.

Behind her, she heard the sound of Drake being sick.

Chapter Sixty-Two

Burnham, Buckinghamshire, waxing moon

The woman appeared from out of a gap in the fence. Griffin dodged back, away from the roadside, but it was too late. He had been spotted. He wondered which way to go, but there were few options. The road was fenced on both sides, and there was no way he could climb in his state. His only choice was whether to try and run, or to stay and face the stranger.

He had been dreading something like this for days. Now that he was drawing close to Stoke Park, it was impossible to avoid built-up areas. There was barely any countryside around here, just towns that merged into other towns, villages that had been swallowed by housing developments, every last available space filled by a retail park or a DIY superstore. This had never been his favourite part of the world, and now it was full of danger.

The woman didn't look particularly threatening at first glance. She was young, and travelling alone. By rights, she ought to have been afraid of him. He wondered how he must look to her. A bearded, grizzly veteran, clickety-clacking along on his homemade crutches, his appearance in no way improved by spending weeks alone in the wilds, muttering to himself and to people no longer with him.

Yet something about her terrified him. Was it the way she walked, so much at ease, her gait loose, like a tiger patrolling its territory? Or was it the cold look in her eyes, like a shark closing in on its prey?

Either way, she scared him to the marrow, and he knew without a shred of doubt that she was a werewolf. He turned on his one good heel, and began to head off down the road in the opposite direction.

After his days of crossing rural England, he had mastered the art of walking with crutches. At the start of his journey, any energetic movement had rubbed his arms raw and left his muscles aching, but now that he had built up some hard skin, and his strength had returned, he could move at a pace, perhaps even faster than normal walking.

Click-clack, click-clack. He powered himself along the tarmac as quickly as he could.

After a minute he risked a glance over his shoulder.

Shark Eyes was closer. Neither running, nor even seeming to exert herself, she loped easily in his direction, gaining on him steadily. She met his gaze with a cold smile.

He had seen that look before, back in the quarantine hospital in London, when he had been tasked with holding the captured werewolves in isolation. He had seen a hundred of those dead stares and sinister smiles.

He leaned heavily on his crutches to power himself forward, and felt the support vanish from under him. With a loud crack, the crutch beneath his right arm split and he toppled forward, headlong into the road.

With no way to break his fall he struck the tarmac with a slap, scraping his right shoulder and arm against the rough surface.

'Aargh!' He gritted his teeth against the sudden pain

and rolled over onto his back. He considered trying to struggle back to his feet, but with a broken crutch he would not get far. Instead he lay there helpless as Shark Eyes closed on him, unhurried.

Her smile grew broader as she reached him, revealing a row of pearly white teeth. But it didn't spread as far as her eyes. 'Well, hello.' She spoke with a London accent. Standard Estuary English. 'Do you need a helping hand there?'

'No, thanks. I'm good.'

Her eyes thinned. 'So, what, are you just going to lie there?'

'What would you prefer?'

'I was hoping for a chase. You know, a little excitement before dinner.'

'Sorry to disappoint you. Perhaps you should find someone with two working legs.'

'Yeah, maybe. You don't look so tasty.' She turned to go. 'Except … now that we're both here …'

His options had pretty much run to zero. He couldn't run, or even walk. Hell, he couldn't even get up. He lifted the only weapon he had available, his crutch. Bracing himself, he swung it sharply in her direction.

She ducked away and caught it with one hand.

He tried to pull it back, but she twisted it from his grip and tossed it to one side. The smile was back on her face. 'That's more like it. You know what? My appetite just came back.'

There was nothing more he could do to defend himself.

She fell on him, making him squeal like a pig when his leg took her weight. 'Oh, that hurts, does it?' she asked. 'Let me give you some more.'

She sat up, kneeling on his wound. He almost bit off his own tongue with the pain.

'This is fun,' said his persecutor. 'I could literally do this all day.'

A deafening shot rang out. A pistol, at short range. Blood from the woman lashed his face. A second shot followed and she dropped forward like a stone. Her body lay heavy on his chest, her mouth now fixed in a smile like a rictus.

With an effort he pushed her off.

Another woman stood over him now, a pistol in her outstretched arm, shaking slightly. This woman was older, and was no stranger to him. And yet …

He wished he had some water to splash over himself, to wake himself up. Was this just another dream? Had the fever seized him once again? He felt her hand grasp his, and knew that she was real. 'You are the very last person I expected to meet,' he said.

She smiled. 'But not, I trust, the last person you ever hoped to meet?'

Chapter Sixty-Three

'You're pretty handy with a gun, these days,' said Griffin to the Prime Minister after she had helped him to sit up, and retrieved his one unbroken crutch for him to lean on.

She nodded. 'It's never too late to learn a new skill. Lifelong education has long been one of my passions. But I have to admit that I'm no expert. I don't even know how many bullets I have left.'

'Let me take a look.'

Her gun was a Glock 17 semi-automatic, the British Army's standard issue side-arm. She seemed slightly reluctant to hand it over to him.

'I promise I'll return it,' he said.

She gave it to him and he checked the magazine. 'Just one round left. The magazine capacity is seventeen rounds when fully loaded. How many have you used?'

'I prefer not to say.'

He understood her meaning perfectly well. He had been lucky to meet only the one werewolf on his journey. 'Well, we have to do what it takes to make it through the day.' He handed the weapon back to her.

She sat on the road beside him. 'What happened to you, Colonel? Tell me everything you know. I have received no word from anyone in almost two months.'

Two months. Had it been no longer than that? Since he'd stopped counting the days, time seemed to have stretched out endlessly. It had been the same as a boy during the school holidays. Six weeks of summer had felt like a lifetime back then. Now that the pressures of modern living had been swept away so dramatically, time had unwound again, slowing from a frenetic gallop to a leisurely trot.

'My helicopter went down in the blasts over London, and I crash-landed in the Surrey hills. I was the only survivor. You're the first person I've spoken to since then.' He indicated the body of the woman who had tried to kill him and eat him for dinner. 'I don't count her.'

'I've met others on my journey,' said the PM, 'but none of them were friendly.'

So that explained the lack of ammunition in the Glock. He marvelled at her ability to pick it up and use it without training. The two shots she had fired to rescue him had both found their target. And using a gun to take a life was not for the faint-hearted. But she had always been resolute and determined. He shouldn't have been surprised.

'Where have you come from?' he asked.

'London. The Pindar bunker.'

He gaped at her. 'Seriously? I saw the explosions hit the city. There must have been half a dozen warheads.'

'Nine. Nine warheads in total.'

'Surely no one could have survived an attack on that scale? I saw the fires spread out and engulf the city, and that was just in the first few seconds after the blast.'

The PM's voice grew quiet. 'London has been almost

entirely destroyed by the blasts and the fire, and then by flooding. Only a few buildings are left standing. But a few people survived. Perhaps they were underground when the warheads exploded. Of course, the Pindar bunker was designed expressly to endure a nuclear attack.'

A silence fell over them, and seemed to grow louder.

'So,' he said at last, 'was it you who gave the order?'

She stared at him coldly. 'Is that what you think?'

'No. But it's the obvious question.'

'The obvious question, Colonel, is who gave the order? And the answer is General Ney. His intention was to wipe the country clean of werewolves once and for all.'

'The country?'

'London wasn't the only target. All of the major cities were destroyed in the attack.'

'My God.'

It was hard to process the new information. He had not truly allowed his mind to linger over the number of people who must have died. To think that the devastation had been unleashed right across the country was simply unimaginable. The Colonel was a warrior and a medic and had seen death and carnage on a horrific scale. Yet everything he had witnessed during time of war was nothing compared with this.

'So who's in charge now?' he asked her.

'I don't know. Not me. But I mean to find out, and to start putting things back into some semblance of order. A firm hand is needed now. Whoever has taken over from me isn't doing their job. As far as I can tell, the government has simply collapsed.'

He knew what was coming next. 'Count me out, Prime Minister,' he said to her. 'My days of saving the world are done. There's only one person I'm interested in saving, and you're not going to talk me out of going to her right now.'

She accepted his protest without comment.

'You're not going to try and talk me into coming with

you?' he asked.

'Where are you headed?'

'The western evacuation centre at Stoke Park. With any luck I should get there either tomorrow or the day after.'

'It isn't far out of my way,' she said. 'I'll walk with you. It looks like you could use my help.'

'No. Thank you. You go and do what you need to do. I'll be okay on my own. I've made it this far without help.'

'Is that right, Colonel Griffin?'

'Apart from just now,' he added sheepishly, 'when you saved my life, that is.'

She stared at him, her sharp eyes boring into his. It was the same look she had given him when he'd been summoned into her office at Number Ten, Downing Street, expecting to hear of his court martial. 'Colonel Griffin, I am coming with you, whether you like it or not, and that is final. Just because I'm not prime minister anymore, it doesn't mean I can't still tell everyone what to do.'

Chapter Sixty-Four

Somerset Levels, Somerset, full moon

It was the twenty-eighth day of April, and Chris watched in bewilderment as snow began to fall from the sky. It had been warm and sunny just a few minutes earlier, but now heavy white flakes gusted toward him as he staggered over the rough grass, his wrists burning where the rope cut into them.

He had been counting the days since Josh had tied him up and accused him of being a werewolf. Three days and three nights, each one spent in complete agony. He doubted that his arms would ever work properly again. He could no longer feel his fingers. Perhaps they would have to be amputated, along with Seth's foot.

His old friend was being carried along on his stretcher by Ryan and Rose, even though Josh and his friends were much bigger and stronger than Rose. But the newcomers had stopped doing any work. Each evening they sent Ryan and Rose out looking for food, then took most of it for themselves. Chris and Seth were being used as hostages, to make sure that Rose and Ryan didn't just try to run away.

Seth had been reduced to a state of almost permanent gibbering, crying about his ankle every time they bumped his stretcher, cringing and wailing if Brittany even went near him. Sometimes she would walk alongside him, whispering to him, in order to torment him.

'I might never be able to walk again,' he told Chris one night. 'My ankle might never heal.'

But Chris had no words of comfort to offer him. 'This is all totally your fault,' he said. 'I hope you'll choose your friends with more care in future.'

'I will,' said Seth. 'I've learned my lesson.'

'And what have you learned, exactly?'

Seth gazed up at him helplessly. 'Um, don't trust the bad guys? Don't trust strangers? Don't trust people you tell me not to trust?'

Chris shook his head sadly to each reply. Seth had still not learned his lesson. 'Don't trust anyone,' he said. 'It's what I've been saying to you since the beginning.'

At least today was the last day they would have to endure this agony. Tonight the full moon would rise, nobody would turn into a wolf, and Josh would be forced to admit that he had been wrong all along. Perhaps then, they would finally be allowed to turn north and continue on the road to Hereford.

But not if it snowed. If clouds covered the full moon, blocking out the moonlight, this hell might go on for another month. Chris lifted his chin to look up at the sky. The white snow fell against his face, but to his surprise its touch was warm. It was blossom, he realized, not snow at all. White blossom from the hedges, blowing in the wind. Spring was in full swing, and everything was growing.

They were trudging across the low-lying fields of the Somerset Levels. The fields here were muddy and bordered by drainage ditches. The area was a wetland, once nothing more than a vast swamp. It had been drained in medieval times, but was still liable to flooding. Chris' feet were thoroughly soaked from squelching through the marshy mud all day.

But at last their destination came in sight.

'There it is!' shouted Josh with glee. 'Glastonbury Tor!'

The steep-sided hill rose prominently above the flat Levels, looking very much like a man-made structure. Yet Chris knew that it was natural. *Tor* was the Anglo-Saxon word for island, and the hill had once been surrounded by a vast tidal lake, connected to the mainland only at low tide. The conical hill was topped by a ruined tower, once a church, but the mythology of the Tor stretched back to much earlier times, even older than the legends of King Arthur and the Holy Grail that Josh and his friends had eagerly discussed, all the way back to pre-Christian Celtic times.

'So,' said Josh, 'what do you make of that, Chris?'

'We should make camp at the base of the hill.'

'That,' said Josh, 'is quite possibly your worst idea yet, Chris. Why would we want to camp at the bottom, in the middle of all this mud? Obviously we're going to camp on top of the hill.'

'If you light a fire up there, it will be seen from miles around. We don't know who's out there. Anyone might come.'

'Do you hear that, Brittany?' said Josh scornfully. 'Smart-arse Chris says not to light a fire on top of the hill.' He pushed his face close to Chris. 'This is your big night, Chris. And I promise you, tonight we're going to party like it's the end of the world! If anyone wants to join us, they'll be welcome. So no more kill-joy suggestions from you, okay?'

Chris trudged on in silence. There was no point talking to these idiots. Instead he watched as the Tor grew larger, until eventually they were at its base and there was nothing to see except its giant mound, rising up from the flats, as if it had been dropped in from on high.

'The only way is up!' cried Josh. 'Come on, guys, let's go.'

Chapter Sixty-Five

Gatwick Airport, West Sussex, full moon

When Liz arrived at Jones' camp, it was obvious that she'd come at a bad time. The Corporal stood outside the Welshmen's tent, his face set in a grim mask, quite unlike his usual jovial self. When she had seen him like this on previous occasions, the situation had always turned bad very quickly. Come to think of it, whenever she encountered Jones it was often in the company of a corpse.

'This is not a good time for you to be here, Liz,' he told her, a warning in his voice.

But before she could respond, the Dogman was coming out of the tent. His face was twisted into an angry scowl. 'You!' he roared. 'How dare you show your face around here!'

'Why? What have I done?' she asked.

'Just go,' said Jones. 'Go quickly. I'll explain later.'

'No!' shouted the Dogman. 'Let's do this now.'

'No, Hughes,' said Llewelyn to the Dogman. 'Cool down. We'll talk to Liz when everyone has chilled a little.'

'Cool down? Chill a little? Don't talk to me like a fool.' The Dogman was furious with anger. Liz had never seen him so enraged. Rock was off the lead, and the dog clearly sensed its master's mood. It thrust its jaws up close to Liz, snarling and barking loudly. Hughes made no attempt to restrain it.

'The Dogman's right,' said the third guardsman, Evans. 'Let's end this now.' He hefted his machine gun and aimed the barrel at Liz.

'End what?' she demanded. 'What are you talking about? What's happened?'

She'd come to see the Welsh Guards in a state of elation, all ready to tell them that she'd found new evidence of the vampire's murderous spree. She'd hoped to recruit their help in identifying the murderer from among the paras. Now she wondered if she was going to leave with her life.

The Dogman lurched toward her, his fists bunched. He spoke loudly and deliberately, emphasizing each syllable. 'What has happened, Constable Bailey, is that our friend and colleague, Griffiths, has just died. From blood poisoning following his gunshot wound, if you want to know the gory details.'

'I'm sorry,' she said. 'I'm so sorry to hear that.' Liz had barely known the guardsman, but she knew how close the Welshmen were.

'Are you?' bellowed the Dogman. 'Do creatures like you ever feel sorrow? Are you capable of feeling anything other than the trickle of blood running down your lips?'

Liz felt the first stirrings of anger at the Dogman's words. There was no possible justification in blaming her for Griffiths' misfortune. 'I don't know what –'

'You don't know what Griffiths' death has to do with you? Is that it? Well, maybe you had nothing to do with his death directly. But I've had my fill of senseless deaths. You may not have killed my friend, but you've killed plenty of others. I've seen you do it. And monsters like you just carry on killing. Well, it's time to put a stop to your killing spree.' He raised his rifle, ready to fire.

Llewelyn muscled forward and grabbed the barrel of the gun, forcing it down. 'I said cool it.' There was controlled anger in his voice, and the threat of violence.

The Dogman narrowed his eyes. Rock switched attention to Llewelyn and began jumping up, snapping its jaws close to his face.

'Are you going to call that dog off?' asked Llewelyn quietly. 'Or do I have to put a bullet through its skull?'

'You'd choose to kill Rock instead of her?' shouted the Dogman in fury. 'You'd take the side of that murderer?'

Llewelyn stood his ground calmly. 'I'd choose to kill a dog before a human anytime.'

The Dogman snatched his arm out of Llewelyn's grasp with a savage jerk. 'Well here's another choice for you to make, then. Me or her. A human or a vampire!'

'Don't be an idiot,' said Jones.

Liz stepped between the two men. 'Stop this! There's no need for any fighting. I came here to prove to you that I'm not the murderer. In fact, I know who the vampire is.'

Llewelyn turned to her. 'You do? Who?'

'It's one of Major Hall's men. A para.'

'You expect us to believe that?' said the Dogman. 'Major Hall is a good commander. His men are brave soldiers. You're just saying that to save your own skin.'

But Jones was nodding. 'Do you have proof of this, Liz?'

'Yes.'

'Don't listen to her!' shouted the Dogman. 'She's a liar!'

Jones rounded on him. 'Just leave it, Hughes. Give Liz a chance to prove her story. If what she's saying is true, then we need to act.'

Evans still had his gun raised uncertainly. 'Yeah, let's do that,' he said. 'Let's hear what she has to say.'

'No. I've already heard enough.' The Dogman gave Jones a vicious shove.

Jones tumbled to the ground. He broke his fall with a roll and was back on his feet in a few seconds, but the Dogman had his gun aimed at Liz again. Rock bounded toward her, jaws slavering, barking frantically, leaping to the attack. The Dogman's fingers curled around the trigger.

Liz knew what she had to do.

She didn't have to make a decision. The metamorphosis began even before she was consciously aware of it. Time slowed to a crawl as awareness of her change grew.

Her teeth came through first, like two piercing spikes dropping into place, their tips sharpened to fine points. Her fingernails extended into razor-tipped blades. Her limbs throbbed with electric power, as the skin that covered them crackled into cold armour. The protective covering spread from her fingers along her hands, fitting like gloves, then sleeves, until it cloaked her entire body. With it came strength, flooding every fibre, muscle and bone.

Her eyes widened, her vision taking on a cool sharpness. She could see every hair on Rock's face, see the drool that glistened on the dog's teeth. Her hearing grew so keen she could hear the breathing of Jones, Hughes and Evans. She could almost feel the beating of their hearts. And she could smell their sweat and other body odours. The rich chemical cocktail of male pheromones, adrenaline and musk washed over her in a powerful stimulant.

The transformation from human to vampire had taken just seconds. It had never happened so quickly before.

But still, she had been too slow. Before she could even move, a shot rang out, deafening at close quarters, every nuance of the sound amplified by her vampire brain. The dog stopped its attack and skidded to the ground, its front paws splayed, its eyes rolling wild with terror. An arc of fine blood sprayed from the animal's side as it crashed forward and rolled across the grass. Rock lay dead before her.

Liz's nostrils flared at the overpowering scent of blood. She turned her gaze to look at Jones.

His SA80 assault rifle was in his hands, the barrel still pointed where he had fired at the dog.

The Dogman's face crumpled in anguish. 'No!'

Time oozed slowly, like thick treacle as Liz watched, weighing the risks. She could move at lightning speed, but would it be fast enough? Three men held guns. She couldn't take them all. The Dogman was the primary threat. She turned to face him.

Already his gun was aimed at her.

She started to move toward him.

But as she moved, the Dogman turned. Slowly his rifle swung in Llewelyn's direction.

Liz powered forward, desperate to stop him.

Jones was on his feet, suspended in motion, trapped in time. His SA80 was braced against his shoulder in firing position, his finger still on the trigger after shooting the dog. He swung it toward the Dogman.

Evans looked on from the side, bewildered, his own gun still pointing at Liz.

The Dogman held his weapon aimed squarely at Jones and the two men faced each other. 'You killed Rock,' said the Dogman. The words came slowly to Liz, like bubbles rising to the surface of the ocean.

Llewelyn nodded. 'I'll kill you too if I have to. Now drop your gun.'

The Dogman shook his head. 'I won't.'

Liz forced herself to slow to a halt. She breathed, resisting the overwhelming urge to lash out. To lash out at someone, anyone, and take their life. The desire to suck blood was all consuming.

I must feed, whispered a voice in her head. *Let me feed.*

But she knew that voice well enough now. *Silence*! she

commanded it.

The Dogman was speaking again. 'You have to choose,' he told Jones. 'Kill her or kill me. There's no other choice. One of us must die.'

'No,' shouted Liz. 'No one has to die.'

She began to spin, whirling her leg out to catch the Dogman's gun with her foot. If she could disarm him, she could bring this confrontation to a halt. But before she impacted, Jones' gun fired again. The barrel jerked in his hand as it spat out a bullet, and a spent case jumped out. The Dogman's body began to crumple even before she caught him with her foot. Blood splashed against her face like rain.

She brought herself to shocked stillness.

The Dogman fell in front of her, his gun sliding to the ground. His eyes registered surprise.

Liz remained motionless, watching as the man died. It took all her willpower to resist the compulsion to fall on him and suck the blood from his dying body.

She breathed deeply and forced herself to return to human form. Her body hungered for blood, but she denied herself the craving. She emerged gasping for breath, exhausted by her brief spell in vampire form. Her limbs felt suddenly drained, and she bent over, breathless. Her energy was spent, and she dropped to her knees.

Before her, the Dogman's eyes dimmed and closed, and Liz knew that he was dead, just like his dog.

Jones lowered his gun, but Evans still held his. He shifted aim between the Corporal and Liz, then back again, not knowing which to fear most.

Jones spoke to him calmly. 'Shoot me if you must,' he said. 'But I did what I had to do. The Dogman forced my hand. It was like he said, someone had to die.'

Hesitatingly, Evans lowered his gun. 'Then I hope you made the right choice.'

Jones looked to Liz. 'Did I?'

'You did,' she said, 'and I'll prove it to you. But I'll

need your help.'

Chapter Sixty-Six

Glastonbury Tor, Somerset, full moon

Rose sat cross-legged close to the fire, Nutmeg lying with her head in her lap, watching as the flames flickered, sending sparks soaring high into the darkening sky. The others sat around the fire, Seth stretched out on the ground, his ankle badly swollen.

Against Chris' advice, Josh had ordered Rose and Ryan to collect firewood and build the biggest bonfire they could manage. They had piled the wood inside the ruined stone tower at the highest point of the flat-topped Tor. The roofless stump of the church made a natural chimney, and black smoke twisted up inside its walls. A cool breeze rushed in from the open doorways of the tower to feed the flames, and shadows danced inside the old stone walls.

'Burn, baby, burn!' said Josh, rubbing his hands together as the clear, starry night unfurled and the warmth of the day gave way to a crisp chill wind. 'You can see for miles from up here, can't you?'

Rose looked out through one of the open stone arches. The countryside was fading to grey now, but before the evening had closed in, it had been possible to see for many miles in every direction. Chris had been right. Anyone within a large area would know they were here, right at the top of the hill, completely exposed. There was no point arguing with Josh, however. It would only end with someone getting hurt, and Rose was tired of that.

'Hey,' he said to her. 'You should grab a beer.'

She shook her head. 'I don't –'

He cut her off. 'Yeah, yeah, you don't drink, I know. Boring. Well tonight, you're going to drink. In fact, you're going to do whatever I tell you. Got it?'

She looked away.

'Fetch the girl a beer, Brittany!'

Brittany lobbed a stick into the fire, sending more sparks flying. 'She can fucking fetch one herself. I'm not her maid.'

Josh jumped to his feet and strode over to where his girlfriend was sitting. He seized her roughly by the arm and jerked her to her feet. 'That's not very accommodating. You have to learn to be nicer to our guests.' He shoved her toward the stash of beer cans and she reluctantly grabbed one.

'Here,' she said to Rose, passing her the can.

As Rose took it from her, Brittany reached out, raking Rose's arm with her long fingernails. 'Oh, sorry,' she said. She bent low and whispered in Rose's ear. 'That's just a taste of what you're going to get if you make any moves on Josh. I've seen the way he looks at you, you dirty little slut.'

Rose rubbed at her arm and put the beer can beside her, unopened.

Brittany returned to her place and Josh seemed not to have noticed anything. He was all smiles. 'So, big night tonight, Chris. Anyone know what time the moon rises?'

'It will be in about an hour,' said Chris. 'Every day it rises approximately half an hour later than the day before.'

'Is that right?' said Josh. 'You know what, Chris? I really hope you don't turn into a wolf, because you are such a well-informed dude. In fact, if you're not a werewolf, I think we're going to keep you with us. I don't know how we'd manage without you.'

'Hey,' said Ryan, 'You promised that if Chris and Seth don't turn into werewolves, then they're free to go.'

'*If* they don't turn? You're not sounding as confident as you were earlier, Ryan, mate.'

'*When* they don't turn,' said Ryan firmly. 'You said we'll all be free to go to Hereford.'

'I did. Are you saying I'm not a man of my word?'

'No. But now you're saying that you might keep us here.'

'Well, perhaps I can find a way to persuade you. It's certainly been a lot of fun having you guys around. Isn't that right, Brittany?'

Brittany said nothing, just hugged herself tight with her thin arms.

Josh threw an empty can in her direction. 'Am I the only one having any fun around here?' he asked, standing up. 'This is supposed to be the party to end all parties. Come on, let's drink, let's make some music!'

The flute player began to play an upbeat folk tune.

Josh stamped his foot. 'That's what I'm talking about. Let's dance!' He grabbed Rose by the hand and pulled her up. 'You do know how to dance, don't you?'

Across the fire, Brittany's face turned as dark as her eye shadow and she glared at Rose.

'I don't want to dance,' said Rose, drawing away from him.

'Yeah?' said Josh angrily. He pulled her back. 'Well perhaps you don't have any choice. Perhaps you have to do exactly what I fucking tell you.'

Ryan rose to his feet. 'You leave her alone! Don't you dare touch her.'

Josh's face was almost black with anger. 'No one tells

me what to do, Ryan. I give the orders around here. You are very slow to catch on. I think you need to be taught a very serious lesson.'

Two of Josh's friends jumped up and grabbed hold of Ryan. They seized his arms and twisted them behind his back.

But Ryan was stronger than them. He wrenched himself free and threw one of his assailants to the ground. The other lunged at him again, but Ryan pushed him away. He turned to Josh. 'Seriously, I'm warning you. You let go of Rose, right now.'

Josh shoved Rose onto the ground, and she drew back into a corner of the building, where Nutmeg came to her, licking her face. She wrapped her arms around the dog's neck and looked on anxiously.

Ryan stood defiantly, his muscles flexing, the firelight glinting in his eyes. He was ready to fight for her.

Josh picked his heavy wooden stick from the ground. 'Come on, then, Ryan. You come over here and fight me, just the two of us, man to man.'

'No, Ryan!' called Rose. 'Stay back! He'll hurt you.'

Ryan stood his ground, sizing up Josh, his big hands screwed into tight balls. He stood an inch taller than Josh and was easily the stronger man. He didn't look too much bothered by Josh's stick. 'All right. If I have to.' He closed in on Josh, his fists raised, his shoulders weaving, ready to dodge blows from the stick.

But Rose had seen Josh's plan. 'Look out!' she cried to Ryan. 'Behind you!'

He turned too slowly. The flute player had launched himself at Ryan from behind and delivered a flying kick to the back of his knee.

Ryan's leg crumpled and he went down. Cackling with laughter, Josh dashed forward and caught him a direct blow on the chin with the end of his stick. Ryan's head snapped sharply back.

Rose screamed.

'Pick him off the ground,' commanded Josh, whirling the long stick between his hands.

Josh's friends hauled Ryan up onto his knees. His face was covered in blood. Josh lunged forward and struck him again with the stick, this time in the middle of the forehead. Ryan keeled over to one side. Josh swung again and delivered a sharp jab to his stomach. Ryan curled into a ball.

Each blow of the stick made Rose cry out. She struggled to her feet and flew at Josh, but he was too big for her and pushed her back to the ground.

Ryan grunted but made no move to get back up.

Josh laughed. 'Your white knight seems to have fallen off his horse, Rose.' He turned back to his friends. 'Tie him up! Tie him to Chris, I want them both bound up together.'

He grabbed hold of Rose and held her as Ryan was bound with rope, and tied back to back against Chris. Seth looked on helplessly from his stretcher.

Josh raised his arm and pointed to each of them in turn. 'If any of you three try to move, I swear I'll throw you into the fire.' He spun around and fixed a smile back onto his face. 'Now, where were we? Ah, yes, Rose, it's time for you and me to dance.'

Chapter Sixty-Seven

Stoke Park, Buckinghamshire, full moon

General Canning crept forward through the darkened trees, his troops fanning out behind him, taking up their positions around the camp. He had rehearsed the plan with them over and over again. Iron discipline and training. That's what the first Wolf Army had lacked. Under Warg Daddy's command, the werewolves had been little more than a loose rabble of resistance fighters, reliant on luck as much as tactics. There had been no overall strategy, other than to seed chaos and to capture weapons. Senseless killing had become an end in itself.

Those days were over. Canning had rebuilt his new Wolf Army into a closely-knit fighting unit. Leanna had urged him to mount a full-scale assault on the western evacuation camp at Stoke Park, but he had resisted until the time was right. Now he was ready, and the attack could begin.

It was true that his troops were small in number, and not as well armed as the surviving human army. But their enemy was perilously weak after months of siege warfare. Besides, Canning had a secret weapon, one that he would deploy ruthlessly.

He waved his soldiers on, and they advanced silently toward the perimeter fence of the camp, dressed in dark clothing, their faces blackened. They would be invisible until the moon rose, and then it would be too late. The attack would already have begun.

The genius of his plan? It didn't matter that his army was outnumbered, and that the humans were better equipped. When the moon rose, none of that would count. His spies had assured him of that.

Aaron, the young man who Leanna had spared from death, had a talent for espionage and duplicity. Perhaps that was why he had lived, while his twelve fellow scouts had perished in the forest. Canning had recognized his skills early, and had made him his spymaster. Aaron had brought him very interesting news from within Stoke Park.

It had been very easy to infiltrate the camp. The soldiers were blinkered in their thinking. They expected an attack at night from armed insurgents, or ravening wolves, not a young man walking openly among them. Once inside the fence – a simple task for a werewolf – Aaron and his other spies had been free to go wherever they pleased, and Canning knew everything about the camp – numbers of civilians and soldiers, deployment of troops, locations of fixed defences, types of armaments in use. He was looking forward to acquiring those weapons, especially the heavy armour that would be critical for advancing his campaign to the next level. He had already planned how he would make best use of it in the battles to come.

And that was how he liked it. Knowledge – it really was power. It was the one lesson he had tried so hard to teach all his life.

His enemy, by contrast, knew almost nothing about the

threat they faced. They did not know the extent of his forces, or how he intended to use them. They did not know the timing of tonight's attack, or even whether an attack would come. And they certainly could not know the one key fact that would guarantee his victory – that half of his soldiers were already inside the camp's fence. Miraculously, it was the humans themselves who had created a new generation of werewolves for him to command.

A hooting owl sounded through the trees and Canning smiled. It was the signal for his army to attack. Inside the camp, the fighting had already begun.

Chapter Sixty-Eight

Somerset Levels, Somerset, full moon

It had been a wonderful, mad mystery tour, taking Warg Daddy and his Brothers up the length and breadth of the country. Sometimes luck had been with him, and the coin had commanded him to kill. Other times, his fate had been to drive on and allow his victims to live. It mattered not to him. Whatever the gods decided, he was happy to obey.

The Brothers were becoming restless however. They were beginning to question his leadership style. They didn't always agree with the decisions of the coin. They longed for the hunt, and the thrill of the chase. Their bellies hungered for meat, and the satisfaction of the kill.

Sometimes he had given it to them. They had murdered their way through the Midlands, butchered near Birmingham, slaughtered in Shrewsbury and tortured their victims in Taunton. Happy days.

But there had been tricky times, like the day he'd made

them release a schoolteacher and her charge of young innocents sheltering in a Devon farmhouse. The coin had commanded him to spare them, and Slasher and Bloodbath had come close to challenging him. There'd been trouble, and he'd had to flex some muscle to keep it from spreading. Slasher still had a black eye to show for it. Bloodbath's nose would never look the same again.

'Why do it?' Vixen asked him afterwards. 'Why choose to spare those people? It would have been easier just to kill the kiddies.'

'Destiny.' It was the only answer that made sense to him anymore.

Just as long as he obeyed the gods, the ghosts that haunted him stayed quiet. And the pain in his skull? It was manageable, especially at night. During the day, not so much. The sun was growing stronger as the year went on. The dark days of winter were long gone. Soon it would be summer. But he didn't know if he would live long enough to see it. No one did.

'We cannot know our fate,' he told Vixen. 'Except by the coin. We must discover it, one throw at a time.'

Why was that so hard for his followers to understand?

When they next came to a fork in the road, he called the Brothers to a halt. They knew the routine by now.

'What are the choices?' demanded Warg Daddy.

'City of Bath,' read Slasher from the road sign. 'Roman baths. World heritage site.'

'Cheddar Gorge,' read Bloodbath. 'Explore Britain's biggest gorge.'

It was not an easy choice. Warg Daddy was glad he didn't have to make it. Instead he flipped the coin. As usual, the gods had no difficulty deciding. 'Cheddar Gorge,' he announced.

They drove on through the English countryside, dusk gathering around them, Warg Daddy pushing his bike to the limit. After all, destiny was waiting just around the next corner. It waited around every corner. The Brothers flew behind him, hoping for good fortune tonight.

After a while he stopped before another road junction.

'Salisbury,' read Bloodbath. 'Cathedral city.'

'Glastonbury,' read Meathook. 'Historic town.'

The coin was a golden blur against the indigo sky. 'Tails again,' said Warg Daddy. 'We ride to Glastonbury.'

He was glad he no longer bore the weight of choosing their destination. But he hoped that the gods had made a good decision this time. He'd had a run of bad luck, and the Brothers were growing hungry. They must have their blood, and soon, or there would be big trouble. He might blame the gods, but he knew that the Brothers would hold him responsible.

The road was straight and his bike was keen. It devoured the distance like the Brothers dreamed of devouring their next victims. The miles vanished beneath him as the sky grew darker. Twilight descended and the first stars emerged, glittering like pinpricks in the celestial sphere – tiny windows to the land of the gods. He had a good feeling about tonight. Did luck have a smell? If so, he could almost sniff it.

Glastonbury. He had been here before. Long years ago on a summer night. He had been young and carefree, back in the old days, before the choices and the bad decisions. His mind had been restful then, and there had been nothing to think of except the next beer, and the next spliff, and the next shag. There had never been a shortage of any of those. It was hard to imagine why he had ever chosen to leave that simple world behind.

In the distance, a single light flickered against the lowering sky. He slowed his bike to a crawl and then a halt. The far-off light on the hilltop was the colour of fire. It was just a dot from here, but already he felt its heat, watched it dance and sway like a will-o-wisp calling across the marshy flats.

Vixen leaned forward to whisper in his ear. 'What is it? What do you see?'

He could hear the eagerness in her voice. He revved his engine hard in reply. 'Destiny,' he told her. 'We have finally found it.'

Chapter Sixty-Nine

Gatwick Airport, West Sussex, full moon

The black cat, Shadow, had escaped onto the roof of the hotel and was refusing to come down. 'Can you lure it back?' Liz asked the boys.

Vijay looked doubtful.

'Is hard to catch,' said Mihai. 'Very fast. Sharp claws.'

'I can catch Shadow,' said Drake confidently 'I'll open a can of tuna. That ought to work.'

'Good,' said Liz. 'You get the cat. I'll wait here. I don't want to frighten it away.'

'What's going to happen then?' asked Vijay.

'Then we're going to catch the vampire at last.'

Liz had already asked Corporal Jones and Evans to bring Major Hall to the hotel. She was counting that the promise of revealing the identity of the murderer would be enough to persuade the Major to come. Llewelyn would insist that all of Major Hall's men come to the hotel with him. One of them was the vampire, and the cat would know which one. She hoped that a hissing cat would be sufficient proof for the Major. If he lived up to his zero-tolerance rhetoric, it ought to be enough to persuade him, even if the murderer turned out to be one of his own officers.

She hoped that it would also be enough to satisfy Llewelyn and Evans too. For Liz, convincing Llewelyn of her innocence was even more important than bringing the criminal to justice. He had shown faith in her by shooting the Dogman, but she needed to deliver hard evidence. She had to prove he'd made the right choice.

She watched as the boys, together with Aasha, rushed off eagerly to the rooftop. She had to admit that they had shown real bravery with their late-night vampire hunting. They deserved credit for showing initiative. Without their help, she would still be a long way from solving the crime.

'You sure this plan's gonna work?' asked Kevin.

'No. But it's my best shot.' She was aware that Kevin had played his part in getting them to this point too. Not that she was going to admit that to him.

'Come on,' she said. 'Let's go down to the foyer and wait for Major Hall to arrive.'

They had to wait a while, but eventually the Major appeared, striding briskly up to the hotel's main entrance. Corporal Jones and Evans accompanied him, and she was relieved to see that he'd brought his entire entourage of Parachute Regiment officers with him. She counted them as they entered the lobby. They numbered fourteen, including the Major.

He smiled thinly when he saw her. 'Constable Bailey. I understand that you have a criminal for me.'

'That's right, Major. Please would you follow me up to the rooftop?'

'The rooftop?'

'It'll become obvious when we get there. Please, just follow me.' Liz glanced at Llewelyn, who gave her a wink in return.

'Are all your officers here today?' she asked Major Hall.

'My most senior officers are here, yes. Is that important?'

'I believe so.'

By the time they reached the door that led onto the rooftop, Liz was beginning to have doubts about the wisdom of this exercise. So many things could go wrong. Major Hall might refuse to believe her story. The vampire might somehow have avoided coming. The cat might not perform as expected. Or perhaps the boys wouldn't even have been able to catch it.

But when she stepped out onto the flat roof, she breathed a sigh of relief. Drake stood with Shadow in his arms, the black cat purring contentedly as Mihai fed it slivers of tuna fish. Vijay and Aasha looked on.

The cat looked up at her with its green eyes, and she was suddenly gripped by a fresh fear. What if the cat hissed at her? Major Hall must never discover that she was a vampire too. She stepped to one side to allow the Major and his men to walk out onto the roof. Kevin stood next to her nonchalantly, his hands in his pockets.

'What is going on here?' Major Hall's voice expressed deep irritation. He stood tall, his hands clasped firmly behind his back, his aviator sunglasses hiding his eyes. 'Some children? A cat? Constable Bailey, is this your idea of a joke?'

'No, I assure you, there's no joke here. This cat is going to identify the serial killer.' She pressed on quickly, aware of how ridiculous that must sound. 'Drake, can you bring Shadow over to the men?'

The cat gazed at her suspiciously, distracted from its fishy meal. Drake carried it toward the first of the soldiers, standing to Liz's left.

The effect was instantaneous and dramatic. The cat jumped down from Drake's hold, landing neatly on the rooftop. Immediately it arched its back and began to hiss at the first officer, a lieutenant.

Liz was startled to achieve such an immediate result. 'Major Hall,' she said quickly, 'arrest that man. He's the killer. I'll explain to you afterwards how I know.'

But the Major made no move to arrest anyone. Instead he watched as the cat slowly turned and pawed its way toward the second officer in the line. This time it hissed even more loudly, every hair on its back standing tall.

'This cat seems very quick to make accusations,' said Major Hall dryly. 'Is that man also a murderer?'

'I don't understand,' said Liz.

She watched as the cat moved once again, now turning its attention to the third soldier in the group. It spat at him viciously and hissed ever louder.

The soldiers looked on in wry amusement.

Drake scooped the cat up in his arms and walked the animal along the line of men. It hissed at every single one, including Major Hall.

Understanding dawned gradually on Liz. They were all vampires, the Major and his men. Every single one.

Chapter Seventy

Stoke Park, Buckinghamshire, full moon

Melanie was driving Ben half-crazy, pacing the ground outside the tent and staring up at the sky impatiently. 'Where is Sarah?' she said. 'It's almost dark now.' She spun on the heel of her boot and marched back toward him.

Exasperated, he grabbed her by the shoulders and stopped her in her tracks. 'For goodness' sake, Mel. She'll be back soon.'

His words did nothing to placate her. 'She ought to be back already,' she insisted.

Ben sighed. He could understand why Melanie was so worried for her sister. Sarah's working day should have finished some hours ago and she had promised to return to the tent by early evening. The full moon would rise tonight and it would be the first real test of the cure that Sarah, James and the doctor, Helen Eastgate, had devised.

Ben had to admit that he was nervous too. He wasn't

alone. Levels of uneasiness within the camp had been growing steadily throughout the day. Now you could almost taste the scent of fear in the cool, evening air. 'Okay,' he said. 'We'll go and look for her. Let me fetch my coat.'

He didn't really need his coat in this mild weather, but it helped to mask the body odour that clung to his shirt and undergarments. Like most other people in the camp, he had not been able to bathe or shower, or wash his clothes properly, in weeks. Some folk had taken to washing in the ornamental lake of the hotel grounds, but with the lake being used for drinking water, that had been discouraged by the authorities. Melanie's solution to the problem was *eau de parfum*. Like him, she was still dressed in the clothes she had been wearing when she left London – red leather jacket, black jeans and black boots. She had lost weight in recent weeks, and the jacket now hung loosely on her slender frame. They had all shed a few pounds. Yet somehow Melanie managed to look more beautiful than ever, her black hair silhouetting her pale skin, her high cheekbones even more pronounced than usual.

Her temper, however, had not been improved by weeks of living under rationing, in a small tent, in close proximity to unwashed bodies. 'Come on,' she snapped, taking him by the hand. 'I'm done with waiting. Let's go.'

'What if we miss her, and she finds the tent empty when she returns?' he asked.

'Then she can wait for us in the tent. She's not an imbecile.'

Sarah certainly was no fool. Ben wondered if half the reason for Melanie's concern was that Sarah no longer seemed to need her in the way she had used to. Since becoming Helen Eastgate's assistant, Sarah had grown hugely in confidence and independence. She was almost unrecognizable from the timid, terrified woman she had been when they'd first arrived at the camp. Ben was delighted at how well Sarah had overcome her phobia, but Melanie seemed less willing to accept the changed dynamics between her and her sister.

'Just because she doesn't need you so much, it doesn't mean you're not important to her anymore,' he said to Melanie.

'I never imagined that I wasn't,' she replied. 'That's not what this is about.'

'Isn't it?'

She stopped and whirled to face him. 'In case you hadn't noticed, the full moon is due to rise any time now, and Sarah is still with those creatures.'

'You mean creatures like James?'

'I do *not* mean like James. I mean a whole new generation of werewolves that are a complete wildcard. Who knows what they might do?'

They had discussed this many times before. Sarah had argued so passionately in favour of using James' blood to treat the sick patients that Melanie had finally agreed to support the project and put her doubts to one side. They had spent days parading around the camp, telling anyone who would listen that James was harmless. They had agreed not to mention the inconvenient occasions when he had ripped out people's throats and devoured their flesh. 'He doesn't do that now,' Sarah had insisted. 'That's all in the past, Melanie. Imagine if I told everyone about the mistakes you'd made, growing up.'

'I sometimes wonder if Sarah actually wants them to turn into full-blown werewolves,' said Melanie. 'Perhaps that's why she hasn't come home this evening. She's decided to stay and watch them turn. You know she has a secret death wish.'

'She does not,' said Ben. 'That's an absurd thing to say.'

'Is it? You don't know her as well as I do. She's always had dark thoughts, ever since childhood. You can't imagine what she's thinking underneath that innocent exterior.'

'Sometimes, Melanie, I can't imagine what you're thinking.'

'What I'm thinking right now,' she told him, stressing each word, 'is that we need to hurry up and find her before anything bad happens. Is that a difficult concept to grasp?' She broke off her scowling and gave him a sweet smile, reaching out to take hold of his hand. 'Come on, you know you always agree with me in the end.'

He flashed her a grin. 'All right. I'm coming.'

The moon was almost peeping above the treeline as they made their way across the camp. Its white light already touched the night sky with a cool sheen. The air was still and quiet, as if the entire camp was holding its breath, waiting to see what would unfold. Ben quickened his pace, seized by a sense of foreboding.

They had almost reached the hotel itself when the shouting began. Inside the building, it sounded like all hell was being let loose. Melanie shot him an *I told you so* look, and dragged him inside.

The reception area of the hotel was as luxurious as the dining rooms and private areas, despite the military presence. Marble pillars, gilt-framed mirrors and crystal chandeliers made an opulent background to the chaotic scene that was now playing out. The hallway was full of activity, with armed soldiers rushing back and forth. A team of four heavily-armed infantrymen had taken up position in front of the double doors that led to the ballroom. The guard who should have been on duty at the entrance had abandoned his post to join them, allowing Ben and Melanie to enter without hindrance.

They watched, taking in the scene, as screams erupted from behind the polished wooden doors. 'Charlie Fireteam, watch and shoot,' ordered the team commander. The doors burst open and wolves rushed through, surging into the plush hallway, snarling and biting at the troops stationed there.

Automatic rifles opened fire, tearing into furry bodies,

spattering blood and bringing beasts crashing to the ground. But the wolves had numbers and crashed through the defensive fire, slashing at the soldiers and biting deep into their necks. The first group of soldiers went down in seconds.

Ben grabbed Melanie and dragged her through an open doorway. He slammed it shut behind them. Back in the hallway, on the other side of the door, more shots rang out, but they were single shots or quick bursts, few in number and didn't last long. A savage howl and shriek brought the attack to a quick end.

'It's the patients,' said Melanie. 'They've turned.'

Ben raised his finger to his lips and drew her away from the door. They were in a smaller reception room, perhaps once a sitting room or a lounge. Now all the furniture had been removed, and the carpet lifted to reveal a bare wooden floor. They tiptoed across it to the exit opposite.

He put his ear to the door and listened carefully. Shouts, gunshots and howls came from outside the building, and from other parts of the hotel, including the upstairs rooms where many of the patients treated with James' blood had been housed, but the room beyond was silent. He turned the handle and pushed the door open.

The large space beyond must once have been the hotel's main dining room. It had been converted to an operations room by the army. Desks were arranged in rows and groups, each one brimming with hastily rigged-up telephones, computer terminals and paperwork. Half of the desks and chairs were overturned on the floor, and bodies lay where they had fallen – a mix of soldiers, civilians and wolves. Nearby a man groaned.

Ben hurried over to him. The man was an officer, wearing air force uniform. He was badly injured from a bite to the side of his neck, and held his hand to the wound, attempting to staunch the flow of blood.

Ben pulled a jacket from the back of a nearby chair and wrapped it around the officer's neck, to help slow the bleeding. 'What happened?' he asked, cradling the man's head in his hands.

The wounded man was displaying clear signs of a severe anaphylactic reaction. His forehead was clammy and bright with sweat. He struggled to speak, his voice rasping and coming between shallow gasps. 'The patients … the lycanthropes … some of them … some of them have turned.'

'How many?' asked Ben.

The man closed his eyes, then forced them open again with obvious difficulty. 'The camp … the attack … the others …'

'What others?' asked Ben.

The man's voice grew weaker. 'They chose … even before the moon … they chose …' His eyes closed again, and he grew still.

Ben let him go.

'We just need to find Sarah and James and get them out,' said Melanie. 'Nothing else matters now.'

Ben nodded. She was right. This was not the time to save the world. If they could save two people, it would be enough.

'Come on,' he said, pulling her behind him. 'Stay close. Don't do anything rash.'

Chapter Seventy-One

Glastonbury Tor, Somerset, full moon

Josh dragged Rose away from the fire and out of the ruined church onto the open hilltop. It was fully dark now and the cool evening breeze had settled, making the night still and crisp. The hot flames behind them cast moving shadows far across the flat hilltop. In the distance, a milky white line on the horizon promised that the moon would soon rise.

Back inside the tower, the flute player had started up a tune once more. 'Oh, yeah, what a beautiful night,' said Josh. 'Just you, me, the music.'

Rose tried to resist, but he was too strong. He laughed as she tried to wrestle free of him.

Nutmeg appeared and jumped up at him, snapping her jaws and barking.

'Ow, that fucking dog!' cried Josh. He gave Nutmeg a quick kick and she yelped, leaving off her attack and giving a low growl.

Rose scratched at Josh's arm with her fingernails, just like Brittany had scratched her, but he gave her a hard slap on the face.

'Don't you fucking try that again. I'll tell you what, Rose, you'd better do just what I tell you, or else I'll kill your dog and serve her as a midnight feast.'

Rose stopped struggling. She didn't doubt that Josh would do just that. 'Run away, girl!' she called to Nutmeg. 'Go on, run!'

The dog cocked her head to one side, puzzled, but then seemed to understand. She disappeared down the side of the hill, limping slightly, and was gone.

'Yeah,' said Josh, 'That's better. What was I saying? You, me, the music. Let's dance!'

He started to jerk her arms in time to the music, wrapping one strong arm around her waist and drawing her close. She felt his body push up against hers, but was powerless to force him away. A sense of panic was building in her, but she fought against it. She thought of all the terrors she had known – the biker gang slaughtering dogs in the kennels where she had worked, the huge black wolf that had nearly killed her on the night of New Year's Eve, and the horror of Mr Canning strangling her brother, Oscar, in his wheelchair. Once, those memories had held a terrible power over her, making her weak, rendering her almost incapable of action. Now they made her strong, for she knew that whatever kind of monster Josh was, he was not a literal monster of the kind she had already faced.

And though she had the body of a weak girl, inside she had a core of steel.

She couldn't push him away, so instead she tried to distract him. 'The moon will be rising soon. Don't you want to see what happens to Chris?'

Josh shook his head. 'Not really. You know, I never really thought he was a werewolf. I was just having some fun. To tell you the truth, I'm still not sure I really believe in werewolves.'

'What? How can you not?'

'Yeah, I know that they were all over the news and everything, but I've never actually seen one for real. You ever seen one?'

'Yes.'

'Whoa! Really? What was it like? Scary?'

She nodded.

'Tell me about it.'

'No.'

'Too frightening to talk about? Yeah, I totally get that.' He brushed the long hair from her eyes. 'I guess we all have some things we can't talk about. Things that happened to us that made us the way we are. It's hard to talk about some of those things, isn't it?'

Rose shivered. If Josh was going to start telling her some sob story in an attempt to justify his behaviour, she didn't want to hear it.

'You cold, babes?' he said, wrapping his arms around her. 'Come on, let's walk a little so we can have some privacy.' He began to lead her away from the tower. She struggled, but he pushed her on relentlessly. 'There's no use pretending you don't want me, Rose. I've seen the way you look at me.'

'I don't want you,' she said. 'I hate you.'

His eyes flared with anger, then he recovered himself. 'Playing it that way, eh? That's cool. I can work with that. But whatever you say, I know what you really want. I can see it in your eyes. I can feel your body language. You've had the hots for me ever since you first saw me. I'm like that with girls, you know? Brittany was the same. Couldn't wait to get her clothes off, the minute she laid eyes on me.'

'You make me sick,' said Rose. 'You –'

The sound of an engine came to her then across the still air. The faint roar of a motorbike. More than one.

Josh had heard it too. 'Now who the fuck can that be?'

The noise of the engines grew quickly louder. They were coming closer. Josh spun around, searching for the approaching bikes. But the night was dark in all directions.

On three of its sides, the Tor was too steep for a bike to climb, but in the fourth direction, the way they had come now, the slope was gentler. A rough track led up from the lower ground to the top. That must be the way the bikes were coming. Rose peered into the darkness, straining to see. As she looked, the beams of headlamps began to come into view beyond the lip of the hill. They grew dazzlingly bright as they approached. Soon there were too many to count. Tyres scrunched on gravel as the bikes ascended the path up the hillside.

Josh raised his hand to shield his eyes as the bikes came up to them. Their engines were now a deafening throaty roar, drowning out all other sounds. The beams of their headlights were blinding.

'Fucking hell,' said Josh. 'Where did these guys come from?'

The first of the bikes pulled to a halt before them. Rose couldn't see its rider behind the harsh glare of the headlight. The other bikes stopped behind the first, picking out a dark silhouette of the lead rider. The man sat astride his bike, hugely built, like a bull, unmoving, saying nothing.

Rose's flesh began to creep. She knew this man. She had seen the bikers before. The Wolf Brothers, they called themselves, and she knew what they were capable of. Back in London, in the kennels where she had helped look after peoples' dogs, she had seen them go about their devilish work. Her legs began to quiver.

Josh relaxed his grip on her. 'Hey there, friends!' he shouted. 'Welcome to the party! Why don't you guys ride on up to the tower? You can share our beer.'

The only answer was the growl of the motorbikes.

The lead rider killed his engine and switched off his headlamp.

Now Rose could see him better. The muscular form, the black leather jacket, the dark glasses behind a black helmet. She knew that a white wolf was picked out on the back of that jacket. She knew that the head beneath that helmet was perfectly smooth, like a billiard ball. She knew that the man who rode that bike was a beast.

The rider dismounted his bike. His passenger, a woman also wearing black leather, followed him. The rest of the biker gang switched off their engines and clustered round their leader. Some of them had rifles or shotguns strapped to their backs. Some of them carried baseball bats.

Josh was looking nervous now. 'Hey, guys! How's it going?'

The leader of the gang removed his helmet, revealing the bald head and black hairy face that Rose knew so well from her dreams. The wolf tattoo on his neck was just as she remembered. Every detail of his face was imprinted on her mind. He rubbed his shiny head with one huge thumb. 'I know you,' he said to her. 'I remember you.'

She nodded, too terrified to speak.

'You know this guy?' asked Josh, astonished. 'Wow, that's amazing.' He offered his hand to the biker. 'I'm Josh.'

The man ignored him and rubbed his head again, making it squeak gently in the silent night. For a long while he said nothing. Josh lowered his arm.

'About the dogs,' said the man in black leather eventually.

Rose nodded. The biker gang had butchered the dogs at the kennels mercilessly, battering them with hammers, skewering them with knives. It had been senseless cruelty and she had been powerless to stop it. She waited for the man to say more.

'That was a mistake,' he rumbled. 'A bad decision. I'm sorry about that.'

'Dogs?' said Josh. 'Hey, is someone going to tell me what's going on here?'

The man in black leather turned to him, and slowly looked him up and down. 'Is this guy a friend of yours?' he asked Rose.

'No,' she whispered.

The biker stared hard at Josh for a full minute. 'Okay. Kill him,' he said.

Two of the other bikers came forward and seized hold of Josh before he could run.

'Hey guys, wait. Seriously,' said Josh. 'You're kidding, right?'

Rose turned away. Soon the night was split with the sound of Josh's screams.

Chapter Seventy-Two

Stoke Park, Buckinghamshire, full moon

Weapons were scattered between the corpses on the floor of the hotel dining room, and Ben picked one up. A pistol. What kind, he didn't know. He gripped it in his right hand, being careful to point the barrel at the floor.

Melanie grabbed one too.

'Do you know what to do with a gun?' he asked.

'Do you?'

'I've never used one before.'

'Me neither.' She aimed the weapon at the body of a dead wolf and pulled the trigger. The gun almost flew from her hand with the recoil, and the noise reverberated off the hard room's surfaces. 'Well, I have now,' she said.

'Why on earth did you do that?'

'Just checking how it works.'

'Well, be careful where you point it.'

A great thunderclap came from outside the building,

followed by a deep rumble. The sky glowed bright white, then red. The glass in the chandelier overhead tinkled as the whole room shook.

'What was that?' asked Melanie.

'An explosion. The camp must be under attack. Stay away from the windows.'

He ducked down himself and crept across the room toward the next exit. Melanie was right behind him.

'Sarah and James must still be inside the building somewhere,' she whispered.

'I think the doctor's lab is this way.' He listened carefully at the door, but couldn't hear anything. 'Ready?'

Melanie raised her gun. 'For anything.'

He yanked the door handle and kicked the door open with his foot. The room beyond was another large dining area, this one converted into crude medical facilities. Low beds were lined against one wall, with medical apparatus stationed alongside each one. He took a good look up and down. The beds were all empty.

'This must have been where they were treating the patients,' said Melanie. 'It looks like they all turned.'

Ben nodded grimly. The floor was littered with the bodies of doctors and nurses. They lay in pools of blood, body parts missing, arms and legs ripped off. Dead soldiers and civilians were mixed in with the carnage, together with one or two dead wolves.

He crept inside the room. A low growl greeted him from the nearby corner. An injured wolf lay sprawled on the floor, blood running from a wound in its side. It rose up onto its front legs as it saw him, its claws clacking on the hard floor. It snarled.

Ben froze. The sheer size of the beast was horrific. Bigger than any dog he had ever seen, the creature's body was taut with muscle and raw strength. It parted its jaws to reveal deadly canine teeth, and its eyes glowed bright in the semi-darkness, like yellow candles. Even in its injured state, it seemed to radiate hate and a lust for violence.

Three shots rang out in quick succession, and the creature fell, the light in its eyes going out as it crumpled.

Melanie put a hand on his shoulder. 'You hesitated,' she said, the gun in her hand. 'If you wait for one of those things to attack, you'll end up dead.'

Ben shook himself together. She was absolutely right. Fear had frozen him, and if it hadn't been for her, he might easily have been killed, even by a wounded creature. He had to do better than that next time. He was supposed to be protecting her. 'I'm sorry. I won't hesitate again.'

He scanned the room for movement, but there were no other signs of life. There was plenty of noise though. In the camp outside, a full-scale battle was raging, with the sound of heavy machine gun fire, armoured vehicles on the move, and distant explosions. Wolf howls and sporadic gun shots still sounded from within the building itself.

Melanie pushed past him toward the next door. 'Come on. There's no time to lose.'

The door led into a corridor running along one side of the building. Through the windows on one side Ben could see the bright flashes of combat. In the darkness it was impossible to make any sense of what was happening out there, but it was clear that the camp had descended into anarchy. If there were wolves loose inside the fence, and perhaps more attacking from outside, then large-scale carnage was a certain outcome.

'The doctor's lab is just along here,' said Melanie, leading the way down the corridor.

A door ahead of them opened suddenly and a woman staggered through. She was elderly, with short grey hair, and wore a white nightdress. She stopped in the corridor when she saw Melanie and Ben. 'I'm hurt,' she said in a frail voice. 'Please, I need your help.'

'Stop!' shouted Melanie, taking aim with her gun. 'Don't move a muscle!'

The old woman lifted her arms cautiously in submission. 'Put that down, dear. Don't point that thing at me. You're scaring me.'

Ben laid a hand on Melanie's arm. 'What are you doing? Don't point the gun at her. She's just one of the patients. She hasn't turned into a wolf.'

'That's right,' the old woman said. 'I'll do you no harm.' She began to hobble down the corridor toward them.

'Stop!' shouted Melanie again. She turned her head to Ben. 'Can't you see? Look at the blood on her.'

He looked closer. The woman's nightdress was spattered with red drops and her chin was bleeding. Her eyes were wild and glinted yellow. 'I'm hurt! Please help me!' she cried, stumbling closer. She was almost on top of Melanie already, her hands reaching out with long nails. Ben looked again. Her fingernails dripped with fresh blood.

He raised his gun and pulled the trigger. The noise was deafening in the narrow corridor, and the strength of the recoil surprised him. But his aim was true. The old woman toppled forward with a desperate cry, clutching at her chest. She fell to the floor writhing, and Ben put a second bullet in her back. She lay still.

He turned her limp body over with his foot. She was dead, but her eyes remained open, still glowing yellow in the dim interior. Her sharp teeth were on display, and the blood that covered her chin and nightdress had clearly leaked from her mouth.

'Another patient,' said Ben. 'Not a wolf, but just as deadly. From now on, we treat everyone as an enemy, unless they can prove otherwise.'

Melanie nodded and pointed to the next door along the corridor. The sign read, *Doctor Helen Eastgate.* She took up position next to it, her gun ready.

Ben lifted his own gun in his right hand. With the other, he turned the handle and slowly pushed open the door.

Chapter Seventy-Three

Gatwick Airport, West Sussex, full moon

The moon was rising now and Liz felt the full force of its tug. The voice in her head began to whisper, inviting her to embrace the change and leave her weak human form behind. She shut the voice out and focussed instead on the rooftop scene.

'So, Constable Bailey, you finally arrived at the truth,' said Major Hall. 'I was wondering how long it would take you to get there. I was sure you would eventually, and I've been observing your progress with interest. But I must confess, that cat came as a complete surprise.'

'You and your officers are all vampires,' said Liz.

They were still in human form, even though the moon was rising. Like her, they had learned to master the transformation. They could use moonlight to power their change, but were not in thrall to it.

Major Hall raised an eyebrow and smiled. 'Vampires? Is that what you think we are? Well, I suppose that if those creatures out there are werewolves, then you might call us vampires. But I prefer to think of us more like guardian angels. Our need to feed is a small price to pay for my men protecting the camp from werewolves, and maintaining law and order.'

'You sick bastard,' said Kevin. 'You're no angels. You're devils. You're as bad as the werewolves, perhaps worse.'

The Major's face hardened. 'You couldn't be more wrong. Without us, this camp would have fallen weeks ago. How many civilians have been killed by werewolves under my protection? I'll tell you – not a single one. In fact, we've largely driven back the werewolves from a wide area around this camp. We're not devils, we're God-damn heroes.'

Liz's hand edged toward the Glock in her holster, but Major Hall's men had already drawn their guns.

'Don't even think about it,' said Major Hall. 'That goes for you too,' he said to Jones and Evans, who were holding their rifles. 'You are vastly outnumbered.'

Fourteen men, Liz had counted. Fourteen vampires. All of them armed with semi-automatic pistols. Too many for Jones and Evans to take on. Far too many for her to handle. And anyway, she couldn't risk the kids getting killed in the crossfire.

'Place your weapons on the ground,' ordered Major Hall. 'Move slowly.'

'Don't do it, Liz,' urged Kevin. 'Don't listen to him.'

'Why should we?' Liz asked the Major.

'I'll make you a promise,' he said. 'You may not like it. But once you consider it, you'll realize that it's the best I can offer. A clean kill. An execution. We're not going to hang you up with the others to have your blood drained. Nor will I feed you to those beasts outside the gates. You deserve better than that.'

Liz's hand was on the Glock. She knew she would never be able to draw it out quickly enough. If she even tried, they would all go down in a hail of bullets, and she wouldn't allow that to happen, especially not to Mihai and the others.

She licked her dry lips with her tongue. 'You have to let the children go free,' she said. 'Promise me that.'

Major Hall nodded crisply. 'You have my word.'

'Liz?' said Kevin. 'You can't let him do this.'

'What choice do we have?'

'We go down fighting!'

'They'll kill us all. And what will happen to the kids then?'

Kevin had no answer to that. 'You trust this Major Hall?' he asked.

Liz studied the face of the Major. She still hadn't seen his eyes behind the aviator sunglasses, but she felt that he was a man of his word. 'I trust him.'

'Blimey,' said Kevin. 'I'll tell you this, love. I ain't never trusted no man less.'

'We have no choice.'

She turned slowly to see what Corporal Jones and Evans made of the exchange. Jones stood motionless, seemingly frozen in place. There was a strange faraway look in his eyes, as if he was somewhere else entirely. He didn't return her questioning gaze. Evans stood beside him, his rifle in his hands, obviously uncertain. After a moment he nodded at Liz.

She breathed a sigh of relief. If another person could accept her decision, she could persuade herself she hadn't totally lost all reason. She looked to Llewelyn again for confirmation, but he was still gazing into the distance, seeming almost oblivious to what was happening.

She turned back to Major Hall. 'All right. It's a deal. We lay down our weapons and you allow the children to go free and unharmed.'

'Agreed.'

'No,' protested Vijay. 'You can't let them, Liz.'

'No way,' said Drake. 'We ain't gonna let them kill you.'

'You have to,' said Liz. 'Look after the others. Take care of Samantha and the baby. They're going to need you now.'

Mihai was almost in tears, his eyes shining in the twilight. He shook his head angrily and refused to meet her look.

But there was nothing more that Liz could do. She could go down fighting in a blaze of glory, like Kevin wanted, and lose everything. Or she could choose to save the lives of Mihai, Vijay, Aasha and Drake. If that was the choice, it was an easy one to make. She raised her hands in surrender.

Major Hall nodded to his men and they began to move out across the rooftop to take the weapons from Liz and the Welsh Guards.

The cat spat at them as they advanced, shifting in Drake's arms, struggling to break free.

'Easy, Shadow,' said Drake.

'Get rid of that odious creature,' snarled Major Hall. One of his officers, a captain, stepped forward, reaching out to take the cat.

'You're the one,' said Drake to the captain. 'You're the vampire I saw in the terminal building.'

The captain grinned, revealing a pair of sharp teeth.

Shadow hissed louder than ever. The cat flew from Drake's grasp and landed squarely on the captain's face with all four paws, digging deep with its claws. The man gave a howl of pain.

Then all hell broke loose.

Chapter Seventy-Four

Stoke Park, Buckinghamshire, full moon

The door to Helen's office swung open and Melanie looked inside. A small group of people was huddled in the room. Sarah and James, together with Doctor Helen Eastgate and Chanita Allen, the camp leader.

'Oh, thank God!' said Melanie. She dashed forward and embraced Sarah, hugging her sister tightly in her arms. Sarah hugged her back, somewhat reluctantly.

'You're safe,' said Melanie. 'Buy why are you crying?'

Dark tear tracks stained Sarah's face, and her eyes were red. 'It's all gone wrong. The patients turned into wolves.'

'Yeah. We noticed.'

'This should never have happened,' said Chanita. 'We were careful to keep the patients indoors, away from the moonlight.'

'They changed before the moonrise,' said Ben.

'They shouldn't have changed at all,' insisted Chanita. 'They should have been like James, able to choose whether to become werewolves, or to remain human.'

'They did,' said Melanie. 'They chose to become wolves.'

Helen Eastgate stood to one side of the others, her face pale. 'This is all my fault. I underestimated the risks. I assumed that the patients would be like James and would make the same choice that he has made. But James is the exception.'

Melanie bit her lip. *I told you so*, was on the tip of her tongue, but she kept it there, not giving voice to the thought. This was no time to start a row. There would be plenty of time for that later.

'I think this must somehow have been planned together with the werewolves outside the gates,' said Ben. 'The camp is under a coordinated attack from the patients within, and from armed werewolves outside too. We heard explosions coming from near the main entrance. The army is fighting back, but I don't know if they can cope.'

Sarah dissolved into fresh tears. 'I'm to blame. I convinced you to do it.'

'No,' said Helen, putting an arm around her. 'We did it together.'

'You certainly did,' said Melanie. 'But there's no time now for wallowing in self-pity.'

Chanita spoke then. 'We must trust Lieutenant Colonel Sharman to keep us safe. He and his men are well armed, and prepared for the worst.'

'But we don't know what size of enemy they're facing,' said Ben.

'There's no point in us worrying about that,' said Chanita. 'Even if the soldiers can't win, they will hold the werewolves off for as long as they can. We need to get out of here and join the other civilians in the camp. Someone needs to keep them in order and stop them from running scared. We may need to organize an evacuation.'

'No,' said Melanie firmly. She stepped into the middle of the room. It was time to put a stop to this nonsense, and talk sense into people. 'The wolves are everywhere. The soldiers don't stand a chance. If we join the others, we'll be like a flock of sheep waiting to be slaughtered. Our only chance of survival is to look after ourselves and get away from the camp as quickly as we can.'

Chanita met her gaze steadily. 'You must do as you wish, but I am responsible for the people of this camp. I won't leave them to die.'

'Whatever,' said Melanie. 'What about you others? Are you coming with me and Ben?'

Sarah gave a quick nod of her head. 'Of course. And James will come too. Helen?'

Helen looked undecided. 'I should stay with Chanita …'

A huge explosion blasted close by, shaking the walls of the building, and making plaster dust fall from the ceiling.

'We need to get out,' said Ben. 'Right now.'

'You'd be crazy to stay here,' Melanie told Helen and Chanita, 'but we don't have time to argue. Come with us, or stay, it's your choice.' She raised her gun and turned back through the door. The corridor was empty and she set off along it, not waiting to see who would follow. She knew that Ben and Sarah would come, and James too. What the others did was up to them. After all, they were responsible for getting them into this mess.

Ben caught up with her after a few seconds and put a hand on her shoulder. 'Stop. I know the quickest way out of this building. Hold this for a second.' He passed her his pistol and she held it while he unlocked a window and slid it open. He stuck his head outside and looked left and right. 'It's clear. Follow me.' He swung his legs through the open sash window and out.

Melanie waited for the others to climb out too. She was pleased to see that all four of them had come. As soon as they had climbed through, she joined them.

Outside all was chaotic. Fires and floodlights lit up the sky, and the full moon shone down over the scene too.

She glanced nervously at James, but the moon seemed to have no effect on him. Crowds of people were rushing in all directions, not to mention army vehicles, soldiers on foot, and the silhouetted figures of wolves running between them. Automatic gunfire bursts and single shots rang out almost continually, punctuated by occasional explosions from the direction of the camp boundary. It sounded like a minor war was in progress.

She turned to Ben. 'Which way?'

His face was creased in a deep frown. 'Stay right here for now,' he warned.

She turned where he was looking. A gang of men and women were coming toward them, shouting belligerently. They looked like a lynch mob. 'What the –' began Melanie, but the crowd quickly surrounded them, blocking any exit.

Chanita stepped forward to address them. 'What is the meaning of this?'

Voices from the crowd called out. 'You did this!' shouted one. 'This was your fault!' yelled another. They were pointing at Chanita and Helen. 'Werewolf lovers!' shouted a third voice.

A hand reached out and seized hold of Chanita by the hair, dragging her onto the ground.

Ben raised his gun into the air and fired a warning shot. 'Stop this! Get back!'

The crowd drew back a step and Chanita pulled herself free. But the baying mob was going nowhere. They quickly regathered their courage and began to shuffle forward again. 'There he is!' shouted a man, pointing at James. 'He's the one who started it.'

Melanie pushed her way in front of James and raised her own gun into the air. She fired off a shot, but this one had little effect on the crowd. If anything, it seemed to provoke them to greater fury.

A woman's voice cried out. 'Get them!' She looked perfectly normal, the kind of woman you'd see choosing organic coffee beans at the local wholefood store, or waiting for her kids outside their suburban school. But her features were contorted into rage. Her eyes blazed with violence.

There was nothing for it. Melanie aimed the pistol between the eyes of organic coffee woman and squeezed the trigger.

Nothing happened. She tried again, but she must have run out of ammo.

The woman's expression turned to triumph. She lunged forward and slapped Melanie's face.

Melanie fell back, more in shock than pain.

No one does that to me.

She dropped the useless gun and rushed her opponent, fingers ready to gouge, manicured nails eager to scratch. Organic coffee woman fell to the ground.

The invisible line that had kept the two sides apart vanished in an instant.

Everyone now was shouting and yelling; everyone was kicking and punching and wrestling. The opposing groups clashed with each other in a tangle of limbs and fists.

A shot went off behind her. Ben was shooting into the air again in a futile attempt to break up the fight. But both sides were well past that stage. The fighting moved up a gear.

Melanie dug her fingers into organic coffee woman's face, drawing blood as red as any nail varnish she had ever worn. The woman struggled to throw her off, but Melanie poked her in the eye and yanked at her hair to subdue her.

A sudden roar cut through the chaos. A roar like that of a lion. Melanie looked up as a flash of pale fur leapt into the melee.

James. He had turned.

He landed on his first victim and bit deep into their neck. A man, or a woman, Melanie couldn't see. But their body crumpled to the ground a second later.

Someone's knee caught Melanie in the side. She flailed out in response, drawing a long crimson scratch down a bare arm. A man screamed as James lunged at him, tearing him open with a savage bite. Helen gave a war cry and rushed into the fight, stabbing a man in the chest with some kind of medical implement. Even Chanita joined the battle, wrestling a young woman to the ground, and pinning her arms in place where they could do no harm.

Still the mob fought on, and others from nearby came to join them.

Ben fired his gun again, and this time the bullet found a target. A man dropped to the ground, dead. The gun blasted again, and again, and more people fell. But the next time, the gun clicked. Ben was also out of rounds.

The crowd began to thin as James jumped from one victim to the next, driving them back with tooth and claw, biting when necessary, slashing with his huge paws, roaring with deafening power. His paws and jaws were slick with blood.

Organic coffee woman broke suddenly free and punched Melanie square in the face. With a shriek, Melanie wrapped her hands around the woman's throat. She locked them together with all her strength, squeezing desperately as the woman choked, not caring what happened next. She was so past caring.

A hand grabbed her arm and hauled her roughly to her feet. Ben. 'Come on,' he shouted. 'We've bought some time. Let's get out of here.'

She nodded and followed him.

And then, as she began to move toward safety, she heard a deep roar from behind. A werewolf had appeared from nowhere – dark brown fur, flashing yellow eyes, and a jaw filled with deadly teeth. The creature ran toward Helen and leapt at her, reaching out in flight with its twisted talons to gouge at her. She faced it with a sharp weapon in one hand, and a look of calm on her face.

'No!' cried Chanita.

James turned and ran toward the brown wolf, rushing to intercept it, and Ben too lunged forward to save her.

They were both too late.

The huge wolf crashed into Helen, slicing her slim body open with razor sharp claws. It landed full square on her chest and bit through her neck in a single ferocious bite.

Sarah screamed and Ben cried out in fury.

James fell on the creature, sinking his claws into its back and tearing its flanks from behind. He brought it to the ground, making deep cuts in the beast's flesh. The brown wolf raised its head and James dealt it a savage blow with his front paws. Still he was not done. With a roar of anger he ripped the wolf's carcass down the middle, splitting it into two bloody halves, and began to savage the remains, ripping chunks from the body with his teeth and spitting them out.

Melanie raised her voice. 'James! Stop that!' But he had lost himself in rage.

Ben edged closer to him. 'James. Come away now.' He reached out a hand.

James lurched sideways, away from the butchered wolf, rivers of tears streaming from his golden eyes. He staggered and landed against Ben, flailing out with his front legs.

Melanie gasped as they tumbled to the ground together.

In a second James sprang upright, shocked by what he had done. 'I'm sorry,' he growled.

Ben rose to his feet too and grabbed Melanie's hand again. 'I'm all right,' he said. 'Now run!'

They ran together, James too, watching their back as they left the remaining mob behind. They fled from the fight, and away from the hotel building, heading across open ground toward safety. The battle was behind them now, and the way ahead seemed clear.

At Melanie's side, Ben began to pant. He slowed.

'What's the matter?' she asked, gripping his arm to support him.

He came to a halt, breathless. 'Can't … run … anymore

…' he wheezed.

His sleeve was torn and a single red stripe along his arm marked where James' claw had caught him.

'No,' she whispered. 'Please, no.'

Ben sank to his knees, gasping for breath.

'He can't breathe!' screamed Melanie. 'Somebody help him!'

Chanita dashed to his side, producing a syringe from out of her medical bag. She crouched next to him, and jabbed it into his arm. 'An adrenaline shot,' she explained. 'It'll suppress the anaphylactic reaction.'

'Will he live?' gasped Melanie.

'He'll live. But –'

James lumbered over, still in wolf form, his eyes bright with grief in the darkness. 'He'll become like me,' he said mournfully. 'Worse than me. Like them.' He gestured back at the camp, now largely in flames. Occasional gunfire still rang out between the tents, but the howling of the wolves and the screaming of their victims dominated now.

Chanita was staring back toward the main building. 'Lieutenant Colonel Sharman and his men will –'

Sarah laid a hand on her arm. 'The Colonel and his men have been defeated,' she said quietly. 'It's time for us to leave.'

'If only Colonel Griffin could have been here.'

'There's nothing more that could have been done.'

Melanie hardly heard them. She dropped to her knees next to Ben and held his hand. His breathing was slowly returning to normal, but his forehead was bathed in sweat. His eyes were shining and feverish and his hand burned hot.

'No problem,' he said. 'It's just a scratch, just a tiny scratch.'

James lay down next to him, his tongue lolling, his paws folded neatly in front. The savagery that had engulfed him after Helen's death had gone completely. 'I'm so sorry, Ben.'

Despite everything, Ben managed a small smile. 'It's not your fault. But make me a promise, James. Take the others to safety. Look after them. And don't let Melanie boss you around.'

'I promise.'

Ben's eyes began to close.

Melanie's eyes were wet, but she shook the tears away angrily. 'Don't you die on me, Ben Harvey!' She shook his shoulder to rouse him. 'If you do, I'll make you regret it, I swear to God.'

His eyes opened again at her words. 'Die?' he said. 'Don't worry. I wouldn't dare.'

Chapter Seventy-Five

Gatwick Airport, West Sussex, full moon

The black cat gouged the captain's face with its claws. From out of nowhere, Kevin produced a gun. Within a second he was pulling the trigger. The shot passed straight through the head of one of Major Hall's men, who was standing right in front of him. By the time the man's body hit the ground, Kevin had unloaded three more rounds at close range. Bodies began to drop all around him.

Liz dived toward Mihai, dragging the boy to the ground with her. 'Get down!' she shouted to the other kids.

From the other side of the roof, Evans opened up with his machine gun. A hail of bullets began to rip indiscriminately through flesh. Liz wondered if the Welsh Guard had any idea who he was aiming at. Blind panic seemed to be his only guide.

A single shot went off from close to Liz. Major Hall stood still, his arm outstretched, his pistol in his hand.

Evans slumped to the ground, dead, his onslaught brought to an abrupt end.

Liz looked for Llewelyn, but the Welshman was still in some kind of trance. He stood near the edge of the rooftop, staring out into the darkness. As she watched, he sank to his knees as if in prayer. What had happened to him? She had no time to wonder now.

She was changing again, transitioning from human to vampire form. The relentless pull of the moon had seized her unawares, and her body began to take on the familiar shape unbidden. *Nosferatu.* Metamorphosis was now her automatic response whenever danger threatened. There was no way to stop it. Her muscles pulled tight as steel cables, her skin remaking itself into armour plate. She felt her blood turn icy cold.

Major Hall's men were changing too. She watched them slip from man to monster, losing their humanity as they took on hellish forms, standing tall against the moon like ghoulish skeletons, with papery skin stretched taut across sunken cheeks.

Major Hall had pulled off his glasses at last. A cold light radiated from them, chilling to see. His face had turned white as bone, with the hollow features of a corpse. He smiled a grisly smile, revealing sharp fangs, and nodded at her in recognition, one undead creature to another. He threw back his head and laughed.

Liz stared at him in horror. Was this how she must look? A living cadaver. A wraith; a ghoul. She examined her own gaunt fingers, glowing pale ivory, twisted into monstrous skewers. The sight of them revolted her. She was a creature made to kill. A slayer, a slaughterer. She had no other purpose.

Then let the killing begin.

This time, she made no effort to resist the beguiling voice. It wanted blood; she would give it blood. She hurled herself at the Major's throat, sinking fangs into his flesh.

This is how it feels, Major. The kiss of a vampire. Do you like it when it's done to you?

But his skin was hard, like scales, and resisted her attack. She clamped down harder and her teeth broke through, releasing thick dark blood that trickled down her throat as cold as ice. Never had she tasted anything as good as vampire blood. She sucked deep and drank hard, the rich liquid filling her with new vitality.

The Major reacted with shocking speed and strength, gripping her with the blades of his fingernails, slashing through her hardened skin, burrowing sharp spikes deep inside her. She screamed.

The Major grinned again and pressed harder. His fingers cut through her flesh, edging closer to vital arteries and veins. With a howl of rage she thrust her own fingers against his face, forcing them right into his eyes, and boring hard into the sockets.

The claws that impaled her sprang free and he grasped her arms instead. He pulled at her with all his strength, drawing her fingers out from his eye sockets. They came away dripping blood. Where once had been yellow eyes, now only empty holes gaped back at her. The Major clung to her tightly, seeming oblivious to the damage she had inflicted. He must know that if he ever released her, he would never find her again. Slowly he dragged her closer, ready to sink his teeth into her neck.

She struggled in his iron grip, but no matter how hard she tried, she couldn't pull away.

Chapter Seventy-Six

According to his father, Corporal Llewelyn Jones should never have become a soldier. He was destined to be a coal miner, like his father and grandfather before him.

His grandfather was a miner all his working life, descending into the pit for the first time at the age of sixteen and working in the bowels of the earth every day until his death. He was a formidable man, whose physical strength, huge drinking capacity and quick temper were unmatched in the South Wales valley where he lived.

Llewelyn's father had worked for only a few years before the mine ceased production, and never found work again. He might have left the village and looked for work elsewhere, but he was caught in a trap of the past, refusing to accept that the pit was closed for good. 'They'll reopen it one day soon,' he would tell Llewelyn confidently. 'When the next government gets in, they'll reopen all the closed mines. They're bound to. Welsh anthracite is the best coal in the whole world.' But the mine never reopened, and his father never found another job.

Llewelyn had never wanted to become a miner and was glad that the mine had closed down. If the pithead in his village had remained open, it would have swallowed him, just as one way or another it had consumed two generations of men in his family before him. Closure of the mine meant freedom, and for Llewelyn, freedom meant the army.

His dream was to join the Parachute Regiment. Instead of descending underground, Llewelyn wanted to go up in the world. The paras were the army's elite, second only in status to the special forces of the SAS. The toughest, bravest men always joined the paras. And Llewelyn had always been tough and brave, just like his grandfather. Yet it took all of his courage to leave the village where the men of his family had spent their lives in the shadow of the pit.

'Why do you want to join the army?' his father demanded. 'The government closed the mine. Now you want to go and fight their wars for them?'

Llewelyn endured his father's drunken raging in silence. The sooner he was gone, the better. He applied to join the British Army aged fifteen years and seven months, the earliest age possible. His father refused to give his parental consent, so his mother had to sign the forms instead. After he left home he wrote to her regularly at first. Every Christmas he tried to send some money to make up for his father's lack of work. But he never saw his family again.

After joining the Welsh Guards and completing his basic training, he volunteered for P Company, the "Pre-Parachute" training and selection process for soldiers wanting to join 16 Air Assault Brigade. It was there, in the demanding test environment of assault courses and endurance races that his dream of becoming a para was brought crashing to the ground.

The problem was heights. Llewelyn had never been

much of a one for heights. As a kid he'd never wanted to climb trees like his friends. It wasn't that he was scared. Anyone who suggested that Llewelyn Jones was afraid of anything would walk away with a bloody nose. There was no question of him being scared of climbing trees. He just didn't want to. What was the point? It was stupid.

Anyway, trees weren't the same as parachutes. Just because he didn't want to climb a tree, it didn't mean he couldn't jump out of a plane. And nobody ever asked him about climbing trees when he signed up for P Company.

The aerial assault course was a steel framework of bars, ladders and platforms reaching sixty feet into the sky. It didn't look much from a distance. Sixty feet was nothing, measured out on the running track. But sixty vertical feet were so much more than they sounded. Close up, the top of the assault course seemed to stretch away forever into the blue sky above him. No matter how loudly the P Company sergeant shouted at him to climb it, his hands remained frozen to the ladder, his feet resolutely stuck to the ground.

He had failed. And he would always be a failure. There were no second chances with P Company. It didn't matter that he had excelled in all the other tests. If you failed the aerial assault course, you couldn't ever join the paras. What use was a paratrooper who was scared of heights?

The world turned and the moon rose. Llewelyn lay flat on his back on the hotel rooftop. The cold, hard surface pressed into his bones, reassuringly solid, yet somehow swelling like the surface of the ocean. Overhead, the sky moved alarmingly. Dark clouds scudded across it like waves crashing on a beach. He tried to fix his gaze to them, but they slid away, seeming to pull him sideways toward the edge of the roof. He pushed his sweaty palms against the bitumen surface, ignoring the grit and gravel that bit into them, willing the ground to stop swaying. If he tried to stand, or even to move, he knew he would fall.

Why did Liz have to bring him up onto the rooftop?

It was P Company and the aerial assault course, all over again. Then, as now, the enemy was fear. Nothing but his own fear.

But Llewelyn Jones feels no fear.

It was an empty boast, just as it had always been. He gripped the roof even tighter than before. It made no difference. Still he felt himself slip closer to the edge. He gripped it harder, ignoring the pain as sharp stones split his skin.

I am as strong as an ox. No man is stronger.

So why could he not stand up? He knew that the roof was perfectly still and flat. Nothing could make him roll toward its edge. Nothing could make him fall. But knowing the facts made no difference to how he felt.

The voice of the P Company sergeant from so many years ago bellowed in his ear. *Get up, you useless piece of dirt! Get up and fight!*

I will fight, he promised the sergeant. *I will get up now, and fight. I will not fail again.*

Liz needed him. They all needed him. Right now this instant. Yet still he lay there, powerless to move.

He risked a glance to his side and wished he hadn't. The edge lay that way, not so very far off. Had it come nearer? No! That was madness. Then, had he rolled toward it? It seemed so close. And over the edge, the precipitous drop … down into the blackness of the deep pit …

He thought of his grandfather, descending into the coal pit every morning in the cage, listening to the clanking in the dark as the winding gear lowered him one third of a mile into the earth's crust. Over the years, a hundred and fifty men had met their doom in that pit, yet still his grandfather had allowed himself to be lowered into it. He had relished it, by all accounts.

You are a coward, boy! It was his father's voice this time. *You ran away to the army because you were afraid of going down the mine. I read your letters to your mam, boasting of soldiering in far-off lands. That was not bravery, it was cowardice that took you away from home. You have been running away every day of your life!*

'No!' he shouted. 'It's a lie. Llewelyn Jones feels no fear.'

Then why are you lying there, while your comrades fight without you?

His father was right of course. His friends were fighting while he lay on the ground. What use was it to be as strong as an ox, if he could not fight? What kind of man was he, after all?

The strongest. The bravest.

Then do your duty! shouted the P Company sergeant.

I shall.

Slowly, he pushed his hands against the rooftop, this time lifting his weight up, not simply in a futile attempt to grip. There was no need to grip. The roof was perfectly flat. He would not fall as long as he kept away from the edge.

He rose just enough so that he could see the battle.

Close to him lay the body of Evans, his eyes closed, his chest still. Blood trickled from a wound in his forehead.

Oh God.

Evans was dead. All his men were dead.

It was enough to make him lie down again.

But Liz still needs me.

Whose voice was that? It was his own. He looked and saw that Liz was grappling with Major Hall. She had his thumbs pressed in his eyes, but he was pulling them out. He forced her to the ground, then rolled with her, closer to the roof edge. Both of them were covered in blood.

You can do this, boy. I know you can.

Another voice this time – his grandfather's. He had never heard that voice before. His grandfather had passed away before he had even been born. But the man had always been there, a towering figure in Llewelyn's life. A legend.

His grandfather had gone into the black pit every day of his working life, facing his fear. Llewelyn had always been told that his grandfather was fearless. Now, suddenly, he knew the truth. His grandfather had been a mortal man, just like him, and he had surely known fear. How could he not? The deep mine had claimed the lives of his friends and comrades. It was a monster waiting to swallow more. But his grandfather had faced his fears, just as he must do, and shown himself to be stronger than fear.

Go on, boy. You are as brave as I ever was.

Llewelyn sat up. His rifle lay at his side. He grasped it and hefted it into his arms.

On the other side of the roof, Kevin was doing battle with the vampires, firing from the doorway that led back down inside the building. The kids must have escaped inside. Kevin was heavily outnumbered and the vampires moved with unbelievable speed, almost a blur as they dodged around the rooftop, returning fire. Kevin couldn't hold them off much longer.

But Liz looked ready to die right now.

Major Hall, or the creature that he had become, pushed his face against Liz's throat and plunged his fangs into her neck. A vision of the dead people in the aircraft hangar came to Llewelyn, their bodies hanging lifeless, two neat puncture wounds in every neck.

The Major was quickly draining the life force from Liz.

Llewelyn rose to his knees and took aim.

He waited for the rooftop to quake beneath him. He waited for the voice of the P Company sergeant to tear him down again. He waited for his father to try once more to heap his own failings onto his son. But the demons in his head remained silent.

He pulled the trigger.

Major Hall tipped over to the side, releasing Liz from his grip. She reached for her own gun and put a single bullet into his skull.

Now Llewelyn turned his gun on the vampire paras and opened fire again. The bullets tore into them, making short work of their crystalline skin. They were fast, but not fast enough for an SA80 in fully automatic mode. By the time his magazine was empty, they were all dead.

I did it.

Once he had said, *I will do it.* But he had let himself down. Then he had been just a boy.

He was a boy no more. He was a man. And a man made different choices to a boy.

A true man faced his fears, and did not pretend that he was fearless.

A true man faced his fears, and knew that he could beat them.

Chapter Seventy-Seven

Glastonbury Tor, Somerset, full moon

When Chris Crohn had worked as tech support guy at Manor Road Secondary School, he had often resented the fact that Seth had a much better job than him. He had envied his friend's position as a software developer in a financial tech start-up. He had coveted his friend's too-small-but-hugely-expensive apartment in trendy Docklands. He had even found himself longing to be part of a disruptive, visionary, hipster business team, just like Seth, even though he hated hipsters and loathed teams of any kind. His secret dream had been to see Seth brought low, so that he and his old friend could once again be equals, just like when they'd been growing up together as kids in South London.

Now Chris' dream had come true. Here they were, both brought low, Chris tied back-to-back against Ryan's beaten-up and barely conscious body, and Seth lying helplessly on the grass nursing his broken ankle. Now he and Seth had the same. They both had exactly nothing. There was a good lesson here, Chris reflected. Unfortunately it had come too late to be of any use.

'What are we going to do?' whispered Seth.

'It's too late to do anything. I told you we should never have lit that fire.'

'No one wants to hear that now, Chris.

'I also said we shouldn't have come with these guys.'

'Chris. No one cares.'

'That's the whole problem. No one ever listens to what I say.'

They waited helplessly inside the ruined tower, listening to the screams and gruesome noises coming from outside.

Josh's friends were in full blown panic. The flute player dashed out through the nearest exit, but a dark shape outside lumbered into view and shoved him back in. The others bolted for the archway on the opposite side, but two more black figures were waiting there. They muscled them into the tower and stood blocking the exits.

Brittany was on her knees, sobbing and shaking. 'Josh,' she kept saying. 'What's happening to Josh?'

Eventually the noises came to an end. The silence that followed was only marginally more comforting.

'What's happening now?' asked Seth in wide-eyed terror. Whatever had happened to Josh, it had taken a very long time for his screams to eventually subside and stop.

'Now they're coming for us,' said Chris.

'Who is?'

'Whoever just did that to Josh.'

The dark figures guarding the exits entered the tower one by one. Men in black motorcycle leathers. Mean, muscular, ugly men. Chris didn't think he had ever seen so much facial hair in one place.

The last man to enter was even bigger and uglier than the others. He had a bald head and wore black shades.

Josh's friends huddled together in one corner with Brittany. They were all shaking, and not from the cold,

Chris guessed. The flute player's face had turned white as a sheet.

The huge biker studied them thoughtfully. 'Take them outside,' he said, 'and kill them.'

The leader's minions began to manhandle the flute player and the others out of the tower. Brittany screamed as one of the men grabbed her and threw her over his shoulder like a rolled-up carpet.

The chief biker glared at her in annoyance. He put up a hand. 'Wait!' He rubbed his smooth head with a thumb. 'Kill them … slowly.'

Chris watched as they were dragged away, kicking and screaming into the night. Before long, Brittany's screams intensified. Chris tried his best to ignore them.

The huge biker removed his shades and examined Chris, Ryan and Seth with interest.

'What shall we do with these three?' asked one of his henchmen.

The giant stroked his beard thoughtfully. He reached a hairy hand deep into a pocket and brought out a coin. He showed both sides of the coin to Chris. Heads. Tails. Both were equally grimy.

Outside the tower, the screams went on, the other guys now joining in with Brittany in a chorus of terror. Whatever was happening out there, it wasn't good. Chris had thought his luck had already reached rock bottom, but now he knew that it could sink even lower. Much, much lower.

Up went the coin, spinning in the firelight. Heads, tails, heads, tails. Chris watched it go, mesmerized by the flickering metal. It seemed to spin for a long time, almost suspended in mid-air, just as his own life hung in the balance. Up, up, went the coin, almost to the top of the roofless tower. Then back down. The big man caught it in his huge hand. He held it out for Chris to see.

'What is it?' asked Seth. 'Tell me what it is. No, on second thoughts, I don't want to know.'

The screams from outside showed no signs of stopping. They had been joined by the chilling sounds of wolf howls as the full moon began to peep through the open archway.

Chris squinted at the filthy coin. In the firelight it was hard to see. 'I'm not sure,' he said. 'It looks like …' He stopped. It looked like tails. But if it were tails, that must surely be a bad thing. Tails couldn't possibly be good. He swallowed. 'I think it's –'

'Tails,' said the hairy biker with a hint of regret. 'Tails, I lose.'

Chapter Seventy-Eight

Gatwick Airport, West Sussex, full moon

Liz had been given the Glock by Dean back in London, almost at the very start of the werewolf troubles. Now, after all these months, she had finally got to use it for real. The thought filled her with no pleasure, but she was glad she'd had the gun when she needed it.

Thanks, Dean.

Her dead colleague had saved her life, even though she hadn't been able to save his.

A short-range headshot from the Glock had finished off Major Hall quickly enough, vampire or no vampire. The dead man lay beside her, still looking like an exhumed corpse, but slowly changing to take on his normal appearance. Liz herself had already changed back from vampire form and was fully human again. Amazingly, the wound in her neck where the Major had gouged her with his long claws had almost entirely healed. It must have been the curative power of the vampire blood she'd drunk.

She looked around and saw mostly bodies littering the rooftop. Then she caught sight of Kevin and the kids, and ran toward them. 'Oh, thank God! You're all alive!'

She gathered Mihai into her arms, and gave Kevin a kiss on the cheek.

'You alive too, Liz!' said Mihai gleefully.

'Yeah, nice work,' said Kevin. 'Good use of teeth, and all that.'

Corporal Jones was storming across the rooftop toward her. She couldn't tell from his face if he was happy or angry. He stopped a few paces from her, eyeing her circumspectly.

Now that she had seen for herself how hideous vampires looked, she couldn't blame him for treating her with caution.

They looked at each other for a few moments, then he stepped forward to embrace her. It was the first time they had ever touched. She let him hold her in his beefy arms, crushing her against his massive chest. She would gladly have kissed him then, and not just on the cheek, but he pulled back to a safe distance before she could act on the impulse.

'You didn't tell me they were all vampires!' he said, eventually.

'Well, how was I supposed to know? You didn't tell me you were afraid of heights!'

'Yeah, well,' he said sheepishly. 'It's not a fact I like to boast about.'

'I'm sorry about Evans,' she said, nodding in the direction of the fallen Welsh Guard.

Llewelyn nodded. 'He went out in style.'

'He certainly did.'

'All guns blazing,' said Kevin.

'He was a hero.'

'It's just me now, then,' said Llewelyn. 'My men are all gone.'

He had lost something, and not just his men. It took Liz a moment to realize what it was. The boyish good looks that the Corporal had always worn were still there, but they had hardened. He had lost more than just his fellow soldier up here on the rooftop. He had lost his innocence.

Llewelyn walked across the rooftop to the body of his fallen comrade and picked up Evans' abandoned rifle. Liz saw him kneel down and mutter some words to the dead man. When he returned, he offered the weapon to Kevin. 'Think you can handle a machine gun, Private Bailey?'

Kevin stood awkwardly, his pistol still in his hand. 'I reckon I probably could.'

Llewelyn held it out to him, but Kevin seemed strangely reluctant to take it. 'Do you think Evans would have wanted me to have it?' he asked.

Llewelyn nodded. 'He'd have wanted it to go to a friend, yes.'

'A friend, right.' Kevin holstered his pistol and accepted the new weapon as if he were being awarded a medal. He headed off down the stairwell without another word. Liz thought she saw a tear in his eye, but it must have been a trick of the light. She could hardly remember a time when her father had cried.

'We need to get off this rooftop,' said Llewelyn, 'and fast. No doubt the whole base has heard our little firefight. And what chance do you think we have of convincing anyone that Major Hall and his officers were vampires?'

Llewelyn was right. They had just killed the base commander and more than a dozen of his top officers. No one would believe their story. They needed to leave the camp immediately. 'We just need to call in on Samantha and the Singh family before we go,' she said.

When they reached the hotel suite, everyone was busy packing.

'What are you all doing?' asked Liz.

'Getting ready to come with you,' said Mr Singh. 'Vijay

told us we have to leave.'

'No,' said Liz. 'I have to leave, and my father, and Corporal Jones too, or we're liable to be shot by the army. But the rest of you must stay. We have to run, and we don't know where we're going. It won't be safe outside the camp for you, especially not for Mrs Singh, and certainly not for Samantha, Lily and the baby.'

Samantha was the only one who hadn't made any attempt to pack. She was sitting on the bed, nursing Leo, with Lily by her side.

'Samantha, I promised Dean that if anything happened to him, I would keep you away from danger. I don't want to break my promise to him, but I can't take you with me now. It wouldn't be safe.'

Samantha smiled. 'I know. You mustn't worry. You've already kept me from harm. And Lily and Leo too. You've fulfilled your promise to Dean. Now you must go. I'll be fine here with the others, especially with Drake and Vijay to protect us. Look at them, they're almost grown men.'

Drake and Vijay both stood up straight, doing their best to look as manly as Samantha had claimed. The boys were not yet men, but she hadn't been exaggerating too much.

'We'll look after everyone,' promised Vijay.

'Yeah,' said Drake. 'We're real men now, yeah?'

Aasha slung her arms around the two of them. 'Don't worry, Liz. I'll make sure these two don't get too cocky. If their heads grow any bigger they might fall off.'

'You should keep Shadow with you, too,' Liz told them. 'A cat makes a good vampire alarm.'

'And a kickass fighter, too,' said Drake, cradling Shadow in his arms.

Mihai had said nothing since Liz's announcement that she was leaving. He was looking up at her, his face sullen, his dark eyes misty with tears. The boy wasn't prone to crying. He was a tough kid, who had been through a lot. More than any child should ever have to endure.

Kevin reached out and ruffled his messy hair. 'You coming then, kid?'

'Me come with you?' His eyes lit up.

'Of course,' said Liz. She gave him a quick hug. 'Did you think I was going to leave you behind?'

He hugged her back, shouting with happiness in Romanian.

'But we've got to go immediately, okay?'

'Sure thing, Liz. Let's do it!'

Chapter Seventy-Nine

'Let's get rolling,' said Llewelyn from the driving seat of the Foxhound.

Liz was sorry to leave her patrol car behind, but if they were going to survive the unknown hazards of the post-apocalyptic world beyond the camp, they would need all the protection that the armoured Foxhound could provide. Besides, there were just four of them now. Herself, her father, Mihai and Llewelyn.

The image of them driving off together as some kind of idealized family unit flashed briefly across her mind, but this was no time for sentimentality. And idealized families didn't usually drive armoured vehicles with crates of weapons and ammo stowed in the back.

'Make sure you're all strapped in,' said Llewelyn. The Foxhound began to move almost before he finished speaking.

Liz had driven in the eight-ton armoured truck once

before. It had seemed outrageous then, to be driving around London in a bombproof vehicle designed to operate off-road in deserts, jungles and mountain terrain. Llewelyn had proudly told her that its heavily-protected V-shaped hull could survive an explosion from an enemy mine, and that it could keep on driving even if one of its four wheels was blown off. She sincerely hoped they wouldn't have to put that to the test.

One feature she hadn't noticed before was the display screen fixed to the middle of the dashboard. It glowed brightly in the darkened cabin, giving a 360 degree view from cameras mounted on the front, back and rear of the vehicle.

'Thermal imaging,' commented Llewelyn. 'Handy for when you fancy a drive in the dark.'

Liz studied the screen and looked nervously out through the thickened glass of the side window. 'How long before someone comes looking for us?'

'I'm surprised they're not here already,' said Llewelyn, flooring the accelerator.

The Foxhound was no sports car, more of a lumbering hulk, and it took its time to pick up speed. But Liz had a feeling that once it got moving, nothing would stop it.

'Look,' said Kevin. 'They're coming.'

She looked where he was pointing and saw a couple of army Land Rovers heading to cut them off. Llewelyn stamped on the brakes and took a sharp turn left. The Foxhound bounced heavily over a grassy hump and onto a different road. The vehicle's huge tyres buffered them from the worst of the bump, but Liz still felt like she'd just jumped a fence on a bareback horse.

'Four-wheel steering,' boasted Llewelyn from the driving seat. 'This thing can go anywhere.'

'It's even less comfortable than it looked from the outside,' groaned Kevin from the back.

'Quit moaning,' said Llewelyn. 'By army standards, this is first-rate luxury. We've even got air-con.' He put his foot to the floor again and the engine din rose to deafening levels, cutting off any further complaints.

'How are we going to get out?' asked Liz. The two Land Rovers had turned to follow them, and another one had appeared further up the road in front. 'Can we drive this thing through the main gate?'

'Not a chance,' said Llewelyn. 'The gate's made from solid steel. It's built to withstand high-speed attacks from trucks.'

'So how do we get out?'

'Too many questions, Liz. You'd better let me concentrate.'

The Land Rover up ahead had come to a halt and was blocking the road sideways on. The soldiers inside were readying their rifles to fire. Liz looked about but couldn't see any obvious way around the blockage. The road was lined with a solid brick wall on one side and a crash barrier on the other.

'Um, …' she said.

'Hush, Liz. Not now. I'm busy.'

The Foxhound approached the Land Rover rapidly. It must have reached around fifty miles an hour and was still gradually accelerating, its engine screaming as the rev counter moved into the red. She doubted that Llewelyn could stop it now, even if he intended to, and stopping didn't look like it featured in his plan.

Up ahead, soldiers were disgorging from the Land Rover and leaping for safety over the crash barrier.

Liz closed her eyes.

The scream of metal and the jolt from the impact left her in no doubt that the Foxhound had collided with its target. The seatbelt tightened hard around her as she was thrown forward in her seat. Behind her, both Kevin and Mihai screamed.

The Foxhound rose up and over the Land Rover, crunching glass and metal as it crushed the smaller vehicle into oblivion. She opened her eyes and for an instant all she could see through the front windscreen was sky. Then she felt a second impact as the rear wheels mounted the squashed remains of the Land Rover and rolled over the top of it. The Foxhound bounced back onto the road surface and carried on as if nothing had happened.

'Fuck a duck!' yelled Kevin from the back.

Llewelyn appeared unruffled by the operation. He peered into his side mirrors and seemed satisfied by what he saw. 'You were asking me something, Liz?'

'Yeah,' she said. 'How do we get out?'

But already more vehicles had pulled into view up ahead, including an armoured vehicle even larger than the Foxhound and equipped with a turret-mounted gun.

'Hey, that's a Warrior,' said Llewelyn with a frown.

'Bad news?'

'30mm armour-piercing cannon bad news.'

The gun turret on the Warrior was already turning in their direction.

Llewelyn spun the wheel and the Foxhound lurched off the main road and onto a service road running parallel to one of the runways. 'We need to make a rapid exit now, Liz. So no more questions, okay?'

She kept quiet and let him do whatever he had in mind. It was best to trust the soldier's instincts and training. He hadn't got them all killed so far.

'Private Bailey!' called Llewelyn. 'I've got a job for you.'

'Yes?' said Kevin.

'Open the roof hatch and climb up on top. You'll find a couple of light machine guns up there mounted on swivel stations. Find a target and start shooting.'

'Yes, sir!' Kevin unstrapped himself and started fiddling with the roof hatch.

'Wait,' said Liz. 'You can't fire on the other soldiers. They're supposed to be on our side.'

As if in response to her plea, the sound of automatic gunfire opened up outside. The army was firing on them. Bullets rattled angrily off the Foxhound's composite armour.

'Someone forgot to tell them we're on the same side,' said Kevin.

Llewelyn swung the vehicle in evasive action. 'You need to understand one thing, Liz. This is the part where we kill or get killed.'

'No,' she said. 'No one else dies tonight.'

She grabbed hold of the steering wheel and yanked it hard to the left. The Foxhound lurched off the track onto open grass. In the back of the truck, Kevin tumbled to the floor. Llewelyn tried to wrestle back control, but she held the wheel with all her strength.

'Okay,' said Llewelyn, 'I see your plan.'

Up ahead the perimeter fence loomed into view. The chain link fence was fixed to steel posts and topped with razor wire.

'Reckon it will work?' asked Liz.

'Let's give it some welly.'

Llewelyn stamped hard on the gas and the Foxhound picked up speed. Bullets began to bounce off the rear of the vehicle again, but the armour was doing its job.

'I think I'll stay down here after all,' said Kevin from the floor.

The fence grew larger until it was all Liz could see.

'Here goes,' said Llewelyn.

The Foxhound jerked sharply slower as it burst through the fence and the six-cylinder engine whined in protest. The steel posts caught the truck like a ball in a net, and for a second Liz thought they would be hurled backward. But then the truck broke free and the fence crashed to the ground as four huge tyres swept over it, squashing it into the mud.

Llewelyn took control of the steering again as they sped off into the night, leaving the airport far behind.

Chapter Eighty

Stoke Park, Buckinghamshire, waning moon

By the time Leanna arrived to inspect her victory the fires had mostly died away, and only smoking vehicles and the ruins of the hotel building remained. The tent city that had filled the lawn in front of the hotel was largely gone. Huge numbers of corpses were strewn across the battlefield, most of them human. It had been a decisive victory for the werewolves.

Leanna strode across the muddy field, gloating. 'You did well, General Canning. Very well.'

Canning walked at her side, matching her brisk pace. 'It was strategy, my dear. And tactics too. A healthy dose of cunning, but most of all, sheer military genius.'

She smiled indulgently at him. She could afford to let his ego run wild, for a day or so at least. Then she would have to slap him back into place. This victory was just the beginning of a long campaign. The southern evacuation centre at Gatwick Airport was much more heavily defended, and as for the core government forces based at Northwood Headquarters …

'There were a few casualties, naturally,' drawled Canning.

'Naturally.'

'But overall we made a net gain in numbers. The new werewolves from the camp have mostly come over to join us.'

Leanna stopped sharply in her tracks. 'Mostly? You mean that some chose not to?'

'It would seem so. They vanished in the night. I cannot imagine why they wouldn't want to serve you, as their queen.'

'Hunt them down,' said Leanna. 'I will not tolerate any kind of disloyalty.'

That was the most important lesson she had learned this whole time. Never tolerate the slightest dissent, else it would grow and spread like a cancer. She would not stand any more treachery. She would not allow it to take root.

Canning seemed doubtful. 'You want me to waste time hunting down rogue werewolves? What about our human enemy?'

She turned on him, eyes flashing. 'The true enemy is always within. Always look for the traitors, and root them out mercilessly. Do you understand? I want those renegades caught and strung up along my castle walls. Do you hear me?'

Canning regarded her coolly. 'I hear perfectly well, my dear. There is no need to shout at me. Have no fear, I will do as you say. Are there any further orders you would like to give me, or may I take a moment to celebrate this great victory?'

She ignored his disdainful tone and calmed herself back down. It would not do to lose her temper now. 'Just one thing. Were there any reports at the camp of the ones I seek?'

'Ah, you mean the traitors. James …'

'There is no need to speak their names,' she snapped. 'You know the ones I mean.'

She had recited their names often enough to herself. James, Helen, Melanie, Ben. Traitors every one. She had no desire to hear them from his lips too.

Canning had returned to his normal obsequious self. 'Indeed, I do. But I did not realize it was a top priority.'

'Finding them is always a top priority.'

'I see.'

She sighed. She had not meant to tear him down. Canning had done well. She ought to have congratulated him on his achievement. People responded positively when praised, she understood that well enough. Rewards, threats, and punishments, that was the way to govern. No one knew that better than she.

Canning cleared his throat. 'There is one body you might like to view. A woman. Youngish, perhaps in her early thirties; long blonde hair. She fits the description, but the corpse is rather badly mangled. It might not be possible to –'

'Show me,' said Leanna.

He led her across the battlefield to a pile of corpses, both humans and wolves. Some bore gunshot wounds, others had been ripped by tooth or claw.

'This one,' said Canning.

A woman's remains lay on the ground, badly mutilated. She had been torn almost in two. Yet there could be no doubt. The long blonde hair. The fair skin. Leanna felt her blood turn to ice. Doctor Helen Eastgate. The smug, earnest look on that dead face.

I swore to kill you one day, Helen.

But not like this. She felt the ice turn to fire, and turned her rage on Canning. 'I told you that the traitors were to be taken alive! I specifically ordered you! I meant to kill them all myself!'

He took a step back, his features contorted in fear. 'I gave orders not to kill them,' he blurted. 'It was not my fault.'

'Then whose fault was it? Who shall I kill in her place?' Of all the traitors, Helen had been the one she had most been looking forward to meeting. She had imagined so many times what she would do. She touched her cheek with one hand, brushing the scar tissue where the acid Helen had thrown had eaten into her face.

Canning noticed the gesture and a look of understanding passed across his face.

Yes, Doctor Helen Eastgate did this to me.

Now her secret was known to him. She would have killed him then and there, had he not immediately lowered his gaze and dropped to his knees.

'I will not fail you again,' he swore. He waited, his neck bowed before her.

Anger boiled in her blood. She could strike him down, vent her rage on him. Or she could let him live and serve her to the best of his abilities.

She bared her teeth. Helen was dead. Her victory had turned to defeat and humiliation. But she must not lose sight of her goal.

'Get up.'

Canning rose, lifting his eyes to hers.

'We will not speak of this again.'

He nodded.

She cast another glance around the muddy field and the smoking remnants of battle. She took no joy from the sight of victory. The ashes that blew in the wind were the ashes of her own personal defeat. There was nothing more for her here.

'Round up any prisoners who are still alive. Remove the weapons and vehicles, and return to Windsor,' she ordered Canning. 'Tonight, I shall throw a feast for my supporters.'

'An excellent idea,' agreed Canning. 'And what shall I do with the prisoners?'

'They are to be on the menu.'

Chapter Eighty-One

Stoke Park, Buckinghamshire, waning moon

Colonel Griffin and the Prime Minister reached the western evacuation camp by early afternoon of the day after the full moon. The Colonel gazed at the burned-out remains, bitter tears stinging his eyes. He could hardly believe what he was seeing.

'They're all dead. Every last one.'

The dead lay singly, or in mounds, shot or bitten or burned to death, each one telling an individual tale of tragedy.

He hobbled around the battlefield on his hastily repaired crutches, searching among the bodies.

'Who are you looking for?' the Prime Minister asked. 'It is hopeless. There must be hundreds here. Thousands.'

Many of the bodies were badly burned, disfigured beyond recognition. How could he hope to find Chanita, if she were among them? And yet, he had to look. If she were here, perhaps lying injured, he had to find her.

Yet every single body he stopped to examine was dead.

'Where is she?' he cried. He had to know. It would be agony not to know for certain what had happened to her. He lurched on, his crutches sinking into the mud, bodies stretched out in every direction.

'Perhaps she escaped,' said the PM. 'She may have got out in time.'

He shook his head. 'Chanita would never have abandoned the people to their fate. I put her in charge of the camp, and she would never have placed her own welfare ahead of duty. If she is dead, that makes me responsible for her death.'

'This was not your fault, Colonel. The werewolves are to blame, and no other.'

Some of the fires were still warm and smouldering. 'It must have happened last night,' said Griffin. 'If only I could have reached here a day earlier. If I had walked a little faster … if I had set off sooner …'

'The outcome would have been the same,' said the PM. 'But you would have died too. You must not blame yourself. You can't always save the world.'

'I didn't try to,' he wailed. 'I only wanted to save one person.'

And yet he had failed in even that.

He sat down heavily on the grass, his thigh screaming in agony. He threw his crutches to one side. What good were they now? He was a broken and useless man, barely able to walk, let alone command a military operation. Even if he could have arrived at the camp before the horror that had unfolded here, what might he have done? How could he have hoped to save Chanita, when he could barely put one foot in front of another?

He remembered the deer with the broken leg he had found as a child. Despite his appeal to his father for help, he hadn't been able to save the animal. He hadn't been able to save Chanita either. Perhaps his father had been right all along. Perhaps sometimes compassion was futile, and death was the only mercy. Perhaps a bullet in his own head was the best outcome now.

'You still have one round left in your pistol,' he told the Prime Minister. 'Put it to good use.'

Her reply came as a harsh rebuke. 'And I intend to keep it there. Do not voice such a thought in my presence ever again.'

He shook his head. 'Then leave me here. Go on your journey. I am no use to anyone anymore. I tried to save one person, and failed at that. Leave me alone in peace.'

She spoke more gently to him this time. 'Don't give up hope, Colonel. Come with me to Northwood. There's always someone else waiting to be saved. Will you try?'

'No. I am done with trying. I have failed too many times.'

He had witnessed scenes of carnage, both on foreign battlefields and at home, but none as bad as this. He no longer had the will to go on. Perhaps it was fatigue after his long journey. Perhaps it was grief at Chanita's loss. Perhaps it was simply too much senseless killing. Whatever it was, he just wanted to lie down and sleep and never wake up. He closed his eyes to shut out the sight of the corpses, strewn where they had fallen.

'Colonel Griffin, the only decisive way to fail is to give up. I will not allow you to do that. For the sake of the one you lost here today, and for all those who still need our help, come with me. There is much work to be done. This country needs a leader, and its armed forces need a commander. Let us be those people.'

'I just don't know if I can.'

She sighed and sat down on the grass next to him, sinking gently into the mud. 'Colonel, you once sent me your letter of resignation. As you may recall, I quickly consigned that to the dustbin, where it belonged. I am an old woman who is tired and has seen too much, and I do not have the energy to convince you once again of your own ability. Instead, let me simply give you an order.

Come with me. Lead my armed forces to victory. I will not accept "no" for an answer.'

He turned his face to look her in the eyes. 'You just don't give up, do you?'

'No. Never. And I won't let you, either.'

'Has anyone ever called you a heartless old cow?'

Faint laughter lines creased her eyes. 'My late husband often did. And far worse. If that's the worst insult you can think of, Colonel, I don't have much to fear from you.' She stood up and reached out her hand to him. 'Now pull your lazy arse out of the mud and start walking.'

Chapter Eighty-Two

Glastonbury Tor, Somerset, waning moon

The bodies of Josh, Brittany and the others, or what was left of them, were scattered over a wide area of the hilltop, and already the early morning flies were gathering to register their interest.

Rose turned away.

Seth had been sick at the sight, and was still looking decidedly green.

Ryan had been barely conscious throughout the entire episode, which was probably a blessing.

Only Chris seemed to be in a cheerful mood this morning. 'They've gone, at last,' he said.

The Wolf Brothers had waited until after moonset before departing from the Tor. They had sped off down the hill path, their bikes kicking up stones and clods of mud, their exhaust pipes belching smoke. Rose hoped she would never see them again.

Last night, as the moon had risen, the bikers had

stripped off their leathers and transformed into wolves, howling at the moon, bathing in blood, and exulting in the savagery of their slaughter.

But their leader had kept his word to spare her, Chris, Seth and Ryan. She had untied Ryan and Chris and had bathed Ryan's wounds. Rose herself was unhurt. She searched around the hillside for Nutmeg, but the dog was nowhere to be found.

A fleet of clouds was sailing in from the west, promising rain. It would be wise to find shelter somewhere until they passed. The roofless tower on the hilltop offered little cover, and she had no desire to hang around this wild and forsaken place any longer.

'Come on, then,' said Chris. 'Let's be off.'

'Which way?' But she already knew what reply he would give.

'To Hereford. How many times have I said it already?'

Ryan was too badly beaten to carry Seth, so she and Chris took one end of the stretcher each.

'No. Wait,' said Rose. 'We can't leave without Nutmeg.'

Chris sighed. 'Okay. Let's find her. But promise me one thing.'

'What?'

'From now on, you all have to listen to my advice.'

'Yeah, whatevs,' said Seth. He had retrieved the flute that Josh's friend had played, and was clutching it to his chest. 'I can learn to play this. It'll be something for me to do while I'm being carried around everywhere.'

'Please don't,' begged Chris.

'Let's just get away from this horrible place as soon as we can,' said Seth.

The flat fields stretched away from the Tor on all sides. In the distance Rose could see the town of Glastonbury itself, but she had no desire to head that way. Chris had been right about one thing – they were safer travelling alone. She wondered if Hereford itself might be too dangerous. Perhaps it would be better to keep away from all towns and villages, shunning the company of others entirely. But what kind of life would that be?

'Hello, there!'

A figure appeared, striding up the side of the hill. An old man, wearing a long coat made of multicoloured patches. He leaned on a walking stick and at his side was Nutmeg. The stranger made his way to the brow of the hill and Nutmeg barked when she saw Rose.

'Nutmeg!'

The dog ran to her, a rabbit in her jaws. She deposited it at Rose's feet and wagged her tail.

Rose kneeled to hug her close. 'Good girl, Nutmeg. Clever dog.' The rabbit would provide a welcome meal once they got a fire lighted.

'Is that your dog?' asked the new arrival. 'I found her this morning. Or rather, she found me. She brought me here.'

'Thank you,' said Rose.

'We should go,' said Chris quickly. 'Before anything else goes wrong.'

'Yes.'

'Don't let me stop you,' said the old man, leaning on his staff. 'Where are you going, by the way?'

'Hereford. What about you?'

'Me? I'm headed to Stonehenge.' He walked over to where Seth was lying on the ground. 'What happened to you, my friend?'

'I broke my ankle,' said Seth. 'I can't walk.'

'Let me examine it. I have some skills in healing.'

They watched as he ran his fingers gently across Seth's foot, ankle and leg. Normally Seth complained loudly whenever anyone tried to touch his broken leg, but for once he seemed content to allow the stranger to do his work.

'I feel the aura,' said the man. 'I have some herbs that will help you.' He reached into one of many pockets in his patchwork coat and pulled out a handful of dried vegetation. Mixing it with water from a bottle, he began to rub the brown paste into Seth's skin. 'Does this hurt?'

Miraculously, Seth shook his head. 'No, it feels soothing.'

'The healing will take time, but this will aid it. I will give you a crystal too, to speed your recovery. Keep it with you at all times.' He passed Seth a small purple stone.

'We have to go now,' said Chris. 'We have a long journey ahead of us. And it will start raining any minute.'

The man looked up at the dark clouds overhead. 'No. It won't rain today. These clouds will pass us by. I know these things.' He turned his attention to Rose again. 'My name is Rowan. I am glad that we met, and I wish you well on your travels.' He turned to set off back down the hill.

Now that he was leaving them, she felt a curious desire for him to stay. He seemed to radiate a powerful magnetism. Nutmeg liked him too. 'I'm Rose,' she called after him.

He turned back and smiled. 'Yes,' he answered. 'I already know who you are.'

Chapter Eighty-Three

Northwood HQ, Eastbury Park, Hertfordshire, waning moon

The last few miles of the journey were agony for Colonel Griffin. His broken thigh bone had become inflamed during his long walk across the country, and he was depending more and more heavily on the diminutive frame of the Prime Minister for support. She was a head shorter than him, and perhaps a hundred pounds lighter. Neither of them could endure much more of this.

'We are almost there now, Colonel,' said the Prime Minister. 'Look.'

A low glow in the distance confirmed the truth of her words, and gave him fresh hope of completing the journey. He had walked forty miles on one leg. Another few hundred yards surely wouldn't kill him.

The Colonel had visited this place on several occasions before. Northwood Headquarters was the UK's principal military headquarters and home to five separate operational HQs, including UK Joint Forces Command. He had not been sufficiently senior to join the permanent operations team stationed here, but he had served as an adviser, and had delivered briefings to commanding officers.

The military complex was one of the most secure locations in the country. A highly fortified twelve-foot steel fence topped with razor wire surrounded the perimeter of the base. CCTV cameras fixed to fence poles silently observed his slow progress, as he and the Prime Minister hobbled together along the road leading to the site's main entrance.

He wondered what sort of reception they would receive on their arrival. The UK's military command was located here, as were the remnants of the government, whatever state that may be in. Judging from the anarchy he had observed as he crossed the country, there was no one competent in charge of anything.

Now they could see the buildings inside the base through the steel fence. Most were low and nondescript. The exception was Building 410, the Permanent Joint Headquarters building, an impressive piece of modern architecture, built on several levels. The light bleeding out from the floor-to-ceiling windows of its imposing entrance hall were the brightest lights Griffin had seen in months. A thousand British staff worked there normally, along with hundreds from other NATO countries. There was onsite accommodation for all staff. A tall radio mast nearby bristled with radio receivers and microwave antennae.

Beyond the office buildings, at the very heart of the complex, was the entrance to the operations room used to control the strategic nuclear deterrent submarine fleet. The order to launch the nuclear attack against London and other cities must have been transmitted from the operations room there to one of the four *Vanguard*-class nuclear submarines.

Griffin shivered. The other *Vanguard*-class submarines in the fleet were presumably still at sea, and fully armed with Trident missiles. They were still out there, somewhere in the North Atlantic or perhaps the Norwegian Sea, ever silent and vigilant, awaiting their orders.

The operations room itself was buried a hundred feet underground in a concrete bunker capable of surviving any kind of attack: nuclear, chemical or conventional. A metal and concrete inner fence topped with rolls of razor wire surrounded the entrance to the facility, which was built into the hillside. The whole area was monitored by cameras, lit by bright floodlighting and protected by armed guards, both inside the fence and inside the command room itself. It was as close to invulnerable as was humanly possible.

Rows of Challenger II tanks were lined up in the spaces between the administrative buildings, along with a host of combat and reconnaissance vehicles. It looked like whatever remained of the army had withdrawn here. A helicopter stood on the main landing pad – a Royal Navy Wildcat, just like the one he'd been flying in when the warheads struck the city. His mind flashed with the noise of the explosions, the memory of fire rolling across the capital, the whine of the helicopter's engines as they struggled in vain to keep it in flight …

He stumbled and almost fell, bringing him sharply back to reality.

'Just a few more steps, Colonel,' said the Prime Minister. 'Can you manage it?'

'With your help.'

'When we arrive, I will see to it that you receive the best possible medical treatment.'

He nodded mutely, knowing that even if he could reach modern hospital facilities, little could be done to repair his injury. The femur was the longest and strongest bone in the human body, and his had snapped in half. He had treated it as well as he could, and would have to make do with one leg and his crutches. They had served him well enough. If he was lucky, he would be able to swap his homemade crutches for real ones very soon.

The main entrance was just ahead. Area floodlighting revealed a high security entryway protected by thick steel gates. Security at Northwood had always been maintained at the very highest level even during peace time. Now a Warrior armoured vehicle was stationed in front of the gate. Soldiers stood behind it, armed with rifles, combat shotguns and machine guns.

'Halt!'

An amplified voice brought them to a standstill just outside the entrance. The Colonel and the Prime Minister stood and waited.

The gun turret of the Warrior swivelled toward them. A group of army soldiers dressed in full combat body armour, and carrying SA80 assault rifles emerged and approached them warily. 'Do not make any sudden movements. Raise your arms slowly.'

'That might be a problem for the Colonel,' said the Prime Minister dryly.

The lead sentry stepped forward under the bright lights. 'Ma'am, is it you?'

'Have I changed so much that you don't recognize your own prime minister?'

The sentry's eyes were wide with surprise. 'They said you were dead.'

'Do I look dead to you? Now, open up these damn gates and let us through.'

When he hesitated she raised her voice, as if addressing an unruly meeting of her cabinet ministers. 'Sergeant, when I give an order I expect it to be obeyed. Now take me to whoever is supposed to be in charge here and tell them I want three things. A glass of single malt whisky. A comprehensive briefing on everything that's happened while I've been away from my desk. And an explanation of how the hell they plan to put things right.'

Chapter Eighty-Four

Maidenhead, Berkshire, waning moon

James was free again. Free of the cold metal cage that had held him captive for so long. Free of the ropes that had bound his wrists and ankles, and of the soldier who had stood watch over him.

He tasted the cold air of freedom and found it bitter. It had come at too great a price.

Helen dead. Ben infected with the same sickness that had brought so much misery to his own life.

A curse. That's what it was. A curse sent from God for his sins. He had repented time and time again, yet still the curse held the power to punish him relentlessly, no matter how much he strived to atone for all his wickedness.

This was no freedom. This was hell itself.

And now he was expected to show more strength than ever before. Ben depended on him. Melanie and the others all depended on him for their survival.

This was not a curse, he realized then. It was a test. A

chance for him to finally prove his redemption. A gift from God.

Yet, still. The burden of the gift was so heavy.

He had led his friends to safety after the battle, escaping into the dark, fleeing from the burning camp, leaving the explosions and the gunfire and the screams of the dying far behind. He had carried Ben on his own back, urging the others on through the night and into the next day. Without him, they might have given up hope.

Ben had drifted in and out of consciousness for hours before finally succumbing to the sickness. Now he would not wake again until the transformation to werewolf was complete. Until that time, Chanita must nurse him, just as she had once nursed James.

He thought of the new generation of werewolves that Chanita and Helen had created. They were his children in a way. He had passed his condition to them, hoping they would make the same choice he had made, to use their power for good.

But at the first opportunity, they had chosen to use it for evil.

They were just like Adam and Eve in the Garden of Eden. The original sin. The wrong choice again. Why did people always make the wrong choice?

And why then was he the one to be punished?

There could only be one answer. The sacrifices and atonements he had made were not enough. They would never be enough. He understood now what God wanted. No ordinary repentance was required of him. He must instead repent for all the sins of all mankind. Like Jesus himself, he would have to make the ultimate sacrifice, and give his life for others. How, and when, he did not know. But it would be soon, he knew that.

At one time the realization would have terrified him, or roused his anger. Now he knew that it was a privilege.

The other werewolves had turned their back on God. Only he had remained true. Yet the true path was not an easy one. It would challenge him even more than the trials he had already faced.

But he was ready for it. He was waiting.

'We must stop,' said Melanie. 'We've travelled far enough.'

He nodded his agreement, and with the help of the others he laid Ben down on the hard ground to rest. Melanie covered his sleeping form with a warm coat.

James stood over them, watching.

He had stayed in wolf form ever since leaving the camp the night before and saw no reason to change now. It seemed safer that way. And more natural. The others accepted it without comment.

'Sleep,' he told them. 'I will stand guard.'

'You need to sleep too, James,' said Sarah.

'No.' He shook his great wolf head from side to side.

He noted the way they kept their distance from him, averting their gaze from his yellow stare. They were right to fear him. He was cursed. And yet, he was blessed too. They could not understand. He must walk his path alone.

It was no longer just his friends who depended on him – Ben, Melanie, Sarah, Chanita – it was everyone.

The true path would be a lonely one, and hard to walk. But he had made his decision. For Ben's sake, for Helen's sake, for everyone's sake, he would not stray from the path.

'Sleep,' he said. 'You are safe with me. No one will ever harm you again.'

To be continued in Blood Moon, the fifth and penultimate book of the Lycanthropic series …

If you enjoyed this book, please leave a short review at Amazon. Thanks!

About the Author

Steve Morris has been a nuclear physicist, a dot com entrepreneur and a real estate investor, and is now the author of the Lycanthropic werewolf apocalypse series. He's a transhumanist and a practitioner of ashtanga yoga. He lives in Oxford, England.

Find out more at: stevemorrisbooks.com